STORM
FRONT

THE **CHARISTOWN** SERIES

LISA N. PAUL

Copyright © 2014 by Lisa N. Paul
Cover design by Mae I Design and Photography
Paperback interior design by JT Formatting

http://www.lisanpaul.com

Printed in the United States of America

First Edition: January 2014
Library of Congress Cataloging-in-Publication Data

Paul, Lisa N.
Super Dandy Publishing
   Storm Front (The Charistown Series) 1st ed
   ISBN-13: 978-0989246538
   ISBN-10: 0989246531

   1.Storm Front–Fiction. 2.Fiction–Romance
   3.Fiction–Erotic Romance

For Jon ~
It doesn't matter what the weather is…
You pack up the shovel, the umbrella, the coats, boots, and sunscreen and make certain we are always prepared. Your presence in my life is the calm that never allows the storm to consume me—for that, I am grateful.
I love you…

PROLOGUE

Early November

RYAN TURNED UP the radio to drown out the awkward silence. It pained him that it was slowly becoming the norm for him and Ashley. The short car ride to Max and Janie's house for Sunday dinner was torture. He chanced another quick glance and saw her hands knotted together in her lap. Ryan sighed inwardly, frustrated with the fact that other than cordial conversations the past few months, their friendship had been reduced to this. Quick glances, hurried hellos, and niceties. He wasn't sure how they'd gotten to this point...again, but he hated it with every fiber of his being. Something needed to change before he lost her again.

* * *

"We're here," Ashley announced walking into Max and Janie's house. Her skin prickled at the fake cheer in her voice. *God, I sound ridiculous, I need to tone down the Mary Sunshine act before I make myself sick.*

Sunday dinner was a tradition that the group had come to love over the past six or so months. Ashley looked around. This was the one time during the week when true peace filled her soul. She watched while everyone stuffed their faces with homemade lasagna, salad, and garlic bread.

Ashley glanced at the couple across from her, and a mixture of happiness and something else, unnamed, churned in her gut.

A few weeks after they'd become an official couple, Janie had moved into Max's house and wasted no time making Max's bachelor pad into a cozy and inviting home. Now that they were together, Janie worked during the day as a middle school teacher. Max finally made the decision to give up his bartending shifts at Danny's and work full-time at *Gage Garage*. It was the finest full service auto-repair and motorcycle rehabilitation garage in the tri-state area of Pennsylvania, New Jersey, and Delaware. It was also the business that he co-owned and operated with Sebastian Gage. Max spent his days working with his hands alongside his best friend, and his nights curled up with the love of his life. Yep, life was pretty fucking great for them.

After dinner, everyone settled in the family room to watch the Eagles game. During the half-time break, Janie, Lyla, and Julie went to the kitchen to get drink refills. Ashley sat quietly on the floor waiting for the women to return. She hadn't been feeling like herself lately. Pretending to be someone she wasn't was taking a lot more effort than it used to. If she were being honest with herself— something she tried extremely hard *not* to do—she was getting really fucking sick of the charade. The people in this house were her friends…no, her family. They would love her even if she stopped pretending, but the real question was could she love herself? Could she ever forgive herself for all of the pain she'd caused? Did she deserve to be happy when he no longer could?

"Every time I see you guys together, I feel so… overjoyed." Julie sounded choked up as she continued her thought. "It's like seeing my kids growing up. You guys are a good pair."

Even from the family room, Ashley could hear the gushing tone of Janie's voice as she replied, "Thank you, Julie. We wouldn't have come this far without each of you."

The three women walked back into the family room just as the meteorologist spoke on the television:

Tropical Storm Leo is gaining strength in the Atlantic as we speak. We are expecting it to morph into a hurricane by Tuesday possibly hitting landfall as early as Wednesday night. Get ready, people. This is going to be a big one.

The world went silent. Ashley's body went rigid and her heart began to thud quickly in her chest. The thundering of her heart and the whooshing sound of blood through her ears were the only two noises that infiltrated the complete stillness of the space around her. She looked down at her hands—completely powerless to stop the fierce tremble of her interlocked fingers.

Out of the corner of her eye Ashley saw Ryan's head pivot down to hers and immediately felt the burn of his gaze. Not wishing to acknowledge him she trained her eyes back to her knotted hands. Her shaking was obvious to her, but she hoped no one else had noticed. Ryan would. Of course he would. He knew her body's reactions before she did. They were that in-tune…or at least they had been.

Was it still the same? She didn't know and right then, she didn't have the mind space to care.

Strong, tattooed arms wrapped around Ashley and a scent that was everything Ryan engulfed her senses. His denim-clad legs moved to either side of her, locking her in place. Giving her comfort that she so desperately needed in a moment when her world was spinning off its axis. She knew she shouldn't let him do this. His behavior was reminiscent of a past she spent years trying to forget, but she couldn't bring herself to push him away.

Ashley moved slightly and Ryan's strong arms tightened in response. Biting down on her tongue, she prayed that her instincts were wrong, but even as she tried to convince herself that everything would be okay, every fiber in her being told her that the coming storm would bring a whole lot more than just rain.

PART ONE

PART ONE

CHAPTER ONE

Something New

Six Years Before, Miami, Florida

"I CAN'T BELIEVE you guys are leaving me here in this hellhole for the next two weeks while you go off to be rock stars. It's not fair." Ashley scooped her long blonde hair into a high ponytail as she watched her brother and his best friend grinning behind her in the mirror.

People always assumed Leo was her twin. It was an easy mistake to make. They shared the same silky, golden hair, the same hazel eyes flecked with green, the same copper skin, and the same megawatt smile. The fact that Ashley had been born a mere eleven months after Leo meant they even spent a small amount of time being the same age. The physical resemblance, however, was where their similarities ended.

While Ashley tended to be quiet in public, Leo loved the spotlight. Ashley excelled in all things textbook related, but to Leo school was a place to socialize. If it weren't for Ashley's patience and persistence Leo would never have even donned his cap and gown last week.

"Sorry, sis, you're the one that chose to be all *responsible* and accept a job the week after school let out." Leo's brows furrowed and he shrugged his shoulders. "Who does that?" He asked of Ashley and Ryan, his teasing tone indicative of the close relationship he had with his sister and best friend.

"Your sister does that," Ryan answered. His sexy warm voice felt like caramel sundae topping sliding over Ashley's skin. Their gaze locked just a fraction longer than usual before he turned to address his best friend. She had noticed more of his prolonged glances lately, but had been too afraid to hope that there was any meaningful reason behind them. There was no way that Ryan would ever see her as more than just a friend.

Running her hand over her long, smooth ponytail, Ashley turned her back to her tormentors and laughed. "Not all of us have musical talent oozing from our pores. Some of us have to work *real* jobs."

Noticing her tennis shoe laces were loose, she bent down to tie them. She knew no good would come from building her hopes up, but she couldn't help but wonder if she may have caught Ryan checking her out in the same way she had been doing to him. With slow, calculated movements she reached for her toes. Without being conceited, she knew her body had changed quite a bit over the past year. She knew those changes had guys looking at her differently. Up until recently, the attention just wasn't coming from the one guy she really wanted it from. She could have plopped down and bent her knees—which would have made tying the laces easier—but where was the fun in that? So instead, she perched her foot on the side of her bed and leaned over, just so... She looped and threaded the fabric with her lithe fingers until she had the perfect bow. Pausing just a heartbeat too long, she raised her eyes and found Ryan staring. BINGO.

"Busted," she teased. Her voice was low as to not gain any attention from her brother, but she knew Ryan heard her when his jaw went tight.

"Oh, shit," Ryan quickly shifted his eyes to the window, but it was too late. Self satisfaction filled Ashley in a way she had never felt before. Ryan Baker found her attractive. She had to bite her lip in order to keep from squealing.

She'd been crushing on Ryan since her freshman year when he'd moved into the cul-de-sac. While he was always kind and looked out for her, he'd always treated her like his best friend's sister. Nothing more. As they got to know each other, their relationship shifted and they became friends in their own right but recently things had started to change once again. She felt differently when he looked at her. She felt it on her skin when he touched her. Yep, there was definitely something new. Something raw.

Ryan and Leo had become fast friends the minute they'd discovered their shared opinions on life's most important issues—school, girls and music. Leo had practically been born with a set of drumsticks in his hands and his voice made all the girls swoon. Vocals and percussion weren't a typical combination and he'd laugh when people told him that drummers didn't sing. "Haven't you heard of Phil Collins?" He would ask. The response was more often than not a puzzled look with a whispered, "no." Leo loved the non-believers. In fact, he lived for them. It gave him the opportunity to prove how good he really was. And he was really, *really* good.

Ryan played guitar. Well, he played several different instruments, but that was his favorite. His nimble fingers could coax wonderful rhythms and melodies out of both acoustic and electric guitars. While Leo's voice was smooth and soothing, Ryan's voice was sultry, seductive and sexy as all hell. His voice along with his incredibly good looks made for a lethal combination. Add to that a killer sense of humor and Ryan Baker was the trifecta of male perfection. The two friends had girls and grown women alike chasing after them wherever they went. What Ashley admired and respected about her brother and Ryan was that they never let the over abundance of attention go to their heads. They were grateful and respectful—never cocky and obnoxious.

The tension in the air was palpable as Ashley watched Ryan visibly swallow. His eyes sparkled and Ashley began to wonder if it were possible that the attraction went both ways.

Not wanting to break their connection, she watched him watching her. She studied his face. His eyes milk chocolate with golden flecks, his lips plump and pink, and his jaw covered in stubble. *So sexy*, she thought.

Leo gazed out of the window, lost in his own thoughts and seemingly unaware of the lightening storm of emotions swirling around him. His words broke the tense silence that had fallen over the room. "Look, Ash, you know we'll always come back for you."

"Um, yeah"—her brows pulled together in mock irritation—"but only because you have to, Leo. Don't try to sound all magnanimous about it!"

Leo laughed. "There you go, always using the SAT words. Can't you talk like a normal person?" He teased.

"Ok, big brother let me rephrase," Ashley beamed. She had recently gotten her braces off and the novelty of flashing what she knew was now a perfect smile had not yet worn off. "I *know* you will come back for me because I write the lyrics to your songs. Without me"—one perfectly arched eyebrow lifted—"no songs!" Ashley giggled and grabbed her messenger bag from the hook on the back of her bedroom door.

"Now wait just a minute, Princess," Ryan scoffed. With her back turned, she let her smile grow large. She knew exactly what Ryan was going say, and by his term of endearment she knew he was going to give her earlier sass back to her on a silver platter. "Who writes the lyrics for *Storm Front?*" His voice was laced with sarcasm but she could practically hear the grin that perched on his sexy lips. She knew he was anything but irritated. Turning around to face him, the challenge in his eyes sent shock-waves up her spine. God, he was hot. She could stay and trade sarcastic insults with him all day, but she had to get to work.

"We write the songs together, oh great one!" She conceded. Hugging her brother, she shot Ryan a flirtatious wink over Leo's shoulder. He made no response but if the pounding of her heart was any indication of the change in their relationship, she knew things between her and Ryan were about to get complicated. What would Leo do if something happened between his sister and his best friend? Ashley shook her head. That was one question she truly had no answer for.

5

CHAPTER TWO

Familiar and Decadent

One month later...

"HEY, BABY SISTER." The voice was like a cold glass of lemonade on a hot humid day—soothing, sweet, and impossible not to embrace.

"Leo! You're back!" Ashley dropped her empty serving tray on the counter and leaped into her brother's arms, wrapping her arms around his neck and her legs around his torso. He laughed as he hugged her tight, her muscles relaxed. She felt the vibration of Leo's laughter vibrate through her as she hugged him harder.

She had been missing him like crazy over the past month, he wasn't just her brother. He was her best friend. The open display of affection may not have been appropriate for the middle of a pizza place, but Ashley didn't care. It was only a job and she finally had her brother home. People often told them it was weird how well they got along, but to Leo and Ashley it wasn't weird. It was just how it was. It was life.

Their parents were well-respected surgeons in a

prominent Miami hospital. Known to the community as decent people, they were very *important* and very *busy*. The doctors Kynde made sure that Leo and Ashley were provided for financially, and that their physical needs were always tended to, but it stopped there. Emotionally, the Kynde doctors were unavailable. Despite the abundance of faceless nannies and babysitters, Leo and Ashley had effectively raised themselves. The siblings had coped with this lack of involvement in differing ways. Ashley lived her young years striving to gain just a moment of her parent's attention, to show them who she really was. Leo on the other hand, grew in the opposite direction. Ashley swore he used indifference as a shield to hide the pain of their parents neglect. Not that he would admit it.

The two of them learned to depend on each other. Over time, their parents became no more than warm-blooded ATMs and signatures on sick notes.

"I missed you too, Ash." Leo laughed as he untangled himself from his sister's embrace.

"Hey, Scott, I'm going to take a break, can you handle my tables?" Ashley asked her co-worker.

"Sure, Ash, anything you need. Take your time." Scott was the brother of Jayson, Leo and Ryan's band mate. "Hey, Leo, welcome home, man." With a handshake and a clap on Scott's shoulder, Leo placed his arm around his sister's shoulders and led her outside.

"Hey, stranger."

Ryan's deep, smooth voice immediately brought goose bumps to her flesh. Yep, the old adage was true. After four weeks apart, his mere presence left her breathless. She tucked a strand of hair behind her ear and walked over to give him a hug. Each carefully orchestrated step

7

felt natural—like she was being drawn toward him. The past four years had contained hundreds of hugs but in recent months each of those embraces felt like so much more. Almost like a promise. She wanted to collect on each and every one of those promises.

Badly.

Stepping into Ryan's outstretched arms felt familiar and decadent all at once. Ashley's thoughts scattered when Ryan lifted her up and twirled her around playfully. The husky sound of his laugh blended with the slight woodsy scent of his cologne had Ashley pressing herself against him in a full body hug. While she had missed her brother fiercely over the past month, Ryan's absence felt like a cold dark cloud, constantly blocking her sun.

Ashley followed the guys' tour progress daily through text messages and phone calls via Leo and Ryan. So she knew that Leo, Ryan and the other two band members, Jayson and Zane, ended up traveling up and down the state of Florida playing in every bar, pub and complex they could get themselves into. Zane's uncle was in the music business and ended up getting the guys recording time in a studio at the family discounted rate of "free", but they had to record when the studio was available and that was at odd hours. Therefore the trip doubled in length going from two weeks to four, but also heightened *Storm Front's* visibility. It was a win/win situation for everyone involved.

Well, almost everyone. Ashley missed her brother like crazy. They'd never been apart for longer than a day or two. The house hadn't seemed big until she was the only one in it. Yeah, she'd see her parents as they passed her room in the morning on their way to the hospital. Sometimes they even took the time to say goodnight...as they left the house at night for banquets or cocktail parties. That was the extent of their communication.

Ashley had found herself working double shifts just to stay busy. While she'd spoken to Leo at least once a day and received multiple texts from both him and Ryan it wasn't the same. Having them home again was a heady feeling. Like the sun had finally come out after hurricane season.

———————————————

"Jesus, Ry, put my sister down. She has legs, and they work," Leo snorted, trying to hold back his smile. Ryan inhaled her coconut scent once more before releasing her slowly to the ground. He couldn't bear to look into her eyes. The fear that he wouldn't see the longing that he felt staring back at him was too great. Instead he stared at the asphalt.

Coward.

Leo laughed loudly before launching into a story about clingy groupies and what lengths the girls would go just to get attention from any musician willing to give it. Sneaking a peak at Ashley, Ryan saw the shear bliss etched on her face. He knew she was thrilled to have her brother home with her. He'd always admired Ashley's and Leo's relationship. He knew that they relied heavily on each other for both emotional and physical support. He had missed Ashley something fierce while he was gone.

Ryan felt the conflict tearing at his gut. He would never, ever want to do anything to jeopardize Leo and Ashley's relationship. Leo was more like a brother than a best friend, and he didn't want to do anything to bruise that relationship either, but holding Ashley in his arms, even if for just a few seconds, was the closest thing he'd felt to coming home since his mother died. Why did she have to be his best friend's sister? He was going to have to talk to Leo. There was no way he could continue to hide his feelings. Leo was his brother, he would understand. Ryan would *make* him understand.

"I gotta get back to work."

Ashley's words were like ice water to Ryan's face, snapping him from his deep thoughts. As he suspected, when he raised his eyes to hers he did not see desire. No. Her green-flecked irises, while outwardly mesmerizing, hid a myriad of emotions. She was lonely. Ryan's chest ached at the thought of her being left behind. He silently vowed to never let her be lonely again. She wielded her bravery like a shield—fending off fear with every ounce of her being, but he knew her too well to be fooled. "Are you boys going to be home tonight? I'd really like us to hang out..." Her voice was barely a whisper as she continued, "I was really lonely without you both."

There it was: her vulnerability. She laid it out for her brother, and for him. It took all of Ryan's strength not to go to Ashley and wrap her back in his arms. He wanted to take care of her, comfort her, but he wasn't sure how Leo would take to him hooking up with his little sister. So he kept his feet planted and used only his voice to comfort Ashley.

"Yeah, Ash, we're not going anywhere tonight. We'll be at your house when you get home." That got him two very different looks from the Kynde siblings. Ashley smiled at him warmly. Leo just gave Ryan a puzzled look and kept all comments to himself.

Ashley excused herself to return to work. Ryan watched through the window of the restaurant as she tied her apron around her slender hips. He saw the way she smiled as Scott said something that must have been funny. To anyone else she looked happy, but Ryan knew every one of her smiles. She may have smiled at Scott, but her smile stopped at her mouth and never quite reached her eyes. Ryan exhaled deeply. The relief he felt over knowing that she wasn't giving her *real* smile to Scott was huge. He needed to talk to Leo. Soon.

CHAPTER THREE

She's Still My Sister

ARRIVING HOME FROM work, Ashley was so excited that she ran straight to Leo's bedroom, leaving the front door wide open. Her huge grin dimmed when she realized that he and Ryan weren't there. From the open window low tones of masculine laughter could be heard. Looking out, Ashley could see both Leo and Ryan in the back yard, about to jump in the pool. She watched intently as Ryan pulled off his t-shirt and let it drop to the ground beside him.

"Mmm." The noise escaped her mouth and she was thankful the room was empty. "It's so unfair to the rest of the guys in the world for one to have so much while others have so little," she muttered to herself. Ryan's body was a work of art on so many levels. Sure, there were guys his age just as tall— as he stood over six feet—but they were all skin and bones. Not Ryan. No. Ryan was all corded muscle and tight skin. His body was chiseled from hard workouts with the soccer team at school. Such was his dedication that even when the season ended he would double his efforts at the gym. Having just turned nineteen, Ryan was one of the older kids to graduate in the spring.

He was also one of the first to get a tattoo without parental consent...legally.

Ashley stared at the ink that graced the left side of his upper ribcage. *Always in my Heart* it read in beautiful script. Ashley wiped at her cheek and a stray tear fell from her eye. She still got emotional when she thought about Ryan's mom and her long battle with cancer. Ryan and his father had moved to Ashley and Leo's area after she died to be closer to the rest of the family. Even though Ashley had never met the woman, she felt deeply for her. How could she not? Look what an amazing son she'd raised.

A loud splash had her looking down at the pool, where Leo had just cannon-balled into the water. The two friends were laughing like big kids. Making full use of her vantage point, Ashley found herself staring at Ryan again. He had the best smile and beautiful full lips that framed his perfectly white teeth. He loved to brag that he never had to wear braces. It frustrated the hell out of her when he talked about his lack of orthodontics, especially on the days when she had just come home from having her braces tightened and her mouth hurt. Were Ryan's teeth perfectly straight though? No! He had one tooth on the top row, just over from the center, that was slightly crooked and that freaking tooth made him even sexier. "It's so unfair," she said a little too loudly to the open window.

"Hey, sis, stop peeping and start playing. Get your suit on and come down. We've been waiting for you." Pink cheeked and more than a little embarrassed about being caught watching them, Ashley left the window and went to get in her swimsuit.

"Jesus Christ," Ryan muttered as Ashley sauntered poolside in her red bikini. The combination of her golden, sun-kissed skin and toned body had Ryan's dick so hard that it could have been used as a diving board. He gazed longingly at her while she put down her towel and mp3 player before slowly descending into the water.

"Dude, I'm standing right here. *And* she's still my sister. Do I need to remind you, again?" Leo smiled, his voice void of any threat or anger.

On their road trip, Ryan had talked about Ashley a lot. Leo hadn't said a word but after seeing the two of them interact at the restaurant earlier that day, Leo had finally confronted Ryan. They'd been sitting in Leo's room when he brought up the subject.

"Ry, I'm gonna ask you something and the only wrong answer is a lie, okay?"

Concerned by the look in his friend's eyes, Ryan croaked, "Sure, Le. What's up, buddy?"

"We were on the road for a month and not once in that time did you hook-up with anyone. The girls were all over you, man. Why didn't you take one? You were like a fucking saint out there. What gives?"

Ryan swallowed hard and closed his eyes. He thought for a moment and looked his best friend square in the face. "There's someone I'm in to. Nothing has happened between us, so far," he quickly added. "But I really care about her. I want her...no, I need her. And when I finally have the balls..." He stopped and took in a deep breath before continuing, "And the blessing to go after her, I wanna be able to tell her that I haven't thought about or touched another woman since realizing she was the one for me."

Leo smiled at his best friend, his band mate, and the closest thing he had ever had to a brother and said, *"You have my blessing, Ryan. I can't imagine anyone better for her. But if you hurt her, I will kill you. Understood?"*

Speechless, Ryan stared at Leo. *"How did you know?"* Ryan lifted his hands in a defensive pose, *"I swear to God, we have never done anything behind your back, man. I swear!"* He lowered his hands and exhaled heavily, *"But, I think I love her. No, I know I do."* Ryan couldn't believe that he was finally able to share the feelings that he'd been bottling up for months. He'd thought he was going to have to hide them forever. Or worse, he'd have to choose. *My God, this was amazing.*

"I'm not blind, Ry. I see the way you look at her. It makes me...well, it makes me want to throw up. I mean, uh..." He paused as if searching for the words. *"She's my sister,"* he offered by way of explanation. *"But I know she feels the same way about you. She's never told me. I know she would never want to make things difficult between the three of us. She would rather never have you than take you away from me. Some would say she's selfless, I say she's stubborn. She'll always put the needs of others before her own needs. But stubborn works both ways, ya know?"*

Ryan's brows pulled together in question.

"I mean that when Ashley loves, she loves forever. And those that she loves will always come first. You see...stubborn! So yeah, the two of you may have tried to hide your feelings for one another, but man when you guys are writing songs together, it's like watching magic. After witnessing your run for sainthood this month, and then seeing you guys today..." Leo mock shivered, *"once*

15

again, makes me wanna puke." He made a gagging sound and Ryan started to laugh. "Look, you have my blessing, man." Their eyes met and they exchanged a silent promise. Ryan to not hurt Ashley, and Leo to step aside and let the relationship take its natural course.

It was a true testament to their friendship that the conversation had been an easy one. Reaching for his best friend, Ryan shook Leo's hand. Leo gave the slightest of nods before pulling him inward and slapping him on the back. And that was it. Permission granted.

Now, Ryan watched this gorgeous girl slide into the pool without any clue as to how every single step she took was one step closer to bringing him to his knees.

"What are you boys talking about?" Ashley said wiping the water from her face, finally joining them at the deep end of the pool.

With Leo's blessing in his proverbial pocket, Ryan knew that he could finally take steps to make Ashley his, and he would start as soon as humanly possible.

"ALRIGHT GUYS, I'LL run out and pick up dinner. I'll be back in about twenty minutes." Leo winked at Ryan as he left the pool with a towel wrapped around his torso.

"What was that about? Do you think he's acting weird?" Ashley asked. Ryan barely heard her questions while he watched as Ashley clung to the edge of the pool, her back to him as he walked through the water to get closer to her. The soft lapping of the water around them gave away his location. She sensed him closing in and shivered. He doubted her reaction had anything to do with the water's temperature. Just knowing that she was affected by him made Ryan grateful for the cover of the water to disguise his growing arousal.

"I think he wanted us to know that we had some time to ourselves." Ryan whispered in Ashley's ear, his warm breath spreading thousands of goose bumps over her wet flesh. She turned around and he got lost in the warmest pair of hazel eyes gazing into his. With the sun setting around them, Ryan loved how her hair looked like spun gold.

She inhaled sharply before speaking, pressing her hands to his chest pushing some space between them. "What are we doing Ryan?" her voice hoarse with desire. His ears perked at the particular way she phrased her question. Employing the use of *we* instead of *he* would suggest that she was already allowing herself to consider this. *To consider him.* While his initial reaction was to roar his excitement, he harnessed his enthusiasm as he slowly moved his way to her again.

"Ash," her name came out as a whisper as he stepped even closer. He ran his hands up her arms and cupped her shoulders, his thumbs stroking the smooth skin around the curved bone. He felt her body tremble and her breath get shallow. Ryan knew she wasn't scared, he could see the desire in her eyes. He could feel warmth radiating from her sweet smile. One hand moved to her neck and one to her jaw, he lifted his thumb, gently swiping its pad over her full bottom lip just a fraction of a second before he placed his mouth to hers for the first time.

His lips were warm, soft and tender. His hard naked chest pressed firmly up against hers, heat sinking into her skin and spreading like the roots of wild flowers. He deepened the kiss as his tongue entered her mouth and stroked hers as if savoring the very feel of her essence. The tug when his fingers twisted in her wet hair sent more thoughts racing through her scrambled mind, could this really be happening? She had fanaticized about this moment for months, even years, if she was being honest.

At first her thoughts were girlish dreams of hugs and pecks on the cheek, but over the years her fantasies had become those of a woman—filled with lust, desire and need. Ashley had never given her body to another person. Not only was she a virgin but other than a few chaste kisses she had remained virtually untouched, saving her body for the one person who held her heart.

As Ryan ran one hand through her hair and the other down the column of her neck, she could feel the flames of desire licking her skin. The feel of his thick erection between her thighs was foreign, but intriguing as Ashley pressed her body even closer to Ryan's.

When a soft moan escaped her, she felt Ryan's body stiffen. He slowly withdrew his tongue from the confines of her mouth and gave her bottom lip a small nip before inhaling deeply and breaking their intimate connection completely. He held her close to him as he looked into her expressive eyes. Ashley felt dazed, confused, and slightly embarrassed. She ran her fingers over her lips, feeling almost uncertain if that heavenly kiss even happened.

"Ryan, did I do something wrong?"

His eyes were filled with desire as he slowly perused her beautiful face, her long neck, her smooth shoulders, her firm breasts, and her taught belly while the water from the pool covered the rest of her body from his easy gaze. But his silence was unnerving. What was he thinking?

"Ashley," she hardly recognized the husky sound of his voice. With his forehead pressed gently to hers he said, "Ash, we need to talk." She looked up at him with a confused but hungry gaze.

"Ok, Ryan, let's talk." Ashley wasn't certain as to what was going on in this beautiful man's mind, but by the steamy look in his golden flecked eyes, she knew, if for some reason she had banged her head when she dove into the pool earlier and she was drowning...she didn't ever want to be rescued.

CHAPTER FOUR

I Know You Do

Two months later...

"I'M SO GLAD you came to your senses and quit your job before school started, Princess," Ryan murmured in her ear. The tip of his tongue traced the edges of Ashley's ear causing chills to run down her spine. The sensations ran through her body like electricity through her veins. The goose bumps on her arms were a giveaway and she heard Ryan's deep chuckle. He knew exactly the effect that particular action had on her, and consequently he did it as often as possible.

"I didn't quit, I took a leave of absence for the month. Mmm, Ryan, you know I can't think straight when you're doing that to me," Ashley purred. Shallow breaths and a racing pulse had her words choppy and hoarse. Her eyes hooded as her long lashes splayed gently across her skin each time she blinked. The couple was in her bedroom writing lyrics for the band's up and coming album and East coast tour. Ashley loved writing the songs for *Storm Front*. While she had no aspirations for stardom, getting her thoughts and feelings down on paper had always been somewhat therapeutic for her. Ashley still rolled her eyes every time Leo tried to use his lame excuse as to how he'd discovered her writing talent.

When she was fifteen, Leo had "mistakenly" found her journal. According to him he had then "accidently" dropped it on the floor, opening to give him access to her secret thoughts. He claimed he couldn't help but to read them, citing his captivation as a half-hearted excuse for his blatant prying. That was when Leo started begging his little sister to write the songs for his new band.

The guys in *Storm Front* thought her lyrics were fantastic and said her hooks were contagious. But Ashley knew that when she and Ryan collaborated the songs they created were unbelievable. So, while she still wrote the majority of the bands lyrics, she and Ryan would get together once or twice a week to work on new material. Since they'd started dating they'd spent a whole lot more time *writing* than they ever had in the past.

That afternoon, they really had started out writing, but as the lyrics became more intense, so did their gazes. With each second that passed, the atmosphere between them became more and more charged until keeping things professional was no longer an option. One glance reassured her that she wasn't the only one having difficulty maintaining concentration.

She still couldn't believe that Ryan Baker was hers. She wanted to lick his smooth tan skin. To graze the tips of her fingers over the shadow of the dark scruff that covered his jaw line. So that's what she did.

At her touch his eyes went molten. "It's hard enough to concentrate when you look at me the way you do, Princess, but when you touch me…" A deep growl sounded at the back of Ryan's throat and he lifted Ashley's face to his, consuming her lips with a deep hungry kiss. The moment he touched her, time stood still. Once his body pressed against hers everything else just evaporated, as it always did when they were together. The outside world ceased to exist. She reveled in the feel of his guitar calloused fingers on her smooth skin.

The expert way his velvety tongue caressed her lips. His hand traveled from her jaw to her neck and continued its descent down to her breasts. It was no secret how responsive she was to his touch. Her nipples were hardened points, straining against the material of her sheer bra and tank top.

———————————————

"You're wearing too many clothes, Princess," he said in a husky voice. Reaching down, he took the hem of her tank between his fingers and swiftly whisked it off. The sun-kissed flesh and blonde hair highlighted with spun golden locks had her gleaming like a goddess, a goddess that was all his. He had planned to tell her that he loved her this weekend, but seeing her draped across her bed with the honeyed rays of the sun streaming in from the window, he couldn't hold it in another second.

Even at nineteen, Ryan knew his love for her was more than puppy love. He had known it for a while. The only reason he had held off sharing his feelings with Ashley was because of her age. He was scared that at seventeen she wasn't yet ready to hear his admission. *No, you coward,* his inner voice chided, *you haven't told her be-*

*cause you're scared that she doesn't feel the same way.
Man up Baker! Tell her!*

"Ry?" Ashley's eyes questioning his. She knew him so well, she always knew when his mind was off somewhere else. Just one more thing he loved about her.

"Ashley, baby, I need you to know something." It was in that moment he realized he wasn't nervous to say the three words he had never uttered to another girl in his life. In his heart, he knew she was the one for him…he had no doubts. "Ashley, I love you."

Tears filled her eyes as she nodded her head and smiled. "I know you do." Ryan smiled back relief washing over his body and then it was quickly replaced by tension. His shoulders pulled up tight, his back went straight, and his lungs lost the ability to breathe… She didn't say it back.

"Ash?" His heart was beating frantically. Had he read her wrong? Did she not feel the same way? He could have sworn….

"Ryan," Ashley placed her small hands on his jaw, turning his face so their eyes met. He dropped his chin, unwilling to meet her gaze. She inhaled, quieted her voice and called to him. "Ryan, love." At the term of endearment his heart began to race. He lifted his gaze to see her cheeks were wet with tears, and her eyes filled with the tears still waiting to fall.

"Tell me what you see when you look at me. Tell me what you've always seen since I was fifteen years old." Ryan just stared at the beautiful woman in front of him.

"Every time you've come into our house to see Leo, every time you've looked at me, every time we've written a song…what have you seen?" She didn't give him time to

23

answer. "Ryan, I have loved you from the start. I have fallen in love with you over the years and I can't imagine my life without you in it. Leo always says I'm stubborn and I guess he's right. I've never given up on you, Ryan. I'm just glad you've finally caught up." The tears rolled down her cheeks, "It took you long enough!" She laughed through the tension but she was interrupted as Ryan took her mouth in the most passionate kiss they had ever shared.

⎯⎯⎯⎯⎯⎯⎯⎯⎯⎯⎯⎯⎯

She tugged at the hem of Ryan's t-shirt, swiping it up and over his head. The sight of his beautifully sculpted chest took her breath away. Exhaling, she ran her hands up his chest and over his pectorals. As her thumbs drew circles over his sensitive nipples, she allowed herself to bask in the way they tightened in response to her touch. Quickly, she repositioned herself.

She sat up with her hands supporting her from behind and inched forward, lowering her lips to the flat discs on his hard chest. With just the right combination of tongue and teeth, she was rewarded with a low groan coming from deep in Ryan's chest. "Oh, Princess, when you put your mouth on me it makes me want to bow down to you...cherish you."

In one swift movement her shorts and panties were stripped from her body and discarded somewhere on the floor. Ryan started his worship at her pierced navel. He tongued the ring and kissed the skin below the indentation. His hands stroked her slim hips as his fingers set off waves of tiny sparks shooting across her skin. He continued to move down her torso until he hit the juncture at her inner thighs. Ashley was still a virgin. She and Ryan had decided to wait until her eighteenth birthday to have sex for the first time. She always complained that having her birthday on Christmas Day meant never having special birthday gifts.

People always assumed that Christmas is a great time for a birthday but in truth her birthday was usually either overlooked or forgotten. This year she wanted to celebrate her birthday by giving *him* a gift. The most intimate gift she could...herself. She knew Ryan wasn't a virgin by any means. He'd had sex before, but he had never made love, so her first time would also be a kind of first for him. Even though they never had intercourse they had done a lot of what they liked to call, "the other stuff."

Ashley's eyelids became heavy as Ryan's lips met her inner thighs. God, the things that boy could do with his lips. "Open your eyes, Ash. Watch me love on you." She looked down at him between her legs and found his milk chocolate eyes staring back at her. Golden flecks of passion swirled as he dipped his head and took his first taste. It was all she could do not to pass out from that first touch of pleasure... She held tight to the sheets and threw her head back. Her body thrummed from the inside out.

"Princess, you taste like the sweetest honey and finest wine." Ashley loved when Ryan waxed poetic about her body. He sounded far older than his nineteen years. All coherent thoughts left her mind when he slipped a finger into her core and licked her swollen clit.

"Oh God, Ryan, you make me feel so good." He continued to pleasure her as he slid a second finger into her. A low moan penetrated the air and he closed his mouth around her sensitive nub and gently bit her. Ashley's gasp at the subtle pain was immediately followed with a mew of pleasure as Ryan laved her clit with long strokes of his strong tongue.

A heady mix of pleasure and pain coursed through her body. She felt her inner walls molding around his fingers as he slid them in just a fraction deeper massaging the magic spot that made her insides melt. Her body shook as her breathing became shallow. "Ryan, I'm gonna come... Oh..."

His voice was rough as he told her, "Let go, Ashley. I'm here to catch you. Let go, baby."

So she did.

And he did.

CHAPTER FIVE

Devil Himself

"YOU SOUND AMAZING, Leo. Every time I think you can't get better, you prove me wrong." Ashley loved her brother's responses when she complimented his progress. He knew that she would tell him if he sounded like shit—she never shied away from the truth—so her compliments meant a lot to him.

"Of course I sound great, little sis. Hello? I'm Leo Kynde! The voice of *Storm Front*." With a smirk and a wink he quickly added, "Don't tell Ryan I said that, he'll kick my ass."

Ashley giggled watching Leo as he got up from behind his drum kit, grabbed a bottle of water from the mini fridge in the garage and drained it in one long gulp. The women were going to swoon over him during the tour. He'd been hitting the gym for daily workouts with Ryan all through the summer and his nights had been spent practicing at the local bars with the guys.

Storm Front was going to be the next big thing—she could feel it in her bones. Wiping his face with his faded Eagles, *Hell Freezes Over* t-shirt, Ashley saw a white gauze bandage covered in plastic wrap on the side of Leo's torso.

"Leo!" She gasped. "What the heck is that?" While Ashley found tattoos extremely sexy on Ryan, she couldn't imagine her brother ever marring his beautiful skin with permanent ink.

"It's just a tattoo, Ash, it's no big deal. You don't seem to have a problem with Ryan's ink." Leo wagged his eyebrows and quickly moved out of the way to avoid a lunging Ashley.

"Holy crap, Leo! Mom and Dad are going to freak out. Did you show them?" Leo quickly tugged down his shirt.

"Wait, I can't see it. Take off the wrap. I want to see what you decided was so important that you thought it should stay forever marked on your body." Ashley crossed her arms over her chest, trying to display an agitation that she just didn't feel.

Tattoos were sexy as hell, but the truth was she was more upset that Leo hadn't told her he was going to do it. Finding out after the fact wasn't the same. It felt like he was slipping away from her and that thought pricked her deeper than she cared to let on.

"First of all, Ash, I didn't need to ask or tell Mom and Dad because I'm eighteen. But, I *did* tell them and they were cool with it. They gave me the whole, 'Go to a safe place and make sure they use clean needles,' talk. Second of all," Ashley could see the tension forming in Leo's shoulders, "I didn't want you to try to talk me out of it."

"Leo." Ashley tried to interrupt him but he held his hand up to stop her from speaking.

"Sweet little sister. I love you more than anyone in the world, you know that, right?" Ashley nodded silently.

"But when you think you're right about something you refuse to see it from anyone else's perspective. Yes, you are insanely smart and as much as I hate to admit it, you're usually right about most things. But you never allow yourself to just follow your heart, Ashley." Leo exhaled loudly, as he ran his fingers through his coiffed hair. "And sometimes that's the only thing that needs to be trusted. Sometimes, all of the black and white points to one answer, but your heart points to something else. Those are the times when you need to follow your heart. I really wanted this, Ash, and I didn't want logic to stop me from getting it."

She was momentarily stunned. "Wow, Leo. That was the most profound thing I've ever heard you say. And I think I understand why you did what you did."

"If you understand then why do you have that look on your face?" Leo ran his hands over Ashley's shoulders the way he had a thousand times before.

"The truth?" She questioned, looking straight into Leo's eyes. The same hazel eyes she saw when she looked in the mirror each day.

"Always the truth, little sister. Nothing between us but the truth."

Trying to hold back the tears that threatened to escape her eyes, Ashley pulled in a deep breath. "I'm scared that I'm going to lose you, Leo. You went and got a tattoo without even telling me. You've never, ever done something so...so HUGE without including me. Next week, you, Ryan and the guys are leaving on your tour for three and half months and I'm scared that this is the last I will ever see of my brother. The real you." The warmth of the tears caressed her cheeks as she felt her body being tugged into the familiar embrace of her brother's body.

"Ashley, you will *never* lose me. I will always be here for you. I love you with my whole heart. It doesn't matter how rich and famous I become and believe me, I will become rich and famous," he chuckled. "You will always be my baby sister and my best friend. When I get too big for my own britches—or in my case, my old concert t-shirts—I'm gonna need you to rein me in. You got it?"

Feeling soothed and loved, Ashley wrapped her arms around Leo's broad torso and squeezed. "I got it, big brother. I got it." Wiping away the remaining tears, she said, "So, do I get to see this heart inspired permanent piece of art, or what?"

Leo lifted his shirt and carefully stripped off the bandage. Catching sight of the ink Ashley understood why Leo needed to follow his heart. He was right. It had led him in the right direction. Scripted beautifully down his ribcage, it read:

The Darker the Storm,
The Deeper the Pain,
The Brighter the Light At the End.
Always Reach for the Light.

———————————

The sound of applause was almost deafening as *Storm Front* finished their last song on the stage at *Riley's Beach Bar and Grille*. This was where the band had played their first gig and this was where they were playing their final show before leaving for three and a half months. Ryan's ears buzzed from the noise and his blood thrummed through his veins. The band's performance was incredible tonight. Zane was on fire with the keyboards, Jayson made the bass his bitch, and Leo melded into his drums as he always did when he played. The way he could sing with the angels and keep a beat with the drums was like nothing Ryan had ever heard before.

He tried and failed to hold back the smile that took over his face as he looked at his band mates. He knew they sounded awesome and he couldn't wait to perform in all of the amazing places they were headed. Sure, the venues would be small and *Storm Front* would be the opening act for the opening act, but they had to start somewhere. They felt like rock stars already.

He looked out into the restaurant and quickly found Ashley. She was sitting at a table with her parents. Ryan thought back to earlier in the week when the Kynde doctors informed them that they had taken time off work to see the show. While Ryan's dad never missed a performance, Leo and Ashley's parents almost never made one.

This was a huge event. Ryan was happy for Leo that they'd made the effort and saw such a great show. Ashley looked so prim and proper in her pink tank top and white denim skirt. Her hair was pulled back in a white headband and her lips shined with pale pink lip gloss. She looked heaven-sent. Ryan felt like the devil himself—his dick stiffening in his jeans as he took in her angelic appearance. He knew under all of that sweetness was his sexy vixen and he couldn't wait to kiss and touch her later that night. He felt his skin prickle as he realized that she had once again caught him staring at her and would likely notice the desire rolling off his skin in waves.

Her parents had left the table to talk to the band's manager, so she sat there alone. Her eyes glittered with lust as Ryan watched her small pink tongue gently glide across her lower lip. With a growl, he hopped down from the stage and weaved quickly through the tables. Lifting her in his arms he spun her around, nuzzling her neck and discretely licking the sensitive place between her neck and her shoulder blade.

"Mmm, Ryan. That gives me chills every time," she purred. "Do you have any idea how sexy you look up on that stage without a shirt on? Singing our songs, playing your guitar, seducing the audience with your eyes?" Ryan felt himself harden further at her sultry words.

"Princess, the things you say to me make it almost impossible for me to keep my promises and wait until your birthday." He groaned when she pressed her body even closer to his.

"Then let's not wait," she murmured, stroking his jaw with a whisper soft touch. "I want you now. Tonight. Let's go back to your house and you can show me how much you want me." The pleading in her voice was almost Ryan's undoing, but the need to do right by her kept his resolve strong.

"Baby, I want you more than music, more than air, more than anything. And we will go back to my house and I will show you how much I want you, but, I really want to wait until we get back from our tour to make love to you. When we finally have sex, I want to claim more than your body. I want your soul, Ashley. And I can't take that and then leave you two days later."

━━━━━━━━━━━━━━━━━━━━━━

His words set her skin on fire and her mind ablaze.

32

How was it possible to love someone more than she already loved the man standing mere inches from her? Wrapping her arms around his still sweaty naked torso, Ashley pulled Ryan in for a mind-melting kiss. All of her senses were engaged in that moment. She loved how he smelled of sweat and the faded woodsy fragrance of his cologne. His milk chocolate brown hair was soft and damp as she ran her fingers through the short messy locks. His broad, naked chest pressed up against her breasts as her hands moved from his hair down his muscled back and nestled into the back pockets of his low-rise jeans.

Pulling in a sharp breath, Ryan dropped his lips from Ashley's and moved them to her cheek and then her ear. "Baby, we need to stop before I embarrass myself in front of your parents, and everyone else. Let's go say goodnight and we can head back to my place." With a breathy groan, Ashley nodded and linked her fingers through Ryan's, following him through the crowd to find her family.

"I think your new tattoo is really sexy, Ry," Ashley said just loud enough for him to hear her over the crowd. Her fingers lightly danced across the top of his back as she traced the heavy black lettering that read *Storm Front*.

Ryan turned, and pulled her close. "I'm sorry we didn't invite you to come with us, Princess. Leo told me you were upset." The chagrined look on Ryan's face spoke volumes. "All of my major decisions from now on will be discussed with you. Okay?"

That simple statement sparked a thousand thoughts through Ashley's mind. *Did he really mean that? Was this really happening? Could we be forever?*

The pause in her step with what must have been a deer in headlights look, had Ryan pulling Ashley close to him once again. "Ash, when I told you I loved you, I meant it. My decisions are *our* decisions. I promise, I won't leave you out again." He placed a quick kiss on her cheek and weaved through the throng of people until they found the Kynde's and bid their goodnights. The next forty-eight hours were going to be busy and Ashley wanted to spend as much time with Ryan as she could before they had to say good-bye.

⎯⎯⎯⎯⎯⎯⎯⎯⎯⎯

Ashley lay sleeping on her bed. Her naked body, covered only partially by the white cotton bed linens, was relaxed and beautiful. Ryan loved how she fell asleep after he'd made her orgasm. Like everything else Ashley Kynde did, when she came apart with pleasure she did it with her whole being. It was the most amazing vision to witness and something he was sure he wouldn't ever get tired of seeing.

With just twelve hours left together before the band was to leave for over three months of small bar shows and opening acts at bigger venues, Ryan was trying to absorb every single detail of Ashley's appearance. She still had to complete her senior year of high school and while she may be concerned with the women throwing themselves at him, he knew for a fact that there were several guys who had been waiting for he and Leo to graduate so they could finally hit on Ashley Kynde.

A shiver of jealousy ran up his spine. Barring a few quick visits until early December, they would be doing the long distance thing. He was going to miss her. Hell, she was lying right in front of him and he already missed her.

Careful not to wake her, Ryan slipped out of her bed and sat down at her pristine white desk. He felt an inane sense of happiness as he perused the many pictures that covered the corkboard hanging above her desk. Images of Ashley and Leo, he and Ashley, and those of the three of them at different times smiled back at him—each one sparking a memory of a time filled with happiness and love, times spent with the two of the most important people in his life.

He stared at the Ashley in the photograph and then turned to the one sleeping peacefully on the bed. She was so feminine and proper, so fragile yet strong. There was so much substance and intelligence all wrapped up in the beautiful gift asleep before him on the bed.

Her heart is stitched upon her sleeve for everyone to see…

The lyrics practically begged to be written. This always happened after he and Ashley were together and they hadn't even had sex yet. What would happen when they finally did? He would probably write an entire album. Maybe even two.

She flutters through my life
sprinkling the magic of her love,
Her heart is stitched upon her sleeve for
everyone to see,
I revel in her openness, her calmness, her desire, yet—
It's her striking hazel eyes that
slowly unravel every inch of me.
Her hazel eyes glow fire green that shock
and hold me tight,
Golden hair has become my torch;

35

My beacon in the night,
She is my princess, my angel—where the fairytales began,
But it's those brilliant hazel eyes of hers—
That makes me thank God that I'm her man

CHAPTER SIX

Tramps, Actually

"LEO, CAN I ask you something?"

Ashley sat crossed-legged on her brother's bed, fiddling with her hair and worrying her bottom lip with her teeth. Leo zipped around his room, emptying his closet and various drawers of their contents and shoving the items—unfolded—into the duffle bags that lay open on the bed.

The hair wound around her fingers bit into her skin, getting tighter and tighter until the tip of the digit was bright purple. "My packing method is making you physically ill, isn't it Ash?" Leo didn't wait for her response. With laughter in his tone he said, "No worries, just take everything out and feel free to fold it nicely and put it back it."

A large and mischievous grin crept over his lips, revealing his plan to have Ashley pack for him from the very beginning.

"Nope, Leo, your *method,* as you call it, is just fine with me," Ashley said through pursed lips. Organization was like breathing to Ashley. In contrast, to Leo chaos was art. However, Ashley knew that Leo counted on the fact that her need for things to be orderly always won out. As a result, his bags, his room, hell, his life, were always perfectly organized. He was forever claiming he didn't know how he would get through each day without his little sis. Ashley's teeth continued to maul her bottom lip. She couldn't seem to stop the nervous twitch that had started earlier that morning when Ryan slipped out of her room to go home and finish his packing.

"Ash."

Leo stopped moving around and sat on his bed, weaving his fingers through hers and bending his head until he was able to meet her eyes with his own. "Ashley Beth, what's going on in that overactive mind of yours?"

Unable to censor her thoughts, she just let them out. "There are so many beautiful girls out there, Leo. Hot girls. Easy girls. Tramps, actually…"

Ashley's lips pursed, her brows pulled together and she sighed in part confusion and part resignation. Her typically perfect posture faltered and her shoulders slumped.

"Do you think…"—her voice faltered slightly—"do you think he'll cheat on me? We've never… had sex, Leo. Never! Do you think…? Do you think Ryan will decide that there are better, prettier, sexier girls out there and forget about me? Or worse," Ashley pulled in a deep breath and closed her eyes before continuing, "lie to me?"

"Oh my God," Leo exhaled, grunted and then he started to laugh.

Laugh!

"Leo!" Ashley shrilled, pushing against his chest with the palms of both hands. "Leo, this isn't funny. I'm being serious here. I'm scared to death. I love him. I'm *in* love with him. Like, the kind of love that makes me think about forever." She exhaled in frustration. Trying to explain her feelings was so much harder than it should be. "It's the kind of love that makes me use the word 'like' in a sentence where it doesn't belong just to drive the point home! I *love* love him, Leo! And I'm not naïve or stupid. I know how groupies are. I just don't know if I can put my whole heart into this and then find out that I was a fool."

Leo's wide smile softened to a warm grin as he leveled his gaze to hers and stared for the briefest of seconds. Appearing to find what he was looking for in her eyes, he asked a question that would resonate with her for years to come. "Ash, haven't you *already* put your whole heart into this?"

"Yeah, big brother, I guess I have. And it already hurts that he's leaving. I would never dream of asking him to stay. I would never want that for you guys. I know *Storm Front* is your dream. But, I'm so scared."

Wrapping her in a tight hug, Leo stroked Ashley's hair and dropped a kiss on the top of her head. He chuckled lightly. Ashley felt his grip loosen and she reluctantly pulled away from the comfort of his embrace.

With complete sincerity in his eyes, a rarity for the fun-loving jovial one of the pair, he began to speak the words that would prove to be the balm to Ashley's soul for the next few months. "Ash, you must not see what I see when I look at Ryan Baker. Because, what I see is a man who is completely and totally in love with you. He worships you. In fact, if you weren't my sister, I would razz him for being completely pussy-whipped. But you are, so I can't. And sis, if that isn't comfort enough, if I ever saw him looking at another chick the way he looks at you, I would shove my drumsticks straight up his pretty-boy ass."

With his patented Leo Kynde wink, he gently placed his hands on her shoulders, pulling her forward and placed his forehead against hers. "He loves you. Ash. Trust me. Better yet, believe in *him*."

Deep and meaningful pep talks were not something people would usually associate with Leo, but as with everything between the siblings, he was able to tap into how she was feeling and say exactly the right thing to make her feel better. Despite the chill that had settled on her skin, she knew he was right. The realization was both calming and unsettling. How was she supposed to cope without Leo around to help her see clearly?

His face searched hers for signs that his words penetrated. Meeting his gaze, she offered a wry smile before clipping him on the shoulder. "My God, Leo, is this what you've stooped to? Stealing advice from fortune cookies?"

"Ssh, don't tell anyone," he grinned. "I prefer it when people underestimate me."

"No one underestimates you, Le," she confirmed with a smile, placing a big wet kiss in the center of his head. She winked as she added, "at least no one that matters. Now go to Ulta and get your three-month supply of hair gel. We can't have those locks going flat during one of your shows, can we?"

With a look of concern that said he didn't quite buy her light-hearted demeanor, Leo ran his fingers through his hair. Forcing herself to maintain her screwed on smile, she challenged him to question her further. After just a few short seconds, Leo exhaled once again running his fingers through his mussy hair. He peered at her from underneath his eyelashes before giving a swift shake of his head and leaving the bedroom. "He is so easy," Ashley muttered, unpacking the disaster that was Leo's bag and sorting everything into neat, perfect piles.

CHAPTER SEVEN

Awful, Plastic Smile

AS THE PRE-DAWN sky changed from black to shades
of reds then burnt oranges and finally brilliant hues of
golden yellows, Ashley helped her brother bring his duffle
bags and milk crates filled with food to the driveway.
Their parents had spent the night at a hotel in Miami following a fundraising gala, so they'd phoned in their good-
byes and good lucks the previous day. While Leo seemed
to take their absence in stride, their indifference was like a
knife to Ashley's gut. So, to fix what she felt was broken
in their family, she went into overdrive. She cooked all of
Leo's favorites for breakfast, and packed a cooler filled
with sandwiches and snacks for all of the band members
for lunch.

She rushed back and forth from the house to the
driveway dragging Leo's boxes while he continued to
break down his drum kit, getting it ready to store in the
small tour bus that was scheduled to arrive in just a few
minutes.

A cold, familiar chill crept through Ashley's veins.
She knew this feeling. This was the sadness that had settled into her gut when the guys had been away this sum-

mer—the figurative cold teeth of complete and utter lone-liness that had eaten away at her soul. While she was thrilled that her brother, Ryan and the other guys were get-ting the chance to live their dream, the dreaded state of invisible always threatened to choke her when they were gone.

Sure, school would be starting in just a couple of days, but without her brother, who would she be? She'd always had a label: *Leo's sister*, or *Dr. Kynde's daughter*. Although known for her academic achievements, she didn't relate to the other people in those groups. She thought of them as stuffy, boring, and two-dimensional, basically nerds.

Without her brother and Ryan around she couldn't even relate to the people who followed *Storm Front* be-cause, well, *Storm Front* was no longer around. As Ashley stacked her brother's things in the driveway, the weight of her impending solitude sat heavily on her shoulders.

"Princess."

Ryan wrapped his strong arms around her waist, ro-tating her until her face was buried in his chest. He needed to hold her tighter, to make sure she knew he loved her beyond all reason.

"Ashley, you looked so sad just now. It's like your body was here, but your mind was miles away. You didn't even hear me calling you. Talk to me, Princess."

The deep emotions unfolded like the plot of a play on Ashley's face, but in true Ashley form, she tried to pull the curtains down before he could see the final act. Nope. No

43

way was he going to allow her to hide behind the mask of perfection for one more minute. He was setting off in less than an hour and he couldn't leave his girl with the lost and broken look that he had just seen on her face.

Lacing his fingers through hers, he guided her to the back porch where—aside from the soft sounds of the birds waking from their slumber and the gentle lapping of the pool water—it was perfectly quiet.

Stroking the backs of his fingers lightly down her jaw, he tipped her chin so her eyes were facing his. "Princess, please tell me what is going on in that beautiful mind of yours. I know you're sad that we're leaving—I hate leaving you too—but I can tell there's more going on than just the physical distance. If we're gonna make this work between us—"

Ryan watched as Ashley's eyes quickly rounded when the word *if* left his mouth and he quickly corrected himself. "I meant in order for us to make this work between us, baby, you have got to be open with me. Please, tell me what's going on. Let me help to ease whatever is making you so damn sad."

The anxiety rolled off her in waves and for the first time in their relationship, Ryan was nervous. In that brief second a small flash of doubt sparked through his mind. *What if she was choosing this moment to break things off with him?*

He had never, not for one second, given that any consideration at all. He'd always known that he was in love with Ashley Kynde and he'd assumed the feeling was mutual. After all, she told him and showed him often enough, but now he was leaving. What if the distance was enough to make her end things? A sick feeling began to churn through his gut. That feeling must have shown on his face because Ashley squeezed his hand tightly while stroking his cheek.

"Does that make it easier for you?"

Her voice startled him. Looking up he saw the sadness that had loomed in Ashley's eyes replaced by ambiguity and fear. Ryan's thoughts were buzzing like a fluorescent light bulb…just before it finally gave out. A single tear drifted slowly down her cheek and stopped at her upper lip. *Wait. What happened? What had she just said to him?*

"Ashley, baby, I'm sorry, I didn't hear you." His tone was sharp but his eyes bled pain. "Is what easier for me? What are you saying?" A jab of panic struck his gut as he saw the crumbled look marring her beautiful face.

Trying her best to keep her mask of perfection solidly in place, she simply stated, "I was saying, Ryan, that maybe it would be for the best if … well, if we broke up while you were gone." Another traitorous tear escaped her stormy eyes. "I don't want to hold you back, Ry…I don't want to keep you from…living." With those words, Ashley stood up from the cozy outdoor loveseat and began to walk away.

"Princess. Do. Not. Take. Another. Step." Ryan unfolded himself from the small sofa and took long strides to meet Ashley right where she stood.

"Look at me, Ash, look me in the eyes." The eyes are so often referred to as the window to the soul and while Ashley was one to keep her window covered with the loveliest curtains around, for him, the glass was always clear. His heart faltered in his chest as he felt—yes, actually felt—her pain…just from looking in her eyes. The sadness overtook him, making the air around them heavy and even harder to breathe. He could feel each pump of his heart as he waited on the answer to his next questions. "Is that what you want? You want to end this? End us?"

Pulling in a deep breath, Ashley continued to stare, the tears had slowed but her cheeks bore a well worn path from the wet pain. "Do you want the truth, Ry?" Those words felt like a dull blade in his gut.

"Yeah, Ash—the truth would work just fine."

"Ryan, the thought of you and Leo leaving for such a long time makes me ache deep down clear through to my bones. I love you both so much and your presence in my life brings me true happiness and joy that goes beyond what any words can say. But, Ryan, having *you* in my life—as my friend, my boyfriend, as my everything...well you touch my soul. Do I want to break up? Heck no! I love you. I want to be with you always, forever. But I understand that your life is about to change."

He watched as she rubbed the edge of her thumb deep into her sternum, he knew the words she was giving were to benefit him. Each syllable was cracking the veneer she worked so hard to keep polished, but he let her continue. "I see the way the girls, heck, the women look at you, like they want to eat you alive. People tell me that women, groupies, will do anything to hook up with guys in a band, Ry..." Ashley let out a small humorless laugh that punched Ryan in the gut at the same time it eased the band around his lungs allowing him to breathe.

"You are so much more than just a guy from a band. You are beautiful and sexy and...gah...everything! I just don't want you to look back on this time and resent me for holding you back."

Ryan stared at the girl in front of him—only seventeen, but more of a woman then most women ever grew to be.

"Princess, don't you understand yet? You're it for me. I know we're young. I know my life is about to get crazy. But you...are...*it*. You are what most guys spend their whole lives trying to find. I just got lucky enough to find you at nineteen. And if you think I'm crazy or dumb enough to ever jeopardize that then maybe you aren't as smart as we all think you are."

Ashley gazed into Ryan's eyes filled with determination, love, and respect, eyes that were staring intently at her, begging her to believe in him...in them. All of her fears melted away like snow cones in August, as he continued.

"I love you, Ashley, only you. You need to trust me and trust that I will take care of your heart even when I'm not physically with you. Can you do that for me?" She felt her smile stretch over her mouth as she nodded her agreement. This felt good. This feeling was the kind of good that pumped through her veins, the kind that would keep her warm while he was gone.

"You know, you and Leo are a lot more like brothers than friends," she mused just before his lips took hers in what began as a simple kiss, but quickly turned into a hungry passionate embrace.

Ryan's strong hand moved swiftly from the back of her head where he had been holding her close, down her neck and over her back. His fingers spread wide covering most of her narrow frame as his thumb caressed the exposed skin where her tank top had risen up. The raw groan that rumbled deep in his throat was swallowed whole by the deep penetrating kisses Ashley bestowed upon him. She couldn't get enough of him. His scent, his tongue, his touch.

"Ahem, sorry to interrupt this adorable, yet nauseating, moment," Leo snickered, not looking at all sorry for the interruption, "but we really have to get going. Jayson just got here with the bus and we still need to get Zane and his two tons of shit and hit the road if we are gonna make any headway today."

Pulling in a deep breath and silently begging herself for the strength to hold her emotions in for just a few minutes longer, Ashley plastered on what Leo often referred to as her "Barbie doll" smile. "Okay, boys, travel safely and kick some serious concert ass!"

"Wow, sis. Did you just say *ass*?" With a hearty laugh, Leo embraced her tightly, making her feel as safe and loved as he always did. "I don't know, Ry, do you think it's safe leaving my little sister here without us watching out for her? We aren't even gone yet and she's already using profane language."

Leo's laughter felt like a warm sweatshirt wrapped over her body. She absently ran her hands up her arms, savoring the warmth before it faded away.

"She'll be fine," Ryan confirmed, his voice more confident than his face looked. From the corner of her eye, she stared at Ryan, wondering if he didn't have fears of his own piling up behind his shield of confidence. She knew that he had nothing to worry about in regard to her, but did he? She gave herself a mental head shake. Of course he knew, she told him often how much she loved him. She'd make sure to continue while he was gone.

"Hello, *she* is standing right here! And *she* is trying really hard to keep it together while *her* two favorite men in the entire world leave her behind. So please, rip off the Band-Aid and go so *she* can cry in peace and then get ready for work." Ashley poked both her brother and her boyfriend in the chest as she tried to bring her point home. All the while repeating to herself, *"Do not cry, do not cry."*

"Okay, sis, come here." Leo pulled her in one last time dropping a kiss to the top of her head. "I will call you every day, I promise. And you know you can call whenever you want. The time will go fast, just wait and see. Between school and work and you hearing from colleges any day now, you have loads to keep you busy. I expect to be your first phone call when you get into the University of Pennsylvania, even before Romeo over there."

"You will be, Leo."

"I love you, sis. Now wipe off that awful plastic smile, it's freaking me the hell out."

With one more squeeze, Leo walked away from Ashley and headed to the front of the house. Almost as an afterthought he called over his shoulder, "Two minutes guys. Seriously, don't make me come back here with the hose!"

Laughing, Ryan moved instantly closer to Ashley. His spicy cologne filled her nose and his touch lit up her skin. Ryan was sensory overload in its finest form.

All traces of laughter were gone as a look of sheer adoration and love washed over his features. Yep, she knew she was a lucky girl. "Ryan, I'll be okay. I want you to go out there and enjoy every single moment of this. You deserve it."

Stroking the pad of his thumb over her bottom lip he whispered, "But what I want is you. I love you, Princess. Please don't forget that."

Staring deeply into his soulful eyes, she knew right then and there that Ryan and Leo were right—trust was everything and she did trust him.

———————————————

The words Ashley spoke next were the elixir that eased his worried mind. "Ryan, I will not forget *anything* about us. I love you too. I always have and I always will. Now kiss me and go be amazing!"

Ryan stared for a brief second, murmuring something unintelligible. Without warning he pulled her even closer to his chest until there wasn't an inch between them. Not even a sliver of paper could slip through.

His fingers weaved their way through her hair, loving the way the strands slipped through his grasp, and he pressed his lips to hers. The kiss was intense and desire-filled from the second it started. He could feel the way her body melded against his, the way she went boneless under his touch. He reveled in the trust she gave to him and in their connection. With just one look from her, he felt ten-feet tall, but when she kissed him, there were no measure-ments to determine that feeling.

"Ash." Ryan's voice was hoarse with emotion. He begrudgingly ended the kiss and rested his forehead against hers. "The only thing I would rather do less than stop kissing you is spend the day riding in a bus in sopping wet clothes because I totally believe Leo when he says he'll be back with the hose if we don't get to the drive-way"—he looked at his watch—"...now." He pressed his lips to hers once more, this time breathing in her scent, trying to capture it deeply in his lungs, his need to keep her with him becoming vital, pivotal to his survival.

Nodding her agreement, she rolled her eyes and linked her fingers through Ryan's and walked to the front of the property to meet up with Leo and Jayson.

The moment he pulled his hand from hers, coolness traveled through his veins. Saying good-bye was painful, but not taking in every last second together was torture. Ryan climbed into the van and took the seat closest to the window. Their eyes locked, his hand ached from the tight fist he had it pulled into. He lifted two fingers to his lips and kissed the pads before pressing them back against the glass. Thank God the guys were leaving him alone, because there was no way he could speak around the enormous lump in his throat. He watched as she brought two fingers to her lips as if placing his kiss directly on her mouth. The bus turned off the street before her first tear fell.

The first of many tears glided down her cheeks. Watching the bus get smaller and smaller as it drove off down the street, Ashley's gut churned. The morning had been an emotional rollercoaster at best. Earlier when she was talking to Ryan about taking a break, she'd been terrified that he might actually agree to it. Nothing could be further from what she'd actually wanted, but she loved Ryan too much not to at least broach the subject. Leo had warned her against it, of course—telling her Ryan would never agree to it, but she hadn't been able to help herself. She needed him to be happy even at her own expense. His complete dismissal of her suggestion gave her the strength to say good-bye without falling apart in front of him. And now her brother and Ryan were off to ride on the winds of the *Storm Front* adventure while she was left standing alone, in her big house, in her small town, all by herself.

"I'll be fine," she told herself out loud. "Just perfect, as always."

CHAPTER EIGHT

Do Ya, Punk

"HEY, PRINCESS, IS now an okay time to talk?" Ryan settled in the beat-up chair on the bus, with his feet resting on the scarred coffee table. Just the sweet sound of Ashley's greeting had his dick hardening in his jeans.

"Hi, Ry. Yeah, I have a few minutes. I'm getting ready for work and after that I have a study group for my Calculus class. How was the show last night? Someone posted a clip on YouTube—you guys sounded amazing, as usual. But, you...you looked delicious!"

Her voice was soothing to his tired throat and his aching muscles. Ryan had never given any thought as to the toll performing on a nightly basis would take on his body. The past four weeks had taught him that no matter how much time he previously spent in the gym, the workouts were nothing compared to the demands of being on tour. The constant moving, setting up/breaking down, on top of their shows was exhausting.

"Yeah, babe, the show was awesome. It feels like we're finally hitting our groove. That first week was tough as hell. I thought Leo was gonna throttle Zane at least twice and Jayson and I had one small fight, but things are smooth now."

"Boys will be boys." The warmth in her giggle traveled through the phone and straight to the core of his body. *God, I miss her. How can I miss her so fucking much?* Those were the thoughts constantly running through Ryan's mind. It took more than a little effort to shake them off when it was time to go from being Ryan Baker, the boyfriend, to Ryan Baker, *Storm Front*'s front man and heart throb.

That was what the argument between he and Jayson had been about. Jayson had said that Ryan's concentration was for shit and if he intended to be pussy-whipped the entire tour then they would have to look for a new front man. Aside from Ashley, *Storm Front* meant everything to Ryan so—on adrenaline alone—he'd thrown and landed a strong punch right to Jayson's jaw. Jayson, being one of four brothers, had no problem returning the jab. Both guys had played the show that night sporting bruised faces and swollen knuckles.

"Ry, you're fading out on me honey, do you need to go?" Ryan knew how much it bothered Ashley when he drifted off during their conversations. He often told her not to take it personally, but she explained it was hard not to take it any other way when phone calls and texts were their only source of communication while he was on the road.

"No, wait, Ash, a couple things. First, I have a surprise for you."

"You do? I love surprises!" The excitement in her voice was palpable. He loved that he was able to put a smile on her face even from so far away.

"Your test is on Thursday, right?"

"Yes, last period, why?" He could hear the gears turning in her head, which increased his own excitement ten-fold. "I know you're scheduled to work both Friday night and Saturday afternoon but can you see about getting someone to cover your shifts?"

Elation bubbled in her voice. "Ryan, what are you planning?"

"Princess, can you get your shifts covered or what?" Confidence oozed from his voice. He knew she was going to love his surprise and he couldn't wait a moment longer to tell her.

"Yeah, Ry, I'll ask Scott if he can take them for me. I'm sure he won't mind, especially since I've been helping him prepare for this calc test."

Just hearing Scott's name sent tiny shards of ice through Ryan's veins. Scott James was Jayson's younger brother and Ashley's co-worker at the restaurant. But Ryan had noticed the way Scott's gaze lingered just a little too long on Ashley. He'd seen the way Scott leaned in just a little too close when he was speaking to her. He'd even heard Jayson and his brother talk when they didn't think anyone was around.

Scott had a major crush on Ashley and while it seemed as though Ashley didn't think of Scott as anything more than an acquaintance, a co-worker, or a classmate, she also hadn't noticed that her aloof feelings were defi-nitely not mutual. Ryan knew when a guy was interested in a girl. Hell, he *was* a guy, and he could spot "game" from a mile away.

"Ash, that's all you're doing with Scott, right?" Im-ages of that smug bastard sitting too close to Ashley popped into his mind before he could control them.

Clearly not hearing Ryan's change in tone, Ashley

giggled. "Oh please, Ry. As if anything would ever go on between Scott and me. I don't think so."

He tried not to snarl when he said, "Great, then get Scott to cover your shifts. I found a cheap flight for you to Jessup, Georgia. It leaves at four on Thursday and the return flight is on Sunday morning. You leave just before we head off to Atlanta. We're playing in a bunch of small towns that weekend so you and I will have some quality time together before the band heads off to Atlanta for the bigger shows. What do ya think?"

As if the squealing wasn't answer enough, he heard the thumping of what could only be her jumping up and down in the cute way she did when she was really happy. "Princess, you excited by any chance?"

"Ahhh! Ryan Baker, if you were here I would be jumping on you instead of looking like an idiot in the parking lot of Penne Plaza! Oh, honey, I'm *so* excited! I can't wait to wrap my arms around you. Oh, shut your trap. You know I'm not talking to you!"

The elated buzz that had him floating on a bubble popped instantly, leaving Ryan flat on the ground, flat-out confused and more than a little pissed off. "Ashley, who the hell are you talking to?"

"I'm sorry, honey. I was walking into the restaurant and Scott heard me gushing and decided to butt into our conversation. But don't worry, I gave him my famous left-hook and he doesn't have anything to say now. 'Do ya, punk?'"

He could hear the humor in the words she spoke to Scott. The tenderness he felt every time Ashley spoke to him remained but even so, his vision was tinged with shades of green. Every muscle in his neck tightened as he heard her turn on the Ashley Kynde charm. "Ryan, honey, let me go so I can see about getting my shifts covered. Will you call me tonight after your show?"

Burying the feelings of jealousy deep into his gut, Ryan replied, "Princess, every time I sing one of the songs that you and I wrote together I swear I can feel you standing next to me, and we've been ending our shows with *Deep Dark Kiss*, so yeah, baby, I'll call you after the show."

"Oh, Romeo." Ashley had taken to calling him Romeo as of late. He didn't mind too much though because although she swore his lines were cheesy he knew they made her swoon nonetheless. "I'll be waiting by the phone." She giggled just before disconnecting the call.

Ryan looked at the screen of his cell phone, a picture of he and Ashley peered back at him. How had he come so far so fast? He gently swiped his thumb over their captured image. *How could one smart, beautiful girl have the ability to turn his entire life inside out? Just as quickly as that thought hit, another sparked in his mind...she could hurt you, man. Be careful. She loves you, but, you aren't there. Things could change at any minute.* Ryan stared at the picture again, and mentally shook his head. *No, she'd never do anything to hurt you. This is time and distance talking. This is your worry about Scott James talking.* He left the confines of the bus and headed to the venue to get some practice time in before the show. Playing always helped to clear his mind.

⊙────────────────⊙

Ashley held the phone close to her chest. *Deep Dark*

Kiss was a song they had started writing before they'd even shared their first kiss. She remembered sitting at the desk in her room staring at her note pad. It had been the day before Ryan, Leo and the boys had left for their summer trip. Ryan sat only a few inches away from her, watching as she wrote each word on the paper. His warm breath sent chills through her body, beading her nipples and moistening her panties.

She'd tried so hard to focus on the lyrics when really all she'd wanted to do was turn her head the slightest bit and press her lips to Ryan's, to swipe her tongue gently across them and taste the satiny smooth skin.

Words swirled through her mind, begging to be released onto the paper, but embarrassment coupled with fear of rejection and sexual frustration kept her hands still, even while her inner thoughts ran wild.

> *Dyin' just to settle in and hold you*
> *a little closer*
> *Dyin' just to sip your lips*
> *Dyin' for your deep dark kiss*

He'd been unusually quiet that afternoon, reflective even. Thinking back, Ashley now knew that his mood was the result of his inner conflict—wanting to finally share his feelings for her, but his loyalty to Leo had held him back.

While the melody had come relatively easy, the lyrics kept evading them. Finally allowing herself to pen the thoughts from her mind onto the paper, she hadn't dared to turn to face him. She hadn't needed to move to hear his breath stick in his chest. There'd been one beat of silence, and then another while she'd mentally berated herself for exposing her cards to a guy who meant the world to her. Worse still, her brother's best friend.

In an almost unrecognizably hoarse voice, Ryan had exhaled and said with a moan, "Ashley, my God." She'd heard the scrub of his hands over his face, and watched from the corner of her eye as he stood from the chair. He'd leaned down and kissed her cheek before quickly exiting her room.

Repeatedly thumping her head against the desk she'd chided herself for allowing him to see into her thoughts, into her heart. The guys had left the next morning for the summer tour, their departure placing an icy feeling in the pit of her belly.

The lyrics to the ballad had sat, unfinished, in her notebook—a direct imitation of the way her feelings for Ryan sat unrequited in her mind. It wasn't until the night in the pool, when Ryan had kissed her for the first time— the night he'd confessed his true feelings for her—that the remaining words to the forgotten song had bubbled out of her like champagne. That night, *Deep Dark Kiss* was completed and to date it remained her favorite *Storm Front* song.

⚫━━━━━━━━━━━━━━━━━⚫

"Dude, what'd that phone ever do to you?" Leo pried the defenseless cell phone from Ryan's white-knuckled grip.

"What? Oh, nothing. I was just talking with your sister." Leo laughed at Ryan's clipped tone and pinched expression.

"So, what'd she do to piss you off? I mean, Ashley

can be stubborn as hell, but she usually doesn't get to you like this. Christ, you usually act like she walks on water."

The two friends started walking from the bus to the small stage they would be playing on later that evening. Ryan watched as Leo climbed behind his drum kit and yanked out a pair of sticks from his back pocket. He loved watching his boy play the drums. Leo made it look so damn easy. Playing was like breathing to him, which is why the two of them had connected so well in the first place—they each saw their instruments as an extension of themselves.

Leo started tapping lightly on his middle tom, leveling his eyes to Ryan and waiting for his friend to talk. The rasping sound of the drum was hypnotic—designed to co-ax an answer out of him. But Ryan was wise to his friend's tactics and remained stoic, lightly tapping his foot in time with the beat. Leo added the deep melodic sound of the bass drum into the mix.

"So, we're gonna play it this way? Cool. I can hammer out the new song while you play the silent, broody guy." Leo laughed and began to go full throttle into his groove giving his arms a full-fledged workout, all the while, keeping his eyes locked firmly on Ryan.

Ryan shook his head. He knew stubbornness wasn't a trait only found in the female Kynde sibling. Leo could wait forever, if that's what it took.

"Grrr, fine, I'll talk. Just stop with the stare. It's fucking creepy, man. Jesus, you and your sister are stubborn as hell when you want something."

"That's true brother but remember what I've told you, stubborn works both ways. We use it to *get* what we want and we use it to *give* what we want. Giving up is never an option for Ash and me. Now spill."

His arms crossed firmly over his chest, Ryan took a breath in through his nose and slowly released it from his mouth. "So, Ash is coming out this weekend."

"Oh, man, that's great. I miss her like crazy. Daily calls just aren't enough." Angling his head in a question-like pose, Leo then asked, "Wait, how'd you get her to agree to that? She has to work two days this weekend."

Ryan loved how happy his friend was. Leo's eyes were round with excitement and his smile was wide, show-ing off the perfect dentistry his parents must have spent a fortune on. "I hate that she's stuck at home alone. Our par-ents suck. They're always working and they never notice when she's feeling down because...well, they're never fucking there!"

Even though Ryan sometimes wished he lived in the Kynde house, he'd never wished to be part of the Kynde family household. He loved his father, and the relationship they had, beyond words. Before his mother died they were the perfect family. Since her passing, his father had done everything a father could do in order to be there for his son. Martin Baker was a great dad.

"So, if Ashley is coming here in less than 72 hours, why do you look like you're ready to rip someone's face off?"

"Two words, man. Scott James."

Ryan watched as Leo processed the name in his mind. The moment Leo's eyes lit up in acknowledgement he continued. "Look, we've discussed Scott several times. You told me not to worry about the punk..."

"Yeah, Ry, I told you that it was Jayson's brother and there was no way you should let your mind go there.

We're a team, man. Jayson wouldn't let his brother go anywhere near Ashley. But none of that matters because Ashley wouldn't touch him with someone else's hands. She loves you. I feel like I'm growing a pussy even having this conversation, but she fucking loves you. Put Scott out of your brain."

"Dude, every time I talk to her she's either with him, or going to meet with him, or just come from seeing him. It freaks me the fuck out. It makes me feel...I just don't like it. That's all."

Leo stood up from his drums and stepped over to the guitar case sitting in the corner. "Here," he said handing Ryan the royal blue electric Fender. "You wanna be jealous, play your freak-out on this."

At that moment, Jayson and Zane walked up onto the stage. They were laughing about who knows what when they saw Ryan and Leo set to practice. "Cool," Jayson smiled, "let's warm up. What do you wanna start with?"

Ryan could feel the fire begging to be released from his body. "*Raging Inferno*," he snarled.

The tapping count of Leo's drum sticks sucked all of the anger from Ryan's body, fueling him with passion and lust for the music. Such was his passion that it continued on into their set that night, rolling off the stage like fog lifting from a lake in the early morning hours.

That night, *Storm Front*'s performance was incredible.

CHAPTER NINE

Good, Then I'm Doing It Right

"HEY, ROMEO. GOD, you're a sight for sore eyes." Ashley had no more than a second to take in Ryan's appearance before he was too close for her to see more than the golden hues of his irises.

Wrapped in his long corded arms, the world spun as he twirled her around and around until dizziness threatened to make her ill. When their lips finally met, it felt like comfort and warmth, fireworks and electricity all strung together. Like New Year's Eve on a tropical island. Breathless, Ashley inhaled deeply, taking in Ryan's rich spicy scent. The air in her chest burned, but by God was it good to *feel* again.

"Mmm, I've missed the smell of your skin." The skin beneath her fingertips tightened and she could feel the goose bumps on Ryan's skin. Raking her nails over his scalp, she felt him harden in his cargo pants.

"Your hair is longer than it was before. I love it like this," she purred, tightening her hold on his hair before moving back in for another deep kiss.

"Princess," he murmured breathlessly into her mouth. She reveled in the fact that his body responded to her every touch, taste, and scent. The need in his voice was palpable as he said, "I want you so bad right now, but we're gonna get arrested for public indecency if we keep this up in the airport."

The second he pulled away from her she felt the loss. She missed the closeness of his body against hers. She felt warmth settle into her cheeks along with embarrassment over her very public display of affection. Pulling her close, he leaned his lips down to her ear and whispered, "I plan on getting indecent I just don't want to share you with anyone. So let's get your luggage—and your sweet ass—out of here."

Her body responded instantly to the provocative words uttered in her ear. "Oh Romeo," she murmured. "It's no wonder the women fall all over you with that silver tongue of yours." Shivering with anticipation, Ashley laced her fingers through Ryan's and they headed toward the baggage claim.

"The only woman I want falling all over me is you, Ashley." He paused before asking, "So are you? Falling?"

Pulling them to a stop, Ashley looked up at Ryan from beneath her long lashes and confidently said, "Ryan, I fell at fifteen and never got back up."

The warmth of her words washed over him and he cupped her face in his hands, kissing her deeply once again. While their breaths mingled and their tongues caressed, Ryan had to remind himself again of his promise that they would wait until December to finally make love. He wanted to wait until he could be with her for longer than just a few hasty days. He would wait until she was eighteen and he could ask her for forever. Just two more months, he thought as he deepened the kiss between them. In the meantime, he planned to enjoy every minute of the time they had together while she was here with him.

⬤————————————⬤

"Sis, get over here!" The excitement in Leo's voice had Ashley shaking with delight. Seeing her brother after more than a month was almost as painful as it was wonderful. Almost. His eyes were bright with eagerness as he took long strides to get to her. His hair, like Ryan's, was longer and streaked with lighter shades of blond— something that always happened to him in the summer. It wasn't unheard of for people to accuse Leo of coloring his hair, but it was really just God paying him a little extra attention in the looks department.

Ashley admired her brother's sun-kissed skin and felt a pang of envy. Between her classes and her work schedule she'd had very little time to enjoy the Florida weather.

"Leo, another tattoo? Really?" There was no anger behind Ashley's question this time. Rather a profession of happiness that her brother was living the life he'd always dreamed of. Examining the new ink she felt a little jab of something deep down in her gut. She couldn't identify it, so she pushed it down a little further and pretended that it didn't exist at all. "What is it Le?"

"Look closely, sis. It's everything that's made me who I am so far." Tears stung Ashley's eyes as the image marked on Leo's forearm became incredibly clear. In between beautiful black flowing ink were the initials LKA, for Leo and Ashley Kynde. The two legs of the "K" were drumsticks and the spine of the "L" was part of a crotchet/quarter note. The "A" was made up of black vines with one small blue flower on the bottom right leg. Twisting around and through the tattoo were random words and symbols that Leo had mentally collected through his life—his treasure chest of thoughts. The piece was large but tasteful and masculine. So very Leo.

"Leo, I love it. It's so you and I love the ceratostigma on the "A". Thank you!"

Ashley was surprised that someone had been able to capture the heart of her brother so perfectly through ink and skin. Without turning her gaze from his arm she addressed Ryan. "And what about you, Ry? Any new artwork on that sweet canvas?"

Having not heard his movement, Ashley startled when Ryan's voice came from so close to her body. "Babe, I told you I would come to you before making any more big decisions. Remember?" Ashley smiled at her brother, her back still facing Ryan. Leo winked and came up with a quick excuse to grab some drinks from the soda machine down the hall.

Slowly turning to face the sexy, dark haired, molten-eyed man who'd captured her heart, Ashley tipped her head back to look Ryan in the eyes. Even though Ashley stood at five foot eight, Ryan was still a good five or so inches taller and he made her feel tiny and protected.

"Ryan, honey, I appreciate your intentions of keeping me in the know about important life decisions, but as long as you aren't tattooing your face or another woman's name on your body, I've decided I'm okay with you inking without my knowledge."

Running one slender finger up his biceps and over his shoulder she felt the shudder that rocked his body. Her finger continued its trail up his neck and to its final destination. His lips. She stroked his plump bottom lip while staring directly into his eyes. Time and place faded away as she heard his breathing quicken with each touch.

Ashley stared into hungry eyes as her body responded to his touch. She couldn't help but to moisten her bottom lip when his heated gaze dropped to her mouth. His chest expanded and his nostrils flared as she watched arousal building like a storm in his eyes. The slight sting of her lip between her teeth brought a surge of pleasure between Ashley's thighs. Reaching forward, Ryan placed his hand in her hair and tugged her toward him. The masculine groan that escaped him was almost her undoing.

"Ash, I need to get you alone, soon." He let out a low growl. "Fuck it. I need you now! I booked us a room for the next three nights. Ready to go?" His hands ran down her back and over her firm ass while he waited for her answer.

Snapping out of the lust-induced fog, Ashley ran her knuckle down Ryan's jaw. "You know I am Ry, but let me tell Leo that we're heading out. I'd like to make plans to see him for a late dinner after the show. I miss him and I want to spend time with him while I'm here."

Ashley spoke slowly, choosing her words carefully. She missed Ryan something crazy and couldn't wait to spend time snuggled in his arms, but she'd missed Leo too. She waited for Ryan's response, hoping she hadn't upset him or worse, made him feel guilty.

"Princess, we don't need to rush." Ryan lifted her chin. A chagrinned look covered his beautiful face. "We can spend some time with Leo and the other guys before we head out. I'm sorry. I just saw you and lost my mind."

"Ryan, I love that about you. Do you have any idea how that makes me feel?"

"No, baby, tell me." Ryan's low seductive voice had Ashley swooning like a fan-girl.

"It makes me feel wanted, horny and loved."

"Good, then I'm doing it right!" He winked, and they went in search of Leo, Jayson and Zane.

"Wow, I thought you two would have been locked away getting down and dirty by now," Zane chuckled. Ryan scowled and Leo threw an empty water bottle at the bassist's head.

"What?" Zane said, genuinely confused. "I'm just sayin' they haven't seen each other in weeks. If it was me, I would be tappin' that ass like crazy!"

When Ryan growled and Leo stood up with clenched fists, Zane realized his mistake. "Dude, I'm so sorry. I look at her and I forget she's your kid sister." Zane held his hands up in a submissive show of respect.

"Fuck you, Zane. Yes, Ashley is his sister, but she's my fucking girl! You don't get to treat her or talk about her like she's a cheap piece of ass. Now apologize. Right. Fucking. Now!" Ryan seethed, his temper reaching boiling point.

Zane's face paled but before he could open his mouth, Jayson piped-up, "Ash, you know we all love you. Zane can be an idiot. Sometimes we still *think* of you as part of the band, or the little sister with braces. But when we *see* you, you're this beautiful grown chick, not Leo's kid sister and certainly not *one* of Ryan's girls..."

The small gasp come from Ashley's mouth had Ryan launching himself at Jayson, backing him against the wall. "What the hell is that supposed to mean? *One of Ryan's girls?* You all fucking know that I haven't so much as looked at another woman since before we did the first set of shows in early June."

Ryan felt the anger and frustration pulsing through his veins like mercury through a thermometer. His mind kept screaming for him to back off but just like the silver liquid when the thermometer breaks, he couldn't quite get a grip on the out of control emotion. "Are you trying to start something, man? Between you and your fucking brother—"

"Ryan!" Ashley's voice broke through his haze, dousing the fire that raged inside of him. "Honey, back down. They're acting like buffoons. They know it, I know it, and if you think about it, you know it too."

She moved closer behind him until he could feel the warmth of her body pressed up against his back. She dropped her voice a little lower when she said, "Let's get out of here, Ry. I know a better way to spend our time."

With the red haze receding from his vision he was able to see the irritated glare Leo was giving to Jayson and the honest shame on Zane's face, but it was the look in Jayson's eyes that gave him a poke in the ribs. There was something there that didn't sit right with Ryan. Maybe it was the fact that Jayson was Scott's brother or maybe it was just that Jayson was acting like an asshole. Either way, Ryan was annoyed.

"Come on, Romeo. Let's get out of here." Hearing

Ashley's sweet voice broke the spell of the tense moment.

"Yeah, Ry, take my sister out for an early dinner. I'll meet up with you before the show and we can all grab a quick bite to eat afterwards." Ryan looked at his best friend and saw tension in what were usually such easy-going eyes and felt his shoulders start to tighten up once again.

Ryan stood stone still. His fingers webbed tightly with Ashley's as he watched Leo approach. Leaning in, Leo whispered in his ear, "Seriously, you guys get out of here. Let me handle this. Go be with my sister and make her happy. And before you think I'm acting all noble, I'm not. Seeing her happy makes *me* happy, so technically, I'm being a selfish ass." He finished his speech with a clap to Ryan's shoulder.

Ryan knew Ashley hadn't heard what her brother had whispered but she couldn't have missed the physical response his words had. Ryan's rigid posture loosened and his angry face went lax. Ryan extended his hand to Leo and went in willingly when Leo pulled him in for a bro-hug. Yep, that guy was his brother in all ways but blood. Leo wrapped his big arms around Ashley and directed her on how to spend the next couple of hours.

"Go take care of my brother," Leo said to her. Ashley giggled when she saw the look on Leo's face as realization of what he said hit. "Mind out of the gutter Ash, Christ, I meant, go take a walk or something…God, I think I'm gonna puke." Letting out a small chuckle, Ryan let Ashley lead him out of the room and back to the hotel. He had no idea what would happen with the guys once they left, but he knew for certain that Leo would take care of it. For now.

CHAPTER TEN

Sweet Ashley

THE FOOD WAS set on a tray in the small hotel room when they entered. "Wait, how? When?" He smiled as her feelings of both confusion and giddiness played out over her gorgeous features.

"Is it possible that I've actually rendered Ashley Kynde speechless?" Ryan's mocking tone earned him a playful slap on the arm and he watched as Ashley sauntered over to the desk and lifted the domes off the plates that were waiting for them.

"Oh, man." Ashley's stomach chose that moment to let out its appreciation for the perfectly made grilled cheese sandwiches and French fries along with the bowls of tomato soup. He knew his girl so well.

"So, I guess I don't need to ask if you're hungry?" Ryan's smile widened with the second growl of Ashley's belly.

"I'm starving, Ryan. I haven't eaten since breakfast—you know I get nervous on big exam days. This looks like heaven."

She eyed the food on the tray before bending over to grab a French fry. As she brought it up to her lips, he felt his insides craving nutrition of a whole different kind. "Um, Ry, where's your food?" She joked as she popped a fry in her mouth.

"Princess, I don't care how hungry you think you are, there is no way you could fit all of that food in your body. But, I would love to see you try." He smirked at her wrinkled nose and pitched brows while she continued to scarf down her lunch. While she ate he filled her in on the most recent shows and various opportunities that had been coming their way, but all the while he could only really focus on her. The way her lips closed around her spoon. Her tongue as she licked the splashed tomato soup from her finger. Her throat as it swallowed each and every morsel of sustenance. His senses were overloaded to the point where he could no longer think of any words at all. Did she even realize how incredibly sexy she was?

"Ryan?" She looked at him, setting the tray aside. His desire mirrored in her eyes.

"Ashley." He hardly recognized his own voice as his body moved towards her without any instruction from his conscious mind.

"I-I need to touch you."

Before her sentence was complete his hands cupped her jaw, pulling her up from her chair and closer to his face. Ashley quickly rose to her toes and pressed herself against him, connecting their bodies. Her small hand traveled to the hem of his t-shirt. With deft fingers she lifted it up over his head and tossed it to the floor. Her hands traveled his torso and traced patterns on his skin. It was like his body was a map and she was marking all the destinations she intended to visit.

"Ah, Ryan, your skin feels so good. My God, it's

been so long." The raspy groan he released triggered something in her and he felt her body against his. His hands moved from her face to her hair. His fingers tugged at the silky strands and she let out a small whimper.

"Christ, Ash, those sweet noises are gonna undo me." He ran his hands from the back of her head down to the waist of her yellow tank top and his thumbs started touching the slight strip of skin between the tank and her shorts. She shivered under his soft touch. "Damn, Princess, I love the way you respond to me. Now lift your arms, you've got way too many clothes on."

Peeling the flimsy fabric from her skin he couldn't suppress his gruff chuckle when he noticed the buttercup yellow bra that matched her tank top. That was Ashley to a T—everything perfect, all of the time. A yellow top meant a yellow bra and he'd be willing to bet fifty bucks—he unbuttoned her denim shorts—yep, yellow panties. "Fuck me."

"Ryan, are you laughing at me while we're making out?" Ashley feigned offense. Some people thought Ashley had OCD, but he wasn't one of them. He appreciated the way she kept herself, Leo and even him organized. And he loved how at anytime he knew underneath the pristine Ashley Kynde was a sexy woman in matching bra and panties.

"No, Princess, I'm just enjoying how well I know you." He wagged his brows, "Now get closer so I can know you better."

He pulled her against his bare chest and slowly walked her backward until the back of her knees hit the bed. "Let me show you just how much I enjoy knowing you, Ashley. Let me show you, just how much you've already taught me."

He eased her down onto the plush beige comforter and began his lessons at her lips. Straddled above her, he watched as hunger flashed through her eyes. It was like looking into an autumn storm where the golden leaves were swept off the trees just before the pouring rain came to wash them away. His tongue entered her mouth as his right hand traveled down the column of her neck and across her collarbone. She whimpered with arousal just before she closed her eyes and turned her head to the side.

"Eyes, Princess." His hoarse voice brought her out of her thoughts with a startle.

"What?" She croaked.

"I wanna see your eyes when I make you come. You hide so much from so many people, Ash, but when I look in those eyes I see everything. Don't hide from me, baby." He looked deeply into her green speckled depths and fell a little more in love than he had been when they walked into the room thirty minutes before. *God, how was that even possible?*

Sliding his index finger under the front clasp of her bra the lacy cups fell away to the sides and he stared down at her full and perfect breasts.

"Beautiful," he whispered, leaning down to cup one firm breast into his hand. He felt her tense as he laved her nipple. Ryan suckled and nipped the sensitive bud until it was tightened and erect before him, then he blew a soft cool breath over the moistened peak and reveled in the small moan that breached her lips. Using his thumb and forefinger to roll and pinch the stimulated nipple, he moved his mouth to her other breast.

"Oh, Ryan. Oh. That feels...so good. Harder, Ryan.

Bite me harder." The plea in her voice had Ryan obeying her demand. He felt himself getting harder in his jeans. He could stare at her forever while she was lost in this place of passion and pleasure.

"So responsive, Ash. So fucking beautiful." He let his left hand leave her breast and travel further south. Her warm, soft skin was spun silk under his calloused fingertips. When he finally reached the waistband of her panties he heard her breathing halt. Slowly he slid one finger under the elastic band to rub the soft flesh of her hip. Her breathing quickened. He couldn't fight his grin, hell, he loved that she anticipated his next move. He loved that she couldn't wait for it.

He slid her panties down her legs as goose bumps covered her heated flesh. Ryan ran his hands from her ankles up to her thighs, stopping just as he got to her moist core.

"Oh, my God!" She hissed loudly when his warm tongue touched her center.

"Princess, you're so wet for me," he murmured, feeling proud.

"Stop talking, Ry." Ashley's plea came out breathless and wanton. She tasted sweet and tangy as he ran his tongue up her seam and over her throbbing bud. He greedily licked and sucked on her clit as he stuck his finger into her wet channel and started to pump. Ryan's cock hardened as Ashley began grinding herself against his lips searching for her release. His scalp stung when she threaded her fingers through his hair and tugged as he inserted another finger into her tight hole.

"Oh, God, Ryan, sweet Jesus! Harder baby, more. Please more!" Her begging was destroying any semblance of the control he clung to. Palm facing up, he moved his fingers deep inside of her and rubbed the sweet spot hidden away, waiting just for him. When he felt the tremor in her thighs he rubbed his thumb over her clit and lifted his head to speak.

"Come for me, Ashley," he commanded. "Let go."

Just as the order left his mouth he leaned in and sucked deeply on her clit, sending her into complete bliss. She came apart piece by piece, shards blowing everywhere, but she didn't care where they landed. Her body quivered as he continued to suckle at her most intimate place and her breath hitched as her mind slowly started to pull itself together.

"That was"—she inhaled deeply—"unbelievable, Ryan. Like, the best it ever was." She watched his smug grin as her kissed up her thigh, her hip, her belly and finally her lips. She could taste herself on his tongue and suddenly her appetite for him was completely unsatisfied. Locking her ankles around his back, she used all of her weight and the element of surprise to flip him over onto his back.

Shock widened his eyes and his brows lifted. "Princess, that was…impressive. Now that you have me as your captive, what do you plan to do with me?"

His voice was filled with love and humor, but she wanted to change that. She wanted to return the lust and sexual gratification that he had just bestowed upon her. In their time together she had experienced a lot of firsts, but Ryan liked to keep iron-clad control of their sexual time together. At first she was fine with his guidance but he tended to keep her from doing some of the things she really wanted to do.

Yes, she'd made him come. They'd grinded and she stroked him off. She'd felt his body quiver and then go rigid until the warm fluid filled her palm and ran down her wrist, but she ached to taste him. She wanted to feel his hard length in her mouth. She wanted him to experience the pleasure that he constantly gave to her. In the past when she'd inquired about performing oral sex on him, she would watch the desire cross over his face only to be quickly replaced by the tenderness of a loving boyfriend trying to care for his girl. She loved that guy but she wanted the other guy too. She wanted the guy who let loose, the guy who burned with lust at the thought of having his woman on her knees in front of him.

She knew the people in her life saw her as *perfect* Ashley, *dependable* Ashley, *sweet* Ashley, but Ryan made her feel *more*. He made her feel sexy, desirable, wanted. He made her feel things that even with her vast vocabulary she could attach no words to. She was ready to show him just how wanton she felt in his presence.

While her hands steadily undid his belt and the button of his jeans she leaned forward, savoring his full lips. Easing down the zipper on his fly she slid her tongue in his mouth, laying claim to the very essence of who he was. When she deepened their kiss, he was so distracted that he didn't even notice her slide down his jeans, using her foot to glide them off of his long, strong legs.

His skin tasted like heaven as she marked a trail from his mouth to his ear. She felt the shiver climb his spine as she sucked on the sensitive spot before raking her teeth over the lobe and biting down. The small nip of pain got his attention, as did the fact that her tiny hands were cascading down his neck and over his muscular chest.

"Did you just bite me, Princess?" His question was barely comprehensible, a mere groan, as her tongue traveled the same path her hands had taken just seconds before.

"Umm hmm," she nodded, "and you taste so good, Ry."

"Sweetheart." Ryan's voice was husky and heavy with longing as she lowered her kisses down his body and closer to his erection. "Seriously, Ashley, what are you doing?" His body was ramrod tight as she lowered his boxer briefs with her left hand and touched his hardness with the soft tip of her tongue. He'd never let her give him a blow job before. They had discussed it, and he explained that he wanted to take it slow with her. He wanted their time together to be about her pleasure first and then he would teach her how to pleasure him.

"Ashley, you don't have to do this."

She held back her giggle. The words leaving his mouth said one thing, but the plea in his eyes screamed another. She slowly peeled down the boxer briefs that covered his long, thick, erection and felt a rush of wetness flow between her legs.

"Ryan, I've wanted this for so long. You think you're protecting me, keeping me, I don't know, pristine or something. But, honey, I want this. I need this. Let me make you feel the same pleasure you give to me every time you touch me." She ran her fingers over his muscular thighs while keeping her gaze trained on his. He needed to know that she wanted this. She was ready for this next step.

His body relaxed, and she once again began to drop light kisses down his torso, down the perfectly etched V under his hips and right to the top of his erection. She heard his deep inhalation and looked up to see his impassioned stare as he concentrated on her every move. She gently stroked his cock with her small hand just before running her soft wet tongue over the bulbous head of his shaft. She felt his body tense as she licked his length like a Popsicle moistening him with her tongue just before sliding him into her mouth as far as she could take him. She took the loud growl that erupted from his throat as encouragement and continued on.

"My God, Princess, where the fuck?" Ryan's thought went unfinished as she slid him further in and out of her mouth, trailing the shaft with her tongue. Each time she would get to the head of his dick she would lightly use her teeth around the rim and then use the slightest amount of suction to pull him back into her warm cavern. Her left hand pumped the length of him in time with her generous sucks while her right hand gently cupped his balls, caressing them with loving strokes.

"Ash, oh my…Ashley." Ryan's hoarse growl came out tense as his body arched, pushing his length further into her mouth. "Ash, I'm gonna come, honey. You need to move."

She knew what was gonna happen, but she didn't move. She wanted what he was gonna give her and she craved it. She continued to suck him deeply. Giving him pleasure was turning her on as well. She held on to his hips even though he tried to push her away. With a loud groan, his orgasm flooded her mouth, and she swallowed down every drop of his release. She could feel him staring at her as she then licked his shaft clean and began to kiss her way up his body.

He watched her completely speechless. She loved seeing that look on his face: a look of utter satisfaction that could only come from complete sexual gratification. She'd given that to him. Lost only for a moment in her thoughts, she felt his calloused palms skim up the sides of her body as he effortlessly shifted her onto the bed beneath him.

"Ash."

Each shallow breath that escaped his mouth made her skin tingle. She'd never felt more powerful, more seductive, more...alive. He parted his lips and she waited for a compliment that never came. Instead, the words that pierced the air around them felt like a dagger in her chest. "Where did you learn to do that?"

At first, she thought his quiet tone was teasing but when she saw his brows pull together and his nostrils flare she knew that his question wasn't a compliment. It was an accusation. A cool wave swept through her belly and her shoulders tightened.

"What?"

If the high pitch of her response hadn't conveyed how hugely he'd fucked up then she was sure the way the sated bliss crumbled off of her face did. Without waiting for a response she scrambled off the hotel bed and started yanking on her clothes.

"Ash, I'm so sorry. I didn't mean—" He got off the bed and stood behind her, reaching one hand out to touch her shoulder. She startled and pulled away, turning around to face him.

"Yes. You. Did." Her eyes glistened like diamonds with unshed tears. "How could you, Ryan? Why would you ever think that I would be with anyone else? What have I done to make you think so little of me?" She crossed her hands over her upper arms rubbing away cold that hadn't been there just mere minutes ago. How could he have said that to her? How could he have even thought it?

"Ash, I'm so sorry. I know that you would never hurt me. I know it. It's just I've been feeling a little jealous lately...and then you give me the world's greatest fucking blow job. I know that we've never done that before. And you've never been with anyone before me..." Ryan's words were coming out jumbled, his explanation weak, but she stood there silently while he continued on. "The earlier scene with Jayson, and you spending so much time with Scott, I guess it just scared me."

"Why are you scared, Ry? Tell me. Because right now I have no idea what you're talking about." She mindlessly rubbed the ache in the center of her chest. Her mind buzzing in confusion as to what the hell had just happened. She just gave him something so special and so sacred, and he accused her of betrayal? Her emotions swirled in her mind... fear, heartache, and anger.

"Ashley, Scott is into you. He has been for a while now. It used to bother me because I wanted you too, but I didn't think I would ever be lucky enough to have your love in return. But now that we're together, knowing how much he likes you makes me...okay, I'll say it, uncomfortable. No. Jealous. Not to mention I've heard that since we've been gone he's upped his game trying to steal you away from me."

She couldn't hold back the humorless laugh that bubbled out of her. Judging by his tense stance and furrowed brow, Ryan must really believe what he'd said. But she knew Scott James. He was just a friend. They worked together and had classes together—that was all.

"Ryan, that's absurd! Scott knows I only like him as a friend. He knows I love you. Everyone at our school knows it. It seems the only person who doesn't know it is *you*!"

Frustration nipped at her gut. Why did she feel like she needed to prove herself to him all of a sudden? Ryan had always been the one person—other than Leo—that believed in her. That loved her for exactly who she was. She felt a small ache in the middle of her chest. It was disappointingly familiar. It was an ache that resulted from her parent's indifference. She recognized it. She was used to it from them.

But never from Ryan.

Ryan hated that she wouldn't look at him when she spoke. He hated that he'd hurt her. Watching her rub the center of her chest nearly brought him to his knees. That was her tell. She didn't even know she did it but whenever Ashley and Leo's parents let them down, she would run the edge of her thumb up and down the middle of her sternum. It was almost as if she was trying to rub away the physical pain. He hated her parents every time he saw her do that, and now he hated himself.

"Ryan, I don't want Scott. But I'm not going to stand here and defend myself for crimes that only exist in your head. Okay, so I gave you a great *fucking* blow job—do you know how? Because I read a ton of books. Yes, Ryan, studious Ashley taught herself how to give a blow job. And guess what, you loved it. And I loved doing it to you."

The first pregnant tear inched down her cheek, tearing Ryan's guts to pieces as he watched it fall. "Now, I trust you," she continued. "I trust you out there on the road with all of those girls throwing their bras and panties at you, but you need to trust me too. Please!"

He just stared mutely at her. Using the palm of her hand she wiped away the droplets that coursed down her face.

"Well? Are you going to say anything?" Her back straightened as she inhaled deeply, pulling herself back together. He'd always admired how impenetrable she could be when she needed to be. Ashley was able to tuck away her feelings in the blink of an eye so that no one could ever see that she was hurting. She'd never been an ordinary girl nor had she become an ordinary woman. While Ryan had spent years marveling that very trait, right now he needed to know if he could get her forgiveness. "Or are you taking a vow of silence to avoid acting stupid in the future," she snapped.

"Ash, I really am sorry." He lifted his palms in surrender waiting to see her reaction. She moved closer to him, extending her hand to his bare shoulder. At her soft touch, his heart began to beat faster. "I honestly never meant to hurt you. I know that you would never cheat on me. I know that you love me. Christ," He smiled devilishly. "I felt it just a few minutes ago." Nothing melted him more than seeing the pale pink blush of her cheeks when he said something suggestive. She was still so new to all things sexual and he loved being the guy to lead her into this life.

"But, I gotta say, Princess"—his brow cocked with humor—"the thing that surprises me the most—more than the sweet kisses, more than the smoking hot blow job, even more than the fact that you let me come in your mouth, the thing that just rocked my world—you just dropped the f-bomb. Really, Ash? I thought cussing was for 'people with a limited vocabulary'?"

Ryan's joke seemed to break the tension in the air. Giggling, Ashley's body eased, her shoulders relaxed and her smile became genuine. "Hmm, let's just say, I'm beginning to re-evaluate that line of thinking. Dropping the f-bomb felt really good in *that* moment."

Even though the mood had lightened, Ryan knew the damage that he had caused and it was eating him up inside. "Ash, please forgive me."

"It's already forgotten, honey. Let's move on. I would love to go and see Leo and I can't wait for the show tonight. Will you end the set with, *Deep Dark Kiss*?"

"Yes," he growled. "And I intend to end the night with a deep dark kiss too."

Pulling her close he cupped her head and kissed her hard and deep.

CHAPTER ELEVEN

She Let Go

"RYAN, HONEY," ASHLEY moaned, "stop." They were lying naked on the hotel bed, their bodies tangled in the sheets. A light sheen of perspiration coated her skin and her body hummed with satisfaction. Despite just coming down from a mind-bending orgasm, Ryan was between her long, toned legs, building her up to another one.

She ran her fingers through his hair and tugged. Hard. When he lifted his face, unadulterated lust and hunger filled in his eyes. The evidence of her previous release glistened on his lips as his tongue jetted out and worked the sensitive nerves. Her body felt like a coiled spring chasing the impending orgasm she had no doubt he would give her. She trembled with desire.

"Ry, I'm leaving in just a few hours and we won't see each other until December. Please, make love to me. I know you want to romance me and make it special, but *this* is special. I love you and I want this so much. I...I...feel like I'm going to explode with want for you."

His grin was equal parts loving and devilish, "Oh, Princess, I am gonna make you explode...*again*. Just hold on tight." As he went to lower his head she stopped him, her desperate stare expressing the severity of her desire.

This time, he lifted up to his knees. "Baby, listen to me. If you think for one second that I don't want to be with you then you're out of your mind. I've been dying to sink into your sweet body since that first night we kissed in your parents' pool. But you're right, Ash, that would be sex, and while that's gonna be fucking hot that's not what I want for us."

His eyes penetrated her as he continued, "At least not the first time. You may be a virgin but I've never had sex with a girl I loved before." Ashley watched as Ryan's face flushed.

"Ryan Baker, are you blushing?"

He ran his hands over his warm cheeks and shrugged his shoulders. "Look, I know you're ready to take this to the next level—and trust me when I say I am too. But I love you, Ash. And, well, I guess I just want to wait until I know that we'll have weeks or months to be able to explore this, once we finally do it. You know that I'll give you anything. I'll give you *everything*. I'll even do as you ask—right here, right now—if that's what you want, but I'm asking you to wait until December. It doesn't have to be your birthday. We can do it the night I get home. But there's just no way that I...I can finally claim you that way and then watch you get on a plane and...and leave me."

Ashley actually felt a weight sitting on her chest. The guy who was always so smooth with the words, so quick with the comeback, was actually stumbling through his appeal. How could she turn down that request? How could she say *no* to that magnificent plea?

"Okay, Romeo, let's wait. But only until the night you get home though because after that little speech, I want you even more. God, I think I almost came...*again*!"

"Well, Princess, I think we both know I have no problems making that happen." Ryan shifted his weight and lowered his head, but Ashley squeezed her thighs together, preventing him from moving any further.

"Honey..." The hesitation in her voice was there but she pushed it back, hiding it underneath her bravado. "During my blow job inquiries I read about something else."

His questioning gaze set off butterflies in her belly. She shrugged before saying, "And since we're kind of pressed for time, why don't I show you want I learned? We can kill two birds with one stone."

Ryan's brows lifted in question but it was his sexy smirk that had the butterflies taking flight in the pit of Ashley's belly. It was one thing to read about things of this nature, but it was something completely different when suggesting them to the most devastatingly handsome man she ever met. Collecting her nerve, she pulled in a lungful of air and took a leap of faith.

"Lay on your back, Ry." She climbed astride his broad body and faced his feet. Bending down to suck on his long, hard shaft, she nestled her core back up to his lips. The deep groan that left Ryan's mouth assured her that he liked her suggestion. Even more so, the way that he feasted on her assured her that she had read *all* the right books.

●————————————————●

Wrapping her arms and legs around him like a monkey climbing a tree, Ashley hugged Leo with all her strength. "I love you, sis." His body shook with laughter as he placed huge kisses on the top of her head. "Hey, Ash, I'm having a hard time breathing." He faked breathlessness as he struggled to put her down.

"Leo, I hate leaving you. I hate it."

As she feigned her tantrum Leo turned to Ryan and said, "Always been so damn stubborn, my sister. Look how she acts when you try to take her favorite toy away."

The two men laughed as Ashley pouted. Leo swept her into another hug and kissed her head again. She loved this gesture—a gesture that was solely Leo's. When he did it she felt alive, needed, loved, and never alone.

When he replied, "Ash, I hate leaving you too. I do," she knew that he wasn't just paying her lip service. Their relationship was the strongest bond either of them had ever made and being apart was just as painful for him as it was for her. They'd already decided that he would move to whatever state she went to for college. If the band became popular he would be traveling a lot, but he wanted his home base to be wherever she was.

"This tour is only seven more weeks. We'll talk every day and before you know it, I'll be home." His smile deepened when he jabbed Ryan in the chest. "I'll even bring this guy with me."

"Yeah, like you could keep me away," Ryan muttered, his mouth turned up in a sexy grin. "My turn, man. You may wanna go check on your sister's flight or something because this here will melt your eyeballs."

"My cue to leave. Call me when you land, sis. I love you." Leo turned away quickly but not quick enough to hide his huge grin.

"Come closer, Princess." Their bodies pressed tightly

together, she could feel his heart beat pounding through his clothes. His scent surrounded her as she buried her nose into his chest and inhaled deeply. He immersed his face in her hair, "I love how you always smell like sunshine and coconuts, Ash. Everywhere you are is home to me." God, how could those words not undo her?

"I'll miss you the most of all, Scarecrow," she joked referencing her favorite childhood movie, The Wizard of Oz, just before pressing her lips to his. "But, honestly, Ryan, walking away from you just feels wrong. It makes me sad inside."

The smile faded from her face and the beautiful glow from their sexy morning together had gone dim. She no longer felt warm and cozy. Leaving Ryan and her brother left her feeling hollow and cold. "I know it's just seven more weeks, but it feels like an eternity."

"You know, if business school doesn't work out, you could always try your hand at acting. You've got drama all figured out, Princess." She knew what he was doing. His pasted on smile didn't reach his eyes and his grip tightened just a little bit more. She loved that he was trying to lighten the mood even though she could see that their separation was painful for him as well.

"Yeah, well, you should definitely keep your day job, Romeo, because your acting skills suck." Ryan smiled warmly as he squeezed Ashley tighter.

"Alright, Ash, your gate is all the way at the other end of the airport, so you better go. Call me when you land. I love you, babe."

"Bye Ry," she blew him a kiss, threw her backpack over her shoulder and headed to her plane.

Had she known how long it would be before she got

to hold him in her arms again, she would have held on just a little longer, but she didn't. She let go.

CHAPTER TWELVE

Stubbornness Works Both Ways

"DUDE, IF I had a camera, I could ruin you right now," Leo teased, not even trying to contain his laughter. Ryan's face must have displayed his confusion because Leo explained, "You are so whipped. And look, as her brother, I am so fucking happy that she found a great guy. But as your best friend, you look like a love sick puppy!"

Ryan couldn't help but to release the laughter he'd tried to hold in. Leo was a *call 'em as you see 'em* kind of guy. It was one of the reasons why they'd remained so close for so long. That was also one of the reasons Ryan had felt comfortable approaching Leo about his feelings for Ashley. He'd known that good or bad, Leo would give it to him straight. There would be no game playing about Leo's best friend and his sister dating.

"Do I look that fucked up, man?"

"Worse," Leo admitted. "Let's go Ry, I think it's time we had a little chat about you and my baby sister." Ryan cringed at the look on his best friend's face as they instructed the taxi to take them back to their tour bus.

The bus was empty when they arrived. Jayson and Zane had taken the day to visit Zane's family in a town about an hour north so Ryan knew they had plenty of time to talk candidly without being interrupted.

"So, here's the deal, buddy," Leo started, setting two beers on the small Formica table in the dining section of the bus. "I get that things between you and Ash are serious—"

"Leo," Ryan went to interrupt but the way Leo lifted his hand and closed his eyes told Ryan loud and clear that this conversation would be one-sided for a little while.

"Man, you're my best friend. I love you like a brother. But. She. Is. My. Sister." Leo emphasized each word. He hadn't needed to. Ryan knew how much Ashley meant to him. He sat in silence, waiting for Leo to continue. "I would walk through fire for that girl. Do you understand?" When Ryan opened his mouth, Leo's *don't interrupt me* stare had Ryan closing his mouth and nodding his head without ever letting sound escape.

Taking a long pull of his beer, Leo closed his eyes in what appeared to be contemplative thought. "I don't know what you two have done, but I know what you haven't...done. I know you've been a perfect gentleman, while she"—color rose in Leo's cheeks—"has tested your willpower."

Shifting his glance to the floor, Ryan allowed himself to exhale the breath he'd been holding. He loved Leo like a brother but until that moment he hadn't realized how important it was that Leo really trusted him with Ashley. He pulled his eyes back up and met his friend's stare.

"I know you love her, Ry, I do. But, you wounded her with that shit you pulled this weekend. Before you ask, yes, she told me about it." Leo cringed. "Thank God she spared me the full details, but I got the highlights. Dude, how could you accuse her of being with someone else? How fucked up is that shit? You and me, we've discussed this. I thought I'd finally got through to you. Scott James is *not* an issue, man. YOU ARE THE ISSUE!" He said as he slammed his hand down loudly on the table, jostling the beer bottles.

Ryan couldn't stop himself from interrupting. "Leo, you have no idea. I'm the one that hears Jayson talking to Scott on the phone. From the sounds of it, Scott is into her. Like *really* into her. And he's making his play. Did you know that they spend a lot of time together, both in school and out? I'm sorry, but I don't trust him any further than I can throw him."

"Look at yourself. Look at your hands."

Ryan looked down to see white knuckles and protruding veins. He could feel the bite of his fingernails as they dug into the palms of his hands. The realization had him unclenching his fists, slowly releasing the tension. "Ryan, she came to me before we left on tour and asked me how she could compete with the women who would be throwing themselves at you and I told her that you loved her and that she needed to step back and trust you to make the right choices."

"I am! I haven't so much as looked at another girl, you know that, Leo! What are you accusing me of?" His heart thumped in his chest as his breathing quickened.

Calm eyes surveyed his face as Leo watched Ryan intently before saying quietly, "Nothing. I'm not accusing you of anything...and neither is Ashley. Do you understand?"

Inhaling, Ryan stared back at Leo unable to form a response. Did he understand? Yeah, he understood. He'd been a complete asshole. He was the one making all of the accusations while Ashley sat back and trusted him blindly. Scrubbing his hands over his face, he tried to wipe away the *idiotic* persona that had taken over his body.

"Do you think she'll ever truly forgive me?" He whispered. Fear froze the air in his lungs, making it almost impossible for him to speak any louder.

Taking a couple more pulls from his beer before answering, Leo smiled brightly at Ryan. "So, here's the thing about Ashley." He drained his beer and set the bottle aside with a clink. "You know she is as stubborn as a goddamn mule?"

"Yeah, I think I may have experienced that side of her a time or two," Ryan huffed although Leo's relaxed face helped to lighten the mood.

"Well, with my sister stubbornness works both ways." Leo chuckled. "Dude, promise me you'll never play poker. Your face shows all of your emotions and you have no idea what I'm even saying. Stubborn works both ways, Ry. When Ashley is angry she's angry with everything she has. But when she loves…well, that girl loves the same way. Why do you think she always forgives our sorry excuses for parents? She's too fucking stubborn to give up on them. Once someone is really truly in her heart, they will live there forever. Now, that doesn't give you the right to fuck with her. Because, best friend or not, you only get so many chances to screw up before I kill you. But, I think you guys are meant to be. So get your head out of your ass and stop worrying about things that don't matter. We clear?"

Ryan nodded. "Crystal." Sitting up straight in the chair, Ryan rubbed his palms over his jean clad legs, stared at Leo and nodded, "You just do me a favor and tell Jayson to keep his fucking mouth shut when it comes to Ashley?"

"You think I didn't already take care of that? Ryan, she's my baby sister." The growl in Leo's voice was not to be mistaken. "I politely explained that if he ever disrespected her in any way, ever again, he'd have to learn how to play bass with his toes."

Even though they both laughed at Leo's comment, Ryan knew that Leo was in no way joking, and he guessed that Jayson probably knew it as well.

CHAPTER THIRTEEN

...As a Friend

"HEY, ASH, WAIT up." Ashley heard footsteps behind her as Scott quickened his pace to reach her just as she was leaving the high school and heading for the parking lot. "I can't believe we're heading into another hurricane. Jesus, this is one of the worst seasons I can remember."

He wasn't wrong. They'd had ten hurricanes and tropical storms that year in Florida—eight of them major. It was the last week in October and the season should have been winding down but according to the Weather Channel it was set to get worse. It looked like October and even November might be filled with tropical storms and hurricanes.

Yuck. Ashley hated being home alone in her big house when the violent weather hit. While she knew she should be used to the creaky sounds the old house made when the winds hit the siding and the leaves on the trees blew angrily, she'd never gotten over her fear of being whipped away by the gale force winds, or drowned by the surge of angry water.

She'd seen so much devastation as a result of the hurricanes over the years and since big storms meant big damage, her parents usually rode out the storms at the hospital, waiting for victims to be brought in. When she and Leo were young, they had nannies and caretakers watching over them. Once they were old enough it had been just the two of them, holding on to each other, waiting for the driving rains and wicked winds to pass.

This season, it had been just her in the house. Alone. On the nights that Leo's band wasn't performing, he'd stayed on the phone with her, whispering comforting words in her ear, and then she'd return the favor if and when storms had hit wherever he was on the coast. They weren't physically together, but they weren't worlds apart. She warmed at the thought, completely forgetting that Scott was walking by her side.

"You're shivering, Ash. Do you want my jacket?" She could see the sincerity in his eyes and watched as he slid out of his rain slicker. "We can't have you getting sick. You have a long shift at the restaurant tonight and don't forget you're covering for me tomorrow," he said with a grin.

"Thanks for the jacket, Scott." She pulled the sides closer together and quickened her steps to move closer to her car. "I'll see you in a few minutes over at the restaurant."

"You know, Ash, on the days we're both working, we really should just drive over together."

His suggestion sounded logical but she knew that it would look bad to anyone that cared to look into it. So she just shrugged her shoulders and got into her car. The sky was a deep gray and thick low clouds sat in wait, ready to crack under the pressure of the water tucked away inside of them. She quickly called Ryan's cell phone as she walked through the kitchen to the staff room, and frowned when his voice mail picked up.

"Hi, honey, I'm heading into work and just wanted to call and tell you that I love you. I can't believe it's been over a week since I last kissed you. I miss you. Call me after your show. Bye."

Turning her phone on vibrate, she put her things in her locker and got ready for her shift. Standing by the mirror, she swept her long golden tresses up into a messy bun and fastened it with a clip.

"Your hair always smells like the beach," Scott whispered into her ear from behind her, sending a gasp whooshing from her body. She hadn't even noticed him standing there until he'd spoken. Placing his hand on her shoulder, he rubbed his thumb lightly along her shoulder blade. "Shh, calm down Ash, I didn't mean to startle you. I was just putting my stuff away and I saw you standing here and, well, you just looked so damn pretty."

"Scott—"

"No, just give me a second, Ash. We've been friends forever and I know you have a boyfriend and all, but he's never around. *Storm Front* is doing really well. Who knows what will happen with them and where that will eventually leave you. Can't you just give me a chance? I'm here and I care about you. I know I can make you happy." He looked so genuine—so sweet—but Ashley only wanted one person, and it wasn't Scott James.

"Scott, I adore you…as a friend. You know that. But, I'm in love with Ryan and I always will be. He holds my heart and soul. I'm sorry. I don't want to hurt you because you're right, we've been friends forever and I'd like to keep it that way. Okay?"

"Sure, Ash, no problem. I'd never have forgiven my-self if I hadn't tried though."

She could see the defeat in his warm green eyes and she felt bad for her friend, but the only thing she could offer him—or any other guy for that matter—was friend-ship. Her heart had already been given to someone and she had a feeling that she was never getting it back.

"Hey, Scott?"

He turned around quickly, longing etched on his face as he waited on her words. "Tell the guys I said hello when you see them this weekend. Wait until you see how much better they've gotten since they started this tour. You'll be really proud of them, especially your brother."

He nodded silently and then went out into the dining room. Ashley followed after him to start what would be a very quiet and marginally awkward shift. *I hope his being aware helps him get over this weirdness*, she thought to herself.

CHAPTER FOURTEEN

Don't Try, Do

RYAN WAS SURE he was going to need to see a dentist by the end of the weekend. Seeing Jayson's brother and the incessant grinding as a response was causing serious damage to his teeth.

"Man, you've gotta relax. You're even sawing your teeth in your sleep." Leo's face was his normal calm, but his words were serious.

It was Sunday afternoon. They'd opened for a pretty well-known band the night before and from the chants and shouts, *Storm Front* had been a huge success. The band's manager, Anthony, had told them that he had a meeting scheduled for them on Sunday evening before the bus left for the next leg of the tour. Everyone was excited and they were all wondering what news Anthony would have. Well, everyone but Ryan. Ryan had overheard Scott talking to Jayson on Friday night when they'd thought everyone else was asleep.

He'd listened quietly as Scott filled his brother in on his ongoing "friendship" with Ashley. He'd clenched his fists and jaw while he listened to Scott explain how he'd asked Ashley out, and how she'd politely declined, but how he wasn't going to let that deter him. He then, heard Jayson—his *band mate*—tell Scott that he should go for whatever made him happy. If it hadn't been for the strong hand that covered his mouth, Ryan would have gone ballistic. Leo had silenced Ryan and quickly led him out of the bus.

"What the fuck!"

The blood boiled in Ryan's veins. He felt like his head might actually explode, and in that very second a haze settled over his vision making everything around him a fuzzy shade of red.

"I'm going to kill that scrawny motherfucker! And Jayson? Jesus Christ, fucking Jayson! He's supposed to be like a brother, yet there he is telling Scott to go ahead and make a play for my girl? I...I..."

Ryan was pacing like a caged jaguar, ready to pounce at the first person to come near him. Clearly Leo wasn't dumb enough to be that person, which was evident by the distance he kept between them.

"Okay, breathe, Ry." Leo spoke quietly. Quietly enough that Ryan had to calm down in order to hear the words he spoke. Ryan's pacing started to slow, as did his breathing. "Ry, Scott is a little fucker—he is—but you need to calm down before you say or do things that you can't undo."

Ryan finally looked up at his best friend and saw that just like him, Leo was visibly annoyed. His words were forcefully escaping his clenched teeth and his eyes swirled with menacing anger. However unlike Ryan, Leo's breathing was controlled and he managed to maintain his composure.

"Ryan, Jayson may be a member of our band and he

may feel like a brother, but Scott *is* his blood. He's doing what he thinks is right and supporting his brother. I didn't tell you about this before because Jayson told me he would never let it reach you or the band, but you were right. Scott has been talking about Ashley for a while. He likes her...no, he wants her and he's been biding his time trying to get her."

The red haze cloaked Ryan's vision once again. All of the progress he'd made to calm himself down in the past few minutes evaporated like raindrops in the desert.

"I knew it," he roared. "I fucking knew it. I'm gonna, I'm gonna—"

Leo moved quickly to Ryan's side. So quickly, in fact, that Ryan stopped snarling to blink at the close proximity of his friend. Had he not been so angry he would have made a joke about Leo's ninja-like stealth.

"Dude, are you like a fucking superhero? I never even saw you move."

Okay, he couldn't let it go.

"Ryan, stop. Just stop for a second. I know what you heard was like a punch to the gut—hell, I'd like to wring little Scotty boy's fucking neck myself right about now—but we've discussed this, Ry. You need to let Ashley deal with this situation. Unless he is physically or emotionally hurting her you need to back off. Man, just last fucking night that blonde offered to tie you up with her panties and suck you off until, what were her words? Until she, 'Blew both your heads off'? I mean come on, man, what do you think Ash would say if she'd heard that?"

"She wouldn't have said anything because she'd have heard me tell that tramp that I wasn't interested in anything she had to offer me because I already had more than

I could ever want."

Ryan thought back to the previous evening. He'd been dripping with sweat—high from the endorphins that always rocked his body after he'd performed in front of a large group of people. He'd wanted to grab a quick shower, a few beers and hang out with his friends, but a bottle-blonde had rushed up to him, fake boobs nearly falling out of her tube top, face caked with make-up and her breath laced with cigarettes and beer. Her hands had been like Velcro as they tried to attach themselves to his body. If he'd listened closely enough, he swore he'd heard the tearing sound each time he'd removed one of her paws from his bare chest.

After first trying to be polite, he realized that brutal honesty was the only thing a woman like that would understand so he told her the truth. Instead of showing any dignity or self-respect, she'd simply said, "It's okay, cutie, your girl can watch."

At that point, Ryan had been so disgusted that he'd pushed the woman off and called security. They'd escorted her out of the back area. Ryan had headed back to the bus for a shower. He'd skipped the hanging out and drinking part of his original plan. He hadn't been in the mood to celebrate.

"But, the point is"—Leo's words cut through Ryan's thoughts—"had she been standing across the room, she would have seen what she saw and thought what she thought. What do you think Ashley would do in that situation?"

Before Ryan could put voice to his thoughts, Leo continued, "I'm gonna set you up for success here, Ry, and just tell you. My hardheaded sister has already decided that you're the one for her. So she would have marched over to the trailer-trash tit-sicle, used a couple of her long and multisyllabic words and made the bleached blonde wonder why she'd ever approached you in the first place."

Ryan could visualize the scene playing out in his head. The thought of his girl staking claim to him in such a primitive way had his heart beating quicker for reasons nothing to do with Scott James.

With a hand firmly cupped on Ryan's shoulder Leo plainly stated, "Ryan, I'm warning you, brother, you have got to put a leash on that temper. Because one day you're gonna let that fucker explode and innocent people are gonna get hurt. I'm telling you, buddy, there comes a time when 'I'm sorry' only buys you a nod from the person you love…as they firmly close the door on your face."

The foreboding in Leo's words left Ryan's mouth paralyzed. It was like his friend was speaking from experience or even worse, seeing things before they happened. *There is no way, I'm gonna let that happen*, he thought to himself, while absently nodding to his buddy.

"I'll try." The whisper was barely audible.

"Don't try, Ryan. Do."

THE NEXT DAY passed without any confrontation. Scott would be leaving in just a few short hours, and then Leo would mediate a band meeting to discuss how Jayson's involvement in his brother's love life was interfering with dynamics of the band. Ryan would simply explain his feelings and hope for a decent outcome.

"Hey, Ash, do you think I could borrow your notes from yesterday's calc class? I got home so late on Sunday night that my mom let me take yesterday off. You know, a personal day."

"Umm, sure, Scott, I'll photocopy them for you and give them to you at lunch, okay?" Ashley's normally bright smile felt wooden on her lips, but she was annoyed with Scott James and the games he was playing. While Ryan hadn't said anything directly to her about the weekend, he'd sounded tense and distant the few times they'd spoken. She'd finally called Leo to get the scoop. In true Leo fashion, he'd given her the low-down with as little detail as possible and made her promise to not just stay out of it, but to try and act as normal as she could.

"Sis, giving a guy like Scott any sort of reaction, big or small, will only egg him on. So do yourself a favor and just go about your business. Eventually, he'll get the hint."

"Le, you know I have no interest in him, right?" It was important for her brother to know that she was in no way encouraging Scott's behavior.

A deep chortle came down the phone. "Of course I know that, Ash. Are you kidding? You don't ever need to defend yourself when you're following your heart, you got it?"

"God, Leo, how is it possible that you did so horribly in school when you're so damn smart in life?"

Her question may have sounded silly—sarcastic even—but she was actually beginning to think her brother was one of the smartest people she knew. Smiling, she shook her head. No, the world would be a scary place if that were the case.

"Nice, Ash. You know you just said that out loud, right?" The laughter coming from the phone was contagious and she found herself laughing along. It was exactly what she needed: something to ease the tension. There you go. Leo—always able to laugh at himself. Amazing.

"Are you okay, Ashley?" Scott looked at her with a warm smile and desire filled eyes.

"Yes, Scott," she said, her tone a little too snippy. "I just need to get to class. I'll get you the notes at lunch."

●———————————————●

"Jesus Christ," Leo's face paled as his eyes went wide like beach balls.

"What's up, man?" A large knot began to form in Ryan's belly. There were very few things that rattled his laid-back, *let's grab the world by the balls*, friend, and in that moment Leo's straight spine, tense shoulders and tight fists scared the shit out of Ryan.

"Leo?" He walked over to where his friend was standing before his eyes locked on the images that left him speechless.

"I'm packing my shit and heading home, Ry. There's no fucking way that I'm letting her weather this hurricane on her own. No. Fucking. Way."

With that, Leo started throwing his belongings into his duffle bag with one hand, calling the airport with the other.

Ryan's voice finally returned and he said, "Shit, that's a big fucking storm, Leo. I can't believe they're still coming this late in the year. I don't know if you'll be able to get a plane into Miami. They might be booked—or worse, blocked. They might not be allowing flights in."

"No, the storm isn't set to hit land for forty-eight hours, and I don't care if I have to fly, drive, or swim. This is supposed to be a Level 4 hurricane. My parents will no doubt stay at the hospital and Ashley will be in that fucking house alone."

Ryan took in Leo's haunted eyes as he heard him whisper, "My sister and I do *not* do storms like this alone. I'm not telling you to come with me. I'm just saying I'm out of here in ten minutes. I'll be back when I can. If they get mad at me for missing shows and they don't want me back—fine. I'll figure it out later." The zip of the duffle signaled an end to the conversation.

The taxi pulled up to the small tour bus and Leo all but ran to the yellow car and hopped in. As he yanked it inward, a booted foot stopped the door from closing. "What the hell, Le? You wanna break my leg?"

The warm smile and slight head nod from his best friend tugged at Ryan's heart, but the sincere gratitude warmed his soul. "Don't thank me, Leo. You guys are my family." He tapped on the back of the taxi seat. "Take us to Philadelphia International Airport, please."

Standing in front of the television in her bedroom, Ashley watched the meteorologist explain how Tropical Storm Wilma had turned into a hurricane just before hitting the Turks and Caicos Islands. It'd then headed toward the Bahamas and was currently on its way to Miami. Turks and Caicos were a mangled disaster—and that was before the hurricane had even hit Level 3. Wilma was now bearing down on the Bahamas, and like the Big Bad Wolf once it was done with the houses made of straw and sticks, it was coming to blow their house down.

A strong chill coursed through her body causing her to shake to the point that her knees buckled beneath her. Thank God her bed had been behind her or she would have fallen to the floor. "Oh, God, this is going to be bad," she whispered.

Tears stung her eyes as she grabbed her backpack and headed to school. She could already feel the knots tying tightly in her stomach. A Level 4 hurricane would most definitely cut off their power for at least a couple of days. A few years back, their parents had installed a back-up generator so she knew she wouldn't be in the dark but she would need to limit all electrical use in order to save generator power. She would have to limit her phone use so as to not wear down her battery. That meant little time on the phone with Leo and Ryan. Her stomach began to twist into knots.

Just as she pulled into the parking lot of the high school, her phone rang. The name on the screen automatically loosened the fist in her gut. She tried for unaffected and carefree when she answered the phone.

"Hi, Leo."

"So, I take it you know about the storm." Clearly she needed to work on her acting skills. "Listen, sis, I know it's a big one."

"Leo, I'll...umm, I'll be okay. Don't worry about me."

"Ashley, have you lost your fucking mind?" In true Leo fashion, the question was sarcastic. "Of course I'm gonna worry about you. Wouldn't you be worried about me? Hell, if the situations were reversed, I'd expect you to drop everything and get your ass home to be with my scared, shaking ass."

She couldn't help but laugh at his description. Her brother was the strongest person she knew but big storms were still his kryptonite. "So that's what we're doing. Okay?"

We? She thought. *We're doing?*

"Wait, Le." She didn't even want to say it out loud for fear of getting her hopes up. "Le, is Ryan with you?"

"I'm right here, Princess," she heard him say from a slight distance. She was hopeful that the shrill squeal that left her throat that no one outside her car could hear. The deep exhalation that left her lungs was so cleansing she realized she must have been holding it since she first heard word of the coming storm.

"So, here's the problem. We're at Philly airport but all the flights are booked out until late tonight. We should get into Tampa around one in the morning. We'll rent a car and get to Miami by six at the latest. Any way we slice it, we should be ahead of that storm because according to the latest reports, it's taking its sweet ass time in the Bahamas. Okay?"

"I don't even know what to say." Her throat was thick with emotion leaving her voice a mere whisper. "Thank you so much. I love you both. Travel safely."

She disconnected her call and went about her day with less fear and more smile.

CHAPTER FIFTEEN

Has. It. Snapped?

THE HEAVY DIP in her bed jolted her out of her dream-less sleep. A smile tugged across her lips before she even opened her eyes.

"Leo, you're home."

Excitement filled her sleep-addled body as she wound her arms around him. "What time is it?" The red numbers on the digital clock sat on her nightstand glowed four-thirty.

She knifed up and glared at her brother. "Leo Kynde, I said to travel safely, you must have been driving at mach speed to get from Tampa to here in three and half hours." Her feigned annoyance made Leo laugh.

"There was no traffic and we were so close that I just wanted to get home. Okay, Mom?" Even half asleep, Leo calling her 'mom' rankled her nerves. She knew he must have caught her stink-eye when he immediately recanted his statement. "Sorry, my bad. You know you're nothing like her, and so do I." Ashley casually looked around her dark room. She was thrilled her brother was there, but where was Ryan?

"Ash, you're about as subtle as a heart attack. Ryan's

not here. He told me to give you a wet juicy kiss—which I'm so *not* gonna do."

He did, however, cup the back of her skull and placed a *Leo kiss* on the top of her head. "He told me to tell you that he wanted to see his dad and help him get his house ready for the storm. He also said he would meet you here right after school. He wants you to call him when you get up later this morning."

Disappointment edged its way through Ashley's mind but her sensibility quickly stepped in when she remembered how wonderful Martin Baker was.

Ryan's dad was such a warm, caring man and such a present father. He was *that* dad: the dad that came to every football game and every *Storm Front* show. He was the dad that supported his son no matter what.

Two years ago, when Martin had suffered a heart attack, Ryan had nearly crumbled at the thought of losing his father, his only surviving parent. But then Martin changed his lifestyle. He started eating healthier and working out, and now he was in much better shape for it. Martin was Ryan's dad, and it's understandable that Ryan should go to him first and help him weatherproof their house. The Kynde's had hired a crew to make sure their house was in shape to withstand whatever Mother Nature threw in this direction.

Ashley and Leo stayed up talking until he could no longer keep his eyes open. He practically crawled through their adjoining bathroom and flopped onto his bed. Ashley could barely contain her happiness as she pulled his door closed and got ready for school.

"HI, HONEY." SHE couldn't help the sugary sound of her voice as she spoke to Ryan on her drive to school. "I can't believe you're home, even if it's just for a few days. God, I can't wait to see you. The end of the day can't come soon enough."

"I know, Princess, trust me, I know. It just about killed me to not come home with Leo this morning and slide into your bed, but apparently the storm will be hitting a lot sooner than they expected. In fact, the wind and rain should be starting as early as this afternoon, so my dad and I have a ton of work to do. Did Leo give you my kiss?" The quick change of topic had her smiling and his silly sexy tone had Ashley pressing her thighs together as she drove.

"Umm, kind of," she giggled, "I'm thinking it's not the same kiss you're gonna give me, but it did make me happy enough until I see you later." Her voice dropped a little lower, got a little sexier, "speaking of later, Ry?"

She knew he heard the meaning behind the question in her voice by the way his breath caught. She didn't care that Ryan was only home for a short visit. It was meant to be. She needed him, it was time. "Princess"—she shivered at his lust infused tone—"we'll have plenty of time to discuss this later when we're alone, sitting wrapped around each other watching the rain beat down on the ground. I can practically smell the coconuts on your skin and feel the silk of your hair twined around my fingers as I run my tongue up your neck and suck on your ear lobe. Maybe our time together will inspire a song or two." She heard him chuckle at her small moan. "Where are you, Ash?"

"I'm sitting in the parking lot at school, honey." Her breathing was shallow and she knew Ryan could tell she was turned on. "Want me to help you take off the edge before you head into that never ending episode of *One Tree Hill*?" She smiled and laughed at his television show reference. He claimed he watched the show under duress and it was just so he could spend time with her, but she knew he actually liked it. "Just sayin' there is as much drama at school as there is on an episode of that show. So, if you need a hand," he chuckled, "I'd be happy to help."

"No," she whispered, "I'll be okay, I think. Just make sure you're at my house when I get home from school to-day." She grimaced when he chuckled at her choked voice.

"Okay, baby. But, Ash, feel free to call me at lunch if you decide to take me up on my offer." His cocky comment snapped her out of her trance and back to reality.

"Whatever, Ryan." She pinched herself when she realized that she sounded like a twit. Everyone knows that the person who ends an argument with "whatever" is the person who lost. However, in that moment she didn't care, because he was home and waiting for her, and she couldn't wait to see him. "I love you, Ryan Baker."

"I love you too, Ashley Kynde. Talk to you later." They disconnected and she went into the school to start the longest day ever.

EACH PERIOD TICKED by slowly, minute-by-minute. The hands on the school's black and white, standard clocks on the walls of each classroom seemed like they never moved, other than the faint Tick tock. Tick tock. Lunch had been a frenzy of hurricane talk and "Power Parties". She'd shaken her head with irritation as her peers discussed the excitement of getting stuck in one person's house for a few days without power. "It's amazing these people get into college," she said quietly to herself as she was pulling her books from her locker at the end of the day.

"Why is that?" The voice behind her, while familiar, was certainly not welcomed.

"Oh. Hey, Scott, I didn't realize anyone was still here. The school emptied out pretty quickly when the last bell rang."

Looking around, she saw just how empty the halls really were. If this were a movie a tumbleweed would have rolled by her Burberry covered feet. The rain had started moving in during last period and all after-school activities had been canceled.

"So, you were saying that you were surprised that the students here got into college. Why's that, Ashley?"

She shrugged, turning back to her locker and removing the last of her books and putting them in her bag. Her stance relaxed as she thought about her peers. "Because every time there's a storm they plan these big 'Power Parties'. They think it's gonna be so cool to be stuck together when the power goes out. But you know what happens every single time? They all get sick of each other after a few hours, but they're stuck together. Couples break-up, best friends hate each other—drama, drama, drama. You'd think that after years of these parties people would learn, but nope."

She shrugged her shoulders and laughed as she zipped her bag. She had all of her books just in case there was no school for a few days and now she was ready to get home to Ryan. *Oh, Ryan.* His name floated in her head and a small sigh left her upturned mouth.

"God, Ashley, your smile is so beautiful, it lights up your whole face."

Scott was staring at her as he spoke and she was all of sudden aware of how close he was standing. "What were you thinking about just now that had you beaming like that?"

"Honestly, I was thinking about Ryan. He's probably at my house waiting for me and I can't wait to see him. He's it for me and that makes me smile. I'm sorry, Scott."

She pressed her right palm against his left shoulder to put distance between them but he instantly clamped his hand over her wrist. His touch wasn't rough. He wasn't hurting her, but she didn't want his hand on her.

When she tried to move her hand he weaved his fingers between hers. Confusion struck hard as she tried to make sense of his actions. Why was he doing this? He'd stopped trying to pursue her after she'd shot him down all those weeks ago.

"Ashley, beautiful," he whispered closely to her ear wearing a small smile on his lips, "he doesn't want you like I do. I would never leave you. I would never let someone get so close to you that he could touch your skin and feel your breath on his face. I would protect you. Drop Baker. Be with me."

Ashley let her exhausted head fall back into the locker with a clink.

"Scott, listen—" but before she could utter another word she heard a litany of curses and the sound of a hand slamming into metal.

"Goddamn motherfucking son-of-a-bitch!" Ryan's face was blazing red. The veins in his neck pulsed with each of his rapid heartbeats and his eyes were wide and glaring—like the devil himself had taken root in his body and was begging for an emergency escape route.

"I knew it. I fucking knew this shit would happen. James, I wanna fucking kill you. I wanna cut your dick off and shove it down your gaping neck! What kind of punk, bastard poaches another guy's girl?"

Ashley was stunned silent. She literally couldn't move or speak. In fact, she was having difficulty breathing. What the hell was going on? She looked from an outraged Ryan to a calm and composed Scott. How was Scott not shaking in fear? She knew Ryan would never lay a hand on her in anger and yet *her* insides were like Jell-o. Her mind quickly flashed back to just a moment before, and the way Scott had touched her face and whispered in her ear. Like a metal spike, realization struck.

"Oh my God." Her voice was soft and brittle. "Ryan," she implored weakly. The eyes that stared back at her appeared fueled with hatred and her stomach churned. "Ryan, you have to listen to me—"

The seething voice that came from Ryan's mouth bore the scalding words that were thrown like darts directly through Ashley's heart. "I don't have to do anything. I knew this would happen. I tried, Ashley, I tried. I trusted you not to cheat on me. I trusted that you wouldn't break my heart and I come here to surprise you and what do I find? The fucking surprise is on me! I'm the asshole because here you are all cozy with this fuckwit."

"What did you think, little girl? Did you think you could play me for a fool? Here I am saying no to women every fucking night for you and for what? You've probably been banging Scotty boy since when? You know what? Never fucking mind!"

Ryan glared at Scott, "You can have her. I'm through!" The clanking sound of his fist meeting the lockers startled Ashley out of her grief-stricken trance.

"You're right about one thing, Ryan Baker, you are an asshole." She watched his back as he froze for a moment and then continued to walk out the door of the school leaving her standing in the hallway alone. Well, alone with Scott James.

Her sobs echoed through the hallway. Hot tears ran down her face. Pain shot through her as she wrapped her arms around herself tightly in the vain hope that it would keep her heart from falling out of her chest.

"Sweetheart, come here. I'll take care of you." Scott leaned in to touch her but the growl akin to that of a rabid animal tore from her throat as she screamed.

"Don't you *ever* fucking touch me again, you piece of shit." She knew she was hysterical. She knew that when she cried it was ugly crying with snot and all but she didn't care.

"Tell me this, Scott," she asked in a voice that she had never heard come from her mouth, "did you know he was there?"

Scott didn't answer. While he was obviously trying to project having some sort of pity for her, the victorious gleam in his eyes was all the answer she needed. "Goddamn you, Scott."

It was official. She had used more swear words in the last twenty—four hours than ever before. But it was also true that they felt great rolling off her tongue.

"Yes, sweetheart, I did know and aren't you glad you saw what you saw? He isn't good enough for you. He's a Neanderthal with jealousy issues." Scott's smarmy smile made her blood boil. "Come on, Ashley, let me take you home. It's raining pretty hard. Let me show you how a gentleman treats a lady."

She didn't know that she had it in her—then again she'd never ever felt that angry before—but when her fist hit Scott's nose the only person more surprised than him by the left-hook and the resulting *crunch* was Ashley her-self.

"Fuck, Ashley, I think you broke my nose," he muf-fled with a nasally voice and tear filled eyes.

However, Ashley was too far gone in her own angst and agony to hear his complaint. "No real gentleman would ever hurt a lady on purpose. And just so we're clear, I would've chosen a Neanderthal dressed in animal skin and carrying a club over an easy-going, snake in the grass, any day of the week. You wanna know why? Because that snake sheds his skin when he's done using it. Just leaves it to rot while he moves on with his life. You're a snake, Scott, and a piece of shit!"

She bent down and with trembling hands, hefted her backpack up onto her shoulder before walking down the hallway and out of the double doors. The fierce rain min-gled with her tears and the wind absorbed her sobs as she walked to her car.

"Ryan," she spoke to his voicemail, "please call me.

It's not what you think." She sat in her car for a moment, replaying the scenario over and over in her head. As she drove home she told herself she hadn't done anything wrong. Why would he assume that she would cheat on him? Why couldn't he trust her the way she trusted him. She'd watched his concerts on YouTube—she knew women ogled him—but he'd promised nothing happened between them. Was she being naïve? Was he jealous because he was cheating on her?

Ashley wasn't sure how she managed to get herself home. All she knew was that she made it there safely, despite the heavy winds and driving rain. The weather outside mirrored the pain that was pummeling her body.

She ran upstairs on trembling legs to Leo's room and felt disappointment crash into her like waves hitting the shore line, when she realized that he must still be at the girl's house he had gone to see earlier that afternoon. Tori something or another. Normally, she'd never bothered him during a booty call, but she needed him home. He'd come home to be with her and just because the worst of the storm hadn't yet hit didn't mean that she didn't need him.

Clumsily reaching into her purse for her cell phone, she pounded in her brother's phone number. "Please pick-up, Leo, please," she prayed out loud.

"Hey, sis."

The familiar greeting was a balm to her battered heart and all the permission she needed to let go. Unable to form words, Ashley sobbed into the phone.

"Ash? Oh my God, what's wrong? Are you hurt? Where's Ryan?" Ashley could hear the fear in Leo's voice and tried to calm herself down enough to speak.

"Leo"—she swallowed past the huge lump forming in

her throat—"you told me to believe in him. You told me he loved me and would never hurt me. But *he* doesn't believe in *me*, Leo." Ashley was once again hysterical. "He doesn't believe in us."

"Ash, what the fuck are you talking about? This can't be about Ryan. He loves you like crazy. He was dying to see you. He couldn't wait to get home. He was going to the school to surprise you. Did he find you?"

"Yeah, he found me. He thought he saw something that wasn't really happening and instead of asking me, he accused me of cheating on him. On us! He said some horrible things to me and then, without waiting for any sort of explanation, he left. He left me, Leo. After all this time, after all my trust and understanding, he just left." She felt like her heart was being ripped out of her chest. "Oh my God, Leo, this hurts so bad."

"Okay, sis, you sit tight. I'm about twenty minutes away."

"I'm sorry to bother you during your time with… *Tor*i?"

Leo chuckled. "Toni. It's okay, Ash. I'm gonna leave here and come home to be with you. And then, I'm going to kill my ex-best friend. In the meantime, stay on the phone with me. I don't want you to be alone."

"No, Le, don't talk to me while you're driving. It's getting bad out there. Just come home, please," she finished on a whisper, "I need you."

"I'll be there soon. We'll figure this shit out. I'll be there in twenty."

Feeling a sense of relief drift over her body, Ashley finally willed the tears to stop falling. "I love you, Leo. Thank you for being the best big brother ever."

His deep chuckle came through the phone. "Yeah, well, I doubt Toni is feeling the same way right now. See you soon."

He disconnected their call and Ashley curled up on her bed and brought her knees to her chest. How did the day go from her having such hopeful expectations, to experiencing such pain? The guy she had spent so many years loving had shattered her hopes without her doing anything to deserve it.

She found a little comfort in the knowledge that he was going to realize what he'd done and would come back to her. Probably tomorrow, but boy was she going to make him grovel.

———————•———————

"Has it snapped?"

"What the fuck are you talking about, Leo? I don't have time for this shit." Ryan white-knuckled his phone while pacing the length of his garage. After starting an argument with his dad as soon as he'd gotten home he'd decided it was better for him to spend some time alone rather than cause any more damage to the vital relationships in his life.

"You better make time," Leo growled. "Has. It. Snapped?"

"I don't know what you're talking about..."

"Your fucking mind? Has it finally snapped? Because that's the only reason why I can imagine you would ever treat Ashley—my sister, your best friend—like a piece of shit on the bottom of your shoe. So I'll ask you again, you sorry son-of-a-bitch, has it snapped?"

In all of the years that the two guys had been friends Ryan had never heard Leo's voice so acerbic. He already knew he'd fucked up, and he already knew the damage would be catastrophic, but listening to Leo's voice told him there may be a body count when this blew over. That wasn't even the part that scared him the most. The thought that paralyzed him was that there was a possibility that he may have lost two of the people that meant the most to him in the world.

His dad had been encouraging him for years to seek help in learning how to manage his anger, a problem that had taken root deep in his gut ever since his mother died. But the jealousy? That hadn't been an issue until Ashley Kynde started looking at him with those hazel eyes and that magnificent smile. When he realized he had someone to love, he also realized he had someone to lose. And he couldn't lose another person that he loved with his whole heart. He just couldn't. Leo had been telling him to get the jealousy under control. He'd warned him, over and over again. Nethertheless, had he listened? No.

"Are you listening to me?" Leo's harsh tone pulled him back to reality. "Christ, Ryan, you broke her heart. What did you say to her? She sounded like she was drowning—and it hasn't got fuck to do with all the rain. I sure as hell hope whatever she did was horrible—unforgivable even—because whatever you said was a punishment that she'll never forget."

The acid that had flooded his stomach for the past two hours rose quickly up the back of his throat. "Leo, I messed up. I saw her with Scott, and...he was touching her. He was—" Images of Scott with his hands on Ashley's face, his lips close to her ear, flashed through his

mind. "He was standing so close to her, whispering in her ear, man, like he had the right to breathe her air. He had that self-righteous look that he sports when he thinks he's better than someone, and he was...so fucking close to her-
..."

"Yeah? So fucking what?" Leo's retort was like cold water in Ryan's face.

"What do you mean?" Exasperation threatened his sanity. He knew exactly where Leo was leading this discussion but he couldn't bear to follow.

"You know exactly what I mean, you blind dick! What did my sister, the supposed love of your pathetic life, do? Did she look like she gave him an invitation to touch her? Was she kissing him? What the fuck did she do to piss you off?"

Pulling in a lung-full of air, Ryan closed his eyes and the sharp sting of his scalp alerted him to the fact that he was pulling hard on his hair. "She...she was backed up against her locker—"

"What? He was hurting her? I will kill that motherfucker!" Leo's anger was palpable.

"No, wait, she didn't look scared, as much as annoyed and...defeated. I was watching through the window of the door. He had his hand cupped over hers, pressed up against his heart. At first it looked like she was trying to pull it away. But then he looked at the door, I thought he saw me...but there's no way that scrawny little punk would actually make a move on her with me standing there, right?"

Ryan didn't wait for an answer before he continued, talking through what had happened for himself as much as Leo. "So, I see a small smile creep over his nasty face and he leans in closer to her and, well, I don't know what he was saying. All I know was that she didn't push him away. She stayed there and let him talk to her. She looked calm and cozy and I lost it, man. I just fucking lost it. I marched in the school, said shit I can't even remember saying and then I told her we were over."

Saying the words out loud caused an instant physical reaction. A sharp pain struck his chest as a memory came to the forefront of his mind. Ashley was standing back against the metal, her eyes round like saucers, pain as clear as her long blonde hair. He remembered her beautiful face as she stared at him in confusion. Now, thinking back, he saw how she'd mindlessly rubbed her thumb up and down her sternum, trying to erase the searing ache that was probably ripping her apart. He had ripped her apart.

"Oh my God, Leo." His voice broke and unshed tears clouded his vision.

"Don't, 'Oh my God,' me. You fucked up, Ryan. You lost your temper and you lost your control…again. I've been telling you to get help. I warned you this would happen. You promised you had it under control. But you didn't. Now, you've hurt my sister and you've hurt me. You've taken a love that was so pure and so beautiful and you've crushed it. Are you happy now?" Leo's voice had adopted a calm tone—something that somehow made the words even more unbearable.

"You're right, Leo. You're so right. What can I do to make this better?" It wasn't lost on him that he sounded like a walking cliché. Every story ever told about an abusive person had them promising never to harm their loved ones again, *but* he meant it. He would do whatever it took to fix what he had broken.

"Please, help me. I'll do anything to make this right for the three of us. You guys are my family. Ashley is the love of my life. I screwed up but I'll get help. Look, where are you? I'll come to your house and maybe you can help me talk to her? I'll go to the anger management classes Dad suggested. I'll—"

"No, Ryan. No. Look, I'm on my way home now. Ash was a wreck when she called me. Honestly, I've never heard her this way before. Let me go and be with her. We can ride out the storm over the next day or two and then we can figure out what the next step is. I think—"

The distinctive sound of crunching metal had Ryan's blood running like ice through his veins and his next breath caught in his throat. Pulling the phone away from his ear to look at the screen he saw that the call was still connected but he could no longer hear Leo on the other end.

"Leo, what was that sound?" Until that very moment, Ryan had never understood what people meant when they said silence was deafening. But the lack of sound roared in his ears louder than any sound he'd ever heard before. Silence.

"Leo? Leo, are you okay? That sounded like a pretty nasty crash, did you hit a guardrail?" Fear crept up Ryan's spine as he prayed for an end to the quiet. "Leo, seriously, buddy, are you okay? I know you're mad at me, but you're freaking me out. Please, answer me." Ryan had to use both of his shaking hands to keep the phone steady.

A faint whisper crackled down the line.

"Ry, it's…bad…"

"Shit, Le, fuck, where are you man? Let me come get you. You're gonna be okay, brother. Where are you?" His body was tense and his lungs were barely pulling in air as he prayed for some sort of response. Already out of his garage and running to his car, the eerie symphony of static, wind and rain filled his ears in what felt like surround-sound.

The harsh, pelting rain soaked his clothes through in seconds and he could hear the sounds of the storm on the other end of the line. "Leo, do you know where you are?" His voice shook with fear.

"Beacon Hi—" Leo wheezed the partial street name as Ryan shut his car door, the deafening silence shrouding him like a blanket made of thorns.

"LEO!"

When his scream yielded no response, he tore out of his driveway and over to Beacon Hill which, thankfully, was only two streets away from his house. With the roads flooding and the leaves flailing through the sky the nor-mally two-minute drive took closer to seven. Ryan had called 911 the minute Leo's phone disconnected and he prayed that the ambulance was having better luck navi-gating through the chaos.

Hydroplaning around the corner, Ryan quickly got control of his vehicle and threw it into park. He opened his door just in time to lose control of his stomach as the im-age in front of him assaulted his senses. There, in the mid-dle of the road, lay a felled ancient Red Maple tree. The old tree that had once stood at about fifty feet tall had cracked in half and landed directly on top of the one mate-rial possession his best friend coveted—his 2002 Jeep Wrangler.

Leo had worked so hard to make sure that the Jeep was paid for entirely by himself. Something he'd purchased without an ounce of assistance from his parents. The day he'd bought the yellow and black Wrangler the two of them had skipped school and gone off-roading for hours. Ryan had never seen Leo look so proud. It was like the carefree façade had penetrated his skin, and Leo was actually living free and happy, out from under the expectations of his parents and the world he and Ashley had been pushed into.

Using the back of his hand to wipe the bile from his mouth, Ryan made his way toward the mangled carcass of a Jeep. The raw sound of someone screaming Leo's name filled his ears. He felt the agony in the voice, but as he looked around and saw no one else present, he realized the screams were his own.

Quickly approaching the driver's side, he saw what looked like a hand clutching the steering wheel. The fingers were clearly broken—the bones poking through the thin skin that was supposed to cover them. The tree's trunk had plunked straight down, crashing through the windshield, through the soft top of the roof, and landing directly on top of what appeared to be Leo. The glass looked like a thousand diamonds scattered over tattered canvas mixed with the liquid red life that slowly left Leo's body, one heartbeat at a time.

"Leo," Ryan croaked, "Leo, I'm here, buddy, can you hear me? Oh my God. Can you hear me, Le?" He carefully reached his hand into the carnage to run his fingers over the swollen jaw of his best friend, his brother.

Trying to contain his tears, Ryan continued to speak, "Leo, I'm so sorry. I did this to you, to Ashley. I did this." His voice shook and the knot in his throat pulled tighter. "Leo, please, please don't leave me. Fuck. I don't deserve you, but she does. Please, don't leave Ashley. You're all she has in this world, Le. You. Are. It!"

The whipping winds and pounding rain hid the sounds of the ambulance sirens until they were practically in front of the wreckage. Quickly, the rescue team and the fire unit worked to lift the tree off of the car. Other than the sound track of Mother Nature and communication between rescue workers, Ryan heard nothing but silence. His brain was numb and his heart was laden with cement.

"Son, do you want to or not? We don't have time to waste," the medic asked him.

"What?" Ryan stared blankly.

"Do you want to ride with your friend in the ambulance? He probably shouldn't be alone." The look in the medic's eyes told Ryan, saying "no," was not an option he would be able to live with. "Just stay on the bench and let us do our job."

Ryan hopped in the back of the ambulance and they sped off, headed for the hospital. He never looked back at the scene left behind. Leo's car was in shambles. His car still running, the driver's door left wide open. None of it was relevant.

Ryan watched in horrified panic as the medics placed two intravenous lines into Leo's arms. The erratic sounds of the heart monitor filled the cabin as the medics hooked Leo up to the pulse ox, placed an oxygen mask over his face, and listed possible injuries to the driver to report to the hospital.

"With that depression and bruise on his chest, we may be looking at a flail segment." The grim way the second medic nodded to the first had Ryan's stomach twisting into an even tighter knot.

"Leo, please, please stay with me," he begged his friend from the corner of the ambulance. As the medics worked to stabilize Leo, Ryan prayed to a God that he hadn't spoken to since the day he'd placed his mother in the ground.

"Ry…" Leo's voice was breathy, broken, but it didn't matter, because Ryan was so grateful just to hear his name that he rushed to his friend's side not noticing the skeptical looks from the medics.

"Ashley…" Leo started again and then groaned as the medic tried to replace the oxygen mask over his face. Leo nodded off the mask and made eye contact with Ryan. One of Leo's eyes was swollen shut but the other was open. It looked determined but full of pain. Leo had something to say and Ryan needed to hear it.

"Tell me, Le. Please, what is it? I'll do anything," he pleaded.

"Make it right." The wheezing became louder as Leo struggled to speak, "sh-sh-she's stubborn…but it works b-b-both ways."

"Shhh, son, you have to rest, try and stop talking," the medic suggested, but it appeared that Leo needed to finish what he started.

"Ry, g-get h-h-help. She'll l-l-love you forever. Ry?" Ryan could barely make out his friend's face through his own tears.

"Yeah, buddy?"

"Not your fault." Leo then started coughing wildly and blood shot from his mouth. The medics shoved Ryan out of the way and began to suction Leo's mouth. Ryan watched from the side as his best friend's eyes rolled in the back of his head and his body started convulsing.

"Leo!" Ryan shouted as he tried to reach for his brother. Red foam began to froth from his mouth. The labored rattling turned to silence.

"Stay back!" The medic screamed at they started chest compressions on what looked like a now lifeless form of what was once Leo Kynde.

"*No!*" Ryan shouted as the ambulance pulled into the emergency bay at the hospital.

CHAPTER SIXTEEN

What Good Are You?

"I AM SO sorry, son."

The medic scrubbed his hand through his hair as he trudged out of the trauma room a short time after arriving at the hospital. Ryan's head was still spinning from the flurry of activity that took place as soon as the ambulance stopped moving. The doors had flown open and the trauma team had appeared as if from nowhere. They, along with the medics, had whisked Leo away into the trauma cube and slid the door closed, leaving Ryan pacing in the hallway, in shock and alone.

After several minutes the medical staff exited the room, stoic looks on their faces as they jotted notes on paper and walked past him as if he weren't standing right there. Acid began to rise in the back of his throat as he saw the medic from the ambulance exiting the room.

With crimson colored vision, Ryan felt his skin prickle with heat as his insides iced over in pain. "You're sorry?" He roared. "What the fuck? You didn't save him. You didn't help him. What good are you?"

"We did everything we could to save the patient—" the older man began to explain before Ryan cut him off.

"He has a name. The least you can do is call him by his name, goddamn it!" His tears stung as they fell, unchecked, down his cheek.

"You're right, we did everything we could to help Leo. The tree hit him hard enough to crack his ribs into small pieces. The pieces punctured his lungs, Ryan. We couldn't save him. I'm sorry."

The venom seethed from his tongue but Ryan didn't have the capability or the care to hold back. "You're not sorry yet," he bit out, "but you will be. You know that was Doctor Mitchell Kynde's son, right?"

Ryan couldn't believe the words and tone spilling out of his mouth, but he also couldn't believe his best friend was dead so he let himself go, not taking in the exhausted and defeated look of the man standing in front of him. The man who'd tried but failed to save a young person from dying on his watch.

"We couldn't have saved your frie—Leo even if he was the President of the United States' kid. I know and respect the Kynde doctors, and I feel horrible about what they are about to endure. Just like I feel horrible for y—"

"You feel bad for the Kynde doctors, huh?" Ryan cut off the medic again. "Poor them! They may have to miss a day of work for their son's funeral. The only person who will really mourn Leo is his sister. This is gonna kill her. FUCK!" He screamed as he punched his clenched fist into the wall: the cinderblock wall.

"Fuck!" He screamed again, hearing the crunch of his knuckles. A searing pain shot up his right arm. The next thing he knew, he was hunched on the floor wailing like a baby. He cried for his pain, his loss, his love, and his life. In one day, he'd managed to destroy his relationship with the only woman he ever loved, and he'd killed his best friend.

How was he going to live?

Furthermore, how was he ever going to face Ashley again?

CHAPTER SEVENTEEN

Leo

ALL THE CRYING must have taken its toll on her body because Ashley woke up still curled-up in the fetal position in the middle of her queen-size bed. The storm whipped around outside, sheets of rain pelted the windows, and debris flailed through the air, slamming into the side of the house. That must have been what had woken her from such a deep sleep. Groggy and a little confused, the events of the day hit her and she knifed up to look at her clock on the bedside table.

"What the—? It's ten p.m? Leo?" She called his name but there was no answer. It had been close to seven hours since she'd spoken with him. Where was he? *Maybe he came in and saw me sleeping and didn't want to wake me,* she thought to herself, but that sounded wrong, even in her mind.

Climbing off her bed, she padded barefoot through the Jack and Jill bathroom into Leo's bedroom. His room was dark and quiet. "Leo?" She whispered, knowing somehow in her heart that her brother had never come home.

"LEO?" She screamed his name praying for a voice

134

that didn't respond. Just as her panic levels were about to hit high-alert Ashley's phone started to bleep. Running through the bathroom and back to her bedroom, she grabbed her cell and stared at the screen.

"Mom? Where are you? Have you heard from Leo? He was supposed to be home hours ago? Do you know where he is?" Ashley fired questions rapidly at her mother, not slowing down enough to give the woman time to answer.

"Ashley." Her mother's voice sounded strange. It was filled with something that was so foreign to Ashley that she almost couldn't identify it but it was definitely there. Was it *emotion*? Leo and Ashley always laughed at their mother because they found it humorous that the woman could be such a brilliant surgeon and businesswoman, but as soon as she left the office, it was like she would shut down. Almost as if she'd used all of her energy in public and only came home to recharge. Whereas their father was a terrific doctor who also had the bedside manner and charm to keep up appearances in all of the right social circles. So when Ashley heard her mother's voice she knew instantly something was wrong, very, very wrong.

"Did you hear me, Ashley?" Her mother asked stoically.

"No, I'm sorry, I think I misunderstood. Can you repeat yourself, Mom?"

"Okay, but please listen, this is important. Hurricane Wilma has hit Miami really hard. Your father was called in twelve hours ago to perform emergency surgeries. I was on my way home—after all, I had put in eighteen hours…" Her mother's voice, while fueled with emotion, was still calm and clinical and it began to piss Ashley off.

"Mom! Get to the point!" Ashley never disrespected her parents—that was Leo's job—but she was worried, nervous and downright frustrated.

"Right, right, anyway, as I was packing up to leave, I got paged to the ER, there had been an accident on Beacon Hill." *Beacon Hill*, thought Ashley, *that's just up the road*. Panic started to bubble in her stomach. "Apparently, the wind had blown a huge tree down on top of a car." Tension crackled through the phone like Pop-Rocks. Ashley waited for her mother to speak, knowing in her gut what the next words would be. "It was Leo's car, Ashley. Leo is—"

Emotion leaked from her mother's voice like water trickling out of the cracks in a dam. Ashley had never, not once in her life, heard her mother's voice sound like this. The hairs on the back of her neck stood on end.

"Mom?" She was finding it almost impossible to speak because of the growing lump in her throat. "Is Leo …okay?" The silence that met her ears didn't answer her question.

"Mom!" Ashley cried, "please, answer me!" The sounds of sobbing ricocheted in her ear. "Okay, I'm coming to the hospital. I'll be there in fifteen—"

Ashley didn't have the chance to finish her statement before her mother cut her off. "No"—her voice was back to cold and clinical—"you need to stay in the house. We have already had one accident tonight. I don't know what your brother was thinking driving in a storm like that. Every news station around is advising people to stay off the roads. You stay home and let us worry about him." With those parting remarks, her mother disconnected the call.

"I don't know what your brother was thinking to be

driving in a storm like that. Every news station around is advising people to stay off the roads."

That statement reverberated over and over in her head as Ashley grabbed her jacket, purse and shoes and headed down to the garage.

———————————

"Ashley, oh my God, how did you get here? Did you drive in this weather?" Ryan knew it was an asinine question—of course she had—but he couldn't bear to think about what could have happened to her now that the winds were blowing over 130 miles per hour and the rain was making visibility practically impossible. Well, at least that was what he'd overheard people saying while he waited to have his hand x-rayed, and then while he'd waited again to have his four broken knuckles and his fractured wrist cleaned up and casted. He gave no thought to the throbbing in his right arm as he drank in Ashley's appearance before pulling her tight to his chest with his left arm, and having her near him after everything that happened with Leo was like honey on a sore throat—warm and soothing. Just as that thought hit him, so did the next one.

"Ash," his voice shook as the chill ran through his bones. "Ash, baby, what are you doing here?" He wasn't sure what she knew about her brother and he didn't know if it was his place to tell her. Maybe her parents already broke the news. She looked horrible. She was soaked through. Her eyes were puffy and red. She looked... broken.

"I-I woke up and Leo wasn't home. He was supposed to come home." As if the dam holding her memories suddenly broke, her body stiffened and she pushed away from him. The pain of her rejection hurt more than the broken bones in his hand.

"Ashley, please."

"No. Ryan. What are you even doing here?" Her gaze dropped to his freshly casted limb. "Oh my God, Ryan, are you okay? What happened? Honey…" She reached for his injured hand but stopped mid-motion pulling her hand back to her body. Ryan could practically see the turmoil in Ashley's face over the simple gesture of touching him. In that second he went from hopeful to crestfallen. "Ry, my mom told me that Leo was in a bad accident. Were you with him?" He wanted to cry, to scream, to rage as she lifted her gaze from his casted arm to his eyes.

"Princess." He reached out to touch her biceps but his fingers never met her skin, and the look on her face just as he was about to make contact nearly made him sick. She didn't want his touch. He'd hurt her too badly. He had finally pushed her too far.

"Ryan." Her voice was soft but missing the warmth it had held since the day they met years ago. "Ryan, where's my brother? I want to go see him. He's probably asking for me. He hates this place."

Oh God, I can't tell her this. How do I tell her that he's gone. I can't. "I can't. I can't. I can't…"

"What can't you do, Ryan?" Her eyes narrowed as the question came out slowly from her mouth again. "Ryan, what can't you do?" He stood there staring at her tall willowy frame and watched her eyes grow more brown than green, searching his face for answers that he never wanted to give her. "Ryan," she snapped. "Where. Is. My. Brother?"

He gulped for air like a fish out of water as panic began to strangle him like a fist at his throat. Was it possible that she had no idea? Slightly, the fingers on the uncasted hand furled and unfurled as his breathing accelerated.

"Ryan," she said, "after everything we've been through, aside from today…before you were," she choked back a sob, "through with me—"

"Ashley, I never meant it, I'm so sorry—"

She put up her hand to stop his apology. "It's in the past, Ry, but if you ever loved me, if you and Leo are the brothers you always claim to be, you'll tell me right now…where is Leo? I need to get to him…now."

He saw the desperation in her beautiful face. He felt her tension. Saw the way her shoulders were squared. She needed to know. "Come on, let's go find your parents. They should probably tell you."

"Goddamn it, Ryan!" Ashley was on her feet, her hands clenched into fists, her eyes wide open in fear—or maybe it was realization—but her voice was loud and insistent. Ryan had never ever heard Ashley use this tone, let alone seen the ferociousness in her face. "Tell me where my brother is or so help me God, I will make a scene so large they will need a horse tranquilizer to put me out. Do you hear me?"

If she wasn't so upset, if the situation hadn't been so heinous, it would have been hysterical. *I can't wait to tell Leo about this. Oh, I can't. I can't ever tell him anything again.*

"Ryan, you're crying." Her bottom lip trembled, "just say it, Ryan." She whispered and tears gathered in the corners of her eyes. "Just say it, so my brain can process what my heart already knows. Please, Ryan."

Inhaling deeply, Ryan sat down on the plastic chair and took Ashley's hand to guide her down next to him. "He's gone. He's gone, Ash. He's gone. He's just.... gone."

The two of them embraced, their bodies woven together like an afghan, and they wept, sobbed, wailed and mourned for what felt like hours.

At some point, Ryan saw two firm hands settle on Ashley's shoulders, and he slowly unattached himself from Ashley to see who had the nerve to disturb them during the worst moment in their lives.

"Dad. Oh, Dad!" She cried as she jumped up and threw her arms around her father. "Dad, he's gone. How can that be?" Ryan watched as she released herself from her father's embrace and stepped back putting distance between them. The sadness in her eyes morphed into confusion and then anger. He could barely hear her voice when she began to speak.

"Why couldn't you save him?" She accused. "All our lives all you did was brag about all the people you'd saved." Her rage was palpable, her volume increasing. "So *those* people get the great Dr. Kynde, but once again, your kids get shit, right? That's how it goes? I don't know why I'm still surprised." Her cheeks reddened more with each tear that fell.

Her father reached out to stroke her arm but she brushed his caress away. "Honey, Leo was already gone when he got here." Her father's eyes were red-rimmed and bloodshot. "Ask Ryan, he was with him in the ambulance. There was nothing anyone could do for him, Ashley. I would have saved him if I could. I would do anything for the two of you. *Anything*!"

"Except be a father," she bit out acridly. Ryan watched as Dr. Mitchell Kynde flinched from his daughter's verbal slap. "I want to see my brother. I want to see Leo, now. Either one of you will take me to him, or I'll find him myself. We've stuck together and loved each other when everyone else let us down"—Ryan watched her eyes focus on him and her father—"I will *not* let him lay in some room alone now. I won't abandon him. He wouldn't have left me either."

Her last blow was aimed directly at Ryan. If he hadn't known from the tone of her voice or the words she spoke, her face would have given her away. "Leo may be gone, but he and I will *never* be through. Ever." She turned away from them to make her way down the hall to the morgue.

RYAN STOOD STONE still as her parting words carved through him like a knife—nicking and slicing with each pass. He'd done this. His anger, his jealousy, and his behavior had broken Ashley's heart and killed Leo. He had ruined the lives of his family. He fucked up.

"There comes a time when 'I'm sorry' only buys you a nod from the person you love as they close the door in your face."

"God, Leo. I am so, so sorry. I know it's not good enough. I know I can't bring you back, I know. I'm just so fucking sorry."

CHAPTER EIGHTEEN

Freight Train

NAUSEA SWIRLED AROUND Ashley's insides as an innate chill encompassed every fiber of her being. There was no way—no way—Leo was gone. Her brain kept repeating that message but her heart felt like lead with each heavy pump. She had just stepped out of sight when the sound of her father and Ryan's raised voices froze her mid-step.

"You're gonna just let her go to that morgue alone? See her brother, alone? What the hell is wrong with you, man?" Ryan's voice was tense with confusion and hurt that she had never heard from him before.

"It would probably be better if she said goodbye to Leo on her own. That's how those two did things. She needs to be alone with him. You wouldn't understand, son. I'm not what she needs. They have—*had*—a connection. Their mother and I raised independent children. They don't need us."

Ashley swallowed the bile that threatened to escape her mouth. He actually sounded proud of himself. How could her father even think that? Of course she needed her parents. She always had. They were just never around.

"Are you kidding me?" Ryan's voice deepened. "You know what, sir? You are one twisted son-of-a-bitch. Your son and daughter did have an amazing connection. They did." Ryan's voice got louder—clearly he didn't care if he was making a spectacle of himself. "They had to because they had two of the worst, most negligent parents around. You and your wife have spent their whole lives being *amazing* doctors, saving lives, smiling for the cameras and donating your dollars. But do you know what people say behind your backs? Do you? They all know what kind of miserable excuses for parents you were—still are. They know that neither of you had anything to do with the amazing people that Leo and Ashley somehow turned out to be."

Ashley listened intently as her father began to defend his actions. "Quiet down, Ryan. We can't have you making a scene in the hospital." There was a brief pause before her father spoke again. "Son, you have no idea what it takes to make it in this world."

"First of all, don't call me 'son'. You had a son, and you ignored him. You put everyone else in the world before him and now YOUR SON IS DEAD!" His voice was filled with angst and contempt. "And your daughter is devastated because not only did she lose her brother, but she lost her best friend."

People around them were quiet and blatantly listening in. She heard Ryan's sneakers squeak on the linoleum floor as he moved closer to her father. He began to speak in a voice that Ashley knew to be lethal. Although outwardly less aggressive, it took on a dangerous edge. "Let me clue you in, you ignorant ass. They did things 'that way' because they only had each other to count on. Yes, you bought them nice clothes and good food, but I'll be honest with you, pal—any father that lets his daughter go visit her dead brother in a morgue alone doesn't deserve *one* child, let alone two. So, as far as I see it, you're half way to getting exactly what you deserve."

Those final words were like icy water being dumped over Ashley's head. New tears poured down her cheeks as she quickly rushed toward the morgue. All these years her parents' neglect and indifference had crushed her inside, but hearing someone else validate the feeling she'd kept locked away made her surprisingly relieved, yet so deeply sad.

The hairs on Ashley's neck stood straight up as she neared the double doors to the morgue. *"I can do this, I can do this."* She repeated her silent mantra as she approached the one place in the hospital she had never seen before.

"Miss Kynde, I am so sorry for your loss." The coroner, a young woman who couldn't have been more than a handful or so years older than Ashley herself, seemed so sincere with her words. She didn't appear to be anyone's lackey. So Ashley allowed the woman's words to penetrate through her deep sadness, anger, and fear.

"I can't imagine what you must be going through right now, but would you mind if I offered a small piece of advice?"

Ashley looked at the petite brunette with the wire-rimmed glasses and the pale blue eyes and nodded without saying a word.

"Miss, Kynde—"

"Ashley."

"Umm, okay, Ashley." The coroner tucked a piece of

hair behind her ear. "I've been at this hospital a couple of years now and I've heard about you and your brother…"

Ashley felt her shoulders tighten and her posture straighten. She had been wrong. Apparently this woman was just another minion looking to score points with her parents.

"Look"—Ashley found the nametag on the woman's lab coat—"Anna, I don't mean to be rude but I don't give a damn if you're trying to impress my parents right now. I just want—"

"Ashley," Anna's voice was soft and gentle, "please know that I mean no disrespect when I say I don't think you should go in there by yourself. Your brother, he's—"

"Leo." His name felt like a prayer slipping from her lips. "His name is Leo."

Anna tipped her head in acknowledgement. "Leo, that's a great name, a strong name. I've heard so much about him over the past few years." She smiled warmly. Well, as warmly as one could smile when working in a morgue. "I'm just wondering where your parents are. You shouldn't be down here alone."

"I…I haven't even seen my mom," Ashley stammered. "My dad saw me in the emergency waiting room, when I found out Leo …d-d-died, but that was all. I told him I was coming down here but he didn't follow me. I…I—"

At a loss for words, her heart slowly sank from the middle of her chest to her feet. "I just want to be with…with him."

The tenderness on the mortician's face was almost Ashley's complete undoing. "I get it, I do. I understand that you want to be with him—that you don't want him to

be in there alone—but, Ashley, I was in there, I saw him."
Ashley looked up at Anna's face and saw a sorrow that
hadn't been there a moment before.

"You saw Leo?" Ashley's voice sounded broken and
small to her own ears.

Anna nodded bleakly and put her hand on Ashley's
shoulder, "Let someone take care of you, Ashley. Please,
don't look at your brother in this condition. From what
I've heard about the two of you, he wouldn't want this for
you. I can promise you that."

Tears welled up in Ashley's eyes just a moment before her body started to tremble. She wrapped her arms
tightly around her frame, and slid down the wall that had
been holding her up. Protected by her own shield she got
lost in her grief and let loose her devastation.

"Ash."

Rivers streamed down her face and she hunched into
a ball with her arms snaked around her legs and her head
resting on her knees. She felt his arms around her and
melted into his embrace, thankful for his presence. *Have I
ever cried so much in one day before?* She asked herself,
but she already knew the answer. There had never been a
day in her life where she hadn't felt loved by Leo—where
he hadn't made her feel alive—so no, she had never cried
like this before. The last twelve hours had been the worst
of her life. With the thought of how many bad days she
had yet to come, an uncontrollable shiver made its way
throughout her entire body.

"Are you cold?" Ryan slipped his body behind hers
and wrapped his long legs around her, holding her closer.
She heard him take a deep breath and felt the warmth of
his exhale on the back of her neck. Anna came back with a

blanket and draped it over them. Ashley was grateful for the gesture but now that she'd lost her sunshine she knew it would take much more than a blanket, or even Ryan's arms, for her to ever feel truly warm again.

———————————————

Waking with a jolt, Ryan clutched at his neck. Falling asleep on a hard floor was never the best idea. As he started to come around he heard Ashley's voice. It was hoarse and thick with emotion and for a quick second he questioned why.

"Ryan, I've got to get home."

"Ouch, what the—" Lifting his hands to wipe the sleep from his eye he managed to bang himself in the eye with his cast. The cast was a reminder of why he was there at the hospital. For a brief second he'd forgotten about yesterday and for that split second he was still Ryan Baker—Leo Kynde's best friend and Ashley Kynde's boyfriend. For just a fraction of a second, life was still beautiful. Then he hit himself in the face with fiberglass and everything came rushing back through his mind like a freight train. Memories of yesterday assaulted his consciousness and practically knocked him breathless.

"You just remembered didn't you?" Ashley's bloodshot and puffy eyes stared down at him and the misery and hopelessness in them damn near broke his heart in two. "I did the same thing when I woke up. You feel like you got hit by a bus, right?"

"A freight train, but same difference," he deadpanned.

"Oh, okay." Her voice sounded empty, hollow—just like her eyes. He stood up slowly, feeling every muscle in his body rebelling against the motion. "Sleeping on the floor sucks. Thanks for staying with me, Ryan. You didn't have to."

"Ashley, of course I stayed with you. I love you. I love Leo—" He felt a tight lump in his throat as he corrected his statement, "I *loved* Leo. I'll never leave you, Ashley. Never."

The shimmer in her eyes nearly broke his heart. What kind of love did he show her yesterday? What kind of love did he show Leo? Guilt lanced through his gut as the events played through his mind once again.

"Ryan, I know you love...*loved* Leo—"

"Ash—" he cut her off, not liking the tone of her voice or where he suspected the conversation was heading but Ashley put her hand up to stay his next words.

"I know you loved him and he loved you. The two of you were amazing together. It was magical and entertaining." The corner of her mouth lifted for a second but her stare dropped to the floor. When she finally looked him in the eyes, all traces of warmth were gone. In its place was detachment and distance. "Please don't ever doubt how deep my love for you ran. It was deep, Ryan. Bone deep. The problem was I don't think you loved me as deeply as you thought you did."

He opened his mouth to interrupt her again but she gently placed her hand on his arm, her touch dissolving all of his words.

"You couldn't possibly love someone with all of your heart and simply toss them away like yesterday's trash. *'I'm through with her,'* that's what you said. I know—I know—you probably didn't mean it. In fact, I'd be willing to bet my life for his"—she pointed to the steel doors separating them from the cold sterile room that held Leo's body—"that you didn't mean it at all. But you said...no, you *screamed* it. And when you did, you broke something in me that you can't fix. I'm sick of being everyone's trash. Do I think you're sorry? Yes, Ry, I know you are. But, sorry isn't going to get you out of this one. I'm sorry I called my big brother crying yesterday. I'm sorry I asked him to come home. I'm so fucking sorry, but he's still gone. I love you, Ryan, but you were right, we're through. So, if you actually do love me, just let me go. I need to be left alone. That's how I'm meant to be." She swiped the steady stream of tears with the palm of her hand. "Just. Leave. Me. Be."

He stood motionless and watched her turn away from him and walk silently down the hallway.

Out of his life.

CHAPTER NINETEEN

Windmilling

"ASHLEY, ARE YOU sure this is what you want to do? My God, Mitchell, can't you say something to stop her?" Judy Kynde paced in circles around her daughter's bedroom while Ashley packed her possessions—neatly—into the waiting suitcases. "Ashley, damn it, you can't just drop out of school during your senior year! You were accepted to the *University of Pennsylvania*. Do you know how *lucky* you are? I realize that life has been hard. It's been hell for all of us. But do you think Leo would have wanted—"

"Don't you *dare* tell me what my brother would've wanted!" She snarled and the whooshing sound of blood flowing through her ears caused a faint spell of dizziness to overwhelm her.

"Ashley, are you okay?" Her father, who had definitely been more attentive in the past five weeks, rushed to her side and placed two fingers to the pulse point at her neck.

"Dad, what are you—"

"Shh…" After a few seconds her father leveled a knowing glance at her and then turned to face his wife. "Judy, we've discussed this already. Why are you making this harder on her? She has all the credits she needs to graduate early, she doesn't want to walk with her class in the Spring, and she's officially eighteen. If she wants to go, we have to let her."

If Ashley hadn't been as shocked as she was, the obstinate and dejected look on her mother's face would have made her laugh. Instead, she stood there with her mouth wide open, catching flies.

"Mitch, have you lost your ever-loving mind," her mother ranted. This was one of Ashley and Leo's favorite *Judy Kynde Rants*. They used to refer to this one as the "Windmill". This was where her mother would swirl her arms in circles while spewing out facts and figures just to shove her point down the throats of anyone who would listen.

Do you see her, Leo? She's windmilling?

"Do you have any idea what people will think of us if our daughter doesn't graduate high school? Do you know—"

That was the straw that broke the camel's back. That was the moment Ashley started doing some windmilling of her own.

"That's it! That is it! I've had enough. Why are you such a bitch?" Ashley felt the heat as it rose from her neck to her cheeks. "Why did you bother having children if you don't give a damn about us? Why? Yes, people *will* talk if I don't graduate. Do you know how I know? Because they already talk about the two of you—they have been for years. They can't understand how two such brilliant doctors could be such horrible parents. And you want to know something else? They're right—you both suck!" She was on a roll now. The words she had kept bottled in for years bubbled out of her like foam from a shaken soda.

Judy crossed her arms over her chest, "Ashley, I don't appreciate—"

"I don't give a damn what you *appreciate*, Mom. The same way you never gave a damn what Leo and I cared about. Yes, you gave us food and clothes. We never went without *stuff*. But that's all it was…just *stuff*."

She quickly swept away the stray tear that barely managed to escape. She didn't want to waste one ounce of sadness in this showdown. She was done letting people see her vulnerable side. Done. "We never cared about the stuff. We just wanted your time. My God. Leo's favorite possessions were the car that he bought himself and that stupid wooden airplane that he and dad made when he was eight." She turned to her father. "Do you even remember that plane? Because it meant *everything* to him. The four hours it took to make that plane were the greatest hours of his life. How pathetic is that?"

She turned to her suitcases and began shoving her clothes in. Not neat. Not orderly. Not at all Ashley-like.

A snort from behind her stayed her hand. "And how exactly do you plan to live once you leave this house? Because money doesn't grow on trees."

God, she hated that expression. That was the excuse every single time she'd ever asked her mother to spend time with her, every time she'd wanted her mother to come to school for an event. Every time she'd wanted her mother to come to one of the *Storm Front* shows. "*Money doesn't grow on trees, Ashley.*"

Her hands gripped the shirt she was holding and squeezed it tightly, twisting and twisting the garment until it no longer resembled anything more than a handkerchief.

"I have plenty of money saved up from all the time

I've worked babysitting jobs and the restaurant. Don't worry about me. I'll be fine. Oh, right, you weren't worried. I must have been thinking of someone else." She zipped up her bag and headed toward her bathroom.

"*You* deal with her," her mother shrilled to her father just before she stomped out of Ashley's room and headed downstairs.

"You're not wrong," her father said in a quiet voice. Ashley was packing up her toiletries when she looked up to see her father staring at her with guilt-filled eyes. His admission left her speechless, so she just stood there silently. "We thought we could have it all, your mother and I. We thought we could have the best careers and the perfect marriage and the greatest children. We thought we could—" Mitchell Kynde ran his fingers through his expensively cut hair. For the first time in years, Ashley actually took the time to look at her father. His golden blond hair was sprinkled with gray, and his skin, once tan all year round, looked ashen. Deep purple bruises lay under his pale blue eyes—evidence that Ashley wasn't the only one in the house not sleeping anymore.

"When we had Leo, we thought we could continue our pace and he would fit into our lives. God, we were so selfish. Life was crazy, and busy and fun. Obviously fun." He smirked. "We had you the very next year. But when we realized that one of us would have to stay back and parent, well, I guess that's when having it all turned into having nothing at all."

Ashley couldn't believe what she was hearing. Her emotions warred within her body. Anger wielded the guns and pain sharpened its knives.

Trying to steady her pounding heart, Ashley inhaled

deeply, letting out a long, deep breath before she gave her response. "So, you mean to tell me, that Leo and I were just an annoyance the two of you needed to deal with. The both of you basically flipped a coin to see which one of you had to 'give up' your career to actually parent your own children. And when neither of you were happy with the outcome, you decided, *'Fuck it, we'll hire strangers to raise them until they're old enough to do it on their own.'* That's pretty much what you're saying here, right, *Dad*?"

If the truth could kill there would be two dead bodies laying on white tile floor right now, she thought to herself as she broke eye contact with the man to her left. She and Leo had always felt like they were the footnotes in their parents' lives, but actually hearing the words—from your own father, no less—was like knowing the range was hot and then actually feeling the burner. The truth hurt like a bitch. The sting of tears threatened her eyes and the lump in the back of her throat faltered her breathing, but she refused to give in. *No, I won't let him see me weak.*

"Ashley, I didn't tell you that to hurt you, even though I know it did."

Lifting her chin, she righted her shoulders. "You don't know a thing about me."

"You're right, I don't." He at least had the grace to look embarrassed by his admission. "And I didn't know a thing about my son either." His eyes went glassy as he continued to speak, "And I will live the rest of my life knowing that my son died thinking I didn't care about him. But I refuse to let another day go by with you thinking the same."

Ashley stared at her father and in a clipped tone said, "You just flat out admitted to not wanting to care for us.

You can't make that better. You understand that, right?" A light clanking got Ashley's attention. She looked down to see her trembling hand holding her toothbrush on the counter. She forced herself to let go of the toothbrush so the noise would stop.

"I never said I didn't care. I said that I didn't want to stop working to take care of my children. And I was wrong, I was selfish, I was a horrible father."

"Keep going, I won't stop you," she snipped.

"But, I have spent every day of the last eighteen years loving you and your brother." *Loving us, ha, what a joke.* Ashley opened her mouth to say just that, when her father leveled her with a stare. "Don't interrupt me." She knew his tone, it was the no nonsense one she'd heard him use often over the years, so she kept quiet to hear what he had to say.

"Your mother and I wanted it all and we gave up everything to have it. In the end, we both achieved amazing careers but guilt and competition have made it so we can't stand each other. We don't even sleep in the same room anymore."

Okay, she hadn't seen that one coming.

"In the end, we were horrible parents, parents who lost our only son five weeks ago. FIVE WEEKS AGO!" He shouted as tears started falling down his face. "I lost my boy and I never got to know him. I never got to love him, but I'm a great fucking doctor. Do you understand, Ashley?"

"No, Dad," she said truthfully, shrugging her shoulders, "I don't. I would never do to my kids what you guys did to us."

"And that is why I support you in your decision to

leave before graduation: because you are a smart girl who will make the right choices when the time comes. I went to school, college, medical school and I made all of the wrong choices. The same with your mother. So you go and do what you need to do. You have your money that you worked hard for but you'll also have an account with money in it, should you ever need it. No strings attached. Before you say it, this is not guilt money, Ashley. It's Leo's college money. He said he didn't want it when he didn't go to school. In fact, I think his actual words were, 'Shove it up your ass, old man,' but I could be paraphrasing." His chuckle held no humor as he repeated his son's words.

Ashley couldn't stop the laugh that escaped her mouth. She remembered the day Leo had told her about that conversation. The sound of gruff chuckling brought her back from her memory. Her father was smiling at his own recollection.

"Anyway, I can't claim to know him well but I know for a fact that he would want you to have that money in case you needed it. So it's yours."

"Thank you, I...I appreciate it." She inhaled deeply, knowing what she was about to do would cause as much pain as it would comfort. "I'm just going to go into his room and take a few of his things, okay?"

"That's fine." He quickly reached out for her arm. "Ashley, I know I don't have the right to ask you for this but—"

"Yes, Dad, I'll leave the airplane." She heard his relieved exhale as he left her alone in Leo's room.

Ryan gripped the steering wheel tighter and tighter as he drove the short distance. He couldn't stay away any longer. It had been almost five weeks since they spoke, almost five weeks since he breathed her same air, since he touched her. He needed to connect with her. He knew that if he just got her to listen to him he could convince her to forgive him. He would never hurt her again. Never.

He pulled up to Ashley's driveway and felt every ounce of oxygen leave his body.

CHAPTER TWENTY

I'll Never Let You Go

SHOVING THE LAST of her bags into the back of her new SUV, a harsh shiver ran the length of Ashley's spine. The air was remarkably cold for December in Miami. *I couldn't be leaving soon enough,* she thought as she shuddered once again, tugging her sweater tighter around her.

"Ash?"

She hadn't heard his voice in over a month and it was aloe and thorns at the same time. Other than the day of Leo's funeral, Ryan had done what she'd begged of him and left her alone. Just that simple question had her insides melting. Closing her eyes, she warned herself not to give anything away.

Stay cold. Stay detached.

"Ryan." She kept the exchange brief in the hope that she could get it over and done with as quickly as possible, without telling him any of her plans. However Ryan had always been able to see through her words and into her soul. That's what had made their songs so incredible. It's what made her love him so deeply. As if her thoughts alone had drawn him to her, Ryan stood barely an inch away. With his close proximity, she could feel the heat radiating from his body. She could smell his woodsy scent —warm and inviting—and she could feel his breath caressing her ear. She shivered again but knew her reaction had nothing to do with the extraordinarily low temperature. On sensory overload, the last several years washed over Ashley as she turned and stared at Ryan Baker.

His life had been tied to her in every way that mattered. He was her brother's best friend, Leo's band mate. He was her first crush and her first love. He was the first guy to break her heart and the person that held her on the worst night of her life. Yet, more than anything, *he* was the reason why she called Leo and begged him to come to her rescue. While she only had herself to blame for Leo's death, she couldn't look at Ryan and not feel betrayal, hurt, and worst of all, longing. That longing was one of the biggest reasons she needed to leave Miami. She needed to start over and bury her past, all of it. And that included Ryan Baker.

———————•———————

"When will you be back?"

He asked the question, but he knew the answer before the words ever left her mouth. He knew she was never coming back. His heart broke once again when he saw the guarded look in her sad and tired eyes.

He'd been watching her from afar over the past month, to make sure she was getting on okay. But what he witnessed was her merely existing, not surviving. She'd clung to him at Leo's funeral, but he hadn't read anything into that. After all, there were close to five hundred people paying their respects to the family. She needed strength to get through that day and he was her rock. He'd stood by her as she had politely greeted her parents' friends and colleagues. He'd helped her console Leo's former class-mates as well as her current ones. They'd held each other when Leo's body was lowered into the ground.

Although after that day, the Ashley that he'd spent years knowing and loving, first as a friend and then as a soul mate, started to evaporate. Little by little, he'd watched as her inner glow dimmed. He'd tried to call her several times but she never answered or returned his calls, and when he cornered her after school, she looked at him with tear-filled eyes and asked him to let her go. So he'd done the hardest thing he'd ever done before and stepped aside. Now she was leaving. What would he do without her?

"Ry, I just have to get out of here." She gestured to the now colorless world around her. "Everything here makes me think of him, of us…"

"Ash, you can't just run away when life gets shitty."

"No, you're right. I suppose I could just stay and be cruel to the people I love, throw them out like garbage and make them feel horrible. Maybe throw in a punch to a wall? Sound familiar?"

Her words stung like a slap to the face. The potency of them left him breathless, but what caused him the most pain was watching her mindlessly rub her sternum with the outer edge of her thumb. Up and down in short strokes she fretted that small area—trying to conceal the agony that this confrontation was causing her.

"I deserved that. I deserve everything you have to throw at me. But, please, don't go. Stay here and fight it out with me, Ash. Please?"

"Don't you understand? I don't *want* to make you feel that way. But I can't do any better. I'm hurt, angry and lost." Turmoil was etched in her face. "Yes, you hurt me, but I loved you. Why would I ever want to purposely cause you pain? Ry, we aren't healthy together because you need help. You're a good person but you have issues, and frankly, I don't have it in me to hang out until you get your shit together. I have my own crosses to bear now." Her statement was harsh, but he knew he deserved no less.

Defeat weighed on each of Ryan's next words. "Okay, Ashley. I get that. I do. I messed up. I will never be able to undo all the damage that my behavior caused, and I'll have to live with that for the rest of my life. But," his gaze hardened with his promise, "I *will* do what it takes to fix the parts of me that are broken. For me. For you. For us." He let out a long, ragged breath. "So, I'll let you leave, but I'll never let you go. I will *always* love you." He reached into his fleece jacket and pulled out a small gift-wrapped box.

"Ryan, I can't…I don't…" Ashley stumbled over her words as she tried to deny the gift he was giving her. He opened her gloved hand and laid the present in her palm. He was supposed to have given her his gift yesterday, Christmas Day, her birthday. Yesterday was supposed to have been magical and beautiful. Instead, he was home with his father wrapped in pain and heartache.

"You, you don't have to open it now, okay? I saw it a couple of months ago and I had to get it for you. Just, please, don't get rid of it until you open it. I really do lov—" She put her hand out to stop him from completing his sentence.

"Thank you for the gift, Ryan." Her voice cracked.

"Take care of yourself."

He watched as she tucked the box into the console of her car. Then she slid into the driver's side, buckled up, and drove away.

It's not forever Baker, do what you need to do. Get your shit sorted out, and then get your girl back. It's not forever. It's just for now.

He repeated that mantra for close to three years.

PART TWO

CHAPTER TWENTY-ONE

Danny's On Main

Charistown, Pennsylvania

Three years later...

"EXCUSE ME, MISS? How long does a guy have to wait to get a beer around here?"

It didn't matter that her back was to the bar. It didn't matter that it'd been almost three years since she'd heard that smooth, cocky tone. It didn't even matter that the voice belonged to the guy who shattered her heart. From his very first word, her entire body responded. Her breathing quickened, her heart raced, and the soft center between her thighs pulsed.

Pulling in a deep breath, she slowly turned around and set eyes on the one person who had owned her heart since she was old enough to realize that she no longer possessed it.

"Well, well, look what the cat dragged in. If it isn't Ryan Baker, songwriter extraordinaire." His smirk hadn't changed a bit nor had the way it affected her, making her insides tingly and warm. She watched as he fought for a response and laughed to herself when he came up with nothing. "So, all this time and you got nothing to say?"

———————————————

Ryan could feel his pulse quicken as he looked into the greenish-brown eyes of the most beautiful woman he had ever seen. For almost three years he had been planning this moment, and now, with her standing just a bar's width apart, he was rendered utterly speechless. For a man that makes his living by stringing together words, lack of verbiage was not something he dealt with on a frequent basis. Her smile was as sexy as ever, but her familiar sass held something new, something less warm, less Ashley. He couldn't quite put his finger on it but there was definitely something different about her, other than the fact that her long, golden hair, and her unadorned sun kissed skin were both things of the past. This Ashley kept her hair shoulder length and streaked with multiple colors, red, purple, blue and black. This Ashley had tattoos weaving along her biceps and her wrists, and a tiny piercing through her nose and a hoop through her lip. Gone was the sweet, pure, innocent girl he remembered. The woman that stood before him now was sexy, sultry, and stunning.

This was not *his* Ashley.

———————————————

"Umm, no, I've got a lot to say. It's just that you look

so...so...*different.*" Handing Ryan a draft beer, Ashley tried to decipher what that comment meant, but his emotions seemed as guarded as his facial expressions. Sure, she could definitely read lust—she'd learned how to pick up *that* signal like a champ over the past couple of years—but she couldn't tell if it was happiness or disappointment in his golden brown eyes. *Oh, who cares,* she chastised herself. *You are who you are. If he doesn't like it, fuck him.*

"So, Ryan, what brings you to Charistown, Pennsylvania? It's a fuckava long trip from Miami." His beer must have gone down wrong because his face went red and he started choking. Quickly composing himself, he lifted his glass to his lips for another sip. *Was he smiling?*

"Christ, Ash, throwing around swear words like a champ now, aren't ya?" His comment rippled through her mind as she thought back to the naive girl she once was. The girl who'd thought that the world was kind, who'd thought that those who loved her would always be around and would always protect her. The girl who'd hid behind her intellect instead of experiencing what life had to offer.

Well, she was no longer that girl. Now, she lived her own life and if someone didn't like what she had to offer, she didn't care. She took care of herself now. Life was great. Yep, great.

"Yeah, a lot has changed over the past couple of years. You look a bit different yourself." She ran her gaze from his head to his boots, using her eyes as if they were fingers stroking his skin. "I like your hair short like that," she murmured almost as if she were talking to herself. "Clearly I'm not the only one with an affection towards facial jewelry." He absently touched the silver hoop that adorned his left eyebrow, while he licked his full lower lip before pulling it between his teeth. She couldn't pull her eyes away from his lips. *God, I miss those lips*, she thought.

"What was that?" Ryan's smirk confirmed her thoughts had not been silent.

"Nothing."

She couldn't just stand there looking at all of the perfection that was Ryan Baker, so instead she started wiping down the already spotless mahogany bar.

•————————————•

Ryan watched with amusement as Ashley mindlessly cleaned the bar top. With yet another swipe of her towel, she casually asked, "So, you didn't answer my first question. What brings you this far from home?"

"Let's just say I'm between homes right now," he answered cryptically as he watched her long sculpted arms cross the bar with smooth graceful motions. Her body had been developed into a beautiful work of art that called to him on a visceral level.

Even though it was early November in Pennsylvania, there she stood in a black ribbed tank top with the words, *Danny's on Main* scrolled across her ample breasts. Her long legs were incased in tight ripped jeans that showed off the firm ass he noticed when he first entered the bar. Even the ink she had chosen to adorn her skin was beautiful and feminine; she just didn't stand still long enough for him to read what it said. "Ashley," his voice husky in a way he hadn't heard in years. She stopped moving for a moment as her eyes met his. He fell into her stare, lost for a moment, free falling through time.

●────────────────────────●

The golden flecks in Ryan's irises stirred long suppressed emotions as Ashley felt her breath quicken once again. How could he still affect her like this after so long apart? "You need another beer?" She asked the question but didn't wait for his answer before pouring the draft and sliding it over to him.

"No, you know damn well that's not what I need. You think I came all this way for a beer?" His pierced brow lifted, adding emphasis to his question.

"How the hell do I know why you came here, Ryan." He stared at her silently, his mouth agape and his eyes filled with emotion.

●────────────────────────●

To make it right, Leo's words echoed in his head.

"Hello? You still in there? I asked, why the hell are you in my bar?"

"Oh really, so it's *your* bar now is it, little girl?" The gravelly voice that boomed from behind Ryan visibly shook him. Just before he turned around to meet the man that came with the voice, he caught the huge grin that spread across Ashley's painted lips.

Standing up to his full height of six-one, he turned around to meet the man who'd made Ashley's eyes sparkle.

"Danny Marcus," the tall man said with an outstretched arm. Accepting the gesture and returning it with a firm shake, Ryan gave the man a quick scan. *Hmm, late forties, not bad looking, owns the bar, he makes her happy.* "And you are…"

"Oh, sorry, man. I'm Ryan Baker. Nice to meet you." Ashley's giggle behind him had his shoulders bunching with tension.

"Danny, this is…umm…an old friend of mine from Miami. We knew each other a long time ago." Her bland explanation of their relationship cut deep, but the way her voice trailed off towards the end, made pain shoot through his heart. He absently reached back to the bar for support hoping the agony her words caused didn't show on his face.

"Sweetheart," Danny rumbled, "You either know someone or you don't. There's no past tense with that. Ryan, any friend of Ashley's is welcome here. Have a seat, I'll get you a burger—they're the best in Charistown. Ashley here will get you another drink. I'll go get my wife, Julie. I'm sure she'd love to meet you." He winked as if he knew the information about his wife would bring some sort of peace to Ryan's fractured ego, and it did. Ryan then watched as Danny disappeared through the double doors.

"I like him, Ash, he seems really…wise." The cool look emanating from Ashley's eyes told him she wasn't necessarily in agreement at that moment.

———————•———————

"Seriously, Ry, why are you here?" His physical presence caused unease in her stomach that she hadn't felt in three years. When Ashley moved to Charistown she'd started over—buried her skeletons and reinvented herself. Yeah, she was hiding, but for now it worked for her. It allowed her to breathe, but now Ryan's presence was like a vise threatening her air. Wringing the rag in between her clutched fists, she lowered her voice so only he could hear what she was about to say. "You can't be here. This is my life. This is where I chose to be. It's not your fucking home, Ryan Baker, it's mine." She wanted to slap the sinful smile off his too-goddamn-sexy face. "What's so funny?"

"I'm sorry, Princess, it's just every time you swear, well…it kind of turns me on." She narrowed her eyes at his statement and then watched as he chuckled in response. "I'm not kidding, it's hot."

She felt like her head was going to explode. She could keep up her façade and pretend that she was who she was, but only if everything stayed the way it had been. She'd built a life for herself. She had her job, her acquaintances, and her occasional dates, but that life was a deck of cards and Ryan Baker was the gust of wind that could blow it all apart.

"Ryan, do not now or ever, refer to me as 'Princess'. I have a name—use it. Or better yet, just hop back in your super-dooper little car and head back to wherever the hell you came from."

She almost dropped her towel when a loud gasp came from directly behind her.

"Ashley Beth Kynde, is that how your mother taught you to speak to people?"

●————————————————————●

Ryan's attention shifted to the petite, strawberry-blonde woman wrapped in Danny's arms, who'd addressed Ashley in the way only a maternal-figure would. She was a good-looking lady, maybe somewhere in her mid-forties if Ryan had to guess. Her smile was bright, her face was kind, and she gave off a motherly vibe that made Ryan want to walk over and give her a hug. At her comment, Ryan returned his glance to Ashley, and Ashley back at him. Her lips twitched just before a giggle escaped her mouth. Ryan couldn't hold back his chuckle and finally they both started laughing uncontrollably.

"Yes. Yes she did," they said in unison.

Their identical answer spurred an even larger wave of laughter between the two of them. Finally, Ashley came out from behind the bar and walked directly into Ryan's waiting embrace.

"Did I say something funny?" Julie asked her husband.

"Apparently you did, beautiful. Apparently you did."

Hours later, Ashley smiled over her shoulder at Ryan as she headed towards the restrooms. "I'll be right back, I've gotta pee. Why don't you order us another round?"

Ryan's gaze found her ass and stayed there until his thoughts were disrupted by a deep voice. "So, Danny says that you know Ashley from way back." He stared skeptically at the large Greek god who'd spoken to him from behind the bar. "Sorry, man, my name's Max. It's nice to meet one of Ashley's old friends."

Ryan shook Max's huge hand, trying not to be intimidated by the man's sheer perfection. "We've joked that she must have been hatched right before she came here, because she never talks about her past." He laughed at his own humor. "Anyway, I'm back here for the rest of the night with my buddy, Kyle, so we'll keep you guys from getting thirsty." Max nodded his head toward the restrooms, "She drinking tequila on the rocks with fresh lime juice?"

"She was, but she's been doing straight shots for the past hour. I think she's probably past her limit. I should probably take her home. I can't believe she isn't on the floor." Worry twisted in Ryan's gut. God, she wasn't even twenty-one yet. Did they even know her age?

"Ryan, my new friend, your poker face sucks," Max laughed. "We all know she ain't legal yet, but that pretty little angel grows horns when she wants to forget. You hear what I'm saying?" Ryan wasn't sure he understood what this guy was saying, but he nodded his head anyway.

"If you know she isn't twenty-one aren't you scared you'll get in trouble? Better yet"—Ryan felt a surge of protectiveness tingle in his mind—"aren't you concerned for her. My God, she can't weigh more than a buck fifteen. She's probably puking her guts up as we speak."

He was having a hard time banking his anger when he noticed Max's shoulders shuddering and saw the flash of white teeth from his megawatt smile. This huge man was laughing at him.

"Dude, are you sure you know the same Ashley Kynde that we know? Because *our* Ashley can drink most men under the table. There's no way our girl is puking in the bathroom right now." The certainty in Max's voice confused Ryan. *Their Ashley? What the hell had happened to his Ashley?*

"Batter's up, Max." Her scent announced her presence before her voice did. At least one thing hadn't changed—she still smelled like coconuts and sunshine. Ashley straddled the bar stool and placed her feet on the bottom rung.

"Your boy says you've been slamming the gold for the past hour, you have any interest in slowing down or do you want another shot first?" Ryan noticed Max was reaching for a clean shot glass before Ashley had even answered.

"I'll take another shot and then I'll slow it down with a margarita. And Max..." She lifted herself so the palms of her hands were flat on the top of the bar making her ass jut out just enough to make Ryan's cock twitch in his jeans. She thumbed over her shoulder toward Ryan as she spoke. "He is not my fucking boy. Get it straight or you know I'll have fun getting even." Her smile sparkled as she lifted the shot in a toast to no one and slammed it down her throat.

———————•———————

Ashley knew she was getting drunk, hell, she just tossed her cookies in the bathroom not five minutes before, but this was the only way she could deal with Ryan's presence. It was taking Wonder Woman strength just to be near him without crawling in his lap and begging him to come home with her. In the parts of her mind that were still thinking clearly, she knew that she and Ryan couldn't be...they could never ever be again. But in all of the other parts, the girly parts that turned to mush every time she thought about him over the past three years, the parts that cried out for him in the middle of the night, the parts that yearned for him no matter what other man was in her bed, those parts couldn't ignore his scent, his smoldering good looks, or his smooth sexy voice.

Christ, she was in trouble.

"Hey, girlie, I'm cutting you off. You're opening tomorrow and I don't wanna hear any bullshit about being hung-over. I'm gonna have Julie call you a cab, okay, honey?"

The gruff Danny from earlier in the day had been replaced with a more loving, paternal figure and Ryan found himself surprised and grateful for the man who seemed to have true affection for each member of his staff.

"Umm, Danny, I'd be more than happy to take her home—if you could just tell me where she lives."

"Max," Danny's voice hardened, "Keep an eye on Ash here for a second, I'm gonna send Julie out to watch her." Danny swung his long thick arm over Ryan's shoulder. "I'm going to take this guy in back for a little chat." Ryan couldn't ignore the questioning glance followed by the smirk Max threw his way.

"Will do, boss," Max laughed, and Ryan watched him pour a glass of water for Ashley before he and Danny turned away and headed for their chat. Slightly curious, and more than a little nervous, Ryan soon found himself in the office at the back of *Danny's on Main* waiting to hear what Danny had to say. *What do you have to be nervous about? This isn't her father. This guy is...is...*

The man staring at him with a level glare and a paternal aura acted more like Ashley's father than her biological one ever had.

"Have a seat, Ryan," Danny requested as he parked himself in the well-worn office chair.

"That's okay, Danny, I'm fine with standing. What is it that you wanted to discuss?"

"Sit down, boy!" The warm smile Danny had worn all day quickly disappeared, leaving an icy stare and a clenched jaw in its wake. His tone left no room for argument and Ryan's ass quickly found the seat behind him. He must have been wearing his what-the-fuck face, because Danny's face relaxed a little as he leaned back in his seat.

"So here's the deal. Ashley's been here just about two and half years now, and she's a good girl with a kind heart. Julie and I consider her ours and we look out for what's ours. Does that make sense to you?"

Ryan stared at the man sitting in front of him for a brief second before answering, "Uh, Danny, to be honest, I'm still trying to figure out how you were able to switch personalities that fast without turning green and splitting your pants, so no, right now nothing of what you're saying is making any sense." He worried his bottom lip with his teeth, trying to figure out how Ashley ended up in this place.

"Nice," Danny snickered. "A Hulk reference. We love our super heroes around here. I can't wait to tell the guys you compared me to the Hulk." He continued to laugh until he saw the unamused look on Ryan's face, and then quickly voided his face of the amusement before proceeding with his lecture.

"Listen up, kid. My wife and I, we only hire special

people—the people with kind hearts and strong souls." Danny shrugged. "It's like a gift we have. We think of our staff like family and Ashley…well, that girl is family. For as long as she's been here she's worked hard, played hard and done everything in her power to make everyone around here happy. But, she keeps her past tucked deep in the back of her closet with the mothballs. We all know it, we all respect it and we all protect it.

I allow her to drink even though she's underage because she is the most responsible person I know and while the irresponsibility of that decision doesn't escape me," the man blushed—he actually blushed, "she has me wrapped around her finger. She hasn't gotten in trouble yet and her birthday is next month so, I'm keepin' my fingers crossed."

Ryan sat quietly, processing the truckload of words this man was dumping out while Danny continued. "It was more than obvious from the moment I saw you two together that there is a shit-ton of history there, and after spending the past five hours with you both, I can see that it's a book that hasn't been closed." With his hands splayed on his knees Danny shifted, coming within inches of Ryan. He lowered his voice, making the gravelly sound more evident. "So my question is: What do you want with my little girl?"

Ryan's head was spinning. How had this man gone from boss, to friend, to scary green guy, to father—all in one evening? How had Ashley ended up tending bar here in a suburb of Philadelphia when she was supposed to be attending U of Penn? These questions rolled around his brain but only one answer left his mouth.

"I love her. I've loved her for years Danny, but I

screwed up and I lost her. I'm not gonna sit here and give you a bullshit list of reasons why it wasn't my fault and why she misunderstood. I deserved to lose her." Ryan scrubbed his hands over his face.

It felt good saying this out loud to someone who cared about Ashley—someone who would hold him responsible for his actions. Sure, he had spent the past two and a half years in therapy, spilling his guts to virtual strangers, but they were paid to listen to him. They were there to take his side and make him feel better. The man sitting in front of him apparently loved Ashley. Danny didn't owe him anything and that's what made this confession so important to him.

"I loved her, but not in the way she deserved. I took and took but I never gave back all of the trust and love that she gave me, and one day I pushed too hard—"

Danny's eyes went wide and the muscle in his jaw twitched as he spoke through his teeth. "Did you lay a hand on that girl?" Ryan could see Danny's white knuckles gripping the armrests of the chair.

"Fuck no! Are you kidding?" Ryan was appalled. He would never *ever* lift a finger in anger to a woman— especially not that woman. She could have clubbed him to death with a bat before he would so much as pinch her in the heat of an argument.

"Danny, I said some pretty horrible things to her. I lost my temper and I didn't trust her. And guess what, man, all of those things I did…they were all just as bad as any physical blow I could have dealt. I broke her trust and I broke her heart. I'm gonna be honest, man, there hasn't been one day in the last three years that I haven't gotten up and gotten out of bed with my only goal being to become a better man. A man worthy of *that* woman drinking at your bar.

Did I do it just for her? No. I did it so I could look myself in the mirror each night before I went to bed. I did it so my mother could rest in peace knowing her son was no longer a fuck-up. But, Danny, hear me when I say, I'm still in love with her—always will be—and I will do whatever it takes to earn back her trust, and her love."

He wasn't sure at what point he had stood up and started pacing around the small office but as new determination ebbed through his body he turned and met the gaze of the man in front of him. Danny sat comfortably, his ankle crossed over his knee and a wide cat-that-ate-the-canary sort of grin tugged at his face. Ryan had no idea what was going through the older guy's mind and quickly let out a lung-full of air before sitting back down in his seat.

Danny dropped his foot to the floor, laced his fingers together and again leaned slowly into Ryan. "Welcome to Charistown, son," he said simply, unlacing his hands and clapping Ryan on the shoulder. "I think you are exactly what Little Miss Spicy needs. So, good luck. But know this—she's family, and you're a guest. You fuck up, we choose her. You got it?"

Ryan nodded his understanding before both men stood up and headed back into the very crowded main bar.

CHAPTER TWENTY-TWO

Lucky Charms

"I HEAR YOU have a house on South Pine Street. Come on, I'll take you home." His voice felt like warm honey dripping down her skin—sweet, thick and desirable. Had she just compared his voice to honey? *Fuck, I must be drunk.*

"You don't seem drunk to me, Princess. You really have learned to hold your alcohol." His smile coupled with the touch of his hand on her lower back made her panties wet.

"Don't call me Princess. Seriously, Ryan, I can take a cab home. I don't live far from here."

"Ash, I promised your boss I would get you home safely and I intend to keep that promise."

Lost in her guilt-ridden thoughts, Ashley made no return remark. She had a promise to keep too. She had promised herself she would leave her past behind. The pain. The heartache. The guilt. But the fact that Ryan Baker was now standing beside her, guiding her gently to the side of his car, smelling all woodsy and masculine with a tinge of beer and mint, she knew she was in trouble. The fact that she wanted to rub up against him like a cat in heat as she took in his scent posed a definite threat to the promise that she had so earnestly kept over the past three years. As his hand hovered over the small of her back while he ushered her into the passenger seat of his 1998 Ford Mustang, she found herself incapable of refusing his offer. It was laughable. The car ride would only be two minutes at the most. Yet, she complied with his request and took her seat.

Allowing herself one more whiff before he closed her in, her heart thundered in her chest as she watched him cross the front of his car. It was suddenly painfully evident that she was very close to breaking that promise. It was undeniable. She still craved him after all these years. Exactly two minutes later, she found herself lightheaded as she finally let out a breath. Her refusal to be assaulted by Ryan's scent resulted in only two short breaths being taken during their ride to her apartment.

While unbuckling her seat belt, she spoke for the first time since the parking lot. "Okay, Ryan, you got me home, safe and sound." She exited the car and quickly walked to her front door knowing full well he was following close behind. "It was great seeing you today and catching up. Be sure to stay in touch...but not too in touch." She snarled her dismissal and turned to unlock her door.

"Ashley."

Her name was a breathy whisper as his hand glided up to her shoulder. The backs of his fingers scorched a trail where skin met skin. A soft moan escaped her lips and thousands of tiny goose bumps spread across her flesh. Her familiar response to his touch sent currents of electricity through her blood.

"Ash, let me come in. Nothing has to happen. I just want to spend more time with you."

Inhaling sharply, Ashley stepped away, disconnecting from his touch and shaking her head to clear the lust that threatened to cloud her good judgment. "Romeo, do you honestly think I don't remember your allure? Please, I know exactly what will happen if I let you in my house. Do you know how I know?" She watched his face, his eyes burned with lust, yet he still shook his head in denial. "I know because I look at you, I see you, and even after all this time, even after everything that happened, I still want you. I still burn for you. I remember what it was like to have your hands on my body and I want more. I want it all."

"I want you to inhale me, consume me, and devour me. I want to come apart knowing that you'll be the one who puts me back together. And when you do, I want to watch you drown in the desire you once had for me. So you see," her eyes ran the length of his body as she tried to keep her thoughts from scattering, "I'm not sure it's a good idea for you to step through my door, because there is no way the reality can hold a candle to the fairytale my memories have created."

Ryan moved closer to her. That one step brought him close enough that his scent once again surrounded Ashley. His warmth embraced her, desire assaulted her. She knew then and there that her self-promise was about to be a thing of the past.

"Princess," his voice raspy as the words finally freed themselves from their prison, he growled, "There is nothing wrong with your memory. Now, invite me into your fucking house."

Before she could protest again, Ryan closed the distance between them, cradling her jaw in his large hands and pulling her closer. He wasn't gentle when he took her mouth for the first time. Her lips were so lush, so warm, so... Ashley. He stroked his tongue across her full bottom lip pulling in the small silver hoop that adorned it. He loved the way it felt against his tongue and his teeth. He threaded his fingertips through her hair and pulled her even closer. His head tilted to the side in an effort to deepen their kiss even more, and she gripped his shirt in return as she stepped further back into her house and yanked his body even closer to her own. The front door was kicked shut with a thud.

They stood in the foyer making out like teenagers. Their bodies pressed tight against one another, their hands set in motion. Her moans sent tingles through his body—further amplifying the desire that had been simmering since the moment he'd first seen her behind the bar. Hell, the desire he had been harboring for years.

Ryan's heart was beating so quickly he was certain she could feel it pumping through his clothes. The deeper their kisses, the faster his heart thrummed. The quiet groans in the back of his throat got louder as she untucked his long sleeved Henley from his jeans and whipped it over his head. *God, is this really happening?* He moved to touch her sweet, smooth skin when she pulled away from his touch.

"Holy shit, Ry." With eyes round like saucers, she stared unapologetically at his naked chest. "Umm, so, obviously, I see what you've been doing over the past couple of years." She purred as she ran her small hands over his chest. Ryan had always had a great body but now he was heavily muscled. He wasn't meaty or overly thick, but he had spent the past thirty-six months improving each part of himself: his psyche, his emotions, and his body. "I'm flattered that you find my body so appealing, Ash," he grinned smugly, "but can you show your appreciation a little closer?"

"Still, cocky, I see," she smiled, rolling her eyes before easing back into his embrace and mapping his torso with her hands and her lips.

"Mmm, Ashley, you have no idea how amazing it feels to have you near me like this again, I…" He stopped speaking midsentence as she looped her tongue through the piercing on his left nipple.

"I love these, Ryan," she whispered, lightly nipping on the steel ring. "Hmm, I see you got some more ink as well."

He wanted to respond to her observations, but once again, his words escaped him while his mind was processing boundless pleasure. His cock was fully erect and demanding release from the constraints of suddenly too tight jeans, and his fingers were itching to touch the creamy soft skin that he knew was waiting under her clothes. Here she was, in front of him, touching him and he could barely put words together as his thoughts scattered through his mind.

"Let's take this upstairs. Follow me," she said with a crooked finger and a wicked smile. He followed as she led him to the staircase. Lust overtook logic as he watched the sway of her hips and admired the lush curve of her ass with each step she took from the first floor of the small house to the second.

Once inside her bedroom, he finally gathered his wits

and pressed his body up against hers. Melted together, his front to her back, he pressed his lips to the nape of her neck.

"Mmm, you still smell so goddamn good," he murmured as he slid his tongue along the curve where her neck met her shoulder. That had always been a hotspot for her. He grinned to himself when her body responded to the soft breath he blew over the moistened area. Her barely contained whimper had his cock begging for a release that his mind wasn't ready for. He wanted to savor every single moment of this night. He wrapped his arms around her, cupping her firm, full breasts over her tank top. Rolling her hardened nipples between his thumbs and middle fingers, he continued to nip the flesh at her neck and shoulders. "You taste like fucking dessert, too. I can't wait to taste all of you, Princess."

———•———

His erotic words were turning her on and setting her off all at once. "What are you waiting for?" She replied huskily and quickly turned around to face him. Her next words caught in her throat as she was struck by the intensity of the beautiful man staring back at her. He was so fucking gorgeous. Why had she ever let him go?

You didn't. He threw you away.

The memory flashed through her mind sending a jolt of pain through her body. "Baby, you okay?" Ryan asked looking at her as if he knew the tremor that moved through her body had nothing to do with pleasure.

"I'm fine," she whispered putting herself back together as she always had before. "Just come closer. I need you." She didn't need to ask him twice.

"I'll come as close as you want me to be." Ryan ran his hands up her bare arms and back down, lighting small fires on every inch of her skin. "Lift your arms, Princess." She heard his sharp intake of breath when she complied so quickly to his demand. He slowly glided her tank top up her torso and over her head, revealing a lacy baby-blue bra that barely covered her full breasts. "Jesus Christ, baby, I didn't think perfection could be improved."

She would have called him out on his tacky line but the sincerity in both his raspy voice and his hungry eyes told her that he believed every word coming from his mouth. "Looks like you got some paint on your canvas too, Princess."

Thousands of goose bumps varnished the surface of her skin the moment his calloused finger traced the ink that scrolled across her ribs. *The darker the storm, the deeper the pain.* Huh? Where's the rest of it, Ash?" He asked, referring to the second part of Leo's tattoo that she had purposely left off when replicating her brother's on her skin. She had known the second Ryan removed her tank that this tattoo would be a discussion, but had hoped he would be too afraid of bringing up the past to call attention to it. As always, when it came to Ryan Baker, he didn't do what she assumed he would.

"I don't know what you're talking about, Ry," she murmured, leaning in to brush his chest with soft strokes of her greedy tongue and effectively ending any discussion about her tattoo or Leo's lost words. As her hands slid down each ripple of his abs, she felt excitement and moisture building between her thighs. God, she had waited for this man for so long—dreamed of this moment for so many years—and now the moment had finally arrived.

He skated his trembling hands from her waist up the plain of her back and deftly unhooked the delicate fabric of her bra. Their eyes met and gazes locked as the lacy straps slipped from her shoulders. Ashley lifted her hands to clutch the cups to her breasts. His eyes were filled with longing and her chest rose and fell with each shallow breath.

"Let me see you, Princess. I've been dreaming of this night for a lifetime." His words were her undoing.

She relinquished her hold of the bra and her body at the same time. The soft sound of the garment hitting the floor was absorbed by the sharp intake of Ryan's breath. She could see the fire burning in his stare as his nostrils flared slightly with want and passion. In the years since leaving him, she had never seen that kind of passion replicated in any other man's eyes and had all but come to terms with the fact that she may go the rest of her life without ever seeing it again.

"Holy fuck, beautiful." She knew why he was smiling and she grinned back at him.

"I'm assuming you like?" She teased.

"You got your nipples pierced too?" She watched as his eyes drank in the sight of the small barbells that ran through her pale pink nubs. "Christ, Ash, I-I don't even know what to say. That's so fucking hot. What happened to the sweet, perfect, Princess I used to know?"

———•———

The smile on Ashley's face faltered, replaced by the plastic mask she was so used to wearing that it almost felt like it was a part of her. "I'm sorry, Ash, I didn't mean—"

"Stop talking, and start doing." Ashley unbuttoned her jeans and eased them down, revealing her lacy baby-blue thong.

"I see some things never change," Ryan grinned moving closer, fingering the lace sides of her thong. "Still like your bottoms to match your tops, huh?" Her sexy smile was the only confirmation he needed.

Taking a final step into her, he closed the distance between them and rested his hands around her narrow waist, practically able to encase the entirety of her frame in his large hands. The pleasure he felt when she shivered from his touch made him feel like a king for the first time in years.

Dipping his head forward, he pulled one of her adorned pink nipples into his mouth, laving the hardened peak with the tip of his tongue. Her nipples had always been highly sensitive but having his own piercings, he knew that she was probably even more sensitive now. Pulling her tight peak into his mouth, he used his thumb and index finger to stroke, pinch, and play with the other one. Her body felt incredible under his touch, it was taking super human restraint not to throw her down and devour her.

"Ahh, Ry, that feels so good. I love your mouth on me." Hearing his name fall from her lips in that sexy, dreamy state had his body blazing with satisfaction and his mind churning with memories. *Stay in the now, Baker, stay here. Don't go back.* He switched to her other breast and let his hand slowly start to travel south. *Keep things moving forward. Don't let your mind go back.*

"Ryan, suck harder. I love the way your tongue feels

on my tits. Please!" He paused, his lips hovered over her puckered nipple, her use of crude language washed over him, making him smile, making him even more aroused. He briefly stared at the perfection before him and then greedily gave her what she begged for. Her body trembled under his touch as he continued to lick and fondle her magnificent breasts.

Red-hot flames of desire danced in her eyes as he stalked toward her, backing her up until the edge of the bed knocked into the back of her legs. "Lie down." By the way her eyes widened and her sweet mouth formed a perfect "o", he could tell his rough command turned her on.

He kicked off his boots and unfastened his belt and his jeans, pushing them to the floor before climbing onto the bed from the bottom and wedging himself between her legs. He ran his hands from her ankles to her thighs and stopped at the waistband of her barely there thong. His eyes moved up her body. Every part of her was inviting, from her silky multicolored hair to her bow shaped lips. His gaze settled on hers. The look of wild abandon was gone only to be replaced with something else.

"God, Ash, you are so fucking beautiful. Seeing you like this…" He closed his eyes and pulled in a deep breath. "I just never thought I would…"

How could he put into words what he was feeling? How sorry he still was. How could he explain that he had spent every day of three years working to get to where he was in that very second? Taking in a deep breath, he decided it was time to tell her the truth.

"Ash-"

"Ryan," Ashley interrupted his thoughts with her sexy words. "I want you to touch me, to lick me, to suck me. I want you to talk dirty to me and most of all, after all of this time, I want you in me. Can you give me that?"

God, who was this woman? Was it the alcohol or something that happened in the last three years that had made her so brazen?

He watched her for a quick second to see if her request was in jest, but desire in her eyes was anything but funny. "Yeah, Princess," He growled, "I can give you everything you need." His nose drifted across the silk of her already flooded panties, and from below, his eyes met hers as he spoke. "Mmm, I can smell your arousal, baby, and just like I remember, you smell amazing."

He pressed his thumbs under the scrap of lace that covered her mound and tugged them off at lightning speed. "I've been dreaming of your sweet pussy for a long time, Ash. The way you writhe beneath me when I lick you, the way you grind yourself into my lips when I plunge my fingers deep inside you and pull your clit between my teeth for a gentle nip just before you come undone. Now, lie back and let me finally taste your luscious cunt, baby."

⸻

His dirty words melted her and scared her in ways she couldn't describe—ways she refused to think about. Was it embarrassment or self-preservation that caused her to snap her legs closed in that moment? She had no idea, but as her body begged for her to give in, her mind screamed for her to stop. She felt herself tense, the warring within her, tightening the muscles of her legs as she brought them together.

"Uh uh, no way, Princess. You opened Pandora's

Box, there's no way to close it now." His smile was sinful, delectable, and captivating and his voice was infused with warmth and kindness. She knew in that moment that she would follow him to the ends of the earth if he asked her to and that scared the shit out of her.

"Open those legs for me, Ashley."

She melted into the mattress as her body won out against her mind. Ryan's warm breath sheathed the skin of her tender folds. He kissed up her hips. "I'm gonna lick, suck, and devour you." His thick finger stroked the seam of her glistening sex and slid down to the warm opening that graciously invited him in. His kisses reached her stomach, her breasts, her collar bones, and then her ear before he whispered, "And when I've made you come around my fingers and my tongue, I'm gonna slide my cock inside of you and finally—*finally*—make you mine."

He added a second finger to the first and slowly slid them in and out of her, using his thumb to stimulate the small bundle of nerves that begged for his attention. Her moans told him exactly what he needed to know in order to slate her desire.

HOW DID HE still know how to make her body feel so damn good? As his tongue grazed the shell of her ear, his thumb picked up speed and the pressure on her clit increased. The muscles in her thighs tightened, shaking under the splendid pressure of her oncoming climax. "Oh,

Ryan, oh, that feels so amazing. Please…"

"Please what, Ashley?"

"Please, please don't stop." Ryan smashed his mouth to hers in an all-consuming kiss as he continued to fuck her with his fingers. Moaning, Ashley bucked her hips off the mattress to meet each thrust of his thick fingers. Her body quaked as the orgasm crashed over her like a tidal wave hitting the bluffs.

She could feel herself clenching around his fingers as he milked every ripple of ecstasy from her hungry body, but still, she wanted more. "Don't look at me that way, Princess," he said, as he eased his fingers out of her body. "We aren't done yet."

"No," she answered brazenly, "we aren't." She rubbed her small hands up his chest and over his broad shoulders and flipped him on his back. The surprised look on his face was priceless.

"This feels familiar," he chuckled lifting his hands to palm her breasts.

"So it does," she quipped. He let out a groan when she pressed her wet sex against his abdomen and sucked on his ear. "It's my turn to do some dirty talking and dirty doing…think you can handle it?" His eyes flared at her direct challenge.

"Yeah, Princess, I think I can handle anything you dish out." His half grin had her giggling.

"We'll see about that."

Letting her hands lead the journey down his chiseled body, she allowed her lips and her tongue to take frequent rest stops. His deep groans fueled every kiss, while his gentle touches to her hair and her shoulders revved her internal engine. His scent flooded her nose. It was woodsy, masculine…and *Ryan*. He was the most beautiful package she had ever laid her eyes on. Strong firm pecs, each topped with a golden brown disc and pierced with a silver hoop. She squeezed her thighs together applying slight pressure to her already sensitive clit. Pierced men turned her on, but *Ryan* pierced? She couldn't hold in her purr-like noise as she flicked each ring with her tongue before moving downward.

Slowing down when she reached his eight pack she took the time to lavish his first tattoo—'*Always In My Heart*' scrolled just below his heart resting under his pec—with extra love and tenderness.

"I've always loved this tattoo," she breathed as she kissed it once more before moving on. She lowered her hand further, sighing as she sank it underneath the waist-band of his boxer briefs.

"Christ, Princess, your touch is like fucking magic."

"Yeah," she giggled, "I can see that, one touch and look, you're hard as stone." She pulled her hand from his briefs and slowly rid him of the last physical barrier be-tween them. "Seems I'm not the only one with Lucky Charms, huh?" His wolfish grin made her laugh out loud. "What the hell made you pierce your dick?"

"I got a Prince Albert four weeks before I came back to Florida." His voice grew softer. "I thought it would be a fun thing to share with you."

Memories of the days before life turned to shit still plagued her thoughts and dreams but she refused to let them rule her conscious mind. So she shoved them back in the metal lockbox she'd created specifically for that reason and slammed down the lid. When she trained her stare back on Ryan she could tell he had been watching her—

waiting to see if she would talk, bring up the past—but she wouldn't. There was no going back.

"That's not a Prince Albert, Ryan." His eyes rounded at her clear knowledge of that particular kind of piercing. She could tell he wanted to ask how she knew about such things and she also knew his pride would never allow him to ask such a question.

"You're right, Princess. And you would know a prince when you saw one," he chuckled. "It's an Apadravya." He brazenly stroked his cock as she stared.

Her entire body clenched as she took in the scene in front of her. The way he pleasured himself with abandon, his guttural moans of arousal. The way he didn't try to hide the fact that he was as turned on watching her watching him as she was. Without breaking eye contact, Ryan spoke to her, his voice hoarse and seductive. "You always did get turned on watching me touch myself. Tell me, Ashley, is your pussy wet right now? Is it getting wetter every second that you watch my hand pump my dick?" At his question, she straddled his thighs once again and dipped her mouth to his hardened length. "Fuck, baby…" Laving his arousal from root to tip she took him into her warm willing mouth. "Oh. My. God."

She loved hearing his groans and feeling his body spin out of control. The few times that she had the opportunity to have him in her mouth were the most powerful she'd ever felt in her life. No other man had ever had that affect on her.

She sucked him deep to the back of her throat and then slowly released him until his crown lay gently on her lips. She sucked on the tip of his shaft just before she ran the back of her tongue up the sensitive spot in the back of the head. Pleas fell from his lips like psalms bestowed up-on her, and she gloried in every one of them.

"Fuck, Ash, I…" Her mouth felt so goddamn good sucking him in and bathing him in her warmth. Tingles spread over his skin making him pray for the blessed tor-ture to never end.

However, if she kept this up it would be only minutes before it did. He could feel his balls tightening as his or-gasm gathered in the base of his spine. "Baby, I'm gonna come."

From between gritted teeth, his warning was feeble at best. He wanted to give her the chance to move but he hoped to fucking God she didn't. That was his last rational thought before his mind scattered and his body came un-done. He swore out loud as his release exploded from his body into hers and he felt her warm mouth greedily accept what he gave her, taking it down with soft breaths and even softer moans.

Finally gathering the energy to open his eyes, he looked at the woman still lapping at his semi-erect cock and their gazes connected. He felt magic of a different kind. "Come here, Princess." She immediately complied and he stroked her hair and laid soft kisses on her lips. "That was…*amazing*."

"Thank you. You know, I learned how to give blow jobs by reading books." He felt a second of guilt pass through him just before she winked at him and smiled. *God, I was such an asshole*, he reflected.

Knowing he needed more of her, he ran his knuckles

down the side of her body. "Let me show you what I learned how to do from this hot young girl I used to date." Ashley started to laugh until she found herself flipped on her back and spread eagle on the bed. "You're quick, Princess, but I'm quicker," he joked.

"Ry, I want you to fuck me," Ashley's raw voice sounded wanton but Ryan knew he couldn't let himself get carried away. He'd waited too goddamn long to rush things now.

"Not yet, baby..." In a slow but calculated movement he brushed his lips over each of her nipples before descending lower. Reaching her stomach he rubbed his thumbs over her hipbones. His touch was light and reverential. "More ink," he observed. She didn't respond and his eyes took in the script that wrapped boldly from one hipbone to the other.

"'Your light will guide me through the darkness, your love will forever be my home.' My God, Ashley, that's beautiful. Did you write that?"

"Yeah, it was the second tattoo I had done. They say tattooing is an addiction...I think I'm an addict." He placed small, silent kisses on each of the words etched on her skin, then continued to make his way to her core.

"I love that you wax." The pads of his fingers grazed over her smooth lips. "It's so fucking hot. Christ, Ashley, there wasn't anything about you from before that I would have changed, yet seeing you like this"—his eyes devoured her—"there's nothing I'd change now, either. No matter what you do, no matter how you change your appearance, you're fucking perfect."

"Yeah, I'm fucking great," she mumbled sarcastically. Her words were lost the moment Ryan's tongue touched her core. She shivered as he spread her thighs wide open and feasted on her like a starving man.

"Ahh, Ryan." She pulled her lower lip between her teeth stifling her cry. He slipped his finger into her tight pussy as he licked her clit with the tip of his tongue.

"Don't hold back, Princess. Let me hear you."

His gruff request seemed to free her inhibitions as she gave voice to the pleasure he was bestowing to her body. Ryan continued to lavish the hardened pearl with long licks and soft nips. He plunged two fingers in and out of her tight entrance, rubbing the soft skin against her pelvic bone. She pressed her pussy up against his hungry mouth and arched her back as she melted around him.

"Watching you come undone is like watching the sun rise, Ashley. It's the most breathtaking thing my eyes have ever seen, yet I know if I'm lucky, I'll get to see it again tomorrow."

Shifting underneath him, Ashley smiled lazily, "There's my Romeo, I was wondering if I would see him again sometime soon."

He looked down into her eyes and saw pieces of their past staring back at him—pieces he wanted to recapture mixed with pieces he wished he could forget. His arms were on either side of her head in a push-up position and she lifted her hands to stroke his triceps. "I want your weight on me, Ry. I want everything you have to give me, right here, right now." He lowered his body to hers absorbing her softness and her heat. His growl sounded almost feral to his own ears, as he pressed the tip of his length into her soft, wet cunt.

She laced her fingers through his hair and pulled him down for a kiss. Her flavor mingled with his scent was an erotic blend. She loved the feeling of his tongue sliding into her mouth. His naked body once again aligned with hers, and his fully erect cock lay nestled between her thighs waiting for the right moment to enter her, claim her.

"Oh, God, Ash. Oh my God, baby... are we really doing this?" After all this time—after everything they'd been through—they were finally at this point. She was finally going to give herself to the only man she'd ever loved. For one night she was going to push the self-doubt and loathing out of her mind for just a little while. She reached between them, stroking him in her palm. "Princess, wait, let me grab a condom." She tightened her hold on him just as he was about to pull away.

"Nothing between us, Ryan. Just this once, I want nothing between us. I'm on the pill and I'm clean. Have you been careful?"

He nodded in the affirmative and leaned forward putting his lips to her ear.

"Nothing between us, Princess...just you and me." Her wish came true, as her thoughts scattered like marbles on a hardwood floor. The feeling of him sliding into her was indescribable in its own right, but add the Apa to that and it was downright euphoric.

"Oh, fuck, Ry..." She whimpered, wrapping her long legs around his waist and pulling him deeper into her. His approving groan made her smile. They quickly found their rhythm as they rocked into each other in a tangle of limbs, lips, and lust. Ryan fucked her mouth with his tongue with the same rhythm he fucked her pussy with his cock, deep strokes followed by almost a complete withdrawal and then slammed back into her with wild abandon. Ashley was lost in a sexual haze that she had never experienced before. She knew it would be like this with him. She knew back then that they'd explode when they finally got together, but it didn't happen then. Thank God it didn't because she would have never had the strength to leave him...then.

"I'm getting close, Ash, I want you to come with me."

"Ryan, I've come twice..." Her breaths were short and quick as their bodies continued to grind into one another's. "It's okay, I'm good." She leaned up to kiss him, but he pulled back.

"You're more than just *'good'*, and you're gonna come again with me." His smug grin showed how certain he was of himself and his abilities. Ashley smiled and pulled him down for the kiss he denied her just mere seconds before. His fingers glided between their bodies and down over her hardened clit. The added stimulation had her pulsing around him as another orgasm started building in her already sensitive body. In and out he pumped while massaging the pleasure spot at the entrance of her core.

"Christ, Ryan"—there was a small amount of humor in her voice—"you are so fucking good." She was close, so when he stroked her one last time she flew apart around him, her inner walls eliciting his release.

Getting a towel from her bathroom, Ryan cleaned up a sleeping Ashley and himself before climbing back into bed with her. She was lying on her side at the far end of her bed, something else different from the Ashley he'd known. When they were younger she'd slept in the center of her bed, leaving a space on either side for the nights when he would sneak in her window. Now it seemed as if she was giving him all the space he needed—as long as he wasn't near her.

Tough shit, he thought as he settled in close to her, pressing his chest to her back. Her warmth seeped through his skin, cradling him into a deep sleep where he dreamt of coconut and sunshine.

CHAPTER TWENTY-THREE

Stud Named Reagan

ASHLEY OPENED HER eyes as the first rays of dawn crept through her window. As she came to, she felt a large hand cupping her breast, and the heat emanating from the warm body behind her and memories of the previous night flooded her head.

It wasn't a dream, Ryan *had* come to Danny's on Main, waltzing back into her life as if no time passed, as if no harm had been done, and how had she responded? She'd just opened her door—and her legs—and let him in. *What the fuck is wrong with me?*

She lay still, not wanting to disturb him until she'd worked out her exit plan, which was going to be tricky since they were in her fucking house. *Shit. Why did I let him in?*

She gave herself a mental slap before letting her eyes wander to the muscular arm that held her tight to his chest. Running up his forearm was a beautiful tattoo that she hadn't noticed the previous night. *Well, of course you didn't notice, you slut,* she held in her snicker, *you were too busy blowing him to look at his arm.* The thoughts of their joined passion brought a small grin to her lips. She had to admit that the sex had been amazing—more so than she'd imagined, and she'd imagined it a lot.

The quote inked onto his forearm was in French. Ashley took French all four years of high school. In fact that was the only class she and Ryan had shared. *Se Souvenir le passé, vivre le presente.* Remember the past, but live in the present. The phrase was so poignant it startled her. Her lungs burned from a lack of oxygen before she realized she had been holding her breath.

"Breathe, Princess. Now that we've got each other everything's going to be okay."

The pads of his fingers ran the length of her arm as he pulled her naked body closer to his. Startled, she knifed up and hopped out of bed. "Ash, what's wrong?"

She knew she was about to break his heart. She could hear the affection in his voice and the concern in his question. She'd seen the love in his eyes last night but had chosen to ignore it, hoping to find peace for just a few hours.

Dressing quickly in her yoga pants and her sports bra and tank, she turned to him. He sat upright in her bed and his mussed hair screamed hot sex. Her resolve also waivered when she saw his whiskered face, begging to be kissed, but, no. She needed to rip off the bandage, and she needed to do it now.

"Ryan." Though her hands trembled her voice was firm. "Last night was great, but it was a one-time thing. It will never happen again." She watched his face and saw the exact moment his confusion morphed into understanding. "Are we clear?"

"Princess, you're right, last night was amazing. But you are so wrong if you think it'll never happen again. I finally got you back and I'm never letting you go again.

I'm guessing I wasn't the first to have your sweet body, Ash—"

Anger swelled inside her like steam in a pressure cooker, and her lid was just about to blow. Stomping over to him, she leaned down and shoved her face into his. "My first? Are you kidding me? No, you weren't my first you cocky arrogant ass. You think I stopped living my life when you dumped me? Do you think I've lived the past three years waiting for you to grace me with your presence? " She poked him in his hard naked chest with her index finger and even through her fury she felt the sparks shoot up her arm. She reacted immediately and took a step backward to place distance between them.

Other than the slight flinch when she jabbed him, Ryan stayed perfectly still and listened quietly as her rant continued to bubble out of her. "No Ryan, you were certainly *not* my first. My first time happened two days after leaving Miami. I ended up in Georgia…" Her eyes grew dark with the memory. "I'd decided to honor Leo by getting one of his tattoo's inked on me and after spending some time up close and pretty fucking personal with the sexy stud of a tattoo artist named Reagan, we went back to his place." She watched as Ryan's brows furrowed in disappointment, how he bit the inside of his mouth, his tell when he was trying to reign in his frustration, and how his chest rose and fell in quick succession as he fought to contain what she could only imagine was disgust at her behavior.

"Yes, Ryan, I can see what you're thinking, it's written all over your face." She knew she was being unkind, she knew her words were cutting him, but she couldn't hold back any longer. With clenched fists and a trembling

203

lip she continued. "Yes, after everything you did to ensure my first time would be special…magical, I lost my virginity to some random guy I just met." Anger and heart-break welled in her belly when Ryan broke eye contact and looked away. "Oh, no, Ryan, you brought this up. You came here, you opened *this box*, too late to close it, remember?" She repeated his words from the previous night. "So after a few drinks, the name 'Reagan' started sounding a whole lot like Ryan. He was sexy and wild, he didn't care that I was a virgin—hell, he didn't know until he was deep inside of me. When we were done he offered to hold me through the night. I slipped out while he slept and was gone the next day. After all, I got what I needed. A little bit of my brother on my skin and a little taste of you under it." She tried and failed to reign in the anger from her tone, all the while knowing that Ryan could read her and would surely see the pain in her eyes.

"Ashley, I'm so sorry. I can't put into words how sorry I am. How knowing that your suffering was caused by me has been eating away at me since the night Leo…" Ashley put up her hand to stop him from saying the words out loud. "That's why I stayed away for so long. You said if I loved you I should let you go. I let you leave…even though every fiber of my being told me I was making the biggest mistake of my life when I watched you drive away."

"So what, Ry? You done loving me now?" She quipped, praying for the strength to keep the tears at bay until she could make her escape.

"No, Princess, that'll never happen. I just spent the past three years figuring out the root of all my anger and jealousy, and I learned how to control it. Now, I can love you the way you are meant to be loved. Now, I can give you what you deserve." His eyes begged forgiveness as he reached out his hand to touch her. Ashley jerked back, avoiding his contact.

"What I want, is for you to get out of my house." She couldn't contain the shrill sound of her voice. "I'm going for a run before work. Be gone before I get back."

Ryan let his outstretched hand fall to the bed. "I was in that bed with you last night, Princess, and you don't want me gone anymore than I want to leave. I won't be in your house when you get back. But you should know that as of yesterday, I am an official employee of Danny's on Main, so get used to seeing me because I'm in it for the long haul."

She tied her running shoes with a growl before jetting out of the room. "Have a nice run, Princess."

"Don't call me Princess, asshole," she relayed as she slammed the door behind her. *What the fuck just happened?* She thought to herself, standing on the other side of her bedroom door. Just before she walked down the hallway, she heard Ryan chuckling in her room.

"Spicy, I think I'm beginning to understand the nickname," she heard as he spoke out loud through private laughter. "And I think I kind of like it." Ashley rolled her eyes and left her house.

CHAPTER TWENTY-FOUR

Wrinkle-Lover

Two months later...

"I'M SORRY, BUDDY, that sucks. You can crash at my place for a couple of days, but I don't do roommates. Been there, done that, prefer to go it alone."

Hearing male voices, Ashley paused at the back door of the near empty bar. Ryan had been in Charistown for a couple of months and other than their one night of scorching sex, she'd managed to keep her distance...at least physically. Late at night lying in her bed, alone, Ryan starred in her dreams and she frequently brought herself to orgasm with her own hand, all the while wishing it were his.

Following a mild meltdown where Ashley expressed her...*distaste* at the fact that Danny and Julie had hired him to work at *her* bar, she had requested that they schedule Ryan different shifts so they wouldn't have to work together. *In fact*, she wondered, *why was he even there?* Thursday's were her nights, damn it. She stayed hidden so she could eavesdrop on the guys' conversation.

"No, that's totally fine, Max, I appreciate the offer—even if it's only temporary." The fact that Ryan's laugh caused a shiver to run up her body pissed her off.

"I don't understand," Kyle, the other bartender and her good friend, piped up, "they're just kicking you out without any notice?"

"Look"—Ryan's voice was laden with defeat—"the rental house is a piece of shit so I'm not surprised they're tearing it down. I'm just happy they are letting me back in to get my stuff. Unfortunately, it was all I could afford when I got to town. I'm waiting on payment for some songs that I wrote to come through but until then, I'm screwed. It cost me a lot of money to find her." What did that mean? Was he talking about her?

Ashley's heart raced at the thought of Ryan spending time searching for her. Why hadn't he just asked her parents?

So here he was tending bar and writing songs for the bands he should be performing in. *What gives?* She would have to ask him... eventually.

"Dude, I'd invite you to live with me, but I already have two roommates—"

"And you really don't wanna live with Kyle." Ashley chose that moment to make her presence known. "He's a dog, and a slob," she hip-checked Kyle while tying the cocktail apron around her waist.

"What are you trying to say, Spicy?" That nickname, along with all of the others the men here at Danny's called her, made her smile. They were so much better than the plain, perfect image she'd been forced to wear her whole life.

"I'm sayin' if it looks like a dog, acts like a dog, and

lives like a dog…WOOF!" She giggled uncontrollably as Kyle lunged forward and tickled her.

"Well, Ash, do you have a better solution to our boy's problem?" She wanted to slap the smug look off Max DeLucca's gorgeous face. She knew what he was getting at—everyone who worked at Danny's did. Ryan had made no secret of the fact that he and Ashley had been a couple. He'd also made no bones about the fact that he'd screwed up and wanted a chance to earn back her trust. They had an unspoken agreement that the specific details of their history would remain between them, so none of the group understood her flat out refusal of any of Ryan's advances.

Pulling in a lungful of air, she regretted her proposal even before it left her mouth. "Ry, I live in a big house. Really, it's too big for just one person. I'm not even sure what I was thinking when I bought it…"

That was a bald-faced lie. After more than six months of traveling up the coast, living in and out of her car, she'd seen the quaint house on the beautiful tree lined street and had to have it. She knew it was much too big for just her, but at the time her brain had been blindly hoping that one day Leo and Ryan would surprise her and come knocking on her door. In reality, she knew that neither would happen, but it hadn't stopped her from buying the house. Nor did it stop her from leaving the lights on by the front door each night. Hope was a terrible thing to lose.

————————————

Standing at the bar with a look of sheer shock on his face, Ryan made a display of knocking the side of his head with his open hand. "I'm sorry, I didn't hear you. What did you just say, Princess?"

She growled out loud at his attempt to make her say the only thing he knew she'd feared saying. "I'm offering you a place to crash, you big pain in the ass. If you'd like, feel free to move your shit in and stay there. But, I expect rent on time. I am *not* your maid or your mom—" He leveled a painful stare at her and immediately she apologized and re-phrased. "Sorry, Ry, but I'm *not* gonna cook or clean for you. So, as long as you keep the place neat, you're more than welcome to dwell there." She stood behind the bar and stared expectantly at him.

Kyle threw his head back and laughed hysterically, "Wow, Spicy, that was some sweet invitation."

"Gee, Ryan, how the hell could you turn down something so...warm and inviting?" Max laughed before he threw his arm around a clearly frustrated Ashley, giving her a quick hug.

Ashley crossed her arms over her chest trying to hide her anxiety with sarcasm. "What the hell? That's what I get for being nice."

"Ashley Kynde, thank you so much for the invitation." Ryan smiled broadly trying to hold back his laughter. "I accept your proposition, and I am eternally grateful."

"Whatever. Fuck you guys. That'll be the last time you see my sincere, heartfelt generosity." With her bottom lip between her teeth she walked away from the deep, riotous, laughter coming from the bar and she went to her locker in the back room. By the time she returned to the main bar the men had reassembled their game faces.

"Here's my key, go make yourself a copy." She tossed the metal to Ryan before heading back through the double doors. "Jerks." The laughter followed her all the way to Danny and Julie's office.

———•———————————————•———

"Holy shit, man, I can't believe she's letting you move in with her. I've been trying for two years to tap that fine piece of ass, but she's never so much as batted an eye-lash at me." Kyle's crude words hit Ryan like a punch to the gut. "Kyle, you fucking idiot, you're like Sophia from the Golden Girls?" Max slapped Kyle on the back of his head before turning his attention to Ryan. "Don't listen to a word this douche says. There isn't a female within fif-teen miles of here that this guy hasn't tried to 'tap'." Max's use of air quotes had Ryan laughing. "Seriously, Ry," Max stage whispered, "rumor has it Kyle Marx here, once got tapped himself by a lady who ended up being not such a lady at all…you hear what I'm saying?" Kyle blushed under Ryan's gaze.

"She…he…whatever the fuck it was, *it* was hot. *And* it was offering a blow job. No reason to turn that shit down." Kyle shrugged his shoulders and started to wipe down the bar. "And Max, you wanna talk shit about me? You watch the fucking Golden Girls, you pussy. So shut your trap, you wrinkle-lover!" At that point, Ryan's chuckle broke out into full-blown laughter.

Finally regaining his composure, Ryan reached over the bar and put his hand on the rag that Kyle was using. "Listen up. I don't care who she dates. I won't like it, but I can't stop it. I love her and I intend to get her back. It's only been a couple of months but I already like you guys, and I see us being friends. That being said, I will mow you down to get to her if the chance ever presents itself. She is not just a piece of ass for me to 'tap'." Ryan sneered using air quotes to drive home his point to Kyle. "She's my everything. We clear?"

Clarity entered Kyle's usually cloudy green eyes, "Yeah, man, crystal." Ryan wrapped his fingers around Ashley's keys and left the bar. Thoughts of living under the same roof together had him giddy like a schoolgirl, yet hard like a teen-aged boy. *This is it, I'm gonna get my chance. I'm finally gonna get Ashley back*, he thought with every piece of hope left in his heart.

CHAPTER TWENTY-FIVE

We Are Just Friends

Four years later...

TIME PASSED QUICKLY as Ashley and Ryan continued living together, platonically. Oddly enough, it seemed to work for them. Even though he'd spent the better part of that time unsuccessfully trying to win her back, they had managed to build an amazing friendship. Ashley dated various men over the years but it was never serious, and never for long stretches.

Ryan never dated anyone. Ashley tried for a while to convince him to go out with women from the bar or from their gym, but he refused and eventually she stopped trying. Everyone from the bar made fun of them about their pseudo-relationship and it pissed her off. They were *not* a couple. She couldn't be with him—she couldn't ever really be with anyone, no matter how many dates she went on. Why couldn't anybody understand that?

"Hey Princess, you gonna stand there all night with your head in the clouds or are you gonna serve the customers?"

"Bite me, Ryan," she snipped shaking the Cosmos for the suits at the far end of the bar.

"What can I get for you two, chickies?" It was a Thursday night in mid-March and the weather was unseasonably warm. Ashley loved the rare warm days Mother Nature tossed out in the still of winter. They reminded her of a lover's gentle tease before the hot, steamy sex.

"We'll have two lemon drop shots with our Lemontini's, please." The women waiting for the drinks had been sitting at the bar for over an hour laughing, joking and having a great time. Lyla and Janie had introduced themselves the previous week when they'd come in to Danny's on Main for the first time. Both were beautiful and friendly, and they had included Ashley in their conversation anytime she was close enough to their end of the bar. She'd found herself hoping they would come back so she could listen in on their silly stories. Since moving to Pennsylvania, Ashley hadn't made that many female friends—in fact, she'd never had a whole lot of friends, even back in Florida.

She wasn't gossipy or girly. She wasn't high maintenance or ditzy. She didn't use a lot of words, and she didn't require a lot of phone time or communication to make her happy. Add that to the fact that she didn't want to share any details about her life—none, nada—that pretty much cut her out of any of the girlfriend groups. There were times when she thought the guys—and by guys she meant Max, Ryan, Kyle, and Danny—saw her more as one of them than as a woman, but, that didn't bother her...too much.

"Janie, I can't believe you are still seeing that fucktard. Richard doesn't deserve you. Dump his hairy ass and move on." Ashley smiled at the candidness of the women's conversation.

"Here ya go, chickies." Ashley poured their shots and one for herself.

"To hot men with tattooed bodies and muscles that flex, but most of all to hot, steamy sex!" Lyla giggled at her own toast before clinking her glass to both Janie and Ashley's and pouring the clear liquid down her throat. Ashley couldn't help but laugh at her goofiness as she followed suit.

"Ly, your toasts get more ridiculous each time." Janie's eyes watered as laughter bubbled out of her.

"Here's some water for you ladies."

Ashley knew, without turning around, exactly who was offering the beverages. Max had noticed Janie last week, and while he was known for his 'Fuck and Release' method of dating, he hadn't stopped talking about the stunning woman all week. Most women threw themselves at him, but not her. She kept her distance and that kept him interested. *Typical man*, Ashley thought to herself.

Janie's aqua eyes went round as she accepted the glass from his hand. "Um, thanks…"

"This sexy beast here is Max. Max this is Lyla and Janie." Ashley watched as sparks zipped between the Greek God and the brunette beauty. "I'll be right back, I need to go take care of those customers." She excused herself from the triad, giving them time to get to know each other.

"So the ladies from last week are back, huh?" Ryan looked over Ashley's shoulder and smirked.

"What's the look for, Ry?"

"What look?" He asked innocently.

"When you're up to something you get this smirk, and you have it now, so what gives?"

Ryan shrugged. "It's just a hunch, but I have a feeling we'll be seeing a lot of those two. They have staying power." Ryan ran his hands through his hair catching the attention of a frizzy-haired fem-bot on the other side of the bar practically begging for a little Ryan TLC. Watching them interact, Ashley was surprised to feel a slight stirring in the pit of her stomach. She couldn't name the feeling, but she didn't like it.

Not one bit.

●————————————————●

"This was such a thoughtful idea. Thanks for having all of us to your home, Lyla," Julie said, handing Lyla a bouquet of roses and a homemade apple pie.

"Thanks, honey, this is much appreciated." Danny pulled Lyla in for a big hug. Ryan, who had arrived at the same time as Danny and Julie, noticed how Lyla's body had stiffened at the contact, but she'd accepted it nonetheless.

"It's our pleasure, really. Janie and I've been having Sunday dinner together for years and when it falls on a holiday it's nice to celebrate. So, thanks for joining our little Memorial Day party. If you wanna know the truth," the sassy espresso haired vixen said, "you're actually helping us. We buy the same amount of alcohol whether there are two or ten of us, so drink up." She winked and led them through to her kitchen.

"She's spunky, I knew she'd fit in perfectly, Danny," Julie stage whispered.

"Jane, guests are here, time to act civilized."

Ryan checked his phone for the time.

"You waiting on a train?" Danny was the master of several things and sarcasm was one of them. "That's the third time you've checked your phone since we walked through the door, what's up?"

"I'm waiting for Ashley." Ryan popped the top of a beer and took a long pull of the cold drink before continuing. "She was arguing with her mom when I left the house. I offered to wait but she insisted I go on ahead. She usually only speaks to her dad, but today her mother intercepted the call before her dad could even get to the phone. I hate that cold bitch. I hate what she does to Ashley, I just…hate it."

Over the years, Ryan had heard several conversations between the women where Ashley's mother had torn Ashley down for pretty much anything—from not graduating from high school, to blowing her scholarship to the University of Pennsylvania, and even going as low as blaming Ashley for Leo's accident. Ryan knew deep down that Ashley's inability to find true happiness and her fear of commitment stemmed from all of the pain she lived through in Florida. He also knew that a fair share of that blame lay squarely on his shoulders. While she'd opened the door to her home for him, she had never let him back into her heart and he was running out of options when it came to getting her back.

"Sweetie, I understand that Ashley's mother is a nasty, unkind, cold woman that hurts Ashley and makes her sad, but *you* need to understand that it isn't your job to make life better for her. Every day that sweet girl lets her past dictate her present is a choice that *she* makes—not her mother, not you, only *her*. *She* has to make the choice to decide when enough is enough." Julie draped her arm around Ryan's back. "And Ry, think about this. Sometimes, when you know that you're so protected that there is no possible way you could fail, you don't even bother to try. Because...what's the point?" Ryan looked into Julie's knowing eyes and received her message loud and clear.

"She's good, boy, pay attention," Danny advised, before he laced his fingers through his wife's and led her out to Lyla's backyard.

Was he standing too close to Ashley? All this time he'd been trying to stay in her focus, but did she even see him anymore? His thoughts were interrupted by the doorbell.

"Look what I found lurking around." Ashley walked through the door with Kyle and hugged Lyla, handing over a tray of cookies as Max and Kyle each kissed Lyla on the cheek.

"I feel so loved," she teased.

"We brought booze," Kyle shouted. The lack of focus in his eyes had the appearance of someone who had already started drinking before coming to the party.

"Is Janie here yet?" Max asked.

"I see you're going for the subtle approach, huh Max," Ryan laughed.

"Yes, and her douchey boyfriend can't make it today. I'm torn up about it. Can you tell?" His smile nearly split his face.

Ashley called out from the deck. "Hey, guys, Janie's outside filling water balloons. Get your asses out here— boys against girls." *After the blowout with her mother, she probably needed some good clean fun to take her mind off*

217

things, he thought to himself.

"Oh, Princess, you are going down." The sexual undertone in Ryan's comment was unintentional but when Ashley's eyes lowered from his face to his shorts, he felt his cock stir.

He felt his cock grow rock hard when she seductively licked her lips and replied, "You wish, Ryan, you wish."

———————————

Splat, Splat!! Ashley's thoughts were rudely interrupted when colorful, thin latex exploded in her lap.

"What the fuck!" She looked up, the shock quickly evaporating when her eyes locked on a very proud Ryan Baker grinning like a fool.

"Don't worry, Ash, I've got you covered." Janie dragged over a tub overflowing with water-filled balloons and Ashley started heaving them at Ryan. One after the other, the balloons hit him like heat-seeking missiles, splashing water in his hair, his face, and his chest. Soon he was drenched and everyone was laughing at the scene.

"It's like watching Frogger," Max roared.

"Holy...shit!"

The sound of awe in Lyla's voice pulled Ashley's attention away from Max's hysterics to whatever Lyla and Janie were gawking at. "Look at his fucking body."

Lyla, who Ashley had learned could maintain a poker face like no other, was blatantly staring at Ryan. He'd peeled of his wet t-shirt and laid it on the back of a chair to dry. "I wanna name every one of his abs," Lyla murmured in a lusty voice.

"Down, girl!" Janie flicked Lyla in the arm, earning

her a mean stare and a playful pinch from her best friend. "Ly, that boy is spoken for." Janie's words instantly pulled Ashley back into the conversation.

"Um, I didn't realize Ryan was dating someone…" Ashley swallowed hard, praying with everything she had that she could keep hold of the pretzels that weighed heavy in her stomach.

Lyla and Janie giggled. "Come on, Ash, cut us a break," Janie and Lyla said in tandem. "We've been hanging out with you guys for a couple of months now. There is *no* way that there isn't something going on between the two of you."

"Between *me* and *him*?" It felt like every nerve in her body was exposed, every button pushed, every memory brought to the surface. Ashley hated when people asked about her and Ryan because it killed her to deny the love she'd once felt for him. Almost as much as it did to deny the love she still felt… but, she had no other choice.

She looked over to where the rest of the group had congregated, with drinks in hand, as if this was entertainment for them. *Why do they enjoy watching my head spin and my heart break?*

"There is nothing—I repeat, *nothing*—going on between Ryan Baker and myself! We are just *friends*, who happen to both live and work together. Period. End of story. Got it?" She pulled her hair back into a low ponytail and turned her back to her friends before loudly stating, "Christ, I need a drink!"

She didn't need to look at Janie and Lyla to know that their mouths were agape. The heat from their stares burned a hole in her back, but she refused to turn around. She needed tequila, and she needed it now. When she heard

219

Ryan addressing the group, she knew one shot wouldn't be enough.

"She loves me, she just isn't ready to admit it yet, right, Princess?" While his joke was exactly what was needed to break the tension, Ashley knew it would be more like three shots before she could show her face in the backyard.

"Whoa there, chickie, save some for the rest of us." She turned around to see Julie, Janie and Lyla standing behind her, each holding their own shot glass. They smiled kindly at her and held out their glasses.

"Look, girl, Janie and I didn't mean to pry." Lyla donned an oddly unnatural and forced grin on her face.

"Shut up, Ly, yes we did. We've been dying to know about you two since the start. And just FYI, look at that ridiculous smile." Janie pointed to the silly smirk still on Lyla's face. "Remember that look, it's her tell. That girl can't lie for shit."

"Fuck you, Janie!" Lyla spewed without a trace of anger in her tone or her crystal blue eyes. "Anyway, what I'm saying is, you want your space, take it. Okay?" Lyla gestured between herself and Janie. "We get it, and we'll give that to you. Now *that's* the end of the story." Lyla handed Ashley, Julie and Janie a shot glass before opening a different bottle for herself. Let's take these shots, cept' I don't shoot straight tequila." Lyla poured herself a vodka.

"To friends," she lifted her small glass. "I love you near. I love you far. But if I need space, and you can't give me *that*," she giggled, "then get the fuck out of my face!"

"*That* was a good one, Ly. You really should write these down." Ashley didn't see the wink Janie sent Lyla at the suggestion. Julie's face was pinched, "Lyla, even after all these years of owning a bar, I still hate the taste of straight tequila. Next time, pour two vodkas, okay?" The women laughed as they watched Julie suck on extra lemon wedges.

"Let's bring this food outside so that Danny and the guys can barbecue." Julie lowered her voice trying to imitate her husband. "It'll make them feel like men." The ladies laughed as they carried the food outside to the grill.

CHAPTER TWENTY-SIX

Burnt Cookies

"PRINCESS, WHAT ARE you doing? We're already late, let's go." Ryan popped his head into the kitchen and couldn't hold back his reaction. It started with a twitch in his abdomen which quickly rose up through his chest, but once it got to his throat there was no way he could contain his laughter.

"It's not funny, Ryan!" He loved when Ashley's cheeks sported a pink blush. Between her reddened face, her little white tank top that was molded just right to her fantastic body, and the newly died blue streaks in her hair, she looked perfect for the Fourth of July festivities at Danny and Julie's house. Every flat surface in the kitchen was covered in a mist of white powder, including Ashley herself.

"What happened, babe?"

"I refuse to answer if you're going to stand there and laugh at me," she said, but the clatter of pans landing in the sink and the sight of blackened discs being dumped in the trashcan answered Ryan's question.

"Ash."

She looked at him with her arms crossed over her

chest as his eyes glittered with amusement mixed with a bit of something else, although his voice was gentle and warm as he continued. "You tried to bake cookies, didn't you?" Her following silence was admission enough.

"Princess, that was so thoughtful. I'm sure Julie would have appreciated the gesture, really, babe." He tried to maintain a serious face, but it wasn't easy containing the grin that threatened to break across his lips. He loved their banter.

"Uh, thanks Ry." He couldn't believe she was falling for his mature act. After all these years, she should know better, geeze.

"No problem. And Princess, for future reference, do you know what Julie would appreciate more?" Ryan finally revealed his wide smile in its entirety before he answered. "She'd appreciate it if you never tried to bake for her again. Seriously, you can't bake for shit. What were you thinking?" His laughter bounced off the walls of the small house as he ran out of the kitchen but he learned he wasn't quick enough when a burnt cookie hit him in the head.

"Ryan Baker, you are such an asshole!" *Maybe*, he thought to himself, chuckling. But hearing Ashley giggle out loud he knew once and for all that there was nothing sweeter than the sound of true laugher coming out of her mouth.

———————————•

By the time they arrived, the party was in full swing. Ryan went directly over to Danny, who was manning the grill, and Ashley delivered her store bought cookies to Julie.

"Look how sweet they are together." Ashley gestured to Max and Janie who were lying together on a yellow blanket spread out on the grass. Deep in conversation, each wore a relaxed smile. It was the first time she'd seen them together and she could see there were some serious sparks between the two. Whether any thing would come from it was anyone's guess.

"I've never seen him look so happy," Julie mused.

"Do you think he realizes the affect she has on him yet, or do you think he's blind to it? I'd hate to see him lose someone like her—she's pretty special, you know?"

Julie turned her gaze from Max and Janie and stared directly at Ashley. "Yes, Ashley, I'm surrounded by pretty special women and so I have it on good authority that it's not just the men who are blind to things that make them happy." Julie placed a loving stroke on Ashley's arm before returning to the house to retrieve more food. Ashley glanced over at her friends on the grass once more. She hoped Max didn't let his past screw things up with Janie. The irony of the situation was, sadly, completely lost on her.

Heading over to Danny and handing him a cold beer, Ashley felt Ryan's gaze on her a moment before she noticed Kyle practically weaving up the slate path that led from the street to the back yard with a woman clinging to his side. Ryan laughed and shook his head in amusement. "Danny, look at that girl with Kyle. She looks at him like he single-handedly hung the moon. What the hell does he do to these poor girls?"

"Hey guys, this is Sheena," Kyle said, introducing the petite, scarlet haired, *young* woman as he approached the group, noticeably off-kilter.

"Um, actually, my name is Shira." Her cheeks were nearly as red as her hair when she sheepishly corrected his mistake. "Sheena, Shira—same difference." Ashley didn't think it was possible for a woman's face to get any redder without bursting into flames but poor Shira's face did.

"Kyle, you dipshit, that's not how you talk about a lady." Ashley couldn't believe that the poor girl had to deal with this level of embarrassment. Kyle had been drinking more than usual lately but this behavior was inexcusable. She was flabbergasted as she watched the woman place her small hands sweetly on Kyle's arm and whisper something in his ear. Kyle went pie-eyed as the dimple in his right cheek winked.

"'Scuse us for a bit," he announced loudly, sliding his arm around Shira. "We're gonna go get our fuck on. Be back soon…but not too soon," he chuckled.

Winking at Ryan and Max, who had left the grass to witness the spectacle, Kyle escorted Shira around the side of the house and out of sight. Ashley looked around, taking in the silent stares and awkwardness that blanketed her friends.

"Seriously? No one's gonna say it?" Lyla started to weave through the group, talking to no one in particular "Fine, I will. That was some fucked up shit!" Ashley watched Lyla's blue eyes dance with amusement. "No, really, let me see if I've got this right. He brings a girl here to meet his friends. He doesn't even know her name. She clearly has the good sense to be embarrassed, unless of course she was suffering from sunburn…yeah, maybe it was sunburn." Lyla paced while everyone listed to her recant the story. "She shows a modicum of backbone by telling him he got her name wrong. He basically tells her he doesn't give a shit. She giggles, whispers some sort of trailer trash voodoo in his ear, and then he announces that they're gonna go fuck? Really? Did that just happen?"

It sounded insane, comical even, but Ashley wasn't laughing. Inside, her heart was hurting for Kyle. Over the six years they had known each other they had shared some drunken nights and some cocktail confessions. She had only been granted bits and pieces of his past, but she knew enough to be able to deduct on her own that there was a ton of pain behind his "Fuck You" persona. Kyle was headed on a downward spiral and she wanted to help but didn't know how. Shaking off the guilt she decided to enjoy the party, but vowed to discuss whatever was going on with Kyle with Danny and Julie in the morning.

As the sun began to set in the sky, and the party was getting ready to move venues, everyone congregated around the table. The copious amounts of food and drink had everyone in a mellow mood. Janie sat between Lyla and Max. Julie was sitting on Danny's lap. Ryan looked around at his friends and wondered how he got so lucky in life and if it could possibly get better than this. Catching sight of Ashley, who was sitting beside him and laughing loudly at something Lyla has said, he knew that, yes, it could get better. The woman next to him could make his life complete. He was just out of ideas on how to make that happen. His thoughts were interrupted by Danny's announcement.

"So listen, before we head over to the park to watch

the fireworks, we should discuss the final details for the fundraiser." Danny's voice had taken on its patriarchal tone, making it clear to everyone around the table that this was a topic to be discussed seriously.

"What fundraiser?" Janie asked, her face full of excitement.

"Ashley, why don't you explain," Julie stated quietly, imploring Ashley to fill Janie and Lyla in on the details, but, Danny must not have caught the subtle hint because he started to describe the event until Julie put her hand over his mouth to stop him.

Ryan's gut clenched. They hadn't had to explain this story in more than four years—in fact, if not for this event, Ryan was pretty sure Ashley would never have spoken of her brother out loud. He subtly moved his hand under the table and rested it over hers. When she gave a slight nod of her head, he laced their fingers together and gave it a squeeze.

"We hold a fundraiser in August each year called *Leo's Lights*," Ryan felt Ashley's leg begin to tremble as she started her explanation. Holding tight to her hand, he was uncertain if he was giving comfort or seeking it.

Ashley took a breath before continuing. "Ryan writes songs for some pretty big labels in the music industry so each year he manages to score some sort of music memorabilia. Actually, how he does it is still a mystery to me. Anyway, we auction off the donated item and all of the money we make goes to helping local kids get the musical training they otherwise couldn't afford. This will be our fifth auction and each year so far we've raised enough money to provide kids of all ages with instruments and musical instruction. In a couple of cases we've donated the extra tuition needed to help the kids who'd earned musical scholarships to college, but still wouldn't have been able to afford it if not for a little extra help." She shrugged her shoulders and her voice got smaller as she said, "I'm really proud of what *Leo's Lights* has accomplished." Ryan was in awe of Ashley for speaking up and explaining the situation to Janie and Lyla, but the way she swallowed deeply and failed to make eye contact with anyone told him that she was only just clinging to her control. He tugged gently at her hand and she brought her gaze to his. No words passed between them but the slight nod that Ashley gave him let him know that she appreciated his support. All these years and she saw him only as support. *Does she even see me as a man? Or am I just her friend?* Exhaling he decided it may finally be time to move on. *How the hell do I do that?*

"If you don't mind me asking, Ashley," Janie leaned forward in her chair, her voice laced with compassion, her eyes full of questions, "who's Leo? You have that beautiful tattoo of his name on your bicep but, well, Lyla and I never wanted to pry."

Ashley felt Ryan squeeze her hand a little harder under the table. She knew that squeeze. She knew he was offering his protection, his support. She also knew that he'd answer the question himself, just to protect her from further pain. Insurmountable guilt slammed into her. She didn't deserve his protection. What she deserved was to feel every ounce of pain her brother had felt the night he'd tried to come to her rescue. Ashley flicked his hand off her lap. *No, I need to suffer on my own.* She squared her shoulders and replied, "Leo is my brother. I run this program each year for him." She stood up and ran her hands over her shorts, as if wiping away the bad memories along with the conversation. "It's getting dark, gang. Let's go get our place on the lawn. I don't want to miss any of the show." She reached over the table, grabbed an almost empty plate of chips and salsa and turned to take the tray into the house.

Her rejection and dismissal cut deep. For over six years, Ryan had allowed her to remind him of his betrayal. For over six years he had shouldered the blame for his wrong doing, as well as the things that had been out of his control. He looked down to his stomach where the knife had been twisted and realized he no longer bled. Yes, his love for Ashley did—and probably would always—run deeper than any love he had ever known, but it was killing him inside to continue this one-sided affair. He knew somewhere inside she still loved him, but after all these years he was just too damn tired to keep digging. *It's time for me to move on,* he thought. *But how?*

Just as the question came to his mind, the answer stumbled over to the table.

"You guys ready to go watch the fireworks?" Kyle ran his hands through his sex-rumpled hair and smiled devilishly.

"Where's your girl?" Ashley snipped as she came out of the house and stopped to look Kyle up and down.

"Who? Shayla?" Kyle smiled as if remembering a

fond moment.

"It was Shira, you fucking pig!" Landing a swift punch to Kyle's arm, Ashley huffed before grabbing her purse and heading back inside. Ryan couldn't hold in the chuckle. There wasn't a thing sexier than a pissed off Ashley. *No, it's time to move on.*

"Hey guys." Kyle, Max and Danny gave Ryan their full attention. "Are any of you available after the show tonight? I thought we could grab a beer, you know?" That was their guy code for they needed to talk.

"I wish I could, son, but I promised Julie I'd finish painting the bathroom by the end of the weekend, and it's the end of the weekend." Danny's gruff laugh made Ryan smile. "But after these two are done giving you their bad advice, let me know and I'll happily straighten it out for you."

"Thanks, Danny. What about you guys?" Ryan didn't realize how much he had been counting on them until they both said they'd be happy to meet up later. Relief washed over him. They would help him figure things out, he just knew it.

RYAN LOVED BEING at *Chopper's* bar. Whether he was drinking, playing pool, or just taking up space, being there made him feel grounded. It reminded him of a time when he was young and playing in the band, they'd played in bars like *Chopper's* all the time. That was back when life was easy—when the only thing he needed to worry about was their next gig, and when he would finally get to kiss his best friend's sister. God, he missed Leo. How different would life be if...

"Hey, man, you got us here, so let's get us some drinks and talk." Max clapped Ryan's shoulder before walking up to the bar and placing their order.

"Dude, we need shots." Kyle looked like he was slightly hung-over from his earlier drinking and Ryan considered advising him not to drink anymore, but, selfishly, he really wanted Kyle's advice and he knew that if he harped on him about his drinking, Kyle would just up and leave. So he kept his mouth shut and walked over to a table.

"Women. They make everything fucking crazy," Ryan mumbled the toast before letting the amber liquid glide down the back of his throat, blazing a trail of fiery frustration straight to his stomach.

"So it's gonna be one of those talks, huh?" Kyle grimaced, as he poured each of them a beer from the pitcher Max had brought to the table along with the shots.

"I'll go get us another round, and tell them to start a tab. I have a feeling we may be here a while." Max smiled as he strutted back over to the bar.

Ryan looked at his friends. Despite their differences, both had become incredibly important to him over the last few years. He'd never thought he'd have a close friend after Leo, but here he was, sitting at a table with two of them.

"Spill, Ry." Max returned and slid a shot in Ryan's direction and waited for him to talk.

"You guys know that I've been waiting on Ashley for

years, right?" Both men rolled their eyes and nodded their heads. Ryan smiled. "But, well, I think I realized tonight that I'm waiting for something that's never gonna happen."

Just saying the words out loud caused an ache in his gut so deep he was surprised he managed to hold himself upright. "So, I guess the reason I asked you guys here is…" He bit the inside of his lip, the sharp pain a reminder of why he was there in the first place. "I need your help moving on." *There, I said it,* he thought as the acid rose up his throat.

"Christ, Ryan, drink this." Max handed him a glass of clear liquid. He braced himself and took a large gulp only to spit it straight back out.

"That was water!" The clean clear substance was a complete shock to Ryan. Pausing only to wipe down the mess he'd made, he drank down the whole glass.

"Yeah, Ry," Max laughed, "it's water. We're not *all* alcoholics." His comment and his gaze shifted directly to Kyle, who chose that exact moment to check out the pair of scantily clad women playing pool. "You looked like you were about to puke so I didn't think another shot would be helpful. Look, buddy, I can't tell you how to 'get the girl.' Hell, I don't ever wanna get the girl again." Ryan didn't believe that for a second. He saw the electricity that sparked every time Max and Janie were together. If Max wanted to pretend it wasn't happening, so be it.

Max continued, "I do, however, know how to move on. And if that's what you want to do, I can help. To move forward, you need to—"

Kyle chose that moment to re-engage in the conversation, chipping in with, "Fuck everything that moves."

"What?" Both Ryan and Max stared at Kyle.

"Don't give me the innocent act, DeLucca." Kyle poured himself another beer from the pitcher and took a long gulp before continuing. "You and your buddy Gage have cornered the market on Fuck and Release. Christ, I think the term F and R just might be in the Urban-fucking-Dictionary by now."

Ryan watched as Kyle pointed a relatively unsteady finger firstly at Max and then at him. "Judge all you want, but neither one of you are better than me—I'm just not afraid to admit exactly who I am. Ryan, you wanna move on from Ashley, good! It's about time. I love that girl— she's a great bartender, a hot chick, and an awesome friend—but her head is fucked up, man. She's goin' down and taking you with her. She can't shake her past." Kyle's eyes clouded over and Ryan saw the familiar sadness that only came out when Kyle was completely wasted. "If she can't shake her past, then it's gonna consume her. You're my boy, Ryan, and you have to know you're too damn good for that. Let. It. Go."

Ryan was completely overwhelmed by the amount of insight Kyle had just offered. Never in all the time they had spent together had Kyle been that clear, and the funny thing was the man was shit-faced drunk. "Not to mention, fuckin' other girls will piss her off," he added. "You get her good and jealous and then stand back with your arms open and your pants down, she'll be all over you like a hooker at a free clinic."

"You couldn't have stopped while you were ahead, could you?" Ryan laughed finishing of his last shot.

"Hopefully he's too smashed to remember me admitting this, but he's not totally wrong," Max agreed. Ryan grinned at the comical look on Max's face. "While I certainly wouldn't go around throwing chicks in her face—because let's face it, Ashley's a tough woman, she might just kick your ass if you do—Kyle's right in that the best way to forget about the past is to move on to something new."

Max poured the remaining beer into the three glasses. "To women, the more the merrier." The three men lifted their glasses and finished off their beers.

CHAPTER TWENTY-SEVEN

Single and Available

"LYLA DALTON, ARE you crazy?" Ashley's heart raced from the two-mile run she'd just taken from her house to Lyla's. If she was being honest with herself, which was something she tried to avoid, her heart had started pumping faster long before she ever tied the laces on her Nikes, and the steamy August air had nothing at all to do with it.

"Some might say so," Lyla shrugged lazily, opening her door and inviting Ashley in.

"Ly, I can't take this." Ashley retrieved the folded paper from her pocket and held it out for Lyla to take, but her friend just crossed her arms over her chest and stared at her.

"Correct me if I'm wrong, Ashley, but that check isn't made out to you, it's made out to *Leo's Lights*, isn't it?" Ashley would have smiled at the mock confusion on Lyla's face if she didn't know for a fact that she was being purposely obtuse. "So, *you* aren't taking anything. The money is going to a good cause and I, personally, love good causes."

Lyla turned her back to Ashley and headed into her kitchen. "Want some water, you look...*sweaty*."

"Yeah, I'll have some," Ashley accepted. "Lyla, that's not the point, this is a shit ton of money..."

"Ashley," Lyla said in a singsong voice, "it's just a one."

Laughing at the silly banter, Ashley responded, "With a lot of zeros after it. Seriously, you write a column in the paper, you can't afford this. Write a check with less zeros and I will gladly accept it." The warmth in Lyla's blue eyes quickly turned to ice and Ashley tried to figure out what she had said to turn the playful discussion into such a painful one.

"Ash," Lyla said quietly, her hands balled into fists and tucked at her sides, her eyes glued to the donation in Ashley's outstretched hand. "I told you before, I won the lottery and I have a lot of money just waiting to be spent."

Lyla's words, although seemingly light-hearted, sounded like they were being forced out of a jaw that was wired shut. "Let me give this to you. Clearly your brother means a lot to you. If I had siblings, I'd want to help them." Pangs of guilt tugged at Ashley's insides when Lyla referred to Leo in the present tense. She knew she would eventually have to tell her close friends the truth about Leo, but she just wasn't ready yet.

Ashley absently rubbed her sternum with her thumb as Lyla continued. "So, just take the money and let it do some good, please."

Raw pain flashed through Lyla's eyes seconds before her ever-present shield came down, covering every stitch of vulnerability that had been exposed. "Besides, if you don't take it, I'm giving it to the Kyle Marx's Drinking Fund." She shrugged before returning the pitcher of water to her refrigerator.

"Well, we certainly can't have that." Ashley smiled. "Thanks, Lyla. I can't begin to tell you the good this money will do."

After a few more minutes, she left Lyla's house and ran the two miles back home. With the evidence of Lyla's generosity tucked in her pocket, thoughts of her brother floated around in her head. *"Look at all the good you're doing, big brother."* Luckily, by the time she reached her front door, no one would be able to tell the difference between her sweat and her tears.

Ryan's deep laugh was the first thing Ashley heard when she entered their house. She took the stairs two at a time to show him the check for the charity.

"Hey, Ry, you're finally awake. It's about time—" Ashley stood frozen in the hallway as she watched the beautiful, blonde-haired woman slip on her shoes. Ryan stood there shirtless, his gym shorts resting low on his hips and his bare feet kissing the hardwood floor.

"Oh, hey, Ash, this is Michelle. Michelle, this is my friend Ashley." Ashley flinched as though cold water had just been thrown in her face. When had Ryan brought this woman home? She'd worked with Max and Kyle last night but Ryan had gone out. He must have picked her up last night. Oh my God, Ryan had slept with someone. Never once in all their time living together had he brought someone home, and now…he had.

"Wow." The word slipped from her lips before she could catch it.

"Wow what, Ash?" Ryan ran his thumb over the very smiley woman's shoulder.

"Um, nothing, I just need to get some Gatorade. It was nice to meet you, Michelle." She raced back down the stairs and headed right to the kitchen. What the fuck? *Well,* she told herself, *it's probably better this way.*

Just maybe, if she said it enough times, she'd eventually believe it.

IT WAS THURSDAY night and Ashley sipped at her drink while watching Max flirt with Janie, when she noticed Ryan shake his head out of the corner of her eye. "What's up with you?" She asked. She was on the opposite side of the bar for the time being, drinking a cocktail instead of slinging them. Danny had asked Ryan to text her on her night off to see if she would come and fill in for Max. Both Danny and Ryan had a feeling the thing between Max and Janie was about to boil over, and as much as Danny had wanted to let Max leave, *Danny's on Main* on a Thursday night needed three bartenders.

Ryan nodded in Max and Janie and Lyla's direction. "Those two are cute, that's all. And Lyla, God love her, she's been trying to make that happen for weeks. I'm not sure who's more frustrated—them or her." He laughed at his own joke and moved away to take orders and pour drinks.

Ashley leaned over and looked to the other end of the bar at her friends and then back at Ryan as he talked to the guys and flirted with the ladies. Every time she saw him smile, little butterflies started flapping their wings in her belly. This had been happening for several months, but it had gotten worse since he'd started dating. *Yeah right, dating. More like whittling his bedpost, but whatever. Bitter much, Ashley?*

"Hey, Princess, talking to yourself, now? Spending a lot of time with Lyla, you're starting to pick up her habits?" Ryan stood right in front of her, his biceps bulging in his black uniform t-shirt, his brown and gold-flecked eyes dancing with amusement—probably at her embarrassment.

"No," she snapped. "I don't have any bad habits, Ryan. And you may want to stop spending too much time talking to me, or your bar flies might get the wrong idea." She gave him her most sugary-sweet smile before taking another sip of her margarita.

"No, they won't," he said shrugging his shoulders aloofly. "They all know that I'm single and available." With a crooked grin and a wink, he left her speechless and returned his attention to the customers. She swore she heard Kyle chuckle but when she looked at him he was busy entertaining the bar bunnies with his sexy looks and bar charms.

She finished her drink and got ready to begin her shift. If nothing else, tonight was going to be entertaining.

———•———

"Ashley, goddamn it! Seriously, did you *see* him?" The look on Lyla's face was priceless. Ashley had known Sebastian Gage for years. He and Max were best friends and therefore he came into Danny's almost once a week. The man was pure and unadulterated sex. He oozed sexy from every pore and there wasn't a woman—or a man, for that matter—who didn't feel the vibe when he was in the room. That being said, Ashley had never, ever, seen Gage approach a woman. Ever. Usually, he sat at his corner booth, almost shrouded in darkness, and the women went to him. The fact that he'd pursued Lyla was almost as shocking to Ashley as it was to Lyla.

"That's Max's friend. You've probably seen him here before." She placed a glass of ice water in front of Lyla, gestured to her cheeks, and gave a devilish smile. "You look like you could use this." She then watched as her friend tried to make sense of the burning lust that was rushing through her body. *Yep, this is gonna get interesting*, she thought to herself.

———————————

"What's got you smiling so big, Princess?" Ryan asked. It was so rare that he saw her happy anymore. It tore him up that the Ashley he once knew was all but gone. Sure, she was still caring, generous and giving, but she no longer turned any of that kindness toward herself.

She, like in Shel Silverstein's children's book, "The Giving Tree," had given so much of herself away, that there wasn't much left but a stump on which to rest. It was like she saw no worth in her person unless she was giving to others, and that broke his heart. Between chairing *Leo's Lights,* volunteering at the local soup kitchen, and working at *Danny's*, she practically worked herself to sleep each night.

They used to be best friends, tell each other everything. She'd been an open book to him, and he to her. However, now the only way he knew how she was feeling was by the color of the streaks in her hair, and even that had been a guessing game until he'd finally figured it out. It was his special inside secret into Ashley's mind and he doubted anyone else had even noticed the correlation.

He'd been relieved when Janie and Lyla started coming around six months before because she'd finally started hanging out with friends again. It hurt that she wouldn't accept him back into the place he used to be, but at least she was starting to let *someone* in. Finally he'd started to see a glimpse of happiness in the beautiful hazel eyes that had once held so much love, and for that he was grateful.

"Did you see Gage approach Lyla just a few minutes ago?" She didn't wait for him to answer before she continued excitedly, "Ryan, that man just rocked her world. I've never seen anything like it! It was like the world stood still when the two of them connected."

Yeah, he thought to himself sadly, *I know just the feeling*. He gave himself a moment to let her excitement penetrate his soul before getting back to serving drinks and *moving on*.

CHAPTER TWENTY-EIGHT

You Hurt Me First

PLEASE BRING HOME flowers for Lyla - A

Ashley heard the front door click shut as she hit "send" and knew she should have texted Ryan the message earlier—as in before he came home—but she was so frustrated with him. He hadn't come home last night after work. She'd had to watch while he chatted up some little bobble-head of a woman all night, including the part where the little tart giggled at his jokes while she planted her boobs all over the bar. Then she'd kept watching, unable to tear her eyes away, as he left the bar with the twit and never came back.

So when he'd come home this morning, she'd made sure to have her earbuds in as she passed him in the hallway on her way to the gym. When she got back, she'd showered and gone straight to the soup kitchen. According to the Post-it note she'd read when she got back, he was at the gym.

Her head told her she was being a bitch—that he had wanted her for years but she'd turned away from him time and time again. She truly believed she wasn't entitled to happiness after what she'd done to her brother, but her heart…God, her heart ached every time she saw him look at another woman. It splintered every time she thought about his lips on another woman's lips, and it cracked when she thought of him making love to another woman's body. She knew she was becoming bitter, but it didn't stop her from tapping out that text.

"Nice try, Ash," Ryan bellowed from downstairs, the playfulness evident in his voice.

"Oh, you're home." Her tone was buoyant with fake brightness as she bounced down the steps.

"Cut the crap, Princess, you didn't send that text until you heard the door open," he chuckled, his smile near splitting his face in two. Ugh. When he smiled like that, she couldn't help but melt. And that pissed her off.

"We're gonna be late for dinner and now we're going empty handed? That's just great, Ryan." She perched her hands on her hips and walked out the door. When she slid into Ryan's car and saw the case of beer sitting on the back seat the warmth of her embarrassment rose to her cheeks.

"Kind of feel like an idiot right about now, huh?" Ryan buckled his seatbelt and leaned over to place a kiss on her head…the same way Leo always had. Ashley froze. Her senses immediately heightened and she heard the faint sound of him breathing in her scent. When she remained still he pulled back enough for her to start breathing again. Pulling her lip ring between her teeth, she felt the blood run from her face, and her skin prickled with anxiety. Ryan's own face lost its color as he murmured, "I'm sorry, Ash. I forgot."

"It's okay, Ryan." She inhaled deeply. "It's been so

long since I had a *Leo* kiss, but it was nice." She nodded her head, trying to convince both of them that the kiss didn't faze her. One brief glance at Ryan told her the attempt was an unsuccessful one.

After a few seconds though, the initial shock wore off and Ashley realized that the contact had actually felt nice. She'd loved Leo's head kisses and had forgotten how special they'd made her feel. Something so small as a brush of lips to the top of her head made her feel loved and appreciated. Ryan's simple gesture created another small fissure in the huge dam around her heart, but it also scared the shit out of her. When Ashley got scared, she got sarcastic and ornery.

"Ryan," she snipped, "stop staring at me like I'm gonna break. It's fine. *I'm fine.* Now drive our asses to Lyla's before we're even later." When Ryan's smile lit up his face, Ashley shifted her body to look out her window because there was no way she'd let him see her smile.

Even though she was.

⸺•⸺⸺⸺⸺⸺⸺•⸺

"See, we're the first ones here," Ryan whispered in Ashley's ear. "Now, either tell me what your problem is or drop your attitude because I haven't done anything to deserve it." The feel of his soft breath on her neck had her nipples pebbling inside her bra and his clean scent had her mouth going dry as her mind drew a blank. She just looked back at him, unable to speak.

This was it, the time to tell him how much it gutted her every time she saw him with another woman. He was giving her the opportunity to come clean with her feelings for him and her fears of losing him or even worse, trying to start something only to see it fail again. However, as he stood before her with the case of beer under his arm and his eyes penetrating what felt like her very soul, she realized she wasn't ready, she wasn't able, and she wasn't deserving. So she did the only thing she knew how to do. She hid in silence behind her mask.

"Okay, Ash, you've got nothing to say?" When she responded with only silence and a slight shrug of her shoulders, he walked away. "Good talk, Princess, good talk."

Sunday dinners were one of the highlights of Ashley's week. Growing up, almost all of her "family" dinners had just been her, Leo and the hired help, so these nights filled her with a renewed sense of belonging. After the encounter she had with Ryan, she needed to belong somewhere. She felt like she could be herself around Lyla and Janie, a feeling that she both loved and loathed. Her spirit felt like when you got pins and needles from sitting in one position too long and then you try to move. Little pieces of her were waking up—it was scary and breathtaking all at once.

She watched as Max tried none-too-subtly to get Janie alone so he could talk to her. Ashley understood why Janie was avoiding him. She would have avoided him too, if he'd pulled the same disappearing act on her. She let her gaze move over to Danny and Julie. They were such an amazing couple—married close to thirty years and still crazy in love with one another. She could see it in the way they spoke, touched, and even looked at each other. A small pang of jealousy zipped through her body. The shock was quick, but unforgettable.

Kyle sat in his chair drinking his vodka, his eyes glassy and his skin gray. She'd spoken to him about his drinking the week before but he told her—albeit lovingly—to mind her own business. Each of the guys had tried to talk to him but had earned the same response. Ashley sighed. She was really worried about him.

Then there was Lyla.

Lyla buzzed around the dining room, serving and removing platters. She wore a smile on her face and was always prepared with the perfect comment or sarcastic retort. Lyla was still somewhat of an enigma, but there was a mutual respect between the two women and Ashley loved their budding friendship. Yet she knew in order to have an honest friendship she was gonna have to be *honest* with her friends. That meant telling them about Leo. A shiver ran through her body. *What will they think of you then?* She wasn't sure she ever wanted to know the answer to that question.

* ——————————— *

After dinner, the whole group sat in the cozy family room and shared silly stories, filling Lyla and Janie in on the bloopers and practical jokes that they'd played on one another over the years.

Ryan enjoyed Sunday night family dinners. While he and his dad spoke regularly on the phone, he didn't get down south nearly as often as he'd like. It was during these dinners that he really saw Ashley's light begin to shine. As dim as it had become it was still there, and it gave him hope for her. Their earlier conversation weighed heavily on his mind. He knew that she'd seen him leave with the woman from the bar the night before, and he knew she'd assumed that he'd gone home with said woman, but the truth was although he had left with her, he'd been bored to tears within the hour and ended up meeting Kyle at an after-hours club. He hadn't gone home because he'd crashed on Kyle's couch. Could he have told Ashley then where he'd spent the night? Yes, but at the risk of sounding like a dick, he was enjoying her snit—it was nice to actually see her give a shit for once. So he'd let her assume. Then, when he called her out on her behavior, he thought for a brief moment that she was going to give him honesty, that maybe she would tell him what was actually going on in her mind. But once again, he was wrong, and all he got was more of the same. Silence.

He was lost in thought when the raised voices caught his attention. His turned to face Ashley, who looked... *angry*, and he was immediately curious as to what in the hell would spike true anger from a woman who had been dancing around her emotions for years. He followed her gaze to Kyle, who had spent most of the evening in such an altered state that there was no way it was just alcohol running through his blood.

"What's not to love?" Kyle sneered, "She writes some advice in a column twice a month, and she doesn't have to worry about employment or money. But not everybody is lucky enough to win the lottery." Ryan watched on as Lyla stared at Kyle, muted by the shock his words had caused her.

Kyle, however, had no such problem as he continued his drunken rant. "We know everyone loves you. We know you love yourself. It's the world according to Lyla Dalton. You always need to put your two cents into everyone else's business. And speaking of cents, yes, Lyla, we *know* you have money. Jesus, could you rub it in our faces anymore?" Kyle spat his words and then tried to stand up but the effects of the alcohol, added to whatever else was still pumping through his system, caused him to stumble.

"Kyle, goddamn it!" Danny shouted. "What the fuck is wrong with you?"

Lyla cut in, her voice raised and her fist clenched. "It's fine Danny. Kyle," she said, turning to face him head on, "I'm glad we are finally close enough to share how we really feel about one another. I've had thoughts about you too. Frankly, I'd been thinking that you were sexy—so hot in fact, that I've spent weeks thinking of all of the ways I wanted to fuck you. Thanks for curing me of those notions." Lyla's face was blazing red, making her sky blue eyes burn brighter. "As for me sticking my 'rich' ass into everyone's business, you're gonna wish I did. You're gonna wish I stopped you from saying all of the shit that just spewed out of your drunk fucked-up mouth."

Kyle's face was blank as Lyla continued her verbal lashing. "I'm not going to hate you for saying those things," Lyla began to rein in her temper and with that her voice, "because tomorrow when you wake up, you're going to hate yourself enough for the both of us." She lowered her face to Kyle's and dropped her voice to a level that Ryan knew to be lethal. "But I will say this and trust me, if you forget what I'm about to tell you, there are six people who are here to remind you. You can try, but you will never be able to take back those words. They are out there. You said them. Now live with them."

Lyla turned to face the rest of the group who stood silent and in awe. "I'm leaving," she said calmly, "please lock up on your way out." With her back facing the group and one foot out the door she stopped but didn't turn around as she said, "Before you ask, Janie, no, you can't come. I need some time. I love you." With that, Lyla walked into the night, alone.

As soon as Lyla left the house, Janie escaped to the kitchen. Ryan watched Ashley stalk toward Kyle, a fire burning in her eyes and anger straining her spine. The Ashley who had lain dormant for so long, hiding all of her feelings was gone. Like a butterfly emerging from a chrysalis. This Ashley was allowing her feelings to radiate all around her in bright shades of color. This Ashley was pissed.

"You stupid fucker," she said, poking him in the shoulder. Standing at five foot eight, Ashley wasn't a slight woman and therefore her poke wasn't a slight poke. Ryan had been on the receiving end of one before, so he knew from experience. In his inebriated state, Kyle's balance was not the greatest, and he took a couple of steps backward to keep from falling over.

"You know I love you, Kyle Marx, but I can't even look at you right now. What you've said tonight disgusts me." Ashley walked past him and headed to the kitchen, with Julie following swiftly behind. Kyle reached out to grab Ashley's wrist and Danny started to step in, but he wasn't quick enough.

Ryan had seen Kyle grab for Ashley and in that moment, his mind traveled back to another place and time. Visions of Scott standing in the high school hallway, caging a young Ashley against the lockers, looping his fingers around her wrist. He remembered the look of confusion and innocence in her eyes—a look he'd chosen to ignore in favor of anger and mistrust. A choice that in turn had led him down the wrong path, a path he still couldn't veer from.

Ryan's vision went red and his fists clenched. The thought of Kyle even attempting to lay a hand on his woman had him wanting to rip Kyle's arms off and beat him with them. The way Kyle had spoken to Lyla, the way he'd just torn her down, making it sound as if they all shared the same opinion...

Ryan felt as if his heart was going to slam out of his chest. Self-restraint was an act of will and strength he had not yet encountered since his rehabilitation, but it seemed as though now was time for him to start practicing. Taking slow deep breaths in through his nose and out through his mouth, he self-soothed his tightly wound temper. As the breathing exercise worked its magic, Ryan slowly un-clenched his fists.

After Ashley left Miami, Ryan had spent three years in grief and anger management counseling. Once he real-ized that his anger stemmed from his mom dying of can-cer, and his fear of losing control, he was able to learn coping strategies to help him gain control of himself, if not the world around him. Seeing Kyle attempt to touch Ash-ley in anger had nearly set him off, but the fact that he was able to regain his composure quickly made him proud of himself. However, Kyle was about to see a side of Ryan that he had never seen before.

Closing the distance, he wrapped his hands around the collar of Kyle's t-shirt and pulled him so close that there was barely an inch between them. "Listen to me, you sorry piece of shit," he snarled between clenched jaws. "Don't you ever—*ever*—speak on behalf of me, or any one of us, ever again. If Lyla even looks at you again then you are one lucky son of a bitch. And if she ever says she forgives you, then she must have finally learned to lie, because no one could, or should, ever forgive the crap you said tonight." Ryan let go of Kyle's shirt and then realized he had one thing more to add so he fisted it again and pulled Kyle even closer than he was previously as he gave his final warning. "And Kyle? If you ever even think about talking to Ashley the way you spoke to Lyla, I will cut out your fucking tongue. We clear?" He waited for an acknowledgment, which he received in the form of a silent nod, before he turned toward the kitchen. He needed to get the hell out of that house.

The coldness of the tile floor mirrored the overall mood in the kitchen. What had been a warm and inviting environment was now blanketed in sadness and anger. Ashley sat on the floor alongside Janie and Julie, feeling helpless as she watched her friend cry. Reaching for the one tool she had in her emotional bag of tricks, Ashley pulled out the one thing that allowed her to relate to people without ever lowering her walls. Humor.

"That boy needs to be castrated, and I'm just the girl to do it!" She let out a maniacal laugh as she recited a list of all the ways she could perform the duty. Feigning a grimace, she said, "Ick, but then I'd have to touch those *testes of STD's* and yuck. We could even get Danny to help! He loves Lyla. If he holds Kyle down, I could wear a thick pair of gloves and use the nut crackers we have at the bar." She laughed evilly. "They crack more than walnuts, you know."

Hearing Janie's giggle, even for the briefest of moments, made Ashley feel so good inside. Knowing she could ease her friend's pain made her feel helpful, useful...meaningful.

"Ash, let's go." Ryan's voice melted through her like butter on a warm skillet. Offering his hand to Janie he pulled her up off the floor and enveloped her in a huge hug.

Once he'd assured Janie that Max had escorted Kyle from the house and that he wouldn't be back, Ashley felt Ryan's hand rest on her shoulder. Without looking back to see his face Ashley stood up from the floor. In that moment, the two of them were in sync—words weren't needed. She knew he was walking a thin line, trying to keep his anger at bay while trying to appear calm. She knew it was time to take care of the man who had spent the better part of a decade taking care of her. She said goodnight to everyone and tucked herself into Ryan's side as they exited the house together in silence.

Ryan knew Ashley would have questions after what had just happened, but he wasn't able to answer them yet. The two-mile drive home flashed by and all too quickly they were sitting quietly in the car in the driveway. The click of her seatbelt echoed in the car as the whoosh of fabric released from its hold.

"Why don't you sit out here for a little while. I'll go get us some lemonade." She moved to open the door but he put his hand on her thigh to stop her.

"Please don't go." He hated how weak his voice sounded, but he needed her, and he needed her to know that. "Please, Ash, just let me hold you for a little while." Eyes focused on the steering wheel in front of him, Ryan found himself unable to make eye contact with her as he made his request. Her rejection would be more than he could bear.

"Okay, honey."

Ryan's head snapped up the moment she acquiesced and his eyes met hers. It had been so long since she'd called him "honey" that he'd forgotten how sweet the endearment sounded sliding off her tongue. She wasn't pushing him away and he knew he should be elated, but tonight he was so physically and emotionally drained that he was just grateful. "But let's not sit here in the car, let's go inside. Okay?" Ryan tried to answer her but the words wouldn't form, so he just nodded his head and exited the car.

Walking through the front door, Ryan went straight to the sofa and after flipping on the television, he sat rigidly on the soft cushions. He listened to Ashley while she moved through the kitchen, pouring each of them a drink and turning out the lights before joining him. The television was on quietly but his focus was on the mantel above the fireplace where pictures of their friends and family members rested. When he declined the drink she offered, she placed both glasses on the coffee table and sat quietly next to him. He realized she was waiting for him to take the lead and he didn't leave her waiting long.

"I was so angry when my mom died. I couldn't understand why she left me," he stared straight ahead as he spoke, knowing that he wouldn't be able to say what he had to if he saw even one ounce of pity in her eyes. "She and my dad loved each other, they were best friends. I saw the way love was supposed to be, not the way it was shown on TV. There was no cheating or abuse. Sure, they would argue occasionally, but they would discuss their issues and figure out ways to get past them. And,"—he paused to scrub his hands over his face—"they loved me. They fucking loved me. I never questioned it. I knew they loved me because they told me and they showed me." He closed his eyes, inhaling deeply, as he gathered the strength to continue his story. Although Ashley knew as well as anyone the ending to his tragic tale, he'd never been so candid with her about his feelings during that difficult period in his life, and he worried that her knowing all of it may change her opinion of him, but he had to tell her. It was time for her to see all of him.

"I didn't know at the time but my mom survived cancer once before, when I was a baby. That's why I don't have any siblings." He turned to face her, willing her to understand why he was an only child. "They wanted more children, but after her treatments they couldn't have anymore." He turned his gaze back to the mantle. "When she got sick *again*, I was twelve, and a typical adolescent, punk kid. It wasn't that I got into big trouble, but I did go out of my way to push boundaries and test limits. When my parents told me mom had cancer, they were so certain that she'd be okay. They explained that she'd gone through it before and she was fine. They drilled into me that I shouldn't be scared, and that everything would be okay. But every day, my mom got more and more sick." Ryan's hands knotted together and his leg bounced mercilessly as his past took on a life in the present.

"I did what they asked—what they demanded. I continued to live like the rest of my friends. I tried to ignore the pain in my mother's eyes and the suffering in my father's." His eyes filled with the unshed tears of the teenage boy he'd once been, and the man he'd grown to be. "Then one day, when I got home from school, they called me into the sunroom. My mom had been sleeping there for over a month in a hospital bed. Thinking back on it, I feel so stupid for not seeing what was really going on, but they were my parents and they told me she was going to be fine, and I believed them. Then mom explained that she was dying. No, she wasn't dying...death was imminent."

Ryan leaned forward resting his elbows on his knees and his head in his hands. He scrubbed his face quietly for a moment before he continued to speak. "I'll never forget the look of defeat on their faces. It was like they'd finally accepted it was time to let go, but what they didn't understand was that I wasn't ready. They'd had so much time to discuss the 'what ifs' and the 'when's', but I hadn't. They'd kept me in the dark. But all of a sudden they wanted me to come and say good-bye to my mom—to tell her it was okay to leave me, okay to stop fighting. Ashley, I hadn't even started fighting yet. They'd never given me the chance to start my fight. I was losing my mom and I was pissed. I was angry. I hurt. And there was nothing I could do about it but say goodbye." Ryan felt the lone tear run down his cheek as he silently cried for the boy who was never even given the chance to fight for his mother. Braving a glance at Ashley, she mirrored his grief, her sorrowful eyes overflowing with the pain of Ryan's loss and regrets.

"She—my mom—told me during one of our last conversations that it was important for me to always speak from my heart. To never assume that people know what I'm thinking, but to say what's on my mind. In a lot of ways that advice led me to song writing. It also led me to loving you, and in a lot of ways it led me to fucking things up with you—the one woman who I have spent most of my life loving. When Mom died, I became a different person, Ash. In fact, if it weren't for Leo, I honestly don't know where I would have ended up. Your brother found me at a dark time in my life and he showed me the light. He just had a way about him."

Out of the corner of his eye, Ryan saw Ashley go rigid when he mentioned Leo's name. He waited patiently for her to collect herself. The moment he saw her shoulders relax, he continued. "I always laughed when you called me Romeo," he admitted, "because I wasn't trying to be smooth, or give you the lines. That was me, just telling you what I was honestly thinking." He let out a choked laugh. "But I guess a nineteen year old kid saying the things I did, probably just sounded like I wanted in your pants, right?"

"Ryan." Her fingertips brushed lightly over his shoulder. He looked up and noticed a gleam in her eyes—one that hadn't been there for a long time. "You were already getting in my pants, so I guess I was dumb enough to believe all of your sweet talking. We were a good pair back then." He was certain the airy tone of her voice was intentional. She was trying to lighten his mood and pull him back from the dark place he was treading so close to entering.

"It took everything I had not to punch him in the goddamn face tonight." Ryan switched topics. *Anger is better than pain any day of the week*, he thought to himself. "I'm not sure what's going on with him, but Lyla didn't deserve one fucking word of the shit he spewed at her. When he reached out to touch you...God, Ashley, if Danny hadn't been there," Ryan's voice dropped to a growl, "everything I worked so hard for, would have been for nothing."

Her raised eyebrow asked the question before her voice did, "What are you talking about, Ry?"

"Ashley, you weren't the only one making changes during the time we were apart. Didn't you ever wonder what I was doing during all of that time?"

In the four years they had been living together, not once had they ever spoken about their time apart. In fact, other than the one time when she'd told him about losing her virginity, they'd avoided discussing those years completely. She never spoke of anything regarding her past— her relationship with Ryan, her brother, or life in Miami. Those were things that were best left in the suitcases in her mind. She didn't need anything in the bags, so why open them?

Shame slowly weaved its way through her chest, wrapping itself around her lungs and gripping her airway. No. She refused to think of those days. They needed to stay in the dark so she could continue to burn bright.

"Ash, really? You never once asked yourself why I didn't come for you?" Complete shock and something akin to disappointment clouded Ryan's beautiful features. "Nice, Princess. Nice to see I meant so much."

"Ry, It's just..." She tried to come up with an excuse,

but how did you explain to the person you once loved more than anything in the world that you wanted to pretend they'd never existed?

"Save it, Ash. It doesn't matter." He shifted on the couch putting a small distance between them. She missed his warmth immediately. "But you should know, in that time, I spent hours—hell, months—working to fix myself." Her eyes flared at him in astonishment. She scanned his face for traces of humor or dishonesty, but all she saw was a man stating the truth.

"I went through grief counseling to deal with the loss of my mother, anger management classes to deal with my need to lash out, group therapy to face the guilt of everything that happened with Leo, and more counseling to handle losing you. Not once did I blame you for leaving me, but I was burying myself with guilt and I wouldn't... no, *couldn't* stop torturing myself over my stupidity. I never stopped loving you. I just wanted to give you a better me—the kind of person you deserved to have in your life. Once I felt like I'd got control over who I was and where I wanted to be, I went to your parents and begged them to tell me where you were."

Ashley was reeling from information overload. She barely remembered any of those months, and here he could probably account for every minute of every day that had passed during them.

"So my parents told you I was living in Pennsylvania and you came here?"

"Christ, no. Your mom just laughed in my face and told me to go to hell and your father told me that while he'd failed Leo in every way imaginable, he'd be damned if he did that to you. He said you wanted to disappear and he would help you do that. He told me that he'd always liked me and that he was sorry for being such a horrible father to his kids, but that he wouldn't help me find you. So I was on my own." Ryan let out a huge sigh and let his head fall to the back of the sofa.

Ashley was speechless. Her father had finally stepped up. He'd let her do what she needed to do and for once he'd respected her decisions. She laughed to herself, bitterly. Had her father known her at all, he would have sent Ryan to her sooner, knowing his presence would have been exactly what she needed. She'd been lost without him, and his love would have made her journey easier. *Oh, well, it is what it is,* she thought. *I got through it on my own and I'm still standing…kind of.*

"So if he didn't help you, how'd you find me?" She knew the answer to this question. She'd overheard him talking about it years ago, but they had never discussed it. But since the past was on the table she thought she'd get some answers.

"Do you really want to know this, Ash?" She tucked a purple strand of hair behind her ear and nodded once, prompting him to continue. "When I realized that your parents were never going to give in, I hired a private investigator. You really were amazing at covering your tracks. We followed a bunch of dead leads before we finally tracked you here. I wasn't shocked that you ended up in such a quaint little town, but I was surprised that you never returned home. Not for me. Not even to visit Leo."

His words were a punch in her stomach. She couldn't contain the cringe they caused and she knew he saw her reaction by the way his eyes rounded. "Ryan, I told you when I left that I felt lost there. I had to go. I'm sorry if it hurt you, but you hurt me first." She winced at the childish way the words sounded coming from her mouth. "And as for Leo, I know he'd understand. He never wanted anything but my happiness."

"What do you think I wanted for you? My God, Ash." His voice was thick with frustration and anguish.

Ashley's heart beat wildly in her chest. She couldn't do this with him. She couldn't start relieving a past that had nearly killed her the first time. She was about to stand up and leave the room when Ryan reached out and grabbed her hand. As he squeezed, the pain and remorse in his eyes was almost tangible. All she wanted to do was reassure him that life would be all right—that *they* would be all right—but she couldn't. She wouldn't. He had changed. He'd learned to be a better man. But her—she'd run, she'd hidden, and she was just barely treading water. She didn't deserve the patient, loving man he'd turned out to be. She didn't deserve happiness at all. Leo didn't get his happiness because she was weak, and she wouldn't allow herself happiness because Ryan had been so strong.

Ashley could feel the color as it slowly drained from her face. Her mind was racing with thoughts. She had to distance herself more. More space, more room, more time apart...

"Princess, I'm sorry, I didn't mean to start with you tonight. I just..." He paused. "I wanted to explain why I was the way I was back then, why tonight pushed my buttons, and why I let you go instead of fighting harder."

"Ry..." His expression was loving - filled with strength and possession. That was Ryan, he wanted to fight harder, but she knew she wasn't worth his fight. She had nothing to give him. He deserved better, a whole person.

Selfishly, however, his pleading look over-ruled all of her notions. If she was going to let him go, she wanted one more night in his arms.

As if he could read her thoughts, he leaned in and whispered softly into her ear. "Princess, please, let me just hold you tonight. Nothing else needs to happen. I just need you in my arms. I need to feel you breathing and know that you're really here…"

He had to know she couldn't say no to him when he looked at her that way. He had to know that the thought of being wrapped in his woodsy scent and held in the shelter of his strong arms would cause a chink in her armor that would take days if not weeks to repair, but he'd asked anyway. There was no way she could turn him down. Not when she ached as much as she did for the security only Ryan could give her.

His shoulders slumped under the weight of the world as Ashley leaned in close and ran her palm down the strong line of his jaw. She noticed the jump of the muscle under her hand. "Relax, Ry. I'm gonna lock up the house—why don't you turn on a movie and we can rest together on the sofa."

She smiled as she turned off the lights around the house and locked the front door. Watching a movie was her way of saying they would sleep on the sofa together. She heard him sigh loudly and then kick off his boots. By the time she returned to the den, their favorite movie was playing and he was lying down with his head perched on his arm. As if it had been yesterday and not years ago, she laid down next to him, her back to his front and allowed herself to meld into his warmth.

Exhaustion seemed to overtake him because once he

had her settled, his arms wrapped tightly around her, she felt his heartbeat begin to steady. The smooth strokes of his thumb on her ribs went from sexy and playful to slow and sedate, until, finally, she felt his breaths whisper soft against her neck. He'd fallen asleep with her tucked into him like a security blanket that he would never release. Not ever again.

Lying there wrapped in Ryan, Ashley was filled with hundreds of thoughts and just as many emotions. She traced the tattoo on his forearm with her index finger. *Se souvenir le passé, vivre le presente.* Well, she wasn't quite living in the present as much as existing, but it was what she needed to do because Lord knew she didn't dare dream of her future when it took all of her effort to hide from her past.

Hours passed as he slept soundly behind her. She knew from years of living together that Ryan didn't sleep well. She knew this because they spent countless nights sitting at the island in their kitchen drinking tea, discussing silly things during the hours most people slept. During the time before he'd come back into her life she'd spent those hours alone, staring aimlessly at the television, praying for sleep to take her. In addition, Ryan's presence had brought her company during the sleepless nights and for that, if nothing else, she was profoundly grateful. Feeling the rise and fall of his chest against her back, and knowing that he was experiencing peaceful sleep for the first time in countless nights, she stayed put, even though her mind begged for her to disengage. *You're getting too close*, it said. *You don't deserve him.*

As the early morning sunlight bled through the windows in the den, Ryan felt coolness seep through his body. Even in sleep he knew the presence that kept him safe and warm through the night was no longer there. He slowly opened his eyes to confirm what his brain already knew.

Ashley was gone.

CHAPTER TWENTY-NINE

Don't Wait Up

WRITING LYRICS TO an awesome musical arrangement always filled Ryan with an incredible sense of euphoria. It gave him a way to clear his mind and say the things he needed to say without facing embarrassment for his unrequited love, or recourse for his anger and frustration. In high school most of the band's songs had been written by him, Ashley, or the two of them combined. Their songs were saturated with feeling and emotion and he truly believed that was the reason why their band gained its following as quickly as it did.

After Leo's death, Ryan never played with a band behind him again. He couldn't bring himself to perform without his best friend backing him up so he decided to step off the stage and write the songs instead. It'd taken him a while to tap into his creative mind after Ashley left Miami, and him, behind. However, once he did, the words began to flow like water from a hot spring. While the lyrics never quite touched his soul like they once had, his songs became relatively popular in the music industry—keeping his mind busy and his pockets lined with cash.

Hearing the clunk of Ashley's car door closing in the

driveway, he peeked out his bedroom window just in time to see her leaning into the back seat to grab her gym bag. The sun had just set, leaving beautiful streaks of oranges and purples swirled through the sky and the iridescent glow of the outside lights to lead her from her car to the house. Quickly, Ryan slid his notebook and recording device into the plastic storage container and slid them under his bed. It wasn't that he was hiding his song writing from her—she knew that he still wrote music—but other than the stuff for *Leo's Lights*, they never discussed lyrics anymore. She heard him play his guitar, she knew he played at open-mic nights, but other than that she didn't ask and he didn't tell.

He wondered if she ever thought about the other guys from *Storm Front*. Did she know that after Leo died and Ryan left the band, Jayson and Zane tried to move on and went nowhere? Did she realize that those he'd once considered his family just turned their back on him when his best friend died? No, she probably didn't because that was the past. They didn't speak of the past. Just another one of those unspoken rules between them. God, he hated those fucking rules.

Ryan clicked on the television in the corner of his room. It was eight-thirty in the evening and unusual in that neither he nor Ashley had to work—something he hoped to use to his advantage. He wanted to talk to Ashley. Actually sit and spend time with her. Not only hadn't they discussed what happened between them on Sunday night, but she'd acted like nothing happened at all—like he hadn't shared the most intimate details of his life with her, and they hadn't spent the night wrapped in each other's arms. She'd stowed away their evening like baggage checked at the airport, and he'd followed her lead and let it go. *You can't keep doing this, Baker. When are you gonna man up?* He grabbed his guitar by its neck and thoughtlessly started strumming a tune he hadn't played in years.

●━━━━━━━━━━━━━━━━●

Ashley toed off her running shoes and slid them under the narrow table in the hallway. The jingle of her keys landing in the metal bowl next to Ryan's was muted by sounds coming from upstairs. "What the hell?" she muttered.

The chords of *Hazel Eyes* drifted down the stairs and through every inch of their home. That used to be one of her favorite songs. Ryan had written that song just for her, and she'd practically swooned every time she'd heard it, but no matter how much she loved it and begged him to share it with his fans, he never did. He claimed it was his private love letter to her and no one but her would ever hear it. He had kept that promise and, true to his word, this was the first time she'd heard it in close to seven years. Sadness and loss washed over her skin like the sand in ocean water, and she felt rubbed raw by the long since played, but unforgotten tune. Shoving aside her sadness, she stomped up the steps and straight into the bathroom, slamming the door behind her. She knew she shouldn't have ignored him, but she couldn't stop to acknowledge him in any way for fear of completely breaking down. So she flipped on the shower and stepped under the spray, allowing the hot water to burn her skin until it finally turned cold.

Not until he was halfway through the melody did he even realize the song he'd chosen. His fingers had begun to play as if they had intentions of their own. Minutes had passed when the realization hit, visions of a seventeen-year-old Ashley asleep on her bed as he penned *Hazel Eyes* played through his mind's eye. His memories vanished with the sound of the bathroom door. Keyed up by the feelings the song had brought to the surface and frustrated with the childish behavior of her silence, he turned his television up louder and relaxed into his bed. Soon after, he watched Ashley leave the bathroom and head straight to her bedroom closing the door behind her. *There will be no conversation between us tonight*, he thought. *God, I'm such a wimp.*

Thirty minutes later, Ryan found himself relocated downstairs sitting in solitude on the sofa, with a beer in one hand and the remote in the other. While absentmindedly flipping through the channels lost in thought, his irritations mounted at their inability to fucking communicate. Just as he landed on the channel he was searching for Ashley suddenly appeared, dressed in her favorite ripped jeans and a black Paramore concert tank top. Disconnecting his stare before she noticed, he forced his eyes to focus directly in front of him, but sensed her movement as she headed toward the door. "I'm meeting Janie at Sombrero. It sounds like Max, fucked up, *again*. Don't wait up." His gaze never left the TV as he purposefully gave an absent nod in response to Ashley's information. He heard the door click closed behind him, and even with the sound of the TV, he found himself drowning in the pain of their silence.

His indifference stung as she pulled the door closed behind her. *He didn't even turn his head to look at me,* she thought. It amazed her how completely attracted to him she remained, even after all this time, yet he was able to act like she didn't exist. He was able to sleep with all of these other women while she barely noticed other men unless she was serving them from behind the bar. That's why she refused to even think about the night they shared recently.

God, that night.

He'd opened up to her in a way he never had before. She'd fallen asleep with him at her back, wrapped in his warmth—his heartbeat in time with hers. Although, just before the sunlight of the morning painted the room, she'd known she needed to get away from him. There was no way in hell she would be able to treat that night like it was nothing. She wouldn't be able to trivialize it—to make it a casual evening that could be forgotten in the daylight like the rest of his flings.

So she'd done what she'd trained herself to do. She'd pushed it down and made like it never happened. Yes, it looked like he wanted to discuss it every day since, but there was no way she'd be able to tolerate any, "Thanks for listening, I'm glad we're friends," bullshit from Ryan Baker. Or worse, what if he wanted to take things further? She couldn't handle a relationship any more than she could handle rejection.

Yep, bury it, Ashley.

Bury it all.

CHAPTER THIRTY

Chucks Not Heels

"THAT MOTHERFUCKER! THAT'S it—he's getting the nut cracker!" Ashley shouted over the blaring music at T*he Sombrero*. Janie sucked down her margarita, sans salt, as Ashley angrily swallowed another tequila shot. The liquid left a trail of fire as it found its way down to her stomach. She listened as Janie filled her in on her accidental run-in with Max earlier that evening at *Chopper's*. She felt horrible for her friend. While Ashley didn't know all of Max's history, she knew enough. Janie was fighting an uphill battle, and Ashley wasn't sure if it was a battle that any woman could win.

"We'll have another round, please," Janie said gesturing to the bartender who quickly filled their orders. Ashley slung back another shot, feeling the sweet alcohol-induced clarity creeping over her thoughts.

"I mean, I *know* what his fucking problem is," Ashley blurted, her speech slightly slurred. "We *all* do." Her gaze went from her empty shot glass to Janie's inquisitive eyes. When her brain finally caught up with her mouth she wanted to kick herself. She wasn't one to gossip, and she certainly didn't tell other people's secrets and Max

Delucca was chock full of them.

"Fuck, Janie, don't ask. I'm buzzed and if you ask me right now I'll talk, and it's not my story to tell." Biting the side of her lip, she downed the full tequila shot. *How did that glass keep refilling?* "I'm a...I'm just gonna go to the ladies room. I'll be right back." She slapped a big kiss on Janie's head and shuffled to the bathroom.

"Yeah, Dad, it was good catching up with you too. I'm sorry we didn't get to talk on Sunday night. Things got crazy here." Ryan smiled at the sound of his father's voice. "No, Ash is fine, Dad. Don't worry about her. Tell me more about Nina."

It had been years since he'd heard the true happiness that was unmistakable in the older man's tone. Ryan spent a few more minutes listening to his dad marvel on about his new "lady friend" as he referred to her, when the screen on his cell phone told him Janie Silver was calling. "Listen, Dad, I need to grab this call. I'll touch base with you on Sunday. Yeah, I love you too, Dad. Bye." He disconnected the call before answering the other with, "Hey Janie, is everything okay?" Nervousness jabbed at his gut when he heard the hesitation in his friend's voice.

"I'm sorry, Ryan. This was my fault and I hate to call you, but you know Ashley, and if I suggest a cab, she'll just try and drive herself home." Ryan could hear the mixture of guilt and complete understanding in Janie's voice as she explained the predicament. She had Ashley pegged.

"Yeah, well, you know Ash, she's as stubborn as they come." Ryan could practically hear Leo saying, '*She's stubborn Ryan, stubborn both ways…'*

"Janie, I'm gonna come down there and pick her up. Just keep her distracted and don't tell her you called me or she'll run like a bat outta hell, okay?" Janie apologized once more for bothering him and thanked him for his help before disconnecting the call. It still puzzled him that his friends couldn't see how much he loved Ashley. It made him want to scream. Why couldn't they understand that he would *always* be there for her? Grabbing his keys, he ignored the little voice in the back of his head reminding him of the revolving door of women constantly entering and exiting his life and his bed.

Ashley made her way—gingerly—back to her bar stool from the ladies room. She would never admit it to anyone but she was definitely more than a little buzzed. She'd used the time away from Janie to get her head on straight, to make certain that she wouldn't spill anything that would cause harm to Janie and Max's relationship, while still being able to give solid advice to her friend. That was not an easy task to do with five shots of tequila and two margaritas running through her system.

"Look, Janie, I realize you've both been through a lot of shit, but here you are ready to try again…" As the words left her mouth, Ashley realized that even though she was the one giving the advice, Janie was the one teaching the lesson. Janie had been hurt before yet here she was placing her heart on a silver platter for Max Delucca, a man who had repeatedly thrown it back in her face.

That was the moment Ashley really understood just

how brave Janie really was, but she continued to voice her thoughts anyway. "My advice, which I'm assuming is why you called me in the first place, is that you listen to the words Max is actually saying, not what you want them to mean. He said, 'It was fun… now it's done,' so let it be done."

Ashley hated seeing the way Max's words made Janie physically cringe, but he'd said them earlier that evening during their confrontation at *Chopper's* and Ashley thought it was time Janie took her heart off her sleeve and tucked it back into her chest.

"But you didn't feel what it was like when we were together. It's hard to believe that I was the only one who felt something." Disbelief and pain flashed through the beautiful aqua eyes staring at Ashley. *Oh, I completely understand what you're talking about,* Ashley thought to herself. *I feel the same way every time I'm within breathing distance of a certain sweet-talking, heart-stopping Romeo.* Although instead of admitting to those thoughts, she continued to discuss Max. However, the more she talked, the more she felt like maybe she wasn't talking about Max at all. "That boy has been closed up like a beach house longer than I've been around. You can't fix him, Janie. You just can't. He needs to want to open himself back up—to take the dust covers off the furniture and open the windows. If at some point he finally decides to do that and you are still available…well, then good for him. Otherwise, it was his opportunity to lose. Do you understand?"

"Seriously, Ash, that's the most profound thing I have ever heard you say. You're so not as twisted as you seem," Janie deadpanned.

"Shh, don't tell anyone…I prefer when people under-estimate me." Ashley whispered the words uttered long ago by her brother. She saluted Janie with her drink and took a long pull. It appeared she and Max had been living in shore houses next door to each other all this time. Huh, who knew?

When Janie's cheeks turned an adorable shade of pale pink and her eyes rounded like saucers Ashley slowly turned her head and followed her line of vision to see what had caught Janie's attention.

"Shit," she muttered as she let her eyes roam the male perfection that was Ryan Baker. "Really, Janie? There was no need to call Romeo here. I am totally capable of getting myself home." The lie sounded ridiculous even to her own ears. The tequila gods must have been laughing at her because as she stood up from her stool she promptly lost her balance, and a pair of muscled arms wrapped around her waist. Large hands subtly grazed her breasts, steadying her body, just before her ass hit the terracotta floor. As if on cue, her heart rate amped up to dangerous levels.

"Yeah, Ash, you seem perfectly fine to drive." Ryan winked at Janie before leading a partially embarrassed, partially annoyed Ashley out of *The Sombrero*. Ashley found herself fighting the urge to nestle her body into his, just to be close to him. *Goddamn tequila, wreaking havoc on my brain*, she thought as she held on just a little tighter.

"Ryan," in her inebriated state she stretched out his name, "you don't need to hold me up. I only tripped in there 'cause my heel got caught in a crack on the floor." Her feet chose that exact moment to once again slip out from underneath her and Ashley caught sight of them, immediately realizing her error. She was wearing her

Chucks, not heels. Shit. She hesitantly glanced up from underneath her eyelashes to see if Ryan had noticed. The smirk on his much-too-handsome-for-his-own-good face told her that he had. Fuck. "Get in, Princess," Ryan chuckled as he opened the passenger side door of his car and helped her in. He buckled her seatbelt and closed her door before walking to the driver's side. The ride home was quiet as she sat silently in the passenger seat trying to decide on the best way to handle the current unusual situation. Although, if she was being honest, unusual was becoming their norm and that wasn't comforting in the least. She was so busy trying to figure out how to regain her composure that Ashley didn't notice Ryan had left the car until the passenger side was opened and his outstretched hand was awaiting hers.

"Ry, you don't have to help me into the house, I'm perfectly capable of taking care of myself," Ashley quipped as her world began to spin. "Ry, did you forget to pay the gravity bill? Cause the house is moving." Hysterical with laughter from her own joke, a small belch escaped her mouth. "Come on, Ryan, that was funny!"

"Come on, Princess, let's get you to bed," he said, guiding her to the stairs and staying close behind her as she started her ascent. She held on to the railing as she took each step slowly, relishing the warmth of his hand on the small of her back. He led her to her bedroom and turned on the lights. "Get undressed, Ash. I'll get some pain relievers and water for you, God knows you'll need them."

She didn't hear the rest of Ryan's statement because she was too busy rushing past him to make it to the toilet in time to revisit her tequila shots. The sound reverberated off the walls, slamming mercilessly against her already throbbing head *Yep, nothing sexier than puking in surround sound.*

"Ash?" Ryan's voice was gentle as he spoke from behind her.

"Shut up, Ry." Her voice was raspy from the violent retching and beads of sweat ran down her spine. "I forgot to eat dinner, no big deal. Let's never speak of this again." Ashley slowly turned her head to see Ryan holding out a cool, damp cloth. As he pressed the cloth to her face his eyes filled with...what? Compassion? Concern? She was drunk so she couldn't be sure. "Thank you," she breathed. The cool sensation felt amazing pressed up against her clammy cheeks.

"You never forget to eat, Princess. What happened?" There was no way she could tell him that coming home earlier that evening to him playing, *"Hazel Eyes"* nearly undid her. She couldn't explain that she thought she may be cracking under the surface and she didn't know if she was going to be alright. So instead she let her sarcastic alter-ego slip out. "Stop staring at me like I'm a zoo animal, Ry. I got drunk and puked. It happens to the best of us. I've even watched it happen to you on occasion. So cut me some slack, okay?"

"Alright then, Shamu." His smile was the fake kind—the kind that shaped his mouth but didn't make the cute crinkles at the corners of his eyes. She accepted his outstretched hand and hefted herself off of the tile floor. "How about if you get ready for bed and I'll go lock up downstairs. I'll be up in a few to check on you."

"You don't have to—" A wave of sadness passed over his face and she quickly changed her response. "But thank you. Thanks for picking me up tonight and thanks for taking care…umm, thanks for helping me out. I really appreciate it."

Ryan turned on his heel and headed out of the bathroom. "Not a problem, Princess."

Gripping the sides of the sink, Ashley lifted her gaze to the mirror on top of the vanity. The person staring back at her made her want to go back to the porcelain throne for another round of tequila shots in reverse. Her hair was matted, her eyes glassy, her lips puffy and reddened, her skin was two shades paler than dead. If that wasn't enough, thanks to the vomit fest, she had little purplish specks spotted under her eyes and at the top of her cheekbones where the blood vessels had broken because of her retching. She truly was a beauty queen. A Princess. The snort that escaped her as she grabbed for her toothbrush certainly wasn't princess-like, which seemed to fit the situation perfectly.

Her physical appearance wasn't the only thing to fuel her wretchedly churning stomach. Sticking the toothbrush in her mouth, she glanced up once again and all she could think to herself was how completely apropos her crumbled image was and how it was an exact replication of how she felt on the inside. She was slowly losing the ability to keep her mask on tightly and even worse, she was losing the desire to do so.

After following up with some mouthwash and clicking off the bathroom light, she padded barefoot to her bedroom and stumbled into bed, fatigue overtaking her before she had the chance to dwell on things any further.

Ryan headed upstairs with a plate of toast and a bottle of water. He hadn't meant to spend so much time away from Ashley, but when he'd gone to lock up and switch off the lights he'd received a text from Janie, checking on Ashley and apologizing again for bothering him on his night off. He'd texted Janie back, which led to several texts back and forth between the two of them while he made a snack for Ashley.

The house was eerily quiet as he walked up the stairs to her room. Lying there, tucked into a ball on her side and sound asleep, was the Ashley most people never got to see. Even after her battle with, and subsequent defeat to the tequila, she was beautiful, and her body was flawless. Although lying there like that she was vulnerable—she was the girl he'd met and fallen in love with so many years before. Before life had become complicated and flawed, she'd been the brave teenager who'd left him when she'd needed room to breathe and grow. Now, she was a grown woman who was scared but strong, fearing the journey forward but knowing in her heart that there was no going back. This was Ashley—his Ashley—but she still wasn't ready for him. She still claimed she didn't want him. He'd promised he wouldn't push her so he would just have to wait a little longer. Date a little more. Love her from afar and hope that she changed her mind. Soon.

Ryan placed the dish on the night table next to her bed and reached for the blanket at the foot of the bed, allowing his knuckle to gently caress the outer side of her arm as he pulled it up to cover her shoulders.

"Sweet dreams, Princess," he whispered softly into her ear, placing a light kiss on her temple before turning to leave her room. He could already hear the lyrics in his head as he pulled her door closed behind him. It looked like it would be a long, but productive night.

CHAPTER THIRTY-ONE

Rainbow Brite

"GOOD GOD, GIRL, do you *ever* stop smiling?" Ashley asked, winking at Janie as she set down martinis for her and Lyla. "I'm glad that boy finally got his shit together," she added, quickly taking a drink order before returning her attention to the girls. It was a Thursday night in mid October and Ashley was tending the crowded bar with both Ryan and Max. *Danny's on Main* was a year-round hot spot in Charistown, but in the fall, with the large windows open and the music playing, Thursday nights were the busiest night of the week.

"No, she doesn't stop smiling. And while it makes me want to puke"—Lyla looked at her best friend lovingly—"I would kill anyone that tried to wipe that happiness off her face." As if on cue, Max, now Janie's boyfriend and self-appointed protector against-all-things-evil, walked past Ashley and leaned over the bar to place a scorching kiss on Janie's lips.

Ashley watched the embrace with a mixture of happiness and weariness. She was genuinely thrilled that her two friends had finally found their way together and appeared to work beautifully as a couple, but watching them kiss as if the world ceased to exist made the small pocket of loneliness in her gut feel a little deeper, and that was a bitter pill to swallow.

"Ahem, this is a bar, and might I add, *my* damn bar. So either go get a room or get back to work, Max." The gravelly voice snapped Max and Janie back to earth and Janie's cheeks flushed pink while Max grinned, running his fingers through his spiky hair before returning to his bartending duties. "Hey, Dolls," Danny said with a smirk. Danny had taken to calling Lyla and Janie "Danny's Dolls" when they'd first become regulars. He'd said the two ladies had wreaked havoc on the male customer's libidos and their relationships. The name eventually became a term of endearment between the owner and the two women.

"I didn't mean to get Max in trouble, Danny," Janie said sheepishly.

"You can't get me in trouble, babe, this is my last week, remember?" Max leaned his huge body over the bar and planted one more quick kiss on Janie's lips before returning to the throng of customers. After the weekend he was going to be working full time at the *Gage Garage*, co-owned and operated, with his best friend, Sebastian Gage.

"Sweetie, you know I'm just messing with you." Danny smiled warmly, "I love that you guys are together. The only people who are unhappy are the ladies who have been vying for his attention for years, trying to win his heart. Now that he's off the market their dreams have been crushed." Danny's eyes glittered with humor as he chuckled.

"Crushed, I say." Lyla and Janie laughed at his sarcasm.

"Oh well, I can't say I'm sorry about that," Janie giggled.

Ashley meandered her way over toward the women with their next round of drinks just in time to hear Lyla say, "Yeah, fuck those chicks."

To which Ashley replied with a plastic smile, "No, that's Ryan's job."

She gave her friends their drinks before scurrying down to the other end of the bar to help the middle-aged businessmen in the corner. Even with the distance between them, she could still make out bits and pieces of their conversation over the noise in the bar.

"Danny," Janie pointed a serious stare at the man whom they all saw as a father figure, "you have got to tell us what is up with the two of them."

"Yeah," Lyla agreed, "we want to help Ashley, but we have no idea about their history." Danny looked at his two girls, and snickered. His laugh held no humor at all.

"Do you two think I'm going to share Ashley and Ryan's personal history with you? Come on! I love you like daughters but of anyone, you two should understand how important it is to keep your secrets and to share them when you're good and ready." He looked pointedly at Lyla. "So, Ly, you ready to show us your skeletons?" Lyla narrowed her eyes in agitation and Ashley knew Danny was right. He knew Lyla wouldn't be sharing anything about her past anytime time soon.

"I have no idea what you're talking about, Danny." Ashley watched as Lyla took a long sip of her martini and Janie tried to ignore the verbal ping pong match between her best friend and her pseudo father. That was one of the reasons why Ashley loved Danny the way she did. He was fiercely loyal and he protected those he loved. He truly was her father in all the ways that counted.

"Nothing to say, Ly? That's what I thought." Danny smirked, "I need to run back to the office for a bit. I'll be back in a few."

Danny retreated and headed to his office but not before Ashley heard Lyla's loud voice shout, "Running away makes you look weak, Danny. Just sayin'."

"Drink your drink, girlie," Danny remarked over his shoulder through laughter.

After his office door was shut, Ashley let out a long exhale from the breath she hadn't realized she was holding. Danny had kept her secrets safe. Just another reason why she loved him so much. The night went by quickly. Pretty soon it was one a.m. and the crowd had finally begun to thin out. Disgust boiled through Ashley as she glared at the Goth girl hanging on Ryan's every word. Fuck that—she was hanging on Ryan, period, like he was some kind of fucking jungle gym.

"Ashley." Janie's voice snapped her out of the semi-violent daydreams she was having about a certain raven-haired, black-lipped monkey who was pawing at *her* man.

Oh, God, he isn't my man. What the hell? I've got to stop feeling this way. I told him to move on. That's what he's doing.

"Earth to Ashley!"

"Sorry, chickies, I...I was just thinking about something."

"Yeah, honey, we see exactly what you were thinking about." Lyla nodded her head in the direction of Ryan and the Goth girl. "Your lip was doing this fucked-up, crazy, twitchy thing. It would have been bizarre if it weren't so entertaining."

"Lyla," Janie admonished her friend. "That was not at all helpful. *True*, but not helpful." Ashley watched as the two women shared a look—a private look that clearly held a message. She wanted to know what that message was and luckily for her, she didn't have to wait long.

"Ashley, are you available on Saturday?" Lyla asked. "Janie and I were thinking about doing pedicures and lunch and we want you to come with us."

Ashley still got excited when Lyla included her in their plans. While Janie and Ashley had become pretty close rather quickly, Lyla was still something of an enigma. Just when Ashley thought she had her pegged, Lyla would do something that totally threw her off. It wasn't that Ashley was desperate for friends, she just valued Lyla's brand of friendship. Open. Honest. No bullshit.

"Man," Ashley winced, "I wish I were. I'm actually busy on both Saturday and Sunday for the next three weekends. It's the annual Coat Drive for the shelter I volunteer at, so between the extra people coming in and out dropping off donations, and the needy coming in to get their winter coats and gloves, the foot traffic nearly triples, sad to say." Ashley saw her compassion mirrored on her friends' faces. Another reason why she loved and respected them as much as she did.

"Oh, that's right," Janie acknowledged. "I'm actually signed up to help next Sunday for a couple of hours." Ashley nodded and gave her a grateful smile.

"And I was told during the fundraising meeting that we received a very generous donation from a 'D. Dolls'." Ashley shot a knowing glance to Lyla.

"I have no idea what you're talking about," she

grinned.

"Really?" Janie and Ashley laughed simultaneously.

"Ly, D. Dolls? As in, *Danny's Dolls*?" Giggles burst from Janie's mouth. "If you wanted to be anonymous, you should have picked a better name. Like, Mike Smith—no one would have guessed that was you," Janie laughed hysterically.

"I know," Lyla conceded, her lip furled and her arms crossed over her chest. "I just wanted to see how long it would take, Rainbow Brite over here"—Lyla gestured to the orange and red streaks in Ashley's hair—"to figure it out."

"Hey, you," Ashley threw a coaster, Frisbee style, at Lyla, "don't get all snappy at me just 'cause a certain tall, dark, and broody guy wasn't here tonight."

"I didn't even notice Gage wasn't here," Lyla snapped back too quickly, and then back peddled as she realized her mistake. "Whatever, there are plenty of bikers on the road, I'm sure I can find one who would love to give me a long hard ride." She punctuated her statement with a wink that had both Janie and Ashley giggling.

"Okay, if you girls are done, I'd like to kidnap this one right here," Max said, swooping Janie off her bar stool and throwing her over his broad shoulder. She squealed and giggled but made no effort to escape the man who had captured her heart. From over his shoulder she and the other two women made spa plans for three weeks from then before Max and Janie left Danny's as they did most nights. Together.

IT WAS LATE and except for the soft glow of the neon lights that hung on the walls, the bar was dark. Ashley closed her eyes and took in the sounds and smells of *Danny's*. She loved being in the bar after closing—when everyone was gone and the place felt like her own private heaven. After Janie and Max had made their grand exit, Lyla found herself a "repeat offender"—a term she used for someone she had been with more than once—and left right behind them. Ryan did his part of the clean up and cashed-out quickly, leaving with Goth girl drooling right behind him. Lastly, Danny and Julie had headed to their office to do the bookkeeping for the night.

Ashley walked out from behind the bar and sat on a stool, remembering the first day she walked into *Danny's*. It was the first day she felt like she finally belonged. This place was home.

After a few moments of reflection, Ashley walked to the back office to tell Danny and Julie that she was leaving. As she lifted her hand to knock on their door soft moans drifted from the other side. *Nice*, she smiled. *After nearly thirty years of marriage those two still have a passion that most people never find, or never keep.*

Sadness swept through her. She had felt that kind of passion once. The corners of her eyes burned with the salty sadness that gathered as she turned and left the bar and headed for the parking lot. She had known what it was like to want nothing more than to breathe the same air of the person you loved. She knew how it felt to have her whole body respond to another person's mere presence. To not even need to see them to know that they were in the same room. She knew how it felt to have the gentlest lips press against hers. To have those same lips turn hungry and needy, as if they could only be sated by the taste of her mouth, her tongue, her taste.

Oh God, Ryan. If I could only turn back time, she thought to herself as she walked to her car. Images of her and Ryan tangled up in each other's arms filled her thoughts, only to be doused by the visions of him leaving with another of his many girls.

She picked up her pace, nearly running to her car. She knew Danny and Julie would be unhappy that she was walking alone in the dark but she couldn't bring herself to bother them while they were stealing tender moments together. Of all people, she knew how quickly life could change. No one ever knew if or when it would be their last time with the one they loved.

TOSSING HER KEYS in the bowl in the foyer, Ashley wiped the sweat from her brow. The four-mile run from the shelter to her house was an incredible cardio workout. Charistown was a beautiful town, full of natural slopes and valleys—perfect for runners, challenging for walkers and magnificent for sightseers. It was a picture perfect day. The early November air was crisp and cool and the brightly colored leaves were falling from the trees like large snowflakes.

As she unlaced her running shoes she heard the squeaks and thumps that could only be associated with one thing. "Fuck, he has someone here, *again*?" While his visitors had definitely lessened, Ashley's jealousy had spiked. With fingers clenched into tight fists, she pounded up the stairs and through the hallway. She slammed her knuckles onto the door that separated her from Ryan's room, and began to shout at the wood divider as if it would give her the satisfaction of answering back.

"Seriously, Ryan, enough is e-fucking-nough!" Ashley's trademark calm had finally snapped. She rarely lost her temper. Her heart raced as small beads of perspiration trickled down the column of her spine. She had trained herself to never let anyone see her get angry, or upset, or sad, or any emotion other than happy or sarcastic. Those were things she could control, and so that's what people were allowed to see. However, right now…right now she was angry. Her mood felt as red as the streaks in her blonde hair.

Using the palm of her hand she banged on his door. "Open your fucking door, Ryan Baker, or so help me God, I will break it down and boot your little 'moaning Lisa' out of my goddamn house!" She slammed on the door once more. "Ryan—"

The door opened quickly and Ashley stumbled into Ryan's bedroom. His arm shot out and he caught her just before her stumble became a fully-fledged trip. Her skin met his hand causing electric charges to shoot up her arms and down her torso. Just a simple touch of his body to hers had the power to affect her on a visceral level. Clearly the affect was not lost just on her, if the look of desire burning in his eyes was anything to go by. Her mind blanked, her angry words vaporized and she gasped for air that had chosen that moment to leave her lungs. "Close your mouth, Princess, you'll catch flies. And by the way, her name is Sue."

"It's Drew," giggled a voice from the bed.

Well, that pulled her out of her lust-induced stupor. Ryan stood in the doorway shirtless, the top button on his jeans undone and his erection obvious. His lazy smile set butterflies off in her belly, which pissed her off even more. How in the hell could she be attracted to this man after all this time—hell, after all these women? She didn't understand it but she was, and that spiked her anger and frustration, breaking limits she didn't even know possible. Would she ever be able to move on? Would there ever be a time when looking at him didn't melt her?

———————•———————

"Ryan," Ashley seethed. Her hazel eyes flashed with anger, her cheeks were pink with frustration and embarrassment, and her fists remained clenched at her sides. *God*, Ryan thought to himself, *she is so fucking beautiful*. "Are you even listening to me?" She yelled.

"Umm, no," he admitted, sheepishly. "Can you repeat that last part?"

"RYAN!" Now she was full on screaming, he had never seen this before. If he wasn't so worried that she might have a stroke, this would actually be funny. "—then you can just get the hell out."

Ryan couldn't believe what he just semi heard. He had been living with Ashley for over four years. "Wait, what? You're kicking me out?"

"Yes! If you can't respect the fact that I live here—that this is *my* house...God, Ryan, what makes you think I need to hear you fucking random girls every day of the week?" His gaze dropped to her fists, balled so tightly they were trembling.

"I can't stand it anymore. I just can't..."

Ryan looked into Ashley's eyes and saw pain. He hadn't seen any real emotion in Ashley's eyes in years and in that moment he wanted to reach out and touch her, to stop the games and finally explain that he had been burying himself in *wrong* just to forget about the *right* that he wasn't allowed to have. As luck would have it, the moment cracked as did the woman's voice when she, again called to him from his bed. With his eyes glued to Ashley's face, Ryan watched as the emotion bled out of her eyes and the ever-present mask slid back into place.

"Ash?" He reached toward her but paused when she backed away from his touch.

"Don't, Ry. Just...don't. Put a fucking ball gag in their mouths, or find a new place to live." She turned around and stormed out and he knew that the sound of the front door slamming was indicative of more than just Ashley leaving the house. He had finally pushed her too damn far.

"Fuck!"

He knew in his heart that he was done playing. It was time to stop being a pussy and man up. He'd hurt his woman for the last time. But how did he help fix what he'd broken? How did he help heal her pain? How did he get her to see that they were meant to be together? Most importantly...

How the hell did he get Sue out of his bed?

CHAPTER THIRTY-TWO

Hurricane Weather

WITH THE GANG all relaxing in the family room of Max and Janie's house—stomachs full and spirits high—Ashley couldn't help but to look around at her *family*. She loved that Max and Janie had finally been able to get their shit figured out and find true happiness with each other.

Kyle was a different story altogether. Between his dry cracked lips, his slightly green pallor, his bloodshot eyes, and his overall rundown appearance, Ashley yet again had a strong suspicion it was no longer just alcohol running through his blood. She'd have to talk to the girls about him in the morning during their Starbucks "therapy" session and then their spa day that they were finally making the time to take. Janie was even taking off from work for this event, which made the day all the more special for the ladies. Ashley found it easier to worry about other people's problems because it kept her mind from traveling to her own issues.

During halftime of the Eagles game, Julie, Lyla, and Janie went into the kitchen to get refills for the drinks. Even though Ashley could hear the giggles of her girlfriends down the hall she couldn't bring herself to smile.

She hadn't been feeling like herself lately and pretending to be someone she wasn't was beginning to take a lot more effort than it used to. If she were being honest with herself, which was something she tried extremely hard *not* to do, and it was something she was getting really fucking sick of. Thinking about the people in this house, her friends, even more...they were her family, she knew deep down, they would love her if she stopped pretending, but the real question was...could she love herself? Could she ever forgive herself for all of the pain she caused in her past? Did she even deserve to be happy when he no longer could?

When the weather forecast announcing the upcoming arrival of Hurricane Leo came on the television Ashley's world went silent as she felt her insides go rigid and her heart begin to thud quickly in her chest. The ba-boom ba-boom ba-boom of her heart and the whooshing sound of her blood through her ears were the only two noises that infiltrated the complete stillness of the space around her. She looked down only to see the fierce trembling of her interlocked hands, but was completely powerless to stop her shaking.

•———————————————————•

Upon hearing the forecast, Ryan quickly dropped his vision to the beautiful woman sitting curled into herself on the plush carpet by his feet. While he couldn't see her face, he could see her arms looped around her long legging covered legs. Her hands were tightly clasped and shaking like leaves on a tree in a windstorm. His mind cleared of any and all thoughts other than protecting the woman sitting before him. Without any care to the consequences of his actions, or the questions in the eyes of the surrounding witnesses, he slid his tall body off of the sofa and onto the floor behind Ashley. As if it were second nature, he pulled her between his jean-clad legs and wrapped his strong tattooed arms around her. Holding her tight, he breathed in her familiar scent and promised himself, this time...this time he would do right by her.

———————•———————

The pair was quiet—not a sound came from either one, but their silence screamed pain. It was evident that not *everyone* in the room was clued in to what just happened between two of their closest friends, but by the quiet that blanketed the once cozy space, it was obvious that the coming storm was going to bring a whole lot more than just rain.

———————•———————

"Ashley, darling." Danny stooped to his knees and cupped her chin in his huge palms. "Look at me, little one. You are not alone. You're surrounded by people who love you." Ashley barely registered Julie's close proximity until she felt soft hands on her own tightened fists.

Julie's soft, maternal tone sent warmth to the pit of Ashley's belly. "This time, sweet girl, we'll get through it together." As fast as the warmth had come, it left, leaving numbness and fear shrouding her like a plastic bag. She needed air. She needed quiet. She needed to get out of the house. Standing on shaky legs, she blindly made her way to the front door.

"Umm, I'm sorry to do this but I need to leave. I'll see you guys later."

Ryan's heart clenched at the complete lack of emotion in Ashley's tone. He did what he promised himself he would always do for Ashley. He got up, rested his hand on the base of her spine and supported her as she silently walked out the door into the dark of the night.

She quickly strode to the car through a haze of numbness until she felt the warmth of a hand on the base of her spine. She knew it was Ryan. While she couldn't express it in words, she was grateful for his presence in the dark night.

God, Ryan thought to himself. *Of all of the names in the world, they name a hurricane that's gonna hit Charistown, 'Leo'? What are the fucking chances?*

Once they arrived home, Ashley quickly darted upstairs and holed herself up in her room, cutting off any contact between them. He shook his head as he began his mental preparations for both Mother Nature's storm, in addition to the storm that was currently brewing on the second floor. He wasn't sure which one would bring him to his knees, but he had no doubt that by the week's end he would be on them.

CHAPTER THIRTY-THREE

There's Juice In It!

"WHAT THE FUCK?" Ashley groaned pulling the pillow over her head to drown out the sound of the doorbell. She was exhausted. Other than a few restless hours, sleep had mostly evaded her. Thoughts of her brother, the storm that took his life and the one heading in their direction whipped around her mind until the sky began to lighten. When the bell rang again and her litany of cursing didn't manifest Ryan, she realized she needed to get her ass up to answer the door. She rolled out of bed and stomped down the stairs. It wasn't that nine-thirty on a Monday morning was early, because it wasn't. Usually at this time she would have been coming back from the gym, preparing to shower and getting ready for—

"Oh, shit!"

"Good morning to you too, sunshine. You look like ass." Janie assessed while she stood cheerfully on the doorstep. "Did you forget about our plans?"

"Hi, Jane." Ashley droned, "Look, I didn't sleep at all last night..." She yawned, not at all trying to hide her irritation of being awake when she could still be snuggled in her bed. "I'm gonna bail on Starbucks today, umm, maybe

I'll meet you guys at the spa later. Sorry, honey." Janie stopped the closing door with her slender body, her cell already up to her ear.

"Hey, Ly, yep, you were right." Ashley watched the smirk on Janie's face grow as she talked to Lyla on the phone. "Yeah," she paused, listening to the voice on the other end of the line. "I know. Ah ha, you got it, I'll tell her. See you in ten. Bye." Janie slid the phone back into the pocket of her jeans and walked into the foyer of Ashley's house.

"Ash, march your sweet ass upstairs and brush your teeth. We don't care if you're dressed or not. We don't care if you look like *that*," Janie ran her eyes up and down Ashley's appearance and crinkled her nose, "or not. But you are getting into my car in"—she looked at her watch —"eight minutes. Now go."

"Janie, I'm too tired, and I'm too cranky. I don't want to be a bitch to my two closest friends."

Janie smiled slowly as she shook her head. "Unbelievable," she murmured.

"What's unbelievable?"

"Lyla said you'd come up with something like that, and she told me to tell you that you haven't seen bitchy yet. She also said if you make her come get you, you'll be praying for *just* bitchy." The sound of Janie's sweet giggle filled Ashley with a sense of kinship and love that she desperately needed this morning.

"Grr…fine, give me five minutes. You'll get fresh breath, and fresh armpits but nothing more." She flashed Janie her patented calm Ashley grin and jogged upstairs to fix herself up.

Stealing a glimpse at her reflection in the mirror as

she brushed her teeth, she noticed today, even more than yesterday that her outward image was beginning to look a lot like the way she felt on the inside. *No wonder Janie looked at you that way.* Gone was the laidback "I don't give a damn" attitude, and in its place was a wounded woman with flaws, cracks and fears. She rinsed out her mouth and leaned over the sink, putting her face closer to the mirror. *Stay put, Ashley Kynde.* She rubbed her hand absently over her ribs, grazing Leo's words. "*The darker the storm, the deeper the pain,*" she whispered to her reflection.

"Ash, your time is up. Get down here, now."

Pasting on her plastic smile she grabbed her sneakers and bounced down the stairs with all the fake enthusiasm she could muster.

"IT'S ABOUT FUCKING time." The sparkle in Lyla's blue eyes revealed more humor than agitation as she opened the door to welcome Janie and Ashley into her house.

"I thought we were supposed to meet at Starbucks, what happened to that plan?" Ashley asked, following Lyla and Janie into the kitchen.

"Not to be rude, honey, but I saw what you looked like when you opened your front door. You weren't planning on meeting us there anyway, so who cares if the venue changed?" There was definitely something off with her two friends, she could see it in the way they were looking at her, and hear it in the tone of their voices. Was this an...

"Oh, hell no!" Ashley turned on her sneakered heel and started for the door. "I can't believe it took me this long to figure it out," she called over her shoulder. "What is this? Some kind of intervention? I love you girls, but I don't need this shit. Jane, thanks for the ride, I'll jog home—"

"Stop. Right. There." Lyla's voice was stern and left no room for misunderstanding. Ashley halted mid-step but kept her back to her friends. "Ashley, we've officially known each other long enough that we feel comfortable saying what we're about to say. We know that you may get upset, but hopefully you care about us enough to listen and hear what we have to say."

"Because, sweetie, you need us right now the same way I needed you not too long ago when it came to my situation with Max," Janie quietly reminded her.

With her back still facing the kitchen where Janie and Lyla stood, Ashley closed her eyes and inhaled slowly. This was it. This was the moment where she had to decide if she was going to finally allow these people in, to show them who she was and what she did. Should she? Or should she secure her mask and put on the performance of a lifetime? *What's it gonna be, Ashley?* Her choice was made easy with Lyla's next statement.

"Ash, you can run and you can hide but we both know that the past will *always* find you. You're better off building an army to help with your defense than fighting it alone. The fact is, even if you think you're sparing those that love you, you're not. They will still suit up, they will still go to battle but they'll fall. You give them no choice.

They'll be armed only with their hearts because you allow them no sight."

Her eyes stung as tears began to fill them. Lyla, the person who hid more about herself than anyone was telling her it was time to open up, and by the sound of her voice, she wasn't only talking about Ashley. When she finally turned around to face the two beautiful souls, what she saw was breathtaking. Janie had wet tracks leaking down her ivory cheeks and Lyla's eyes seemed truly open for the very first time. Yeah, maybe it was time to start letting people in.

"Okay, how about if I share some of my story," she looked pointedly toward Lyla, "and then you finally give me some of your goodies."

"Yeah right," Lyla said, her tone dripping with sarcasm. "Today is all about you, Spicy." Lyla held her hand up to ward off Ashley's frustrated response. "The one who needs, gets. Today is your day, but I'm sure my time will come. And when it does, you can throw all of my words right back at me. Deal?" Lyla gestured to the family room, "Now, you two go get cozy and I'll be right in there with refreshments." Lyla turned her back to them in dismissal while Ashley followed Janie into the other room.

Ashley slumped to the floor in front of one of Lyla's huge, overstuffed chairs. Letting her mind wander for a moment she realized that her friend's taste in décor reflected her personality—outwardly large with its commanding presence felt, but when settled in, it was comforting, cozy and familiar. Panic bubbled in her stomach and her fingers laced together as she waited for Lyla to return.

"Honey, after that scene last night, Lyla and I decided that we can't let you push us away a second longer." Janie handed Ashley a shot of tequila and a lime wedge off the tray Lyla had brought in from the kitchen. The three women sat on the floor around the coffee table in the cozy family room.

"Christ, Janie!" Ashley grinned, "It's ten o'clock in the morning and you're giving me alcohol?" Ashley looked from Janie to Lyla with pleading eyes. "Has she lost her mind? Is she trying to add a drinking problem to my growing list of issues?"

Lyla snorted. "As if, Ash. We *know* what that body of yours can handle, so don't try the puppy dog eyes on us." Lyla squatted down next to Ashley with a slightly guilty look on her face, "For the record, I did tell her this wasn't the best way to get you to talk but she disagreed, something about *The Sombrero*? Whatever, drink up, buttercup!"

Ashley shot a quick scathing look to Janie before Lyla continued to talk. "As for the time of day—ten a.m. or ten p.m.—as long as there's a ten in it I think we're good to go." Lyla giggled at her own joke while Janie smiled brightly and handed the shot to Ashley.

"Fine," Ashley said accepting her fate, "but if I'm drinking so are the two of you."

Ashley found extreme satisfaction in watching Janie's face go pale. "Are you crazy? It's ten o'clock in the morning," Janie complained. Laughter poured from Lyla's slender frame as she and Ashley stared at one another quizzically and then both at Janie. When Janie realized what she had said she started giggling too and then Ashley joined in. The three women laughed until tears rolled down their cheeks.

Lyla picked up her shot of vodka, making Ashley

giggle. Every time Lyla refused tequila shots, she couldn't help but remember the story Lyla had once shared about the time she'd thrown up all over the beautiful man who was going down on her in the back seat of the expensive town car he had rented for their first date. Every. Single. Time.

"Here's to booze to make us chatty, instead of food that makes us fatty." Lyla giggled out her toast and saluted her friends before throwing the alcohol down her throat. She sucked on a lime that had been covered in sugar and waited for her friends to follow.

When they didn't move she narrowed her eyes at them, "You know how much I love revenge so if you know what's good for you, you'll take those fucking shots." Knowing Lyla as well as they did, Ashley and Janie quickly followed Lyla's lead.

After the first round of shots Lyla disappeared into the kitchen and then came back with a cold pitcher of Screwdrivers. "What?" Lyla asked shrugging her shoulders. *That girl has perfected her innocent face*, Ashley thought to herself.

"There's orange juice in it, so technically it can be considered a breakfast treat." Lyla grinned as she brought the glasses along with some bagels to the table. After setting them down Lyla prompted, "Ashley, what happened last night? What's going on with you and Ryan and more importantly...what's going on with *you*?"

Maybe it was the alcohol, or Janie's presence, or maybe it was the uncharacteristic gentleness of Lyla's voice...she wasn't sure, but whatever it was, Ashley felt her walls sway a bit in response to her question.

In an attempt to re-fortify them, Ashley let out a long

sigh as she set her glass on the table and then ran her hands through her newly blue-streaked, blonde hair. The colors in Ashley's hair were the only outer indicators of her mood. If people didn't take the time to notice that then that was their problem, not hers. To her, her "hair moods" were as clear as the tears that other women cried. Although people rarely made the connection, or just didn't take the time to notice.

Taking her glass back into her hand, she finally responded with, "What are you talking about? I'm fine." Ashley took a healthy sip of her drink and tried hard to maintain eye contact with her friends.

"Blue is not fine..." Lyla said gently. Ashley froze. She could handle obnoxious Lyla. Crude Lyla was fun. Rude Lyla was downright entertaining, but gentle Lyla? Gentle Lyla could break her into pieces.

"Blue?" Ashley whispered.

"What Lyla is trying to say honey," Janie intervened, "is that the streaks in your hair are blue. When you do blue, it means you're sad. So do black and gray. Purple usually means you're feeling bored and in need of an adventure, and—"

"Red means you're really fucking pissed off," Lyla finished. "You've been sporting a lot of red streaks lately. But over the past week, you've gone blue and...well, we're really concerned."

Lyla's questioning eyes penetrated Ashley's armor and she felt those walls sway once again within her, clear to the point of crashing down. And here she'd thought her feelings and emotions were hidden. She thought no one noticed and no one cared to. She should have known better. She should have known that these two women could see into her soul. They would understand her pain. Could she finally unload some of her burden? Some of her guilt?

Downing the contents of her glass and pouring another, Ashley wringed her hands and pulled in a deep breath. "So Ryan and I..." She looked at Janie and Lyla and realized she would have to go back even further for her story to make sense.

"Alright, are you sure you want to hear this whole story?" She rolled the empty glass around in her palms trying to figure out the best place to start when the glass slipped and fell onto the wooden table. The clattering sound it made when it collided with the tray startled her.

Janie squeezed her hand and said softly, "Of course, honey. Please, share with us."

However, it was Lyla's, "Christ, Ash, if you want more tequila just ask for it. There's no need to get all dramatic," paired with her inviting eyes that made Ashley realize she was safe with these girls. With her friends. It allowed her to finally unlock the suitcases of her past.

"Okay," she began, "here we go. I met Ryan when I was fifteen. He was my brother Leo's best friend..."

THE THREE WOMEN sat on the floor for hours that Monday, listening to Ashley's history—from her very first kiss with Ryan right up until the weather forecast the previous evening.

Tears flowed from three pairs of eyes, gasps escaped

from three different mouths, pain expressed from three different women, but by the end of the afternoon the story had been shared between them and Ashley felt like a weight had been lifted off her shoulders. Not enough to make her forgive herself entirely, but enough that she felt like she could finally swim instead of merely keeping her head above water.

"Oh, honey, my God, you've been holding all of that in for more than six years."

"Janie, don't look at me that way. This is why I don't tell people about it. I can't deal with the pity looks. It's over. It's done. I've moved on. But, I can't be with Ryan. I just can't let myself love him. He'd be better with someone else."

"Six," Lyla said out loud, smirking.

"Lyla, what the fuck are you talking about?" Ashley knew before she even asked the question that she wasn't going to like the answer but, stupidly, she asked anyway.

"It's actually impressive, Janie. I'm impressed with her," Lyla said addressing Janie but staring only at Ashley.

"Ly, don't do this, she needs comfort not confrontation." Janie winced at Lyla's glare.

Ashley sighed dramatically, "Okay, I give in, I'm listening."

"In that short, ridiculous statement, you lied six times. *Six!* That's a lot of bullshit for such a short statement, don't you think?"

"What the hell, Lyla?" Ashley felt the flush creeping up her cheeks. She should have known she'd never be able to hide anything from Lyla. When you spent your life keeping your own secrets you become amazingly adept at sniffing out other people's.

Lyla leaned in closer. "You, my sweet, kind, caring friend, are full of shit. It's not over. It's not done. You haven't moved on, and you *should* be with Ryan. I've never seen a connection deeper than the one you two share. He isn't better without you, Ashley, he's merely surviving—the same way you are. You want to feed yourself garbage, fine, but don't serve it to us and call it chocolate...cause we know it's shit!"

The statement hit Ashley somewhere deep inside and she squared her shoulders and glared at her friend. "You're one to talk, Lyla—"

"Okay, girls, let's rein it in." Ashley could see the nervousness creeping its way onto Janie's face.

"Listen, Ash," Lyla's voice softened a fraction, easing some of the jagged edge off of her tone, "I know I'm being a complete hypocrite. I realize that, okay? But you're fucking up something really, really special." Lyla ran her long fingers through her ebony hair in what appeared to be frustration. "My God, Ash, how often do you find someone that devotes their life to you? That man has spent more than six years listening to you say no. But eventually he's going to give up. Is that really what you want?" The pure pain and frustration in Lyla's voice was as clear as the sun in the sky. She really did want to see happiness for her friends. However...

"Lyla." Exasperation filled Ashley's tortured body. "Where have you been? That boy has been whoring around for close to six months now. He's had more ass than a public toilet seat. He *has* given up. He *has* moved on."

Saying it out loud finally made it real, and the agony flooded her heart, making it hard to breathe. The dam that had been holding back all of her feelings for Ryan since she was eighteen years old—shattered, and she was left hanging on to a branch in the middle of the water, praying for survival. Tears poured down her face.

"I don't deserve him after all I've done. I've been horrible to him for *years*. I pushed him away and locked him out and he's finally moved on. I refuse to be like the selfish twits in all of those romance novels who suddenly decide they want the guy and rush back to him—not giving a damn that he's happy without them. I won't do it." Her voice cracked and she accepted the tissue from Janie's outstretched hand.

"Well," Lyla shrugged, "you've definitely been a bitch to him, no doubt about that...Ouch! Janie, don't pinch me." Lyla pierced Janie with a frosty stare. "I was agreeing with her. Let me finish before inflicting bodily harm. Sheesh."

Lyla turned her attention back to Ashley with her eyes soft and tender, the way they had been at the beginning of the conversation. "Sweetie, you deserve only good things. What happened with Leo was *not* your fault. Look at me."

Lyla paused and waited until Ashley brought her eyes up to hers before saying, "It wasn't your fault. What *is* your fault is the time you are choosing to let slip away from you and Ryan. That you *can* control, that you *can* claim. Seize your time, Ash, because you of all people know that it doesn't always last forever."

Ashley swallowed the lump in her throat along with the advice her two best girl friends had so willingly offered. The three women decided to forgo the spa for a day of hanging out with movies, junk food and talk of the upcoming storm.

There was something freeing about sharing the burden that had lain solely on her shoulders for so long with people that she trusted. However, just because the weight had been lightened didn't mean it had been completely lifted. The guilt she still harbored over surviving when Leo had died trying to get to her was still suffocating. The pain she felt over the years of anguish she'd caused Ryan was still tormenting, and the feeling of not being good enough still loomed above her head, like thick black clouds preempting a great big storm.

No, she wasn't ready to take off her mask, or step out from behind her curtain. And thank God she didn't have to yet. She still had her house, her friends and *Danny's on Main*—her one true home—to keep her grounded until she was finally ready to take those steps. And after the day's events she knew the time was coming.

She just didn't know how soon it would be.

CHAPTER THIRTY-FOUR

She Likes Bribes

"GO HOME, BOYS, thanks for helping handle stuff around here," Danny grumbled appreciatively, clapping Ryan, Max, and Gage on the back before walking them to the front door. They had congregated at the bar, Tuesday, as per Danny's request to take some storm precautions. Ryan looked around and took in his surroundings—taped windows, stowed awnings, booths covered in plastic, tables and chairs hugged tightly together in the center of the bar. Yes, this place was braced for a storm. But was he?

"Ryan," Danny called from across the bar, "don't forget to tell Ashley not to come in tonight." He looked out of the storm-prepped window at the driving rain, "The winds are already picking up steam and the worst of the storm isn't supposed to hit for another six hours or so. I'm gonna stay closed until the storm passes. No reason to have any of you guys coming here when it's unsafe. No one will be out anyway."

"Have any you heard from Kyle?" Max questioned. Danny and Ryan both shook their heads.

"Gee, what a pity," Gage deadpanned. The only thing that had stopped Gage from beating the shit out of Kyle—

on multiple occasions—was their mutual friendship with Max. Gage often said that if it weren't for Max, Kyle would have disappeared somewhere where no one would ever find him. Ryan wasn't hundred percent certain if Gage was joking about that statement. He was definitely mysterious enough to be scary, so Ryan never deemed it important enough to ask.

"Gage?" Max lifted his brow.

"What the fuck, brother? I've had my own shit to deal with. Kyle, fucking Marx, ain't on the top 100 of my 'to do' list this week, so don't look at me like that." Ryan watched as Max laughed out loud at Gage's response. Most people found Gage intimidating—Ryan was one of them—but not Max. Max laughed at Gage's little rant.

"Brother, I can't take you seriously when you go all badass like that with me because when you bite back your smile, the fucking dimples in your cheeks show. What kind of badass biker has dimples? I mean, really?" Max was howling at his own humor. Ryan watched as Gage pulled his brows together in what should have been a scowl, but the twitch in his mouth kept the look from appearing menacing and what did you know, Max was right. As Gage's lips drew up into a smirk, two big old dimples miraculously appeared, giving the larger-than-life biker a soft, more human-like quality.

"They really are kinda cute," Ryan teased.

"I prefer scary," Gage rumbled, his thick arms crossed over his even larger chest. Max's snicker turned into a full on laugh, which had Gage laughing too.

"He's not machine, he's man," Max snorted quoting his favorite line from Rocky IV. "Yeah, Gage, badass? Whatever."

"Hey, Max, wanna talk about being a big badass?" Gage asked, with a glimmer in his crystal blue eyes. "Hey, guys, did DeLucca here tell you about the sweet little book he wrote—"

"Okay, okay," Max interrupted Gage's story. "I'm sorry, man, you're a big, tough guy." Max faked a shiver. "Look, I'm all scared of you and shit." Gage crossed his thick tattooed arms over his huge muscled chest and quickly snapped his brows back together.

"So like I was saying, *Maxy* here wanted to win Jane back, so—"

"Gage." Max shot a warning look. "Stop. I'm not the only person this story would embarrass. Think about it man." Ryan watched the interaction between the two men and saw the exact moment the realization clicked in Gage's face.

"You're so fucking lucky I...you're just lucky, DeLucca." Gage ran his hand through his shoulder length hair and reached a long arm over to the bar to grab his leather jacket. "Alright, guys, I've gotta head back to the track to make sure it's secure before heading over to my grandmother's house. Max, you're gonna head to the garage, right?"

"Yeah, brother, I'll make sure shit's tight before I head home."

"Drive safely, man." Ryan shook Gage's hand and watched him run out to the parking lot through the sheets of rain.

"I'm gonna get going too. I told Janie I'd stop at the market before I go home. I don't want her driving in this." Max wore the look of a man completely and totally in love as he talked about the mundane task of going to the mar-

311

ket. Ryan was happy for his close friend, but he felt a small pang of jealousy deep in his gut.

Sure, he had spent the past six months fooling around with different women, but that's what it was—fooling around. All of the relations were consensual and fun, but they were also empty and meaningless. He'd been playing a childish game to get the attention of the only woman he wanted, but it had backfired. She barely even looked at him anymore, let alone spoke to him. Their friendship had suffered to the point of no return and he was miserable. He needed help. He needed someone who could point him in the right direction.

"You better get going too," Danny said handing Ryan his jacket.

"You don't want her being alone too long in this weather." The knowing look on Danny's face had Ryan sliding his arms through his jacket sleeve and rushing out into the rain.

"Max!" He called, trying to shout above the roar of the whooshing wind. He held his hand to his face to shield it from the debris that had been blown up off the street... "Wait up!" Max heard his call and pointed to the passenger door of his jeep. Ryan quickly climbed in, his clothes drenched despite the brief journey.

"What's up, buddy?"

Ryan ran his hands over his face wiping away the stray droplets that rested on his long dark lashes. "I can't continue living this way—being with all these women, pretending I don't care. It sounded like a bad idea when you guys suggested it back then, but I went along with it. But Max, man, it's killing me, and she won't admit it but I just know it's hurting Ashley too. What the fuck do I do?"

Max's head fell back to lean against the headrest of the driver's seat. "Christ, Ryan, I forgot all about that night. That's what this has been all about? Fuck…"

Anxiety started clawing its way up Ryan's spine. "You…you forgot about that night? Really? The night you and Kyle told me to move on and fuck other women, I believe your toast was, 'The more the merrier.' You're a dick! Jesus, Max, this is my fucking life…and you *forgot*?"

"First of all, Ryan, now that you mention it, I believe I told you that I *wouldn't* march random women in front of Ashley. In fact, I *know* I told you that she's a tough chick and she scares the hell out of me when she gets pissed. Second, I was in a bad place myself. You were the one taking love advice from me and Kyle. Are you crazy? And third, you're an adult, dude. At any point you could've stopped that crazy shit and reevaluated, but you didn't. Don't blame that on me, that's all you."

"Shit." Ryan released the breath he was holding. "You're right. I guess I'm just looking for someone to blame, but it's not you. I fucked up. I'm just so tired of being shut out, and I thought if I made her jealous enough I'd win her back, but instead I've lost her completely. Other than picking her up a couple months ago when you and Janie were still trying to get your shit together, I haven't spent any time alone with her. We're either with the group or she avoids me. What do I do?"

"No way am I touching this subject because, clearly, I suck at giving relationship advice. I can, however, point you toward the person who saved my life." Ryan waited for Max to continue, but the silence inside the vehicle stretched on as the rain pounded on the hood of the car.

Realization and Max's stare hit Ryan square in the face.

"Wait, Lyla helped you with Janie after you tortured that poor woman, right?" Max nodded his confirmation.

"Lyla is pretty fucking smart when it comes to this shit. My only advice— she likes bribes, so don't go over there empty handed."

"I need to *pay* her for her services?" Ryan was flabbergasted.

"No, you idiot. Don't you pay attention to anybody besides Ashley?" Ryan thought about that question and the answer was honestly, no. Ashley's wellbeing and happiness always came first. Everyone else came much further down the list.

"No, man, I don't."

Max clapped Ryan's shoulder as he turned the key in his ignition. "Raspberry truffles, Ry. The ones in the gold box from the store down the street. Now get out, I've got shit to do."

Ryan exited the car and stood in the rain, watching Max drive away. Energy filled his body as the possibilities started to flood his mind, *Lyla, huh? Okay. I'll go see Lyla.*

The grocery store was mobbed with people trying to fill their carts with bottled water, bread, eggs, and batteries. Ashley had purchased the water and batteries two days prior so she was just trying to stock up on non-perishable items in case the power lines snapped. Memories of her youth swept through her mind—images of her and Leo eating Fruit-Roll-Ups and dry cereal until their bellies hurt. Usually by the second or third day without electricity they would be sick of the junk food and be begging their nannies for fruit or peanut butter sandwiches.

Her memories floated away as, "Demons" by *Imagine Dragons* started playing on her phone.

"What's up, Ryan?" She said cheerfully. Keeping up the faux-friendly tone was becoming increasingly difficult as their relationship became more and more strained over the past month or so. She had contemplated discussing her feelings with him, but it felt like he'd been avoiding her. She had barely seen or heard from him other than text messages or Post-It notes in days. I mean, really? Who used Post-it notes anymore?

"Where are you, Princess?" Just the sound of his voice asking that simple question affected every part of her body.

"I'm at the market getting food in case we end up losing power during this thing." She couldn't even bring herself to say the word 'hurricane'. One of the reasons she'd chosen to stay in Charistown, Pennsylvania was because of the infrequency of major weather events—this was the first hurricane to hit the small town in the years since she had been living there. "Is there anything specific you want me to pick up for you?"

"No, Ash, anything you get we'll make do with until we can get out after the storm passes. So hurry up and get home."

Ashley froze mid-step, what did he mean by 'we'll make do with'? The thought of having to deal with one of his many bar flies or music groupies made her want to vomit. There was no way, she was going back to her house if she was gonna be trapped there hearing them all day and all night. It would kill her. "Ash, you okay?"

With her mouth suddenly bone dry, Ashley tried to swallow before responding. "Ry, listen, I know that you and I aren't..." She searched her vocabulary, trying to find the right words to convey her thoughts but, like the moisture in her mouth, they escaped her.

"We're not what, Ash?" Ryan's voice sounded dark, serious, and maybe even a little nervous.

"Umm, I don't even know what we are any more, Ryan, I'm not even sure if we're friends at this point. God...look, it's ridiculous to discuss this on the phone while I'm standing in the market and you're...where ever the hell you've been lately. But all I'm asking is, can you please not bring one of your, and I use this term loosely, *women* back to the house tonight? Who knows if we're gonna get stuck in tomorrow, and I just can't deal with another one of your Wailing Wendy's screaming through the wall. Okay?"

The pause on the other end of the line felt endless. Was he upset with her for asking him to put a pause on his pussy party? Tough shit. It was her house. Her name was on the mortgage not his, so if he didn't like it he could do as she'd suggested and move the hell out. Yet, as soon as that thought hit her consciousness, panic struck just as hard. What if he left? How would she move on without him?

"Ashley," Ryan's gentle voice interrupted her internal dialogue. "I understand why you feel the need to make that request. I can't tell you how it makes me feel, but you have every right to lay it out there. But, Princess, I've been around a long time. I know how these storms affect you. You may question the status of our relationship but there is one thing you should never doubt, and that's the fact that I

316

will always be your very best friend. Before anything else in this world, I am your friend. And, as your friend, I would never let you down in a storm." His voice became not much louder than a whisper when he added, "Ever again."

Relief warmed her body like the sun on an August afternoon. He was still her friend. Yet, as soon as the warmth hit, a frost penetrated her tender skin. Friend, he'd said. *I am your friend*. He'd finally moved on. She finally managed to push him away. She was relieved but heartbroken. The nausea that came with her back and forth thoughts was unsettling, so she decided to table them until she got the shopping done and got home safely. The last thing she wanted to do was be out driving once night fell.

"Okay" was the only word she could manage before disconnecting the call.

———•———

"Fuck!" Ryan's voice boomed in his empty car the minute Ashley hung up. "Why wouldn't she question whether or not you're gonna bring home a random chick, Baker?" He argued with himself as he pulled out of the chocolate store's parking lot and onto the main road. "She doesn't know if we're even *friends* anymore? What the hell?" His clothes clung to him and rain water saturated the driver's seat. This did nothing to improve his rapidly souring mood. The only thing that kept him from boiling over was that he finally had some semblance of a plan. Now he just prayed it would help.

When he pulled into Lyla's driveway he felt a vise grip his gut. What if she didn't want to help him? Christ,

Max had thought he'd been acting like a dick and he'd been the one to give him the advice in the first place. What would she think? *Here goes nothing*, he thought.

Ryan unclicked his seat belt and once again stepped out into the storm. *Be quick*, he told himself, *and get home to her.*

When Lyla didn't answer the doorbell the first time he rang again, cursing a blue streak for not thinking to call ahead instead of turning up unannounced. Just about ready to give up, he heard the clink of the deadbolt being released and the jingle of the chain sliding off of the latch.

"Who the…? Oh, Ryan…" Confusion marred Lyla's face for a second before a slow closed lipped smile spread across her mouth. Awareness flashed through her eyes when they lowered to see what he was holding in his hands.

"Oh, Max, my wonderful protégé," she muttered. Her small smirk became a full grin as she opened her door widely, motioning Ryan in from the rain. "Stay right there, I'll run and get you a couple of towels. You're dripping like a wet dog." Before turning away, she reached down and swiped the golden box from Ryan's drenched hand. "No reason to let a perfectly good bribe get ruined." Ryan didn't bother to stifle his chuckle as he watched her move quickly down the hall and out of sight.

A few moments later Lyla returned, arms full of fluffy towels and a sweatshirt. "Why don't you take off your jacket and shirt, Ry, and I'll throw them in the dryer for you?" She scoffed at his raised brow. "Get real, Baker. You may be nice on the eyes but you're not my type."

"I've seen you with a lot of men, Lyla Dalton," he inspected the XXL sweatshirt he was about to slip over his head, "and this sweatshirt isn't even yours so my question is, what exactly *is* your type?"

Lyla wrapped his sodden clothing up in the equally wet towels and looked at him thoughtfully for a moment before turning her back on him and walking back down the hallway into what he guessed was the laundry room. Just when he thought Lyla had avoided yet another question, she glided back through the hall and threw something directly at his face.

"Think fast."

Ryan's hand shot out and caught the folded up ball of...socks in his right hand. "Your feet are probably wet too. Put those on. As for my kind of man, I'm not looking for the white horse or the right guy, I'm just looking for the smooth moves and the right now. As long as he doesn't belong to someone else, that's all that matters to me." She sidled up close to Ryan and he thought to himself that their height difference would have been laughable, had the mood been different.

"You, my friend, have belonged to someone else for far longer than I've known you. So, while I can appreciate the painting on the wall I would never dare touch the artwork. Come on into my kitchen, I'll make you something warm to drink."

"That sounds great, Lyla, thank you. But I can't stay long." He swore he heard her smile even though she made no verbal response to his statement. He followed her quietly to the kitchen.

"Ryan, I didn't invite you and I'm not trapping you here. You can leave whenever you want. Although, the fact that you turned up on my door with raspberry truffles means you've been talking to Max and, knowing him, that can only mean one thing. You need my help." She shrugged, "So stay, leave...whatever." Her shrug of indifference was like the shiny, sharp curve at the end of a fishing line. Hook, line, and sinker. There was no way he was leaving without some advice from this sly vixen.

Ryan could understand why Ashley had grown to love this woman as quickly as she had. They were very similar creatures—both smart, both tough, and both hiding something painful on the inside. He knew Ashley's secrets but he wondered if anyone knew Lyla's.

He watched as she moved fluidly around her kitchen. She looked different today. Usually she was the image of perfection from her hair to her toes—even when he saw her at the gym and she was sweaty from her workout she seemed purposefully put together—but today he saw a different Lyla. It could've been because she wasn't expecting company, or maybe she wasn't feeling well, but her hair was piled on the top of her head, with a pair of black-rimmed glasses perched at her crown. She wore a battered Batgirl t-shirt that looked like it had been around since the first Gulf war and a pair of tattered sweats. Without any make-up on her face, she looked much younger—more innocent, more vulnerable.

"Ryan, what are you staring at?" She ran her hands over her face and up her head. She quickly pulled off her glasses and placed them on the counter behind her. He watched as her cheeks turned a pale shade of pink just before she turned her back to him and poured their coffee.

Hmm, that was an interesting reaction from their tenacious friend.

A loud whistle drew Ryan's eyes to the picture window that filled the kitchen wall. Large gusts of wind whipped through the trees, swiping the remaining colorful leaves off the Oak that stood proudly in the yard that faced the breakfast nook. The sound of Lyla clearing her throat reminded him that he was here for one reason and one reason alone.

"I was told that you were the lady that knew how to fix stuff," he grinned just before he sipped his coffee.

"I may be," she answered while opening the candy box and removing one dark chocolate morsel from its sleeve. "Max is a smart man, sending you here with my kryptonite. He knows I can't say no to raspberries and dark chocolate."

Pure bliss overtook Lyla's features as she bit into the sweet confectionary. "This has been a long time coming, Ryan. But the weather won't hold out for long, and you and I both know Ash won't wanna be left home alone once this shit gets worse, so let's make this quick, okay?" Surprise rippled through Ryan. Had Ashley opened up to Lyla and Janie? How much did they know? He absently squeezed his hands around the coffee mug, trying to find the right place to start.

"Ryan," Lyla called his name firmly but kindly. "I know your history, okay," she confirmed. "What I don't know is why you've been acting like a ride for the penetrated-impaired." Her face stayed somber but her eyes glimmered with humor.

How could he not laugh at that? The woman came up with the best one-liners he'd ever heard. His whole body shook with the force of his laughter until he felt stinging in his eyes. He was an emotional wreck. He felt his amusement turn to despair as the past steamrolled through his mind.

"I had it all." Ryan tried to rein in the overwhelming sadness before it threatened to flatten him. He cast his eyes back down at his mug as he admitted. "And I fucked it up. I lost her. No, that's an understatement. I lost *every-thing*…and cost her everything in the process."

He felt the familiar weight of his failures settling firmly on his shoulders. "But here's the thing, Lyla. I've spent years repenting for my sins, years trying to earn her forgiveness—hell, trying to forgive myself. But I can't keep living in the past. Leo, would…"

Just saying Leo's name to anyone but Ashley felt like awkward and unjust. "Leo would be so pissed at what's happened between Ashley and me." He looked blindly out the big picture window. "Stubborn, that's what she is. Her own brother said it time and time again. He said that she was stubborn *both ways*. He said that when she got angry she stayed pissed, but when she loved, she loved forever. I guess he got the first part right."

He turned to leveling his gaze on Lyla. "She's never forgiven me, and loving me forever seemed to have had an expiration date. I tried giving her time and space but it was never enough. So I finally realized it was time to move on.

About six months ago, when I was out with Max and Kyle, I told them how I was feeling. Max suggested I move on and Kyle said the best way to do it was get with as many girls as possible. He reasoned that if Ashley saw me moving on, she might change her mind about me."

Even as the words left his mouth, he knew they sounded childish and asinine, so Lyla looking at him as if he had sprouted a second head didn't come as a shock.

Her standing up, walking to her cabinet and grabbing a bottle of vodka and a shot glass, sure as hell, did.

"Lyla, I don't need a drink. I have to drive home and the roads already suck." If looks could kill, he would have been lying on the cold hard floor.

Her eyes flashed with irritation as she twisted the cap off the bottle. "Ryan, this drink isn't for you—it's for me. This drink is so I can deal with the rest of this conversation in a clear and level headed way, so give me a minute, would ya?"

Filling the small glass to the brim she lifted it to her lips and emptied the clear liquid into her mouth. Ryan watched on silently as she repeated the process. Seemingly content with the amount she consumed, Lyla poured one more and then returned the bottle to the cabinet. She brought the tiny glass back to the dining table and took her seat and stared at Ryan wordlessly. After a few seconds, his eyes fell to his lap.

"Seriously, what in the hell would possess you to go to Kyle for anything other than the latest information on cunnilingus?" He knew her question wasn't sarcastic or disrespectful, and that's what bothered him.

Frustration coursed through his already tense body. "Look, Lyla, I was out of options and I was desperate, okay? That guy always has women lining up to be with him—"

"Oh well, excuse me," Lyla cut him off as she threw her hands in the air, her irritation evident in the tone of her voice. "I thought we were talking about Ashley here, not some brainless chick looking to ride the log flume that is Kyle Marx. My God, Ryan, don't you see? Yes, Kyle has his line of girls looking for a spin, but have you noticed any of them buying a second ticket? No, you do not! Because one ride is enough for any self-respecting woman."

She curled her fingers around her glass and shot back the second splash of vodka.

Ryan could tell that Lyla had more to say, but she kept her mouth shut, as if waiting for Ryan to make the next move. So he did. "Then you tell me, what do I do when the woman I love more than life is completely finished with me? Tell me, Lyla, because I'd love to hear your sound advice on this? I am so sick of playing games and waiting for the right time. When is the right fucking time? I'm sick of hoping that she'll wake up one morning and decide I'm worthy of her again. I've been worthy for years! I love her, but I'm dying inside. This has got to stop." He scrubbed his hands over his whisker-roughened face as he tried to hold back the tears that threatened to fall.

"Ryan," Lyla's voice had taken on a tone so soft, Ryan found himself quickly looking up to see if it was the same person still speaking. Her gentle eyes captured his attention as Lyla spoke in the way that only *she* could. "Do you have any idea how smart you are when you aren't acting stupid?"

He clearly wasn't as smart as she thought because he had no idea what the hell she was talking about. He shook his head silently and hoped she'd continue to speak.

"You just answered all of your own questions. First of all—and think before you answer—do you honestly, in your heart of hearts, think Ashley is finished with you? Do you think a woman who hasn't dated in…well, at least the eight months that I've known her but I've heard it's been longer, is done? Is a woman who turns green with envy each time she sees another woman get your attention, over you?"

He was stunned speechless, which was perfect because Lyla continued to talk. "You're sick of playing games? Well, thank God for that! Because your games suck ass, Ry. Yes, you made her jealous and *that* probably did work in your favor, but I would venture to guess that, had you just had an honest conversation with her months ago, all of this would have been avoided."

"That's bullshit, Lyla." A new wave of irritation swelled through Ryan's system. "I've tried to talk to her for *years* but she's slammed the fucking door in my face every single time. I've told her how sorry I am. I've begged for her forgiveness. What more can I do?"

"And that is where the two of you keep failing." Now she had his attention, what was he doing that kept the wheels of failure spinning? "Ryan, you've spent years apologizing for your mistakes. Yes, you fucked up. Yes, your actions had consequences. But did you ever stop to think that she'd already forgiven you?"

He could have sworn he heard the "click" as Lyla's words took root in his mind. What she was saying actually made sense. "I can't sit here and heal your relationship because you two need to do that yourselves, but I can say this. Leo's theory about her is spot on—she is stubborn as hell. Think about this. Maybe, just maybe, you're not the one that she's holding the grudge against. Maybe you're not the one she's punishing. Maybe it's not *you* she deems unworthy."

Lyla slowly stood up from her chair and traipsed through the door to the right of the kitchen. She came back a moment later holding Ryan's clothes. "It's getting really bad out there, you should get home."

Ryan stood up and took the warm clothing from Lyla.

His mind reeled from their conversation. "Ry." Lyla stared at him, concern heavy in her eyes, "It's important you get home safely. So bank our chat until you get there, okay?"

There was so much sincerity in the small package that was Lyla Dalton, he was embarrassed and even a little ashamed that he hadn't taken the time to get to know her better. *Well*, he thought to himself, *that's gonna change*.

He stood at the opened door and watched the sheets of rain falling sideways from the sky. Turning to her he said, "Thanks for everything, Lyla. Even if I don't get the answers I want, at least I'll get the answers I need." He looked at his booted feet. "It's time I move forward one way or another."

"It's time you got your ass out of my house—you're letting the rain in." Her soft smile belied her sarcastic wit and he nodded and ran quickly to his car.

CHAPTER THIRTY-FIVE

Answer the Call

THE SOUND OF the ticking clock in the hallway could be heard even above the noise from the wind and rain outside. Whether it actually was, or she was just watching the time so closely, Ashley didn't know. Pacing the floor, she stopped every minute or so to look out of the window, noticing the ever darkening clouds that were closing in around the house. "Where are you, Ryan? Why aren't you home yet?" Nervousness clawed at her belly as she moved from the den to the kitchen. She ran her fingertips along the granite counter top, the cool stone permeating her skin as memories of the day they installed them played in her mind. She had wanted so badly to upgrade the outdated kitchen but didn't think she could afford the renovations. Ryan had refused to let her give up and had talked her into making it a DIY project. He convinced her that, since he lived in the house too, he should be able to sink his money into it. After weeks of hard labor and various disagreements, she had the kitchen of her dreams. Leaning up against the refrigerator door her eyes moved to the green digital numbers of the clock on the microwave oven. It had been more than two hours since she'd spoken to him.

Where was he? Was he okay?

Since Ashley's cell phone was completely drained and resting on the charger, the shrilling sound of the land telephone line in the kitchen first startled her and then had her rushing to pick up the call.

"Ryan?"

"No, sweetie, it's Julie. I just wanted to see if you were holding up alright." Julie's voice lowered as the true reason for her call surfaced. "I also wanted to know, if maybe you wanted me to come and stay with you tonight?"

"Thank you so much, Julie, but Ryan should be home any minute. We'll be fine." Ashley heard Danny's voice in the background. She couldn't make out his words, but she knew that he needed his wife's attention. "Jules, go be with Danny. I'm fine. We'll chat later." She hung up the phone and continued to pace, waiting for Ryan's return.

The house creaked with the massive gusts of wind, while heavy waves of rain and debris slammed against the side of the quaint, brick-lined house. Anxiety ricocheted through her, sending sweat down her spine and nausea up her throat.

Another half hour passed without word from Ryan. "No," she said out loud, "there is no way this would happen again." Pieces that had been held together for so long began to wiggle loose as she felt her body slide down the stainless steel door and into a puddle on the kitchen floor. Quiet sobs wracked her body as the fear and pain swelled within her, shattering the locked box where she kept it hidden away.

"Ash, I'm home. Sorry it took so long, the roads are a mess and I have no cell service." So wrapped up in memories of the past and the horrific thoughts of what could have happened, she barely heard Ryan call out his greeting.

It wasn't until she heard her name again that she managed to call out her response, "Ry?" Hearing the pounding footsteps scurrying through the house gave her comfort that he really was home and safe.

"Baby," his voice was soothing and thick with emotion as he settled behind her, wrapping his long legs around her frame, in a position that was all too familiar to her. "Are you sick? What's wrong, Ash, tell me, I'll make it better, Princess, I swear."

His presence was a balm to her tormented soul. She slowly lifted her head from her arms and turned to face him, the anguish in his eyes stealing her breath away.

Tears burned her cheeks. Her teeth gripped the small hoop that pierced through her bottom lip. Snuggling tightly into his arms, she quaked when his thumbs touched her face to sweep away the tears. The familiarity of this moment unleashed a whole new round of tears.

"Princess, please talk to me," Ryan begged. Then, just like the thunder crashing through the atmosphere her words came crashing through the room.

"I...I thought something had happened to you." She couldn't hold back her thoughts, or her fears. They were lava erupting from a volcano—hot, molten, fire that needed to find air in order to cool. She vigorously wiped at her face, trying unsuccessfully to remove any evidence of her meltdown.

"I'm so sorry, Ash. After we spoke, I had a few errands to run. I figured we would probably be stuck in for a couple of days so I wanted to get a few things taken care of." He pulled her closer to him sitting her on his lap as he stroked her back and whispered comforting words in her ear. After a long while filled with only their warm breaths and rapid heartbeats, Ryan cleared his voice.

"Come on, Princess, let's get out of here. My legs are beginning to cramp." She noticed that his smile didn't quite reach his eyes, but she didn't care. Gratitude for his safety was the only thing that mattered to her.

She took hold of his offered hand and on shaking legs followed him towards the den.

"I had a few errands to run. I figured we would probably be stuck in for a couple of days. So I wanted to get a few things taken care of..."

In the space of mere minutes, the meaning of his explanation morphed in her mind. The words evolved, his simple statement turning into a detonated bomb as it ricocheted, leaving shrapnel scattered all over her exposed skin. Hurt and anger pulsed through her and she pulled away from Ryan's touch, wrapping her arms around herself to protect her body from further damage.

Ryan recoiled at the sudden change in Ashley's demeanor. "Are you okay, babe? Are you hurt?"

"Oh, so *now* you give a shit if I'm okay," she hissed. "You didn't seem to care while you were 'taking care of things.'" She hated it when people used air quotes but this seemed like the perfect time for them so air quotes it was.

Ryan's face changed as he realized what Ashley was saying, but she didn't give time to react before she continued her hysterical rant, the words flowing from her mouth at break-neck speed. "I asked you—nicely, I might add—not to have any of your lady-friends over here for what, Ryan, a day or two? I didn't want to be stuck listening to you getting your whistle blown, or hearing how rough Sally can ride…but obviously that was too much to ask. You had to go out and sink your dick in whatever Fun Dip you could get your hands on to hold you over till after the storm."

Ashley flailed her arms in Kynde Windmill style as she marched past him to the stairs. When she hit the bottom step she turned around to face him, her eyes glistened with unshed tears and her thumb rubbed up and down over her sternum as she stared directly into his eyes and said in a low voice, "Did you even think for one second about me? Did you think about how I was feeling, sitting here in this house worrying about you? Thinking back to the night my world changed? Did you give two shits about me while you were fucking some bobble-headed Barbie, or were you too goddamn busy 'taking care of things'? I'm gonna guess you were too busy playing Ken." She spat before turning away from him to head upstairs.

•————————————•

Anger brewed in his already aching chest and with three steps he closed the remaining distance between them clasping her on the shoulder and spun her in his direction.

"Oh my God, you're unbelievable. Did I ever think about you?" He roared, staring her deep in her bloodshot eyes. "You've *got* to be fucking kidding me, Ashley."

Taking a small step backward he released her and inhaled deeply, holding it in before releasing it slowly. "Did I ever think about you? Princess, I've spent every minute of every fucking day since I was *nineteen* years old thinking about you. Hell, if were being honest, even before

331

then." Even though controlled, his voice was sharp, his stance was rigid, anger, frustration, and years of holding back coursed through his veins. He refused to play these games anymore, he made a promise to Leo, to Ashley and to himself and it was time he lived up to it.

Ryan closed his eyes and whispered, "He asked me to make it right with you." Leo's broken voice played in his mind. "He knew I loved you, he knew I'd live my life trying to earn back your trust, so making that promise to him was the easiest thing I'd ever done. So yes, Ashley, you're all I've thought about." His gaze tightened as he willed her to understand.

Ashley returned his stare and he knew from her face that she was stunned by his outburst but experience told him that she was still too caught up in her own animosity to see his point of view. He stalked closer to her, needing to feel her warmth around him, even if the heat came from anger and despair.

"I fucked up, Ashley. I was a stupid, punk-ass kid who made a horrible mistake. Did I deserve your anger? Abso-fucking-lutely. Did I deserve for you to dump me on my ass and never look back? You bet. But, did any of us deserve what happened with Leo? No! I didn't, he sure as hell didn't, and as much as you would love to stand there and shoulder the burden for the rest of your life, you didn't either."

Ryan pumped his fists open and closed, trying to encourage the blood to flow through his fingers. He wasn't angry. He was afraid—afraid of actually losing her for good, after all these years of fighting to stay in her life.

He watched her lip curl up in disgust. She crossed her arms over her chest and her nostrils flared subtly. She was still refusing to listen to him—he knew she couldn't hear what he was saying because she was too engulfed in pain and anger. Ryan's chest tightened as he watched Ashley rub her fist over her sternum in small circles.

Make it right...Take care of her, Ryan...

Leo's words reverberated in his head like a dream. Better yet, like a prayer.

"You," she jabbed her finger into his chest, "are an arrogant asshole." Her face was flushed, her eyes burned with hurt, filled with years of guilt and sadness. He watched as her body shook with...what? Fear? Frustration? He didn't know, but he *did* know that now was the time to push—he couldn't back down now that they had finally come to this point. He needed to see this through. Something screamed at him, warning him that if he pulled back he would lose her forever.

Make it right...

Leo's voice rang through his head. *Yeah, buddy,* he promised his best friend, *I will.*

"What makes me an asshole?" He ran his hands through his hair, "I can't wait to hear this," he snapped sarcastically, moving so that he was only inches from her frame as he stared intently into her eyes. "Seriously, Princess, please enlighten me, because this is how I see it. From the time I met you, you have yet to follow your heart....ever! Sure, you listen to that big ol' brain of yours, you let it make every single *smart* decision, but you haven't actually *lived* one day of your own life in twenty-four years."

He watched as Ashley blanched at his accusation, but it didn't take long for her to react as he felt the full-force of her anger and the venom in her words. "Have you lost

333

your mind? Clearly, all of the stupid women you've been fucking have rubbed off on you because I've been living my own life since the day I left Miami!"

His stomach clenched. He knew his next words would hurt her. He knew they were unkind but she needed to hear them. She could choose not to hear him—hell, she could choose to never speak to him again—but he couldn't stand in the corner wishing for things to be different any longer. It was time to face the past and move on, either together or apart.

Inhaling deeply, he ran his fingers through his hair, stopping to massage his scalp.

"I didn't say that you weren't living on your own, Ash, I said you haven't been *living*, period. You've never once followed your own heart. Leo knew it, he told you so himself, didn't he?" Ryan watched as Ashley took on the far-away look she got when thinking about the past. He assumed she was getting lost in memories of her brother, but he needed her with him…now.

"Ashley, are you listening to me?" She startled when he called her name and the tension that had momentarily left her shoulders returned. Ryan softened his voice, he needed her to hear him. "You spent your childhood trying to be the perfect daughter, and then spent your adulthood following the dreams Leo had mapped out for himself before he died. When have you ever just been *you*?"

Ashley visibly flinched, and Ryan knew the words he just spoke sliced through her heart like a knife. The pain was evident as her mouth dipped down and her chin began to tremble. In a matter of mere seconds, the pain transformed into fury, and her injured expression became a vengeful sneer.

"You want to know when I was me?" She seethed. "I was me when I loved you! I was me when I gave you my heart, my trust, my love…EVERYTHING, Ryan!"

She palmed away the salty sadness of her unchecked tears and continued speaking in a raspy, broken voice, "I gave *myself* to a guy who didn't return my love, or my trust. He didn't cherish my heart, he gave it back to me— broken into jagged little pieces. That's when I was me, Ryan. You were the first and only man who got a piece of the real me. And do you wanna know what I learned? I learned I wasn't good enough."

Each word crippled him. They punched at his diaphragm, stealing his breaths. She had *always* been good enough. It was he who never measured up. He who didn't deserve *her*.

No. This wasn't about his insecurities. This was about getting her to move forward.

"Ashley, do you want to know where I was tonight?"

She looked down at his feet before she replied, "No. I don't care where you were, or who you were with."

"That's bullshit and you know it." His gaze penetrated hers. "I was trying to figure out what to do about you…about us." He could see the argument forming on her lips so he pressed one finger to her mouth and continued to speak.

"I've been trying for years to get you back, but I finally realized *I* didn't lose you, Princess…*you* did. I don't care what you say or what you think, you stopped living the day Leo died. You're half a person and that half isn't even you, it's…Leo. It's his piercings and his tattoos. But come on, Ash, let's be truthful, you're not even showing the honest side of your brother…" Her stone still posture

335

and shocked stare told him he had her attention, even if it was laced with excruciating pain, and it forced him to proceed.

"It's not the side that made him proud, it's the side you're choosing to recall. You're rewriting history, Princess, and while you've remembered the battles, you've forgotten the victories." Ryan stroked his knuckles down the side of Ashley's jaw, "Leo would be heartbroken to see what's happened to you."

Ashley swatted his hand away from her face and glared at him, "How dare you," she sneered, "you son of a bitch! How can you stand there and talk to me that way after everything I've been through. My God Ryan, I thought you loved me. I thought you'd always be there for me but once again—once *again*—you stand before me and crush what's left of my heart!" He could taste the venom in her words and it became increasingly bitter with each swallow.

They were interrupted by booms of thunder and streaks of lighting, which struck in time to the argument that was raging between them. If Ryan had been a religious man he would have surmised that God himself had orchestrated a symphony building up to this—their final blow-up. Ryan's insides churned at her toxic words and her fractured glare. She batted his outstretched arm away as he tried to embrace her crumbling form.

"I do love you. Can't you see that?" He could hear the plea in his tone but at this point he wasn't above begging if it would make her listen to him. "Look at me, Ashley. Really *look* at me...for once. I'm standing here telling you the things you need to hear even if, in the end, your knowing them makes you hate me. I'm not trying to crush your heart, Princess, I'm trying to put it back together.

You've spent almost seven years in mourning. Seven years blaming yourself for things you had no control over. It's time to let it go, Ashley. You need to move on. Leo loved you with his whole heart—you were his soul—and he would never have wanted you to live your life mourning his. He would've told you to, 'Reach for the light at the end, Ash.' He lived by those words."

He knew it was a little low to quote Leo at this moment, but he needed her open, raw and ready to start over. Leo was the one person who truly had the gift to do that. Although the devastation and pain in Ashley's eyes told him he may have pushed too hard too fast.

The ringing of the phone broke the silence but not the tension. He didn't want to answer the call, the only person that mattered in the moment was standing in front of him, but the second and third rings seemed to get progressively louder.

"Answer the call, Ryan," Ashley requested, her tone flat her eyes red. "It could be Lyla and she's home by herself. She could need something."

Ryan knew that Ashley wanting him to answer the call was about more than Lyla. He knew she was trying to put space between them but as much as he wanted to push her—to continue to make the progress that he knew they could—past experience dictated that he needed to let what he'd said thus far settle. So, he'd give her space…just not too much. As soon as his back was turned his thoughts went to who could be on the phone. Memories washed over him as he remembered the night so many years before, when he'd taken the call from Leo. God, he hoped it wasn't anything bad, if not for his sanity, for Ashley's.

He knew if anything happened to anyone from the bar, including Kyle—because even though he was a huge pain in the ass, he was still family—then Ashley would most likely never recover. He quickened his pace the last few steps and grabbed the receiver.

Such was his focus on the telephone that Ryan forgot about Ashley. He forgot about the woman he'd torn open and left alone in the hallway. He forgot about her innate impulse to run away from her fears. The lights flickered as the storm whipped around them. The wind howled and sent the rain crashing against the house. Such was the noise that Ryan had to press the receiver tight to his ear to hear the person on the other end. Such was his concentration that he didn't hear the one noise he should have been listening for. The sound of the front door opening and closing.

"WHAT'S UP, DANNY?" The hairs on Ryan's neck stood up when the caller I.D showed the Marcus' home phone number.

"Ryan…" The older man's voice sounded strong but thick with emotion. "I just got a call from the fire company." The silence that followed that statement spoke volumes.

"Tell me what happened, Danny." Ryan squeezed his eyes closed as he once again scrubbed his hand over his scalp. How could this night get worse? Julie's soft cries in the background alerted Ryan that he wasn't going to like what Danny had to share.

Danny's gruff chuckle sounded forced and Ryan heard him comfort Julie before he described the domino effect of the 140 mile per hour winds that had snapped the tree, knocking it into the utility pole, which in turn had split the pole and sent it—and its still-live wires—crashing into the bar, thus sparking the fire that had ultimately consumed *Danny's on Main*.

"What?" Sorrow cracked Ryan's voice.

"According to the fire chief it wasn't burned to the ground," Danny sounded like he had aged during the length of the conversation, "but what wasn't ruined by fire was destroyed by the hoses and the hurricane. The bar is totaled, son. I wanted to call each of you personally, because God forbid you find out on the news." The shudder in Danny's voice was audible.

Tears filled Ryan's eyes. *Danny's*. Both the place and the man had been home to him for more than four years. It had been the net that caught Ashley when she was lost and flying blind, and the place that had kept them together for so long.

"Oh, fuck, Ashley!" Ryan's grip tightened on the receiver, and the phone shook against his ear as he spoke. "Danny, I don't know how I'm gonna tell Ashley. As much as I love the bar, as much as it's been my home, it's been her safe place for almost six years. Christ, Danny...."

"Go, talk to her, son. I've got another call to make. We'll catch up tomorrow once the storm passes. Ryan, I know it was our home and Julie and I are...well, we're sick over this, but it was just a place, son. What really matters are the people who comprise it, and that's all of us..."

Ryan heard Danny's voice break just before he cleared his throat. "We'll be okay. I need each one of you to believe it...for me."

"It's gonna be fine, Danny. We'll make it fine." Ryan tried to make his tone confident with false enthusiasm. It wasn't until he disconnected the call that the soundlessness of the house screamed for his attention.

"Ash?" He called, taking the stairs two at time to the second floor, "Ashley?" He knew, he just knew, before he'd even called her name a third time that she had left their house. She'd left angry, hurt, sad, and in the midst of a hurricane named after the one person in the world that had never let her down.

"Ashley Beth!! Fuck!" Ryan ran down the steps barely stopping to shove his feet into his boots as he headed for the door. It was nearing on midnight, where the hell could she have gone?

Memories of a similar time flashed through his mind as he raced through the living room. "Where are my fucking keys?" His shout went unanswered as it echoed through the house. Ryan wracked his brain for where he might have left them. He knew that he *always* left them in the bowl on the entryway table. Always. He knew that Ash knew— "Goddamn it Ash!" Realizing she'd taken his keys—most likely to stop him from following—he threw on his jacket and raced out the door. As he calculated the time of his phone call with Danny in his head, he knew that, with the weather the way it was, the ten minutes he'd spent on the phone wouldn't have given her that much of a head start.

His mind was spinning with possibilities as to where she might have gone. The small town had been all but evacuated—every business was closed and every road was littered with branches and fallen trees. The wind pulled at his hair while the rain slapped his face. It felt like he was running against a wall because the harder he pushed, the less he moved. Memories of racing to find Leo crashed through him like the wind and the rain but, just like years before, neither slowed him down.

CHAPTER THIRTY-SIX

Into the Light

THE WINDSHIELD WIPERS swished quickly from left to right, but it didn't matter. Even though they were on hi-speed, Ashley still couldn't see more than a foot or two in front of her. Her car felt more like a boat as it rocked and swayed from the pressure of the wind. *Probably wasn't my best idea leaving the house in this weather*, she chastised herself as she finally pulled her car onto Main Street. A fallen tree prevented her from driving any further on the road, but she needed to get there. She needed to get to *Danny's*. Her safe place. *Danny's* had been the warm embrace that had saved her when she'd been ready to give up on herself which now seemed like a lifetime ago.

Tired and hungry, she'd pulled into Danny's parking lot for the first time about seven years prior. She'd had no intentions of ever going to the *University of Pennsylvania*—hell, she hadn't even formally graduated high school—but she'd wanted to torture herself by visiting the campus that she would never attend. She'd wanted to remind herself of one more thing she didn't deserve, one more thing that would never be. On the way to Philadelphia she stopped in Charistown for a bite to eat. When she walked into *Danny's on Main* she found her home.

All these years later, it was still her home. She'd chosen to hide her weaknesses from most of them—not because they wouldn't accept her, but because she couldn't bear the look of pity they would have on their faces if they knew she still harbored guilt for Leo's death. Danny and Julie would be crushed if they thought she still blamed herself after all these years.

Wrenching her keys from the ignition, she stepped out of her car and started to make the rest of the journey on foot. Danny and Julie had given her, Max, and Kyle their own set of keys to the bar about four years earlier for Christmas. Ashley smiled when she thought of the card attached to the keys—*You never knock on the door of your own home*.

The rough bark of a fallen tree trunk cut into the smooth skin on the palms of her hands as she hefted her body over it and on to the street on the other side. She tried to wipe the rain-matted hair from her eyes so she could see where she was going but the wind refused to cooperate and she lost her footing and slipped, falling to the ground. It wasn't the sting of the cut on her leg, or the knowledge that the warm liquid she felt trickling from her knee wasn't rain but blood, but the acrid smell that filled the air and the loud sounds of people's voices over Mother Nature's tantrum that caught her attention.

"What the hell?" She took off running down Main Street towards the smell and the shouts, until the swirling lights of the fire trucks came into view.

"No. No. No." Screams filled the air as she arrived in front of *Danny's on Main*…or, what was left of it. "NO!"

She wished her screaming would stop. Her limbs

shook uncontrollably as her chest heaved, trying to allow her lungs to take in the thick, wet, smoke-filled air around her. She closed her eyes tightly and shook her head, hoping to jar the images in front of her from her brain.

"There's no way this can be happening," she cried into the night.

"Miss, are you okay? Can we call someone for you?" She opened her eyes to see the hand that lightly touched her soaked shoulder, led to an arm that was covered in fire retardant gear. She stared at the fire fighter but was unable to form words, unable to process what was happening in front of her. "Miss, you're screaming and shaking and I'm worried you're going into shock. Please, tell me your name."

Ashley shrugged out of the man's grip and walked closer to the disaster that had once been her lifeline. "I'm sorry, Miss, but we can't let you any closer to the site. Even though the fire is contained, the building isn't stable. Please, it's pouring, this storm is tenacious and it's not going anywhere," he shouted over the wind. "You need to get to a safe place. Let me call someone for you."

"I don't have anyone," she whispered, her tears mixed with the rain streaming down her face. "I have nothing left. I'm all alone now."

Trembling, she slowly made her way to the ground, her legs drew up tight and her arms wrapped tightly around them. "I have nothing left. I'm all alone now," she repeated as she rested her head into her knees.

———————•———————

There she was. Sitting on the sidewalk, curled so

tightly into herself it was painful for Ryan to witness. He knew exactly what she was doing. She was trying to shield herself, to make herself numb to the inescapable agony surrounding her. He could recall the first time he'd seen her coiled in tightly like that. It was the night she had built her fortress—the night she had sat guard outside the morgue and created walls too high for him to climb and too thick for him to break through. They had a close friendship for a lot of years, and even that took a lot of patience and a very large chisel. Now thanks to his stupidity, he had all but lost the small opening he had made with her. And this, this was his own private hell.

His heart splintered as he watched her from a distance, but the damn thing cracked clear in half when he got close enough to hear her cries. Seeing her car at the top of the street had the memories of Leo's wreck slamming into him like a freight train. Seeing Leo's car shattered and flattened under the tree. His body broken and mangled, hanging on for mere minutes, if only just to give Ryan advice on how to love Ashley.

Breaths that were ultimately wasted on advise that had gone unused. So the only thing that stopped Ryan from a full-blown melt down was his deep need to get to Ashley—to make sure she was well, to wrap his arms around her, to protect her from going through any more pain alone. He'd left the abandoned vehicle and ran like the hounds of hell were chasing him to get to her.

"I have nothing left, I'm all alone now." He watched her body tremble violently in the cold, wet, stormy night and his eyes quickly traveled to the remains of their touchstone. If *his* loss felt insurmountable he could only imagine what Max and Kyle would be feeling right now. And

Danny and Julie, oh God, their pain. Shivers ran through his own solid frame as he thought about their loss. Even as his family's hurt weighed heavily on his mind, thoughts of everything but the beautiful heartbroken woman before him vaporized the minute he heard her sobbing, "Leo, I'm so sorry. We had everything in each other.

And Ryan…God, you must hate what I've done to him." Her words became jumbled as her sobs wracked her body. "I deserve what I've become, Leo." Her words were killing him, her tears sliced him, and his emotions bounced all over the place, making it impossible for him to settle on just one. Was he sad? Hurt? Confused? Angry? He didn't know. All he did know was that he needed to get to her to comfort her. He needed to alleviate her pain, to somehow absorb it. He didn't care how he did it, as long as he never had to see her look like that again.

●————————————●

She felt his presence a split second before a Mylar blanket slipped around her shoulders and his firm body pressed up against hers. She hadn't realized how cold she was until there was a modicum of relief from the bitterness.

"Ashley, baby, why are you apologizing to Leo? Why, even for one second, would you think that he would blame you for what happened to him? And what, besides being a stubborn pain in the ass, have you done to me?" *I love him,* that was the first thought that shot through her mind. Her insides were bleeding, her soul was crying but this man made her want to smile. *Still.* Two times in one night, the box labeled "past" was being dropped at her feet and the key placed in her hand. She knew then, in that moment, that it was time. It felt like Leo himself was begging her to finally open up and let go of the burden she was carrying. Looking at the devastation in front of her and feeling the warmth and love of the man beside her, she knew, she'd never be granted this chance again.

The cold rain sluiced over her face as she turned to stare in the dark pools of understanding. The only lights were those still set up by the emergency units. Her mind buzzed with hurt, pain, and guilt, but she couldn't escape the need to watch the beautiful man sitting there, unwavering in his support like he had been through most of their lives. As she eyed him, she found the hurt, the pain and the guilt replaced with the warmth, the security, and the peace that was...*home*. Wrapped in the arms of the only man she had ever loved, Ashley Kynde allowed the impenetrable walls that had been separating them for so long to finally come crashing down.

"Everyone expected perfection," she said, staring at the rubble while the cold rain poured down her face. "I expected it too. Leo, he was the free spirit...everything I was too scared to let myself be. I was busy trying to make my parents see me. *Really* see me. Leo should have been enough—I realize that now—but I wanted them too. By the time we were in high school, everyone saw me as sweet, innocent Ashley who could do no wrong." She turned her head and met his soft brown gaze, "Do you have *any* idea how hard it is to keep up with that expectation?"

"Princess, I never saw you the way you saw yourself, but we can get into that later." He cupped her hands, his skin felt so warm on her frozen fingers, "please continue."

Before she could say another word a police officer approached and told them they had to evacuate. He gave them both a ride to Ashley's abandoned car and Ryan carefully drove the pair of them home. Lost in her thoughts, Ashley continued to speak and he continued to listen.

●————————————————●

"When you and Leo became friends"—he watched as her eyes danced with the memories—"I was so happy. Not just because you were super hot, but because Leo finally had someone he could relate to—someone like a brother. He always told me that our parents' neglect bothered me more than it did him, but I couldn't imagine how that could be the case. So, you were like the family I'd always wanted for him."

Ryan wanted so badly to interrupt. To explain to her that while she and her brother had been as close as two siblings could be, in some ways she really hadn't known Leo that well. Leo was a glass-half-full kind of guy. While he thought his parents sucked, he'd stopped being affected by them at a young age and the only thing that bothered him was how deeply their indifference hurt Ashley. She'd spent her time worrying about him for no reason, but he kept his mouth shut, and let her speak and she did so for quite a while.

Once they were safely tucked inside their house, Ryan built a fire in the brick fireplace while Ashley stripped out of her clothes in front of him. Gone was her sense of decorum or modesty, and in its place was the cold chill from the rain mixed with raw pain of freshly open wounds. Clearly, she had no problem letting him see her in nothing but her bra and panties, he thought, because tonight, he was seeing so much more than just her skin. He was finally seeing her soul, stripped down, and laid bare. No more hiding. This was her. He drank in every inch of her beauty even after she slipped the fleecy sweatshirt over her head and eased into drawstring sweatpants.

"Ash" he said quietly as they sat on the pallet hearthside, "what I don't understand, is why you think any of this is your fault? Why have you been able to forgive me for the accident but not yourself?" He couldn't begin to imagine the answer that was going to come out of her mouth. Even hearing Lyla suggest it felt strange, though seeing the look of complete resignation on Ashley's face, he knew Lyla had been correct.

"Ry, you hurt me and you lost me. We both lost in that game." He watched as Ashley dug her long fingers into the soft blankets on the floor, but didn't try to offer her support. Something inside told him she needed to take this step on her own.

"But you paid a price so much steeper than just losing the girl. You lost your best friend, your brother. He didn't just leave you. God, you found him trapped in his car with his life flowing out of him along with I don't even know what else, because I've spent years being too damn selfish to ask you." Tears rolled down her cheeks as the trembling words left her mouth.

"You stayed with him during the last minutes of his life, Ryan. How could I *not* forgive you for anything you said to me? My brother died with family by his side… because of you." She looked at him, her eyes brimming with tears. "Not once in all these years have I thanked you for being there with him. Not once did I ask you if you were okay or give you the opportunity to unburden your pain. He was *my* brother, and it was *my* loss, *my* grief. I was so selfish and I am so sorry Ryan. I'm not sure if it means anything after all these years, but thank you. Thank for being there with my brother."

He wondered if she could hear his heart beating. Did she know that her words—her absolution—were healing something deep inside of him he hadn't even realized was still broken? He allowed his tears to fall without embarrassment or shame and listened as Ashley continued her confession.

"Then there's me—'Perfect Ashley'. I got my heart broken by a guy and was too weak to deal with it. So I called my big brother to rush to my aid. I knew the hurricane was coming. I knew that driving was dangerous. But I wanted him with *me*. And look what happened? Had I just been tougher, just been stronger and held back my emotions, he would have never been out that night."

In that instant, the realization struck him hard. He finally understood why she'd become the tattooed, pierced, swearing, closed off, snarky Ashley. It was her self-inflicted punishment for Leo's death.

"I just can't forgive myself for that kind of selfishness. I'm no better than my mother." She turned, staring back toward the fireplace, and wiped at the steady flow of tears.

His body was thrumming with conflicting emotions as he watched Ashley melt into a puddle of her own guilt and dismay. It wasn't until he heard her gasp, that he realized he had cupped her upper arms and turned her whole body ninety degrees to face him.

"I can't stand it anymore, Ashley. I came to this town more than four years ago to find you and, yes, you were here, but you also weren't. There were so many changes it was almost hard to recognize you. Don't get me wrong, parts of the transformation are amazing—like the way you've learned to stand up for yourself and how you throw your sass at just the right time."

He ran his gaze from her eyes to her crossed legs and breathed in her scent, "Physically you were always stunning, but in the time we were apart you grew into a sexiness that I never even knew existed—but Princess, that's where the good changes ended. I still saw the old Ashley in you—your generosity and your kindness—yet all of your warmth?" Ryan snapped his fingers. "Gone. All of your openness? Gone. All of the softness that made you, you? Gone. While I've seen a little of the old Ashley creeping back in since you've become closer with Lyla and Janie, you still keep yourself at arm's length from everyone. Even yourself. Ash," He reached over and lifted the side of her sweatshirt, exposing her inked ribs. "Leo's words weren't meant to lead you into darkness, you know that, Princess. He always looked toward the light." He paused for a moment, hoping that his words were sinking into her, praying that she was not only hearing him but believing him.

"I told you earlier, that you've been re-writing history, and I could kick myself for letting this go on for as long as I have." His warm finger lifted her chin as he stared into her soul. "Have you honestly forgotten why he came home in the first place? And it wasn't so he could fuck 'what's her name'"

"Toni." Ashley answered, her voice hoarse and quiet.

"It doesn't matter—listen, the point is, he didn't come home to be with her. He came home to be with you, because he hated big storms as much as you did. He couldn't stomach the thought of you being alone in that fucking house. He was leaving Toni's house regardless of your call and I'm sure you've conveniently blocked this out of your twisted version of history as well but, Ashley, Hurricane Wilma tore Miami apart. There were hundreds of downed trees and electrical poles. If it hadn't been the one on Beacon Hill it could have been another one, on another street." She opened her mouth, he assumed it was to interrupt him, but he gave her his "No-Nonsense-Bar-Tender" look and she closed her mouth without saying a word.

"You think you were being, what was your word, 'selfish' because a *guy* broke your heart?" Was she insane? He fucked up back then. Him. And she's found a way to claim that blame as well. "Are you fucking kidding me?" He knew his tone was sharp, but he was bleeding for his part of the pain she shouldered all this time.

"That guy promised to love you and to keep you safe. That *guy* promised you forever and asked you to trust him with your heart and your soul, and then…" He swallowed the large lump in his throat, "That guy took everything you gave to him willingly and threw it away, so of course you were hurt, of course you were heartbroken. That didn't make you weak or selfish…that made you fucking human."

"Ryan," she reached out to touch his arm, but he flinched just before she could make contact, her touch was like electricity and he needed to ground himself before he let her skin touch his. He saw the look of rejection and hurt pass over her face as she moved to pull her hand away. He needed her touch more than he needed to protect himself, so he placed both of his hands over hers and pulled her closer to him, pressing her palms on the left side of his chest.

"Do you feel that?" His question was broad, the answers were endless. The look on her face told him that she was feeling so many things all at once.

"Do you feel my heart, beating, Princess?"

She nodded, her eyes never leaving his, her touch making his already racing heart pound even faster. "You said we both lost the game. You said that I just lost the girl and my brother too, but you're wrong, Princess. Yes, I lost my best friend, my brother, but I didn't *just* lose the girl that day—I lost my heart.

"When I first came here and we made love, that's exactly what it was for me. Me *loving* you. And after that happened I thought we would finally get our happily ever after."

Ryan let his mind tumble back to that night, when he thought he'd finally found his woman and his happiness. When he thought he'd finally found heaven after living in hell, only to have it ripped away after one incredible night. He stared into the fireplace watching the flames caress each other in the most erotic and seductive dance. He remembered what it felt like to have her heat wrapped in his even for just one night.

"I was devastated when you told me that it was nothing more than fun for you, but in the same breath, I was grateful. Because that was the day that my heart started to beat again. I may have lost the love of my life the day I threw it away, but my mistake has brought me pain every single day since. You're not the only one who's consumed

353

with self-loathing, babe, because I've made myself watch as I lost more and more of you each day."

"Okay, Romeo." Her comment brought him a dash of hope that was quickly squashed when she removed her small hand from his chest, breaking all contact. His body mourned her touch and he tensed further as she slid back on the pallet, creating distance between them. Even with her puffy eyes and tearstained face, her beauty overwhelmed him, and it took mammoth effort not to reach for her to pull her back into his embrace.

"Okay, what, Princess?" He knew there were land-mines awaiting his approach but he had no idea where they were, or how to avoid them.

"So, you've loved me forever, you've hated yourself for hurting me, and you've watched me suffering for years? That's your story, right?"

BEEP! BEEP! BEEP!

Alarms were blaring in his head and he noticed her eyes dancing with mischief. *She's baiting me. This is a trap.* His thoughts ran rampant as panic started to rise, but then, just as quickly, that same panic ebbed and dispersed. When was the last time he'd seen true openness in the hazel gems reflecting back at him?

"Yeah, Ash, that's my story and it's the truth. Why are you questioning it? Haven't I proven my loyalty to you?" Ashley looked at him as if she was deciding whether or not to believe his explanation.

"Hmm…" He watched as she tapped her finger against her bottom lip. "Romeo, oh Romeo, why did you fuck so many damn Juliets?"

BOOM!!

He watched as her internal thoughts played out on her

face. When she let her guard down he was able to read her like a beautifully written book. She had finally let him crack her cover and now he needed to return the favor. While she'd posed the question as more of a joke, he saw her need for a genuine answer and he was going to give it to her.

So, after taking in a deep breath, he explained everything. All about his talk with Max and Kyle, and all about trying to move on without Ashley by replacing thoughts of her with random women.

"W-wa-wait," Ashley's laughter interrupted her, causing her to repeat herself. "You went to *those two* for advice about women? About me? Ryan, eight months ago Max and Janie were a *disaster*, and Kyle...well, he's Kyle." She rubbed her hand over her eye and shook her head. "Okay, I can only imagine the sage advice those two idiots had to offer."

"I'll be honest," Ryan said, small laugh lines crinkled at the sides of his eyes, "Max did warn me that it would be a bad idea to parade random women around you. But..." The soft crinkles left his temples. He needed to be serious for a minute.

Her soft touch felt like satin on his skin, soft and smooth. "But what, Ry?" Knowing he would always choose honesty between them, he responded with the only answer her could. "But the thought of you feeling jealous, angry, or even pissed off at me was better than knowing you felt nothing at all." The admission, while childish, made him feel lighter and freer. As he took what felt like his first deep breath in months, Ryan glanced at Ashley. He couldn't decide how she was feeling so he waited patiently for her to speak.

Ryan's confession filled Ashley with a sense of elation and deep sadness all at once. Here he was, admitting that his love for her was and had always been solid and strong, but it was her indifference that finally pushed him too far.

Indifference. The one thing that had paralyzed her as a girl—the thing she'd sworn she'd never become—was her weapon of choice against the only man she ever loved. My God, this man, this man had been here in front of her *all this time*. So much wasted time.

"I couldn't agree more, Princess." She hadn't realized that she had voiced her thoughts, but she was glad. "I don't wanna waste any more, Ash. Do you understand?" He bent his head to the side his eyes locked with hers. "You're everything to me Ashley, and I want us to move on… together. Please forgive yourself, and let's move forward."

One small nod led to another until—finally—she let him pull her shaking, sobbing frame tightly into his. Chest to chest they sat on the soft blankets, her legs wrapped around him, her fingers threaded together behind his neck, her face pressed lightly against the soft cotton of his t-shirt as she released a cleansing cry. She was being held by her one true love. She was finally letting go, but she was no longer scared. She knew he would catch her no matter what.

A loud, boom sounded from somewhere outside in the distance followed by complete darkness in their house. The only light came from the red and orange flames that licked the walls of the fireplace. His arms held her tighter when she startled from the loud noise followed by the blackout.

"It's okay, baby, I've got you." His breath tickled her neck just before he grazed her ear lobe with a small lick. The tiny hairs on her neck tingled as he laved the shell of her ear with the tip of his tongue and nipped the sensitive skin. When he slowly moved his kisses down from her ear to her neck, a shiver pulsed through her body.

"Ashley?" His voice was hoarse, his question clear. She knew he wanted to make certain they were on the same page this time. She had a feeling neither of them would survive if they weren't.

"Ryan. I have loved you from the start... " Ashley cupped his face in her hands as she repeated the words she said to him when she was just seventeen years old, and then added the words that were begging to come next, "I fell in love with you when I was fifteen and I've lived my life without you. I survived it, but I hated it. It was lonely and hollow. Leo always said I was stubborn and I guess he was right, because in my heart, I never gave up on you ...on us. I know it seemed like I did, but I think—no, I know—that's why I've been such a raving bitch these past months. I couldn't stand to see you with all of the other women. I know it sounds horrible, I did want you happy, honey, I swear...but I wanted you happy with *me*. I just didn't feel like I had the right to ask for you back."

She stroked her thumbs over his whisker-roughened cheeks. "I know you, and I know you're probably scared to place your bet on me, but, Ry, I'm in this. I'm here. And I'm not going anywhere, ever again. I love you."

CHAPTER THIRTY-SEVEN

Wilma and Fred

THERE SITTING ON the soft pallet in front of the warm fire, while the hurricane wrecked havoc on the world outside, Ryan lifted onto his knees and crawled closer to the woman facing him. "Lift your arms, Princess." Her round eyes questioned him but her no words escaped her mouth. "Lift them, honey, or I'll rip your favorite shirt clear off your body. I've been waiting years for this moment, I don't give a damn how soft and fuzzy that fleecy shit is."

Soft humming of blood swishing through his veins immediately filled his ears when she quickly complied. His cock grew long and firm in his track pants as his hands felt her warm, soft skin for the first time. He eased the top up and off her body and threw it onto the sofa.

His gaze settled on her silken skin and her lace covered breasts.

"Oh, Ashley," his voice was rough as her name rumbled out in a prayer. "My God, you're so fucking beautiful. I want you, God, how I want you." His words were short and direct, not at all like the silver-tongued stud she had known all her life. What was missing from his words, he knew from her softened look, must have been written all over his face—lust, adoration, desire, need, and love. He *loved* her. He was in love with her, and he always had been.

●————————————————————●

"Your turn, Romeo. I need to feel your skin on mine." She reached for the hem of his t-shirt and pulled it up over his head. She would never get tired of looking at his body. It was perfection—taut, bronze skin over bulging muscles. She traced each of his tattoos with her fingertips before rising to her knees and caressing the art with her tongue. His moans reverberated through her chest and traveled down to the sensitive area between her thighs.

"Ryan, you have no idea what it does to me when you moan like that," she panted.

"Tell me, Princess, what does hearing my pleasure do to you?" His growl affected her even more. "Does it make your panties wet?"

"Yes, Ry," she exhaled, moving around to his back, tracing each letter of his *Storm Front* tattoo with the tip of her tongue. "My pussy is wet, my clit is pulsing, my nipples are hard, and my whole body is begging to be touched…by you."

She leaned forward and her lace-covered breasts pressed up against the hard plain of his back as she whispered in to his ear, "So, what are you gonna do about it?"

In an instant, she found herself sprawled out on her back beneath him. Barely a second later Ryan was on his knees, between her legs. Her teasing laugh was caught in the warmth of his mouth as he devoured her lips in a searing kiss.

"What am I gonna do about it, Princess?" His voice was pregnant with desire while his eyes burned with lust, "I'm gonna show you exactly what happens when you poke the dragon who's spent his whole life in love with the Princess." He paused for just a brief second before stripping her out of her sweatpants and lacy panties all in one fell swoop. She let out a strangled giggle as his hands stroked the arches of her ticklish feet.

"The more things change, the more they stay the same," he smirked. "I've missed touching your soft skin ..." His tongue traveled up her shin to her knee. "Mmm, I've missed tasting you."

With each of his seductive statements, Ashley felt the moisture pooling at the juncture between her thighs. "I smell you, Princess. I could never forget your sweet smell." The tip of his index finger made the final trek from her knee to the soft flesh of her pussy lips. He trailed the digit from top to bottom, spreading her open and slowly dipping his thick finger inside her.

She quivered under his touch, his voice, his scent. With her eyes closed she thought of her few sexual encounters over the past years. No other man had ever turned her on the way this man did. "Oh, Ryan, please..."

She opened her eyes when his ministrations stopped and watched as he brought his finger, glistening with her arousal, up to his mouth. She couldn't hold back her whimper when she saw his tongue dart out and wrap itself around his thick digit, pulling it into his mouth.

"So, good, Princess. So sweet." The desire she saw in his eyes was as clear as the ink on his beautiful skin. "Tell me, Ash, what do you want?"

"I want you, Ryan, I need you. Please touch me." In

an instant Ashley watched as his desire morphed into hunger and his erection grew thicker between their bodies.

"Tsk, Tsk, beautiful, I haven't forgotten about that sassy little mouth of yours. Tell me what you want, Ashley. Tell me in the spicy words you use so well." His fingers lightly grazed her opening, his touch barely a whisper. "Tell me and I'll give you exactly what you want, Princess." He moved down her body, dropping kisses on her bare stomach and nipping at her hipbones, blowing warm breaths over the wet trail he left behind.

The sting of her teeth biting into her bottom lip and the comfort of her tongue rubbing the ring that pierced through it were the only things keeping her grounded in the moment. She wanted nothing more than to have Ryan wedged between her thighs, but words were nearly impossible to form.

"Tell me." He inched his mouth closer to her bared sex and ran his tongue from her opening up to her pulsing clit. "Mmm, say the words, baby." Need coiled in her belly. She reached between her thighs and ran her long fingers through his midnight hair before tugging firmly on the locks, letting him know what she wanted. His eyes met hers and she saw her hunger mirrored in his gaze. Words flowed from her lips like air.

"I want you, Ryan. I want to feel your mouth on my cunt, I want you to eat me like I'm the first meal you've had in years. I want you to make me come apart and when you do, I want you to know that you are the only man that has ever made me feel that way. So, fuck me, Ryan. Fuck me with your mouth, your fingers and your cock, and know that I intend to take you with me on every single ride."

His eyes flared as each erotic word dripped from her mouth. Each syllable causing visible jolts of excitement to ricochet through his body. Ashley licked her lips as she watched Ryan stroke his cock, enraptured by her verbal plea.

"Spicy enough for you?" She grinned wantonly.

"Forever, I've waited for this," he mumbled just before he released himself and ran his tongue from her seeping entrance to her swollen clit. "Mmm." As his piercing flicked her hardened bud she sent up a small prayer to the gods of tequila, who she knew were responsible for this wondrous addition to his already talented tongue.

"Oh, God, Do. Not. Stop," she pleaded as he fucked her with his fingers and cherished her with his mouth. A swarm of butterflies took flight in her belly, her thighs twitched and her core pulsed. Each time his warm tongue lapped her clit, tsunami waves crested over her. "Oh, Ry… oh…my…"

She felt him massage her sweet spot once again while sucking her pulsing clit into his mouth. The twin stimulation, along with the knowledge that it was *her* Ryan giving her this pleasure, was like the perfect storm. In the span of a few moments her world went silent, frozen with the power of the stimulation almost too much to bear, and in an instant, waves of pleasure crashed over her bathing her in bliss she had never known before.

"I've always loved watching you come apart," he mumbled pressing soft kisses up her inner thighs, her hips, and her toned tummy. "Knowing it was me that had made you look like a ravaged sex goddess always brought out the caveman in me…guess it still does." He slid up her body, rubbing his fully erect cock against her belly.

Ashley ran her hands up the muscled arms of the man leaning over her. While her climax had been unbelievable, she wanted more. She'd never tired of him when they were younger, and she'd never tire of him now...not ever. "Honey, while misguided, your caveman protection was the only way you knew how to love back then. That's not the case now, so bring on the caveman, Ryan, I want it...I crave it." Her hand left his arm and traveled quickly from his shoulder to his chest, down his abs to his raging hard on.

"Oh...fuck, Ash." His groan was guttural as she watched his eyes flutter closed.

"Lie down, honey, let me show you how Wilma treats Fred." As if all of his strength had magically disappeared, his body gracefully poured to the floor. Like a panther, Ashley stalked on all fours to settle between his legs making sure her eyes never left his. Her hands skated along his bare flesh, moving slowly over each ripple of taut muscle. Her lips followed closely behind with teasing licks and naughty nips.

She kissed his lush, full lips, taking the bottom one into her mouth and sucking it between her teeth. "I love you, Ryan." It was a simple statement that needed no more words attached. His hands cupped her face and his hooded eyes turned serious.

"Ashley, the love I feel for you runs so deep, so strong and so true that it's hard to breathe when you're not around—hearing that you feel the same way...God. I would go through all of these years of pain all over again knowing that we'd end up here together, right now."

"Oh, Romeo." She dipped her lips to his once more kissing the mouth that had given her the words to soothe her soul. She moved smoothly to his ear then to his neck. She ran her tongue from his neck down to his beautiful tattooed chest and as she played with the ring that scored his nipple, she felt his deft fingers unhooking her bra.

"I need to feel all of you against all of me, baby," he said by way of explanation. In return, she rubbed her breasts against his warm skin. If the deep moan was any indicator, he was extremely happy with her moves. She continued her journey down his long body until she rested between his strong legs.

She stroked his impressive erection, loving the weight of it in her hand. "Mmm." She licked her lips and pumped his length, her smile widening when his breathing labored.

"Princess, please." His hoarse plea brought fresh moisture to her already drenched pussy.

"Please what, Ryan? I wanna hear you ask for what you want." She teased him by mimicking his earlier command. "I wanna hear you use your dirty words, honey. You know they turn me on."

"Fuck," he roared. "Princess, put my dick in your mouth and suck it down. I want your lips around me, I wanna feel your tongue. Baby, please suck my cock." His body tensed the moment her tongue touched the sensitive head of his erection. "Ah…" He released a pent up breath as she pulled him slowly into her warm wet mouth and hissed as her tongue laved the sensitive spot just underneath the head. His fingers twisted through her long silken locks as she fucked his dick with her mouth with all the hunger of a starved woman, and the tenderness only true love could possess.

"Ashley," he moaned. "Princess, you need to stop, baby, I'm gonna come." But she didn't want to stop, she wanted him in her mouth, and she wanted to give him everything he'd given to her. He writhed underneath her.

"Ash, please baby." His pleas were different, like he actually *wanted* her to pull away. So she did.

Confusion must have shown on her face because Ryan quickly palmed her cheek, gaining her complete attention. "No, Princess, I love everything you're doing to me," he chuckled, "maybe a little too much. I don't wanna come in your mouth this first time, baby, I want to come in you, with you. Okay?"

"I want that too, Romeo," she sighed happily. He reached for her, placing his hand behind her head, and slammed his lips to hers. Their kiss was not gentle, sweet, or kind. It was hungry, and it was ravenous.

They sank deep into each other as their bodies wound tightly together. Ryan lowered them to the ground, side by side, mouths still joined, and pushed her knees apart with his thigh. His fingers quickly found their way to her hot core and he inserted two into her with ease.

"So ready for me. I love that, Princess."

"I was made for you, Ryan," she whimpered as his thumb rubbed circles over her engorged bud. Climax quickly rippled through her body, robbing her of thought and breath. When she floated down from her orgasm-induced haze she looked at him through hooded eyes.

"Nothing more incredible." He said on a heavy breath as he palmed her naked skin causing goose bumps rise under his touch.

"Ry, I want you. I want you inside me. Make love to me." Her short sentences were the result of both breathlessness and an overwhelming desire to be joined with this man. His voice was low and thick with lust. "I have to go get protection, baby." She reached out to stop him before he moved to get up.

"You know I'm on the pill...the question is, how careful were you during 'Operation Piss Off Princess?'" While she meant for the question to be light-hearted, she could tell by the way his brows furrowed that she had struck a nerve unintentionally.

"Ashley, my heart has *always* belonged to you. I've never had an encounter with a woman where I haven't been properly protected—not once, not ever." His tone told her that he spoke the truth and she knew exactly what she wanted.

"Then nothing between us, Ryan." His nostrils flared when her meaning became clear.

"Are you sure?"

"Nothing between us ever again," she clarified and brought his face closer to her own. His weight felt amazing pressed up against her naked skin and she melted underneath him, his kisses turning her to liquid while his touches set her ablaze.

"More, Ryan," she begged. "Please, please...more."

Her pleas were like a lighter to a gas tank, each one igniting a spark while Ryan waited for the motherfucker to blow. He reached between them and placed his hardness at her opening and Ashley lifted her hips to drive him in. Flames exploded around him and his mind melted, not just at the feeling of being inside of his woman but being inside her bareback. He thanked God he'd only ever experienced this with her before, and now with her again. This was what men fought for—what they died for. This was heaven. This was him and Ashley.

He rocked into her and felt her tight walls grip him as he kissed her breasts, her neck, and her sweet lips.

"Ash, I fucking love you."

Her legs wrapped tightly around his waist, clasped at the ankles, and she lifted her hips to pull him in even deeper. They both groaned. Faster, he pumped into her and the sting of her nails scoring his back turned him on even more.

He growled when she licked at the sweat that ran down his neck. He could feel his release brewing at the base of his spine, and his balls pulled up tight against his body, so he reached between their joined torsos and grazed her sensitive clit.

"Oh, oh, God, fuck, Ryan…"

"Let go, Ash, give it to me. One more, baby, let me have one more." Her walls tightened around his shaft as she blew apart, bringing him with her. A perfect union. No, a perfect *reunion*.

TAKING ANOTHER LOG from the pile and throwing it onto the fire, Ryan fanned the flames while Ashley lay snuggled on the floor, wrapped in one of the many blankets they had put down at the beginning of the night. He watched out of the corner of his eyes as she pulled her bottom lip into her teeth, her gaze firmly on his ass.

"Staring again, Princess?" He taunted.

"Ryan, I'm never gonna not stare. You are male perfection, and you're all mine. Now get back over here. I'm cold." She lifted the blanket and he slid in next to her. As his naked body touched hers it sent a shiver through her.

"Come closer, Princess. Geez, you *are* cold. Come here, let me warm you up."

"So smooth with the ladies, Romeo," she teased and his body tensed.

"Listen to me, Ashley." He lifted up on his forearm, and used his other hand to take her chin between his thumb and index finger. "I fucked up, I know I did, but there are some things I think you need to know—"

"Ryan," she cut him off. "It's okay. What you did when we weren't a couple is your own business. I was wrong to bring it up, and I won't do it again." Regret filled her eyes.

"No, you need to hear me out." When he was certain that he had her attention, he moved his hand from her chin down to her arm, sliding his fingers up and down her soft flesh, and then stopping periodically to trace the "*Leo*" tattoo on her bicep.

"Did I sleep around this past year? Yes, I did, but I didn't hook up with as many women as you think. I couldn't, Ash, because I only wanted you. It was childish and asinine, but true. The nights I didn't come home I crashed at Kyle's on his filthy, germ-infested couch. So," he shrugged, "in essence, maybe I did sleep with people those nights too."

They both laughed before Ryan continued. "I stayed out because I was drunk, and I knew if I came home I'd make a fool of myself. Not once did I stay the night at some random chick's place."

He saw the questions in her eyes, "I never wanted to give any woman the impression that what we had was anything other than sex. Does that make me an asshole? Yeah, I guess, but the only woman's bed I wanted to wake up in was yours." Ashley's mouth opened in what Ryan assumed would be a classic Ashley rebuttal.

"I know, I know," He jumped in like he was reading her mind, "I was a dick, parading women around to make you jealous." He squirmed under her narrow gaze. "I can't change what I did. And I know it sounds like I'm trying to make it seem less disgusting, but, really, I'm not. I've been a whore but you'll never know how sorry I am. What I did with those girls was never based on love—not once, not ever—and I need you to believe that. It was just me trying to move on from the only woman who has ever owned my heart. Please, tell me you can get past that?" The tension slowly left his body as Ashley gave an understanding nod.

Leaning forward, she gently kissed his lips and smiled. "Yeah, Ry, I can get past that. I'm already over it. So let's let it go. Okay?"

Lying on his side behind her, they both watched the dancing flames of the fire. The grandfather clock that stood in the corner struck five, as his eyelids grew heavy. So much had happened in the past twelve hours, so much damage, so much destruction, and so much pain, but things had also begun to heal and for that small favor he would be forever grateful.

"Ry?"

"Hmm?" He wasn't yet asleep but he was emotionally and physically spent from the events of the day.

"Is *Danny's* really gone?" He felt the pain that laced

her question.

"No, Princess, just the building is." He placed a soft kiss on the round of her shoulder. "Buildings can be replaced, and as soon as the weather clears up we'll help Danny rebuild." The rain and winds whipped around outside and aside from the incandescence in front of them, the house remained in darkness. "But right now, baby, let's try to get some sleep, okay?"

"Okay, honey." She wiggled her bare skin closer to him and he felt her body relax when sleep finally claimed her.

CHAPTER THIRTY-EIGHT

Destruction And A Bet

"OH GOD." JANIE'S voice was filled the emotions that everyone else was feeling but were too stunned to verbalize. It had been twenty-four hours since Hurricane Leo had hit Charistown with its one/two punch before making its way up the coast to take on its next opponent. Ryan, Ashley, Max, Janie, and Lyla had agreed to meet Danny and Julie at the wreckage so they could all deal with the tragedy together.

"Come here, sweetheart," Danny grumbled. His red-rimmed eyes, accented with purple smudges, suggested how little sleep he'd had the night before. He extended his hand to a quietly sobbing Ashley. Wrapped tightly in Ryan's arms, she gave him a loving squeeze before walking over to Danny and Julie. They enveloped her in an embrace that to any outsider would look like parents consoling their child and together they mourned their loss.

A few minutes elapsed and the embrace between three expanded to include, Max, Janie, and Ryan, all forming a circle around the couple who had become so much more than employers over the years.

"Lyla, girl, get your ass over here. You know this

family isn't complete without you." Clearly Danny's cracked voice held no less authority than normal because with no more than a loud sniff, Lyla slowly walked through the sodden rubble to her family and melded into their warmth.

Pulling away, Ryan looked around the dilapidated wreckage. "Hey, where the hell is Kyle?" No one had seen or heard from Kyle in days, which was strange in its own right, but after such a big storm where it was public knowledge that *Danny's on Main* had been destroyed, even Kyle should have checked in. "Look, I know he's been off—getting worse for months, even—but this isn't like him." As if on cue, Danny's cell phone rang.

"Hello, this is Danny." The group was quiet as Danny spoke to the caller. It quickly became clear by the look on Danny's face that the news he was hearing wasn't good. "Motherfucker. Yeah, Nixon, uh huh, I understand. But he's breathin' on his own, yes?"

"Who's Nixon?" Lyla whispered to Max.

"Kyle's younger brother, now shh."

"Okay, boy, I hear ya. No, I'll tell everyone. When can he have visitors? Yep." Danny continued to listen and answer briefly. "You got it, Nix. Anything you need, son, okay? Nixon Marx, listen up boy, he's my family, which means you are too, so hear me when I say, *anything you need*, got it? Okay. I'll call you later. Bye, Nix."

When Danny ended the call, he closed his eyes and absently shook his head. The room stayed quiet, as if everyone decided to give Danny a moment to clear his head, without ever having to discuss it.

"Honey," Julie lovingly stroked his forearm, "what did Nixon want? Where's Kyle?" Ashley felt her insides tighten—a cub scout couldn't have tied a better knot. Danny and Julie were standing in the middle of what used to be their livelihood, they'd lost everything in the last forty-eight hours and now, Danny had the weight of something else on his broad, but not unbreakable, shoulders. He needed her. No, he needed *all* of them. They were a team, a family.

"Danny, talk to us. We may be like your children, but we're adults. Let us help you for a change." As the words left her mouth, Ashley felt strength firing in her blood. This was her time—her time to put away the past, and start moving on in the present in all aspect of her life. *Reach for the Light.* She felt warmth in Leo's words and the strength in those around her.

"Fuck, I don't know how to tell you all this—especially the two of you," Danny shot a quick look to Ryan who now had Ashley wrapped tight in his arms.

"Kyle got into a car accident last night. They found his car wrapped around an electrical pole. According to the paramedics who first responded, he was semi-conscious when they first arrived but, he was also pretty goddamn drunk. Once they were able to get him on the stretcher, he went unconscious and hasn't woken up since. Nix said that in Kyle's case, being drunk probably saved his life because his body was so limber it just kind of went with the flow of the car. He never tightened up, never fought it."

Danny shook his head in what appeared to be sorrowful disgust. "That boy is tempting death every single day and this time death nearly won. Jesus Christ. You should have heard the list of things damaged or broken in that boy. Nix has been at the hospital all night. Kyle has had two emergency surgeries. Nix sounds beat." He turned to

Julie, "We should head up there, sweetheart. There's nothing we can do to this place today."

"Of course, Danny, but you didn't tell us, where did the accident happen?" Julie questioned.

"He was on his way back from Bethlehem."

"Fuck!" Max groaned pinching the bridge of his nose with his finger and thumb, and sent a look of understanding in Danny and Julie's direction.

"What the hell is in Bethlehem?" Lyla asked a question that not only Janie, but Ryan and Ashley also, had no answer for.

"I'm sorry, Ly, I just can't tell you that." Max pulled Janie close to his chest and kissed the top of her head. "I hate to fall back on the standard answer, but it's not my story to tell."

"Christ." Lyla shoved her hands in her leather jacket. "We could write not just one book but a whole damn series when you put all of our shit together. Fine, don't share, but is he okay?" There was no misreading the depth of the sincerity in her question.

"He will be, Lyla girl," Danny mumbled.

"Ahem." Julie cleared her throat in a loud and purposeful fashion.

"Jules," Danny grumbled, a smirk creeping across his handsome face. "You can't possibly be thinking about our bet now, while all hell is breaking loose in our lives?"

"Danny Marcus," Julie grinned, wiping the last stray tear from her cheek. "You, my sweet husband, have always preached about finding the silver lining when the skies are at their darkest and here it is buddy. Now pay up. The rest of you too. Don't think you can get away with stiffing the boss lady."

The confusion that marred Ryan's sexy face was comforting to Ashley because she had no freaking idea what the hell was going on around her. "Ry?" She asked, but he shrugged his shoulders and they both watched silently as Danny, Max, Janie, and Lyla each slapped a twenty-dollar bill into Julie's waiting palm.

"What the fuck, guys?" Ryan pulled Ashley closer to his body. She went willingly, loving how his innate protective instinct reappeared overnight.

"Son, no need to get upset." Danny wrapped both arms around his wife. "Julie, here won the bet, that's all."

"The *bet*?" Ashley sputtered through barely contained giggles.

"Yeah, she said you guys would find your way back to each other during the storm. Something about a 'Power Party'? We all thought she was crazy."

Julie laughed. "Not looking so crazy anymore am I?" Her gaze leveled on Ashley. "Pedicures on me, Spicy girl."

The solemn mood was lifted slightly as the seven of them carefully maneuvered their way out of the mess that was once *Danny's*, and headed to the hospital to see their friend.

CHAPTER THIRTY-NINE

REALLY Thankful

"I CAN'T BELIEVE we're having a real Thanksgiving dinner, here at *our* house, as a couple, with *our* family." Ashley's face ached from all the smiling she had done since waking up before the sun to start preparing for their feast. It was late morning and the two of them were moving in what looked like a well-practiced dance around their kitchen, even though this was the first home cooked dinner party they had ever prepared together.

"I know, Princess." Ryan slid behind her and as his hard frame pressed up against her back he twirled satiny strands of her gold and pink-streaked hair around his fist and pressed his lips firmly against the nape of her neck. "This is everything I've ever wanted."

His murmured words sent goose bumps down her arms as his fingers slid over her shoulders to her firm full breasts. He could feel the warmth of her skin radiating through the fabric of the thin sleep cami as he rolled her puckered nipples between his index finger and his thumb.

After a mere teasing touch, he let one hand continue down the firm contours of her tummy and straight beneath her boxers. His thick middle finger slid between the sensitive folds of her most intimate place and moisture coated the digit while he slowly pumped in and out of her greedy body.

"Mmm, Princess, you're so wet and ready for me."

"Ah, that feels so…so nice." Her head fell back lazily against his chest as he sunk two fingers in and out of her warm, wet pussy.

"Ashley, baby, I'm not looking for nice," he growled as his thumb rubbed circles over her pulsing clit. "I'm looking for *great*, *wow*, or *so fucking good*, but nice? No, Princess, *nice* isn't gonna work." He quickly spun her around and yanked the boxers down her legs.

"Ryan," she giggled as arousal spiked through her body sending fresh wetness between her thighs. Before she could say another word her feet were lifted from the ground and her naked ass was planted firmly on the cool, smooth granite countertop. Ryan sat before her on a barstool, pure unadulterated hunger and determination glimmering in his chocolate eyes. His big hands parted her knees as he leaned forward and pulled her closer to his mouth. When he licked his bottom lip, her body melted.

She could smell her own arousal and by the look in his eyes, she knew the fragrance was affecting Ryan too. Hunger seeped into his gaze as he inhaled deeply and licked his bottom lip once again before taking her into his mouth. He ran his tongue from slit to clit, collecting her moisture and swallowing it down.

He'd told her often how he loved having her in his mouth, on his tongue, weaving through all of his senses. She was like the blood that pumped through his veins, vital to his survival. Back when they were teenagers she laughed off his romantic musings, but since being back together, she realized that everything he said was true. Every time they were together she felt his energy flowing through her and she knew that he was her soul mate in every way.

"Oh, fuck, Ry..." Her whimpers were his inspiration. Nuzzling her engorged nub, he slid his fingers, knuckle deep, into her core, stroking her sweet spot and making her writhe against his hand while she called out his name. She pulsed around his fingers, coating them in fresh sweet cream as she continued to fuck his face, searching for the release that was only a breath way.

"Give it to me, Princess, let go," he demanded gently as he pressed his tongue firmly to her clit using his fingers to coax another climax from her. She felt her legs shaking and her breaths were shallow as moans left her body quickly without her permission. She palmed her breasts and squeezed her nipples as her climax built in her body like a fireball.

"Fuck, Ryan, I'm gonna come..." She screamed her release as she pressed herself against his face one last time.

Her sated body felt boneless as Ryan lifted her off the counter and carried her to the sofa. He placed a kiss on her lips as he lowered her to the cushions and smiled. "Well, Princess, how was that? *Nice* enough for ya?"

"Not bad, Ry," she giggled, "not bad at all."

As a dark scowl crossed his face and she couldn't help but laugh at his expression. Glaring at her was the most beautiful man she had ever seen, standing there looking down at her like a panther stalking his prey. Dressed in sweatpants and a vintage Aerosmith concert t-shirt, he looked downright edible and she was hungry. She slinked her arms around his hips and brought him closer to her.

She lifted her gaze from the arousal in his sweats to his sexy face standing far above her.

"Ryan, I have so many things to be thankful for this year and all of them lead me back to you. I promise to give the emotional Thanksgiving speech later, but right now, I just want to show you how grateful I am."

———————————•

Mesmerized by her hazel eyes he lowered himself to the couch and pulled the chenille blanket over their partially naked bodies.

"Princess"—Ashley snuggled closely to his body, her legs tangled in his as her hand ran up his torso—"I can't begin to tell you how thankful I am for you." His normally smooth voice was rough with emotion as he spoke around the lump forming in his throat.

"I would have enjoyed anything we did for Thanksgiving as long as I was in the same room with you, but spending it together, with you, as your..." he paused, waited a breath and then continued, "boyfriend, is fucking amazing. I love you, Ashley, There is nothing in the world I am more grateful for than you."

"Romeo," Her eyes filled with tears and her voice thick with feeling, "you always say the most wonderful things." Then, true to form, she added, "Do you write this shit down ahead of time?" Deciding that they'd done enough talking, Ryan launched himself at her, pinning her beneath him and using his talented fingers to tickle her ribs while she squirmed and gasped for breath.

"Ryan," she laughed gasping for air, "I'm gonna pee myself, you have to stop...please!"

"Okay, Princess, I'll stop." Obeying her command he slipped his tongue in her mouth and started a torture of a whole different kind, one that neither of them had any desire to stop.

CHAPTER FORTY

Unconditional Love

"SERIOUSLY, ASH, DOES he always walk around that way? Or is he doing it just for our benefit?" Lyla stared at a shirtless Ryan as he made his fourth round-trip from the basement with the final box of Christmas decorations.

Ashley giggled at her friend's dry humor. "Hey, Jane, you're sitting closer to her, do you wanna wipe that small spot of drool off her chin?"

"Oh, screw you, Ash," Lyla whispered without any anger. "You know his body is like a work of art."

"Of course she knows my body's hot," Ryan said as he walked over to the sofa and placed a soft kiss on the top of Ashley's head. "In fact, I think she decided to name each of my abs." Ryan winked at a wide-eyed Lyla before he chuckled and headed upstairs for a shower, leaving the women to continue their coffee therapy.

"You guys seem so happy together." Janie beamed. "I'm so glad you finally, you know...worked everything out." Ashley wrapped her hands around her mug. The past month and a half had been the happiest she had ever been.

"I am happy, girls. I'm really happy."

"EVERYTHING WAS DELICIOUS as usual, Julie. Thank you so much for having us all for Christmas dinner." Ashley tucked a green streak of hair behind her ear as she carried the bread basket from the dining room into the kitchen.

"Yeah, Jules, the food was fab and your tree is gorgeous." Lyla swiped her index finger through the icing on the chocolate fudge cake. "Ouch, Janie! That hurt. You didn't need to flick me in the head, you could've just asked me not to stick my finger in your cake."

"Technically, it's my birthday cake," Ashley piped up, laughing, but Lyla and Janie were already staring each other down.

"Okay, Ly," Janie smiled devilishly, "*please* don't stick your finger in my cake."

"Umm, it's my cake," Ashley interjected again.

"Ouch, stop it!" Lyla squealed when another flick followed her second swipe. Ashley laughed at the two women. It still amazed her how far they'd all come in just a year. Last year she hadn't even met Lyla and Janie and while she'd spent Christmas Eve with Danny and Julie, it had been a quiet celebration and she'd spent most of the time trapped in her own thoughts. And Christmas day—her birthday—was spent mostly alone and then with Danny and Julie for a small dinner. Even Ryan had gone home to see his father. Everything was so different now.

"Speaking of *gorgeous*..." Julie's statement intruded upon Ashley's thoughts. "Tell us about the gorgeous boy you brought with you tonight, Ms. Dalton." Julie herded the women to the kitchen table so they could speak freely without the threat of being overheard by the men, who were now settled in the family room having after-dinner drinks.

"Honestly, there's nothing to tell." Lyla occasionally brought what she liked to refer to as *strays* around to family dinners. While she claimed she did it because the men had nowhere else to be, Ashley assumed it was because almost everyone else was paired up leaving Lyla and Kyle the odd ones out.

Even though Lyla's walls were up and she was always standing guard, Ashley noticed the sometimes far-off lonely look in Lyla's sky blue eyes. "Rick's nice, he's great in bed and he's harmless. We'll use each other for a little while and then move on without hurt feelings when it's over. No biggie." Her shrugged shoulders may have seemed nonchalant, but Ashley could sense Lyla felt something else entirely and it pained her to not only feel it but to realize there was nothing she could do about it.

"What about Gage?" Ashley blurted. "It looked pretty damn steamy between you guys for a bit and then what...?" Was she imagining the pale pink flush that rose in Lyla's cheeks?

"Gage is, well...he's..." Ashley had seen Lyla Dalton in all kinds of moods, states, and situations, but never had she seen her in a state of speechless fluster.

"He's what, Ly?" Janie goaded their friend with a light elbow to the side.

"For the love of chocolate, Jane, if you lay a hand on me one more time tonight, I'm gonna twat-pop you! We clear?" When Janie acknowledged the open threat, Lyla continued to explain her relationship with the sexy and illusive Sebastian Gage.

"He's sexy as hell, okay, I'm a big girl and I can admit it. But the man comes and goes. He's like the fucking wind." She flipped her sable hair over her shoulder and sighed. "And it's fine. I'm not looking for anything thing serious." Ashley wasn't sure who Lyla was trying to convince with that little speech, but it certainly wasn't convincing her.

"Hell," Lyla continued, "I'm not looking for anything more than a night or two. But Gage says he won't give me that. So as far as I'm concerned, he can keep blowing past 'cause I don't need any boy drama in my life."

Danny bellowed from the family room bringing an end to the girly chat. "Ladies, get your fine behinds in here. It's time to open presents."

Flames crackled in the fireplace and the Christmas music playing softly in the background enveloped the group in warmth and love that could only come from being around honest love and friendship—a family made of choice, not of force.

Sitting on the plush rug that backed up against the soft leather sofa, Ryan leaned forward and placed another soft kiss on the top of Ashley's head. Her sweet scent traveled up his nostrils and splintered like a firecracker in a hundred directions through his body. With her sitting between his legs it was hard to hide the affect she had on him.

So when she shimmied herself backward, closer to

the apex of his hardening center, and giggled nonchalantly at a comment Max had made, Ryan knew she was playing a little game with him. She was throwing down the gauntlet. Warmth ebbed through his body as he leaned forward, breathing in her citrusy smell. She wiggled herself a little closer. *Oh yeah, she started this game, but I'm gonna finish it,* he thought to himself smugly.

"Keep it up, Princess," he whispered huskily in her ear, "because I have no problem with lifting you over my shoulder and leaving right now. I'll fuck you in the car, in the snow, hell, in the goddamn street—anywhere just to see if you're still giggling when my cock is plunging in and out of your sweet cunt."

Her gasp was inaudible but he didn't miss it, he couldn't. Her chest rose and fell at the same time that goose bumps lined the skin of her arms. Nipping at her ear, he heard the faintest whimper and knew his sexy words combined with his nearness probably had her all keyed up and wanting.

"I can smell you, Ash. I can practically taste your anticipation," his low voice was barely a whisper, "so keep giggling, I dare you."

"Ahem, I know you all wanna get home and get to your own gift giving," Danny cleared his voice and chuckled, "but Julie and I have a little something we'd like to give each of you before we go our separate ways." Ryan watched as Danny linked his fingers with Julie's and twirled her closer to him. They were his idea of the perfect couple, so much like his parents were, and everything he aspired to be if he and Ashley ever got married.

Julie handed small wrapped boxes to Max and Janie, Ashley and Ryan, and Lyla. There was one box left that had Kyle's name written on the tag.

"While I'm pretty sure you each know how Danny and I feel about you, I know for a fact that you can never hear enough how loved and appreciated you are." Julie's eyes glowed with the dancing flames in the fireplace and shimmered with tears. Ashley felt her throat tighten as Julie continued to speak.

"We love each of you as if you were our own children. While the three of you—she addressed Max, Ryan, and Ashley—"have been around for many years, you two women"—she looked carefully at Janie and Lyla—"have the same unconditional love, trust and respect as if you'd been here forever. Even Kyle, who we all know has been a little difficult lately, is our son and we will love and support him in whatever way we can." Tears rolled down Julie's porcelain cheeks.

"Alright, sugar." Danny rested his big hand on Julie's petite shoulder. "What my beautiful wife is *trying* to tell you kids is that we would have never been able to make it through this past month and a half without each and every one of you. Plain and simple, you are our family."

Ryan was trying to understand what point Danny was trying to make, but he couldn't see through the emotions to understand the words. "Julie and I are going to start rebuilding *Danny's on Main* but, well…we'd like it if you were all part of the process."

CHAPTER FORTY-ONE

Queen of Hearts

"RY, I'M SHOCKED. Did you have any idea they were gonna do that?" Ashley rotated the shiny, new key between her fingers.

"No, babe, I was just as shocked as you were."

They were on their way home from the Marcus' house and were both still taken aback by the overture that Danny and Julie had made. They wanted each person in the group to be a partner in the bar—silent or otherwise. Danny explained that they didn't need the financial backing to re-open, but he wanted to make the bar a family owned and operated establishment. And they were family. He and Julie had given each person a key—more a symbolic gesture as there wasn't actually a door yet—to not just the building, but to the operation itself. If they wanted in, they would love to have them. If not? No hard feelings.

"I want in, Ry." From the moment the offer was placed on the table, Ashley knew that she wanted— needed—to be part of rebuilding her home, her life.

"Of course we're in, Princess." The complete certainty in his voice was just another reason why she loved the man sitting to her left with all of her heart.

"Ryan," her voice got smaller as she pulled in a breath. They pulled into their driveway and Ryan turned off the ignition before shifting to face Ashley. Even though he had no clue as to what she was going to say, the concern was evident on his handsome face.

"Princess, let's discuss whatever's on your mind inside. It's freezing out here and while it would be my pleasure to warm you up, I'd rather look you in the eyes while we talk about what's bothering you."

"Okay, Romeo, let's go inside."

Hearing the click of the coffee machine, Ashley poked her head into the kitchen and saw Ryan as he stood at the Keurig, staring intently at the clock on the microwave and muttering to himself. "It's 11:15, I still have plenty of time. So long as whatever she's worried about isn't horrible... "

"What, honey?" Ashley slipped behind him, skating her hands up his abdomen and over his broad chest.

"Nothing, Princess, here's your coffee." He had put the cream and sugar in her cup exactly how she liked it and by the time he'd done that, his own coffee had finished brewing. "Now, tell me what's on your mind."

Ashley sipped the hot liquid but her nerves kept her from really tasting it. Over the years they had discussed many things and in the weeks since they had been an official couple they had discussed many more, but other than the time they'd renovated the kitchen, they'd never discussed their financial situations. However, if they both wanted to buy into the bar, then it was time they did.

The problem was, how did she discuss this with Ryan without making him feel inferior? She was a bartender at the same bar and while they made good money, they certainly wouldn't have the kind of money they'd need in order to keep their house and invest in *Danny's on Main*. In addition she *needed* to invest in her future—in *their* future.

Unless...

When she left home, her father had given her access to Leo's college money. She had been using that money along with donations to fund *Leo's Lights*. However, her father had also been putting money in trust for her as well but Ashley had sworn she'd never use it. She swore her life held no value without her brother, but she was finally *reaching for the light*. It was time to start building a future, and she wanted to share it with Ryan.

"Ash?" The concern in his voice was unbridled.

"Oh, sorry, I got lost in my own thoughts for a second." The clink of her mug on the granite ricocheted through the room. His face looked serious, not sad so much, but concerned and worried. Fear gripped his lungs, making each breath a chore instead of a right. "Ry, I just want you to know that I have a lot of money. A lot of money."

"Okay...well," he exhaled, relief practically rolling off him in waves, "thanks for telling me, Princess." He looked at the clock on the microwave. "It's getting late, you ready to go up to bed?"

"Oh, shit, Ryan, that's not what I meant! And it's not even midnight, I hardly think we'll turn into pumpkins if we stay up a little longer." Exasperation had Ashley running her fingers through her hair. "Let me start over." She pulled her bottom lip between her teeth, the small hoop wavering with the movement of her tongue. She wanted to do this right, and she wasn't off to a great start.

"Ry, I know how much money we make working at

the bar, but I have a large chunk of change that's been waiting for me to"—her eyes stung and she took a breath—"start following my own heart. I may have ended up in Charistown by accident, but my heart has kept me here. I learned how to breathe in this town, how to trust in this town and my God, Ryan, I learned how to love again in this town. So when I said in the car that I want in...I meant, *I want in*. But, I want you by my side. So if you were worried about money, then don't. Worry, I mean. I—sorry, *we*, have enough to invest and carry on living here."

She looked up and expected Ryan to be confused at her rambling—she'd managed to confuse even herself a little—but instead she saw a small smile tipping the corners of his lips before he glanced at something over her shoulder. "Ryan Baker, are you even listening to me? This is important. What the fuck are you"—she turned to see what could possibly be so important behind her that he couldn't stay focused—"looking at? Oh my God, is there a spider? Ick, Ryan, you know I hate those things. Is it big?" She started to move away from where she was standing.

"Relax, Princess, just checking the time." He chuckled, taking her hand in his and lacing their fingers together as he dragged her from the kitchen toward the stairs.

"Why the hell are you smiling like that? And you've looked at the clock four times. Do you have some place better to be?" His smile was breathtaking as his eyes narrowed. She felt like he was staring straight through to her soul.

"Ashley," His skin felt so warm on hers. Absently, she followed him up the stairs while he said, "You're not the only one who's been saving their pennies. You forget I'm not just a beautiful face with a penchant for pouring mean cocktails."

She wondered if he could hear her heart as it picked up speed in her chest just from the way he was looking at her. The exaggerated wink and the way his pierced brow lifted in question made her want to melt into a puddle at his feet but just as quickly as his flirt came on, it was swept away by the serious look that overtook his eyes.

"Ashley, when I came to Charistown you knew I was selling my songs to record labels and, baby, that hasn't changed. Between royalties and new songs, I've been collecting steady paychecks for years. My landlord"—Ryan pulled her close to him so their bodies touched—"wouldn't let me pay for more than a small kitchen renovation and monthly rent. So, I'm set to go. I'm all in." His knuckles gently grazed her chin lifting it up so her eyes met his. "Okay?"

Relief flooded her body. *He's all in*, she thought. *This is really happening. We are really happening.* She smiled at Ryan only to catch him looking at the time…again!

"Ryan, again with the clock! What the fuck? It's really starting to piss me off. What's going on?" With their hands still joined Ryan led her to their bed and sat her on the edge. The relaxed stance he held only moments before had been replaced with shoulders tight with tension, sitting atop of a rod straight spine. "Ryan?"

"Ashley, baby, it's Christmas Eve. I know you've always hated having your birthday on Christmas because you feel like you get gypped on both occasions—and in your family, with your parents, you did. But, Princess, I want you to know that will never be the case again. I would like to give you your Christmas present right now and your birthday present tomorrow. Is that okay?"

A familiar box came into sight as Ryan lifted it out of the night table drawer. Confusion clouded Ashley's thoughts. It was the same box he had given her when she'd left Miami seven years previously. A box she had never opened but also never discarded. A gift that had, like her heart, stayed shut tight.

"Ryan," she whispered hoarsely, "I don't...I don't understand. When did you find this? I've had it hidden for years."

"Princess, I've known where this box was since the first week I moved in." He shrugged, seemingly unembarrassed by his snooping. "But I took it a few weeks ago. I need for you to open this, Ash. I need for you to see what you meant to me all those years ago so that I can explain what you mean to me now."

Raw need was etched in the contours of his beautiful face—a desire so deep that she wanted to reach into his chest to massage his beating heart. She wanted to promise him that everything would be all right, but instead she opened the aged paper that covered the oblong box.

"Oh, Ryan, it's so beautiful." Tears stung her eyes as she withdrew the gold necklace from its velvet bed. The dainty diamond-encrusted princess crown had tiny pink topaz stones at the top of each point and a small round diamond hung proudly from the center. Words failed her as she fingered the delicate gift that was meant as a token of love for a teenage girl but was now an important link to a past that she, as a grown woman, had tried to forget.

"Ryan," she croaked, "I love this. It's like you've given me back a piece of our past, and"—she looked down at the glimmering crown and pulled it to her chest—"I can remember us without hurting. I can feel us without the pain that has haunted me for so long."

"You've been my Princess forever, Ashley. I've loved you since the day we met. You were right when you broke up with me back then. I wasn't ready. I didn't love you *the way you deserved to be loved,* but that didn't mean I wasn't loving you with everything I had to give. It just meant that *I* wasn't enough for you—not then. When I finally found you, Ash, I figured it out. I knew who I was and who I wanted to be. But I wasn't a complete man, because I didn't have you in my life. So I waited and waited"—he grimaced as he wiped the faux sweat from his forehead—"and waited. But guess what? Even all of that time was put to good use. Because the Ashley Kynde that I found here wasn't the sweet princess I grew up with. No, she had evolved into a spicy, kind, sexy, beautiful, smart woman that I am proud to call my best friend."

It felt like the words Ryan had spoken were floating in the air, she could see each and every one of them as they drifted in front of her, cradling her heart as they sunk into her head. As he continued to speak, he unbuttoned his shirt. He started from the bottom button and worked his way up. Perplexed, she watched as his fingers deftly remove each button from its eye.

"Ryan, what are you doing?"

"I love you, Ashley. I'm in love with *all* of you—the girl that you were, and the woman that you've become. While I may call you *Princess,* you're so much more than that."

As if in slow motion, Ryan leisurely peeled open his shirt and there prominently displayed over his left pectoral was a new tattoo. The Queen of Hearts was branded upon the skin that covered his heart. Bright hues of color topped each point of the crown that rested upon her head, the same brilliant colors that had been entwined in Ashley's hair over the past handful of years. Every emotion she'd ever felt was right there, permanently etched into his skin.

She leaned in to examine the fine details of the art. Ingrained in black fine-point lines around the queen were words but before she could begin to read them, Ryan's voice pulled her out of her head and into the space they shared.

"It's 11:57, Ashley, look at me." The commanding tone of his voice told her how important her complete attention was to him. She breathed in his unique scent when he leaned forward to clasp the necklace around her neck just before he took a small step back, looking so deeply into her eyes she could swear she felt him touching her with his glance.

"Back then I loved you. You were a part of me that I didn't think I could live without." He pulled her palm to his chest and placed it over the top of the fresh ink, "Now, as you once said to me, I know I could live without you... but I never want to again. This tattoo is your Christmas gift. It's our story—it's you, and me, and it's Leo. It's Miami and *Storm Front* and Charistown and *Danny's*. It's each of us as individuals and the two of us as one. You own me, Ashley. You own me heart and soul. You're not my princess, you're the queen of my heart."

Before Ashley could formulate any sort of response, Ryan was lowering himself to one knee. As if by magic, a small black box appeared in his hand.

"Holy Shit, Ryan...what? What are you doing?"

"It's after midnight, Princess. Happy birthday. I love you, Ashley Kynde and I will never *ever* stop loving you.

Will you please do me the honor of finally becoming my wife?"

His insides were trembling as he asked the question. Not because he feared her answer, he knew she'd accept, but because he'd been waiting for what felt like forever to ask this question and he could taste it on his tongue. It tasted sweet, like honey and chocolate. It tasted like bliss. The only thing that would taste better was the heavenly sound of her acceptance.

●————————————————————●

"Oh my God, Ry...Yes. Yes! Yes, I will marry you, Ryan Baker!" Ashley cried, shaking as he placed the engagement ring on her left hand. The one-syllable word repeated over and over again through tears, both his and hers had her heart slamming into the wall of her ribs. As she laid the hand donning her new engagement ring against his chest, she knew his reaction to her answer was the same.

Her legs began to give way but, as always, he was there to catch her before she fell. "I love you. I've *always* loved you," she cried shaking as excitement filled her body.

"I know, Ash, I know. And I've always loved you...we just took the scenic route to get here, Princess. And now that we have each other, I can guarantee I will never let you go again."

His first kiss was soft but filled with intent, filled with promise. He slid his hands down her torso to the hem of her dress and whipped it up and over her head before lifting her up and lying her down in the center of their bed.

"Mmm, not playing around here are you?" Ashley

asked with a breathy tone as she shimmied out of her leggings.

"No, babe, I'm not." The lacy red bra and panty set covering very little of Ashley's body, had captured all of Ryan's attention. "I've been dying to make love to my fiancée for almost two minutes now. How long are you gonna torture a man?"

Staring at his woman dressed in nothing but scraps of red lace and his ring was the best Christmas present he could have ever wished for. His cock hardened in his slacks, begging to be released from its prison.

"Is your chest sore?" She asked through a lust filled haze, as she pointed to the new ink that he had to have gotten either last night or earlier that day when she had spent long hours at the shelter, preparing for the influx of people.

"No more than any other tattoo, baby."

"Then come here, because I need to feel you." He joined her on their bed, lying back with one arm behind his head and the other flat on the comforter. Her fingertips felt amazing on his warm skin. Every time they touched it felt like a gift. He moaned when she placed her soft kisses and long licks across his chest. He couldn't hold back the deep groan that vibrated deep in his chest when she tongued the hoop through his nipple and undid his belt at the same time.

The sound of the zipper being lowered ever so slowly made him want to scream in anticipation, but instead, he slowly lifted his hips to assist her in shedding his pants.

Just as she was about to lean in and take his hard length into her mouth she looked up at him. Her eyes were blazing, her soul was pure, and the best parts of her past were now entwined with her present. She was perfect. She was his future.

She leaned forward and licked the weeping head of his thick cock. Slowly she took him into her mouth, taking the time to lick and suck until she could take him no further.

He moaned when she hollowed her cheeks and he groaned when she took him to the back of her throat. His hands weaved through her hair encouraging her quicker pace. "Oh, Ash. Oh my...*fuck*...Ash..."

As he continued to thrust into her mouth, she used her right hand to pump his shaft as his thighs quivered with his impending release.

"Ashley," he growled, "oh, fuck, baby, I'm gonna come." She deep throated him again and then used shallow sucks and strokes until his entire world went silent. There was no sound, no sight, and no breath. When his lungs begged for air he realized he hadn't been breathing. Panting, he opened his eyes to see a very beautiful, very happy, and very horny woman licking her lips and touching herself.

———————————

"Whatcha you doing, Princess?" While the question came out lazy and sedate, she found herself on her back and under him before she had the chance to answer. "Because it looks to me like you got really worked up sucking me off, so now it's my turn to return the favor." He kissed her neck, her collarbone, and her chest and his strong hands cupped her breasts just as his face leaned in to inhale her cleavage. "Fuck, you always smell amazing,

Ash."

Lost in his dark eyes, she felt her bra loosen from the back as a smirk pulled up one side of his mouth. His tongue drew circles around her tightened nipple, the sensations heightened by the small metal bar pierced through it. "Christ, Ash, your tits are incredible." His dirty words turned her on almost as much as each sensual touch. "Your body is perfection, every single inch of it." His hands skated over her breasts to her taut abdomen. "One day, when you have our babies, your body is gonna be even more perfect."

Snickering, Ashley covered his hands with her own. "My belly won't look like this after having babies, Ry."

Shaking his head, "What I'm saying is, it won't matter if you're no longer cut with muscle or exactly how you are now, because you will always be perfect for me." His thumbs hooked the sides of her panties and dragged them down her long legs. The ragged hitch of his breath was the sexiest sound she'd ever heard, but not nearly as delectable as the look in his eyes when he took in her naked form, lying in wait on the bed beneath him.

"I want you Ryan, I need you inside me." Her desire for this man knew no bounds and she had a feeling it never would. His mere presence turned her on, a fact made evident when his fingertips made their way down her torso to the juncture between her legs.

"Baby, you're already so wet, you're dripping." His fingers glistened with her arousal. "Mmm, you taste amazing." He licked her juices off his fingers before inserting them back into her drenched pussy. The slight brush of his thumb over her pulsing clit had her mewling with need. Her body was already primed from blowing him, and she was euphoric from the proposal and his beautiful words. She was a firecracker ready to burst—all she needed was a spark, and good thing for her, Ryan Baker was the match.

"Please, Ryan. Please."

"Please, what, Ash?" He taunted as his fingers pulsed in and out of her wet heat, bringing her closer and closer to the edge. "You want me to make you come, baby?" Without waiting for a response Ryan dipped his head down between her thighs and licked her slit with the flat of his tongue. Her loud moans were unconstrained and pleading as he plunged two fingers into her opening and gently pulled her clit between his teeth.

"God, Ash, your pussy is so fucking sweet." Tremors traveled through her body, shaking her limbs and catching her breath. Her climax was so close, so damn close. She shamelessly rubbed her core against his face as she sought the ultimate release. As he licked at her clit he sunk his fingers into her once more, hitting just the right spot at just the perfect time.

As her body shook and her insides quaked, Ryan slid his hard cock into her magnificent wet heat. "Oh, Ry. Yes, thank God, honey." She purred in appreciation when his hand slipped between them and massaged the small bundle of nerves at the top of her sex. With a strangled moan, Ashley squeezed her ankles tighter around his back and came apart at the same time Ryan rode to his own incredible climax.

And together they finally found their happiness.

After the storm and into the light.

EPILOGUE

"GOD, YOU LOOK like shit, man."

"Ryan, don't be an ass." Ashley pulled her bottom lip between her teeth trying to come up with a better adjective to describe the sight in front of her. "Kyle, you don't look like shit, you look…" she paused, "you look better than the last time we saw you."

"Nice save there, Princess." Ryan chuckled, roping his arm around her shoulders. It was New Year's Eve day, Ashley and Ryan were visiting Kyle who had just arrived back to his apartment from his prolonged stay with Nixon in Philadelphia.

"Knock, knock!" Janie announced as she and Max entered the apartment. "We come bearing food."

"Ugh, and cleaning supplies. It's fucking disgusting in here," Lyla said, pinching her nose and wafting her hand through the air.

"Seriously, open the windows—and get rid of the dead body."

"People, give the poor man a break, he's been gone for almost two months, so of course this place smells like shit." Ashley kissed Kyle's whiskered cheek. "It's great to have you back."

"I hate to break it to you, babe," Ryan grinned, "but this isn't much worse than what the place smelled like before."

"Dude, fuck off." Kyle lazily flipped Ryan the finger before letting his head drop to the back of the sofa.

Ashley had visited Kyle a few times over the past month and a half, and each time she left him she'd hoped that the next visit would show more improvement. While his cuts and bones were mending, he still seemed so off, so sad and broken. Uncertain as to what it was that he needed, she'd tried to make herself useful without becoming overbearing. Kyle, like the rest of them, had his skeletons and sometimes they came out to play. He had always managed to shove them back in the closet but over the past year, she—along with everyone else—had noticed his decline. She wanted do what she could to help him get through his dark period, starting now.

"So at the risk of getting tomatoes thrown at my head, or worse, Lyla mixing cocktails for me," Ashley fake shuddered, "how about if we girls go about cleaning this shithole...oops, I mean *apartment* up and let the guys do some bonding?"

"I'm all for that," Janie agreed easily.

"Sure, but I'm not going near the bathroom," Lyla announced. Ryan shot Ashley an appreciative glance and the women dispersed, leaving the three men huddled together by the sofa.

———————●———————

"Dude, seriously, how are you feeling?" Ryan twisted his hands together. His friend's bruised face wasn't the only thing that was raising red flags. Kyle, whose demeanor had changed over the past year—between the excessive boozing and rapid mood swings—had Ryan certain there was more than just an alcohol addiction to be dealt with.

"Ky, at the risk of sounding like the women"—Max looked behind him to make sure none of them were within ear shot—"we're your family, man. Talk to us. What the hell is going on with you?"

Kyle grimaced as he tried to reposition his body on the sofa. Not an easy task, with a cast on his left leg and another on his right arm.

He glanced out the window, and a faraway look settled over his face. "I'm not okay. I'm not ready to go there yet, but I know I'm not okay." Ryan bit the inside of his mouth to avoid probing his friend for answers he was clearly not ready to give. Quietly Kyle continued to speak, "And then there's *her*. She comes to me every night."

He scrubbed his left hand over his beard. "Every fucking night, man. She's fucking radiant, with her flaming red hair and her whisky eyes. She whispers to me, begs me to hold on. She tells me that this world is better with me in it and it's time to fight, and then she floats away like a fucking...Christ, I don't know an angel? Maybe? It sounds insane, I know, but when I go to sleep, she's there. I've seen her. I can smell her, she smells like gardenias. And I swear, she's the only reason I didn't die in that accident."

Ryan studied and watched in awe as a lone tear slowly trickled down his friend's cheek. "Fuck," Kyle griped, swiping the wetness away with his fist. "These meds are making my eyes water. How about if someone gets me a beer?"

"Dude," Max stared at Kyle with stern eyes, "you're on pretty heavy drugs. I don't think you should be drinking."

Kyle growled, "Max, if I needed a mother, I'd have asked for mine. Now get me a beer or shall I get up and get it myself?"

Conceding, Max left and returned shortly after with the drink. "Here's your beer, you stubborn fuck. Just know that you are going to crash again—I just hope you're lucky to survive another brush with death, you arrogant asshole." Max slammed the bottle down on the table, called for Janie, and hastily left Kyle's apartment.

Ryan watched in silence as Kyle took a few deep breaths and then opened the beer. Within a couple of gulps the bottle was empty. Max wasn't wrong. Kyle was going down and whether or not he would get back up was anyone's guess.

Kyle Marx was suffocating in a hell created for him long ago. One he couldn't seem to escape, and didn't believe he should. A bent man, he looked for temporary reprieve any way he could get it. What Kyle had yet to realize was that merely surviving wasn't good enough, and bending only gets you so far. Sometimes, the mold needs to shatter in order for change to take place...

Sometimes you have to break, so you can breathe.

Book 3 in the

THE CHARISTOWN SERIES

BREAKING to Breathe

ACKNOWLEDGMENTS

I REMEMBER WRITING the acknowledgement page(s) for *Thursday Nights* and feeling so blessed for both the people and the MIRACLE that took place in order for that book to have gotten written and published so... beautifully. Yes, it was difficult learning the process, that first time around, but in my ignorance to the way things worked, I was blinded to how hard it would be to not just repeat the process but to make it even better the second time around. I learned quickly, it was NO miracle at work the first time. It was AMAZING people helping me to learn the ropes and this second time...wow...even they rocked my world.

Storm Front WOULD NOT be here in your hands if not for the people I'm about to mention. Each of them truly made the words appear on the pages, whether it is through inspiration, editing, support, understanding, love, and/or laughter. My gratitude is endless...so is this list... sorry ;)

When *Thursday Nights* was first released I was a basket case. My words, my heart and soul were out—exposed for all the world to see and it was...well...scary as hell. The only thing that could have been scarier than people reading my story, was people NOT reading my story. But, thanks to **Brandee Veltri** – from **Brandee's Book Endings,** *Thursday Nights* kicked off with a grand blog tour that landed my story on the pages of so many incredible blogs. Through those blogs, I found people who enjoyed my book and who I quickly got to know and adore on a much deeper lever. After almost a year, I can say a lot of the strangers I met through TN's blog tour, are now much adored friends.

It would be virtually impossible for me to name all of the blogs that have supported both *Thursday Nights* and me, as an author, over the past year. I can say, however, that I am and will be eternally grateful to every single one of you. You have shared my words, my sales, my teasers and my general silliness time and time again. I wouldn't be here if not for you. There aren't enough "Thank you's" for all of the work you do. (Curtsy)

Speaking of teasers... For those of you who follow me on Facebook, by this point you are probably very familiar with all of my Charistown teasers. They are sexy, sassy, sophisticated, and they take my breath away every single time I see them...**Juliana Cabrera** – you are a magical lady. I give you a mere sentence or two and you find the perfect picture...every single time!! I don't know how you do it, but you do. I swear you wield a magic wand. I don't want to steal it...I just want to marvel at your amazing work. Thank you for sharing it with me.

In *Storm Front*, there was a scene...you know... THAT scene...the one you probably hated me for. While I didn't enjoy writing it, I wanted to make certain all of the medical information was correct. So I sent out a call on Facebook and who came to my rescue? The extraordinary **Rhonda Raymond Dennis**! She patiently stayed on the phone with me and answered all of my questions while allowing me the opportunity to write down her answers.

She was kind and sweet, I got off the phone with her that night feeling confident and secure that my sad and tragic scene was at least accurate. Thank you, Rhonda!!

I know there is an ever-going question about whether or not Facebook friends are in fact REAL friends. Some people question how one can possibly be friends with people they never met before. In the past year, I have found some of the most wonderful people on Facebook. When you find people with common interests, desires, and/or needs as you, the friends grow the same as any other "real" friendships do. They were there when I needed to rant, laugh, play and cry and when I needed to do it in the comfort of my home behind the privacy of my screen. I can honestly say, that I don't know what I would have done this year without some of my FB friends.

My fellow *Dummies* – Where would I be without you? There are too many of you to name, but each of you is special to me in your own way. I have loved meeting you in person and I can't wait to meet the rest of you in the up and coming months.

To the *Tapas* group – It doesn't matter how long I knew you, just that I did. It doesn't matter how much I love you, just that I do. Your very presence improved my life at a time when I needed it most. So thank you…I'm grateful and I miss you.

To my Beta Readers – I'm not sure if people understand how hard it is to be a great beta reader. Being a Beta reader *isn't* about liking a pre-published book. It's about finding every single possible flaw, inconsistency, character issue, story plot problem, over-all positive and negative issue with the story. Once they have found those things, they then need to find the best possible way of informing the author. It's one thing to write a negative review on a book already written, it's another to contact a writer and tell them all of the things you think they should fix/change in their story. It isn't an easy thing to do and we, authors, depend heavily on our Betas. I can say with great confidence, I have the GREATEST Betas EVER!!! Thank you, **Cary Bruce**, **Kathy Sizemore**, Ilsa Madden-Mills **Jenn Wolfel, Amy Barber, Jessica Sharff, Jennie Wurtz** and **Carey Heywood.**

Cary Bruce, I was so lucky when I found you during the final days of my TN editing. You came on and offered me amazing encouragement. (Shaking my head) Poor you, got sucked in for the rest of the series. You have offered me amazing feedback and wonderful pep talks throughout this entire process. Your help is so appreciated. I'm thrilled to have you on my team!

Kathy Sizemore, you are such a gift. From Lisa's Reads to *Thursday Nights* to Las Vegas... meeting you was such a treat. You are a fun and wonderful woman. You read my words with enthusiasm and excitement...you offer wonderful feedback and such a great way of looking at things. I adore you Kathy. Thank you so much for finding me!

Ilsa Madden-Mills, You my friend have been the sweetest breath of fresh air. I can't remember how we met, maybe in one of the writer's groups, but I am really freakin' grateful that we did. Your input on SF was wonderful. You told me what you loved and gently told me what you thought would make it better. I've grown so fond of our chats, your sweet southern voice brings a smile to my face each and every day. Thank you for coming into my life!

Jenn Wolfel, It has been such a pleasure getting to know you. I love discussing books with you…your take on the stories is refreshing and honest, that's why I was thrilled to include you to my team. You've added so much with your opinions and suggestions. I know I tend to get lost in my "ho'house" when I'm writing, but you've kept tabs on me. You didn't let me disappear…thank you, Jenn. I appreciate you.

Amy Barber, Oh, Amy – How anyone can say that people can find family on Facebook has never met us. You have given me so much support in these many months, I can't begin to explain how I feel about you. So…I'll stick to the book. Your time and dedication to all things Charistown has been flat-out amazing. I feel truly blessed for meeting you. I can't wait to spend some quality time with you.

Jessica Sharff, I met you during TN and I was thrilled when you wanted to stay on for SF. I knew I was going to run the Beta process differently the 2nd time around and you were so patient with me. Jessica, you have no idea how helpful your patience was. When you finally got the MS, your reaction was priceless. Thank you for sticking by me. I'm thankful for you.

Jennie Wurtz, Meeting you in Vegas was great, but playing Dirty Minds with you on Friday nights…the best!!! So when things started to get funky and I needed extra help, you were there and I will be forever grateful. Jennie, your feedback was spot on! I'm thrilled that we discussed, "REALLY THANKFUL" I think the whole chapter is better thanks to you. What can I say, I'm RE-ALLY THANKFUL! ;)

Carey Heywood, Ahhh!!! I love you!! Thank you for

believing in me. You read SF in its early stages and you offered great feedback. You stood behind me when I wavered and you stood beside me when I chose to change things you wouldn't have. You are a true friend. Thank you!

To my Editing Team – **Ryn Hughes, Toni Pirrello, Ellie Folden, Nicole Tway,** and **Robyn Petrilli, Pamela Moseley and Gary Patrick**—Wow, people,—I'm not even sure of what to say. This was a truly a marathon. **Ryn**, your content edits were beyond amazing. You taught me how to see my work from a different point of view (haha) and I am grateful. You were right…it all makes perfect sense. **Toni**, you are and will always be my Pretty-Maker. Seriously, how do you do it? **Ellie**, you stepped up when I was frantic and you calmed me down. Thank you for giving me the confidence to know it would be ok. **Robyn** and **Nicole,** You girls are like my power-play…you came in and kicked ass just before the timer buzzed. **Pamala**, you saved me from complete hysteria, I will forever be in your debt. **Gary**, my semi-colon God, without you…my life would be fiilled with ;;;;;; - There are not enough words to thank the group of you… Well…there are 107 thousand+ but you know what I mean.

So, the coolest thing happened to me…two days *before* Thursday Nights published, I got an invitation to sign at the very popular, extremely anticipated, Naughty Mafia – Sunday Sinners 2013 Signing Event in Las Vegas. I was in shock. I looked at the email and laughed. I then wrote back to the sender and told them they sent their letter to the wrong person. Did I want to go to that event? HELL YES!! But I was nobody. My book wasn't even released. I then received another email from **Ellie Lovenbooks**. She explained that her blog read Thursday Nights and loved it. And they wanted to invite me to sign during the Sunday signing. I accepted and went on to experience my first ever author signing. It was the greatest weekend!!! I got to meet so many talented authors, fantastic bloggers, and incredible readers. I will forever be grateful and indebted to **Ellie** and to **Lovenbooks.** They changed my career and my life. Xoxox!

One of the most important things on my "to do" list for Las Vegas was to finally meet in person my soul sister, **L.b Simmons**. I had been talking to her since February 2013 almost every day and I was finally going to get to hug my girl. Never in my life have I met someone who looked more like me. Not only did we act alike, people kept thinking we were sisters. What a compliment for me! (She's pretty gorgeous). L.b Simmons, you came into my life when it was dark and you shined your light all over it. You make me laugh, you make me smile and there are not enough words to thank you for all you have done for me. I love you, I truly do.

When I'm not absorbed in my computer, I actually have a three dimensional life. I have an amazing **family and incredible friends**. I don't tell them enough how much I appreciate them, but I do. They have supported me through all of my book "stuff"…but there support has been so much more than a pat on the back or an obligatory question. They are excited for my stories and interested in what's coming next. Without them, there would be no stories. Thank you for your love and support, it doesn't go unnoticed. I love you back even harder.

To my little boys – I know, I'm writing AGAIN. No,

you can't read over my shoulder because it's totally inappropriate. That being said, I love you to pieces and I am super proud of you.

To Jon...you got all sorts of love at the beginning. That's it for you.

To my readers, While Storm Front is over 107 thousand words; there aren't enough words to describe the heartfelt gratitude I feel toward you. I am blessed. Every review, every PM or message, every "like" has warmed my heart. You truly have no idea how your voices have rocked my world. Thank you.

XO,
Lisa Paul

ABOUT THE AUTHOR

LISA PAUL IS A wife, mother, daughter, sister, friend, reader, writer, blogger, and self-proclaimed comedian—just not always in that order. Ever since she was a little girl, she has devoured books. Falling in love with the Sweet Valley High series at a young age drew Lisa to series books and inspired her to write her own. *Storm Front* is the second book in her Charistown series following *Thursday Nights*. When not writing, Lisa can be found eating french fries and Godiva raspberry truffles or hanging out with her husband and two sons. Visit her website at **http://www.lisanpaul.com**